STORIES BY CANADIAN WOMEN

STORIES BY CANADIAN WOMEN

Edited by Rosemary Sullivan

Toronto
OXFORD UNIVERSITY PRESS

Oxford University Press
70 Wynford Drive, Don Mills, Ontario M3C 1J9
Oxford New York
Athens Auckland Bangkok Bombay
Calcutta Cape Town Dar es Salaam Delhi
Florence Hong Kong Istanbul Karachi
Kuala Lumpur Madras Madrid Melbourne
Mexico City Nairobi Paris Singapore
Taipei Tokyo Toronto
and associated companies in
Berlin Ibadan

For my mother
LEANORE GUTHRIE SULLIVAN

CANADIAN CATALOGUING IN PUBLICATION DATA
Main entry under title:
Stories by Canadian women
ISBN 0-19-540468-8
1. Short stories, Canadian - Women authors.
2. Canadian fiction - 20th century.* 3. Canadian
fiction (English) - 20th century.* I. Sullivan,
Rosemary.
PS8321.S86 1984 C813'.01'089287 C84-099302-1
PR9197.33.W65S86 1984

4 5 6 7 8 99 98 97 96 95
Printed in Canada by Webcom

Contents

Acknowledgements

EDNA ALFORD. 'Tuesday, Wednesday, Thursday' from *A Sleep Full of Dreams*. Used by permission of the author. MARGARET ATWOOD. 'Polarities' from *Dancing Girls* by Margaret Atwood, used by permission of The Canadian Publishers, McClelland and Stewart Limited, Toronto. ROBERTINE BARRY. 'La Gothe and Her Husband'. English translation © Patricia Sillers. SANDRA BIRDSELL. 'The Wednesday Circle' was first published in *Night Travellers* (Turnstone Press, 1982) and is reprinted by permission of Turnstone Press. MARIE-CLAIRE BLAIS. 'The Forsaken' used by permission of Marie-Claire Blais and Louise Myette, Literary Agent. English translation © Patricia Sillers. MONIQUE BOSCO. 'The Old Woman's Lamentations on Yom Kippur' used by permission of Monique Bosco. English translation © Patricia Sillers. DIONNE BRAND. 'Sans Souci' which first appeared in *Fireweed: A Feminist Quarterly* (Summer/Fall 1983), used by permission of the author. SHIRLEY FAESSLER. 'A Basket of Apples', copyright © 1969 by Shirley Faessler. Reprinted by permission of McIntosh and Otis, Inc. MAVIS GALLANT. 'The Moslem Wife' from *The Fifteenth District*, used by permission of Macmillan of Canada (A Division of Gage Publishing Limited). ANNE HÉBERT. 'The House on the Esplanade' used by permission of Editions du Seuil. JOY KOGAWA. 'Obasan' which first appeared in *The Canadian Forum* (March 1978), used by permission of the author. MARGARET LAURENCE. 'The Rain Child' from *The Tomorrow-Tamer* by Margaret Laurence, used by permission of The Canadian Publishers, McClelland and Stewart Limited, Toronto. LOUISE MAHEUX-FORCIER. 'Discretion' originally appeared as 'La Discrétion' in *En Toutes Lettres* (Le Cercle du Livre de France Limitée). Used by permission of Editions Pierre Tisseyre. English translation © Sally Livingston. JOYCE MARSHALL. 'So Many Have Died' from *A Private Place*, used by permission of the author. CLAIRE MARTIN. 'Letter to Werther' appeared originally as 'Lettre à Werther' from *Avec ou sans Amour* by Claire Martin (Editions du Renouveau Pedagogique Inc.). Used by permission of Editions Pierre Tisseyre. English translation © Patricia Sillers. ALICE MUNRO. 'The Peace of Utrecht' from *Dance of the Happy Shades* by Alice Munro. Reprinted by permission of McGraw-Hill Ryerson Limited. HÉLÈNE OUVRARD. 'The Angel' used by permission of Hélène Ouvrard and Louise Myette, Literary Agent. English translation © Patricia Sillers. P.K. PAGE. 'Unless the Eye Catch Fire...' from *Evening Dance of the Grey Flies*, used by permission of the author. GABRIELLE ROY. 'The Satellites' © Fonds Gabrielle Roy. This story was first published in French as an introductory chapter to *La Rivière sans repos* (1970). Used by permission of François Ricard, Agent. JANE RULE. 'Invention for Shelagh' from *Theme for Diverse Instruments*. Copyright © 1975 by Jane Rule. Reprinted by permission of the author and Georges Borchardt, Inc. GLORIA SAWAI. 'The Day I sat with Jesus on the sundeck and a wind came up and blew my kimono open and He saw my breasts' used by permission of the author. ELIZABETH SPENCER. 'I, Maureen' from *The Stories of Elizabeth Spencer*. Copyright © 1976 by Elizabeth Spencer. Reprinted by permission of Doubleday & Company, Inc. AUDREY THOMAS. 'If One Green Bottle...' from *Two in the Bush and Other Stories* by Audrey Thomas, used by permission of The Canadian Publishers, McClelland and Stewart Limited, Toronto. ARITHA VAN HERK. 'Never Sisters' © Aritha van Herk. Used by permission of the author and Virginia Barber Literary Agency, Inc. SHEILA WATSON. 'Antigone' from *Four Stories* (Coach House Press, 1979). Used by permission of Sheila Watson. ETHEL WILSON. 'Mrs Golightly and the First Convention' from *Mrs Golightly and Other Stories*. Used by permission of the University of British Columbia Library.

Every effort has been made to determine copyright owners. In the case of any omissions, the publisher will be pleased to make suitable acknowledgements in future editions.

Introduction

'Mask', by Gail Geltner, which provides the subject for the cover of this book, is one of those mysterious paintings that seem to alter while the viewer looks at it. Initially the face appears vulnerable and pained, as though uncomfortable under scrutiny; and yet, as one looks further, the eyes strengthen and begin to turn on the viewer—at first, in accusation, then with understanding, and finally, with a comprehensive compassion that acknowledges and comforts. 'Mask' is a portrait of woman as lover, as muse, as creator; with its remarkable emotional energy it suggests the range of this collection of short fiction by Canadian women.

This book spans a century of writing and includes stories by both English-speaking and (in translation) French-speaking authors. Representing a cross-section of the best writing in the genre by women, the stories demonstrate a wide variety of styles, from the realistic to the symbolic and experimental. All are about women: in childhood, adolescence, maturity, old age; in relationships as daughters, sisters, lovers, mothers; in a variety of social and political contexts. Though the authors are Canadian, by birth or by choice, nationality and gender have different meanings for each of them. Some write as nationalists, whether Canadian or Québécoise; some write as militant feminists; others avoid these categories entirely. Yet all are shaped by these two facts of being.

Canada has produced an unusual, even a predominant, number of women writers. The study of women's writing is too new to have taken us far in examining why this is so. Motivations for writing are always mysterious. The writer writes because she has the talent, the compulsion, the luck, and the environment that make writing possible. Were we to examine in detail the biographies of these writers, we might find patterns of early and unexpected encouragement. Almost every author in this collection has spoken of the problem—for the woman writer—of self-confidence. How does a woman, once she begins to write, find the courage to believe in herself as a writer, and how does she find the confidence to continue? How does she resist instinctive self-censorship, and learn to trust her own authority as an interpreter of areas of experience that, traditionally, have been dismissed as female. It is possible that the status of being a colony—as women are often described—within the Canadian colony has given a particular impetus to women writers in this country. As a writer in a colonial context, where the writing of literature was itself a presumptuous act, women could claim equal authority with their male colleagues. Sara Jeannette Duncan was motivated by the desire to create a new literature in Canada, and took encouragement from the fact that the new cultural experiment welcomed all practitioners. Even for the modern Canadian writer, cultural identity remains an issue. Once the writer focuses on the confusions over national identity, colonialism can, paradoxically, be turned into a source of strength—the writer discovers a new sense of cultural responsibility: to define a people to itself. The circles of identity—personal, cultural—conflate. The compulsion to understand one's culture feeds and is fed by the need to understand oneself; it may be that Canadian women have been doubly motivated.

It is clear that the writers in this collection have learned to write confidently and eloquently of their own experience as women. And it is not of crabbed eccentric situations they write but of universal experience. In the call for a literature written by women there has been a tendency to expect a radically different story. John Stuart Mill, in 1869, urged originality from women: 'if women lived in a different country from men and had never read any of their writings, they would have a different literature.' It is characteristic of a dominant group or class to demand self-definition of a subgroup, but acceding to such injunctions denotes dependency. We find that the large extant body of work by women deals with familiar human themes: love and hate, progeny, culture, politics, and power—all expanded to incorporate the perspective of the previously silent majority. Today the focus has shifted to reveal the experience, from within, of the woman alone, the woman with a man or another woman, the projection of men through women's eyes, of the woman as mother. This declares that the human story is being rounded out; it is no longer androcentric. The most significant shift in emphasis—an obsession with redefining the power politics of the couple—has profound implications, striking at the issue of the use one human being makes of another and, ultimately, at definitions of the self. When colonials rebel, the parameters and structures of reality must be redefined.

The alteration of subjects and tactics by Canadian women writers over the past hundred years can be seen in the stories collected here. Not only has the social context changed, but so have notions of self-definition and of acceptable subjects for fiction. In the nineteenth century, women writers in English Canada shared common social backgrounds and experienced common social constraints. Their background was educated, genteel. Turning to writing as a career, they began publishing in their twenties or earlier: Isabella Valancy Crawford to earn a precarious living for herself and her mother; Sara Jeannette Duncan as an ambitious journalist turned novelist; and Susie Frances Harrison—who was also a professional musician and folklorist—as a reviewer at the age of sixteen. Their stories in this collection are fascinating as much for what they leave unsaid as for what they say. Though the authors attack subjects that women write of today, they do so by covert excursions rather than by candid assaults. Crawford, for instance, satisfying the sentimental formula demanded by readers of the newspapers in which she published, offers melodramatic portraits of types arrayed on a battleground of opposites—good/evil, loyalty/betrayal—reconciled by sacrificial love. In 'Extradited', a simple story of betrayal, the men are stereotypical projections of female fantasy. More interesting is the woman—a jealous, petulant, narcissistic daughter of Eve, who curls 'serpent-wise' in her husband's strong clasp. Crawford directs her resentment at the image of woman sketched by conventional society, woman as small-minded, half-educated, and self-congratulatory in her pettiness. Harrison's romantic vignette, 'The Idyl of the Island', coalesces mysteriously around its central symbol, while her splendid grasp of the texture of the Canadian wilderness creates a psychological landscape. A man briefly encounters his perfect ideal of the lover—a woman forever inaccessible, a kind of benevolent La Belle Dame Sans Merci. Again, the portrait of the woman is extraordinary. Asleep, cushioned on the edge of her island—a small oval-shaped allegorical space—she is an unconscious and consummate image of female sexual passivity; trapped in an arid marriage, she is imprisoned in her body. Harrison does not mount an attack on the rigidities of the institution of marriage, but grieves instead for one of its unfortunate victims. The bravest and most powerful of these three early writers, Sara Jeannette Duncan, launched her journalistic career early, eventually becoming the first woman editorialist with a major Canadian newspaper, the Toronto *Globe*. As a feminist, she believed in 'careers, if possible, and independence anyway—marriage is an incidental.' Though more aware than most that the writer needs to engage feeling and cultivate the ego, she spent the greater part of her life in British Imperial India—stuffy, provincial, dedicated to a stultifying decorum. This sharpened her satiric gifts and located her focus on the moral and creative cost of failing to realize one's talents and emotional needs. 'A Mother in India' reunites a mother with her daughter, whom she has seen only twice in twenty-one years. Neither polemical nor strident, the story is a witty, subtle, and extremely intelligent study of a woman who learns that her notions of herself are at odds with a maternal role imposed on her by social demands. 'Men are very slow in changing their philosophy about women. I fancy their idea of the maternal relation is firmest fixed of all.'

French-Canadian literature in the nineteenth century offers few examples of the short story—by women *or* men—though it predates English-Canadian literature and can boast of several impressive fiction writers, including Laure Conan. Robertine Barry ('Françoise'), editor of *La Patrie*, wrote *contes* inspired by rural Québec life. She saw herself as a cultural anthropologist, with an interest in recording the traditions, attitudes, and language of the *habitant* before they disappeared. In 'La Gothe and Her Husband' she brings two young girls from the city to visit an old servant. The core of the story is the girls' interest in a young *habitant* woman, La Gothe, who describes her marriage to a man who 'slaughtered' her with beatings. Barry conveys La Gothe's mute rage against this man through an elaborate metaphor of a menacing summer storm breaking over the placid meadows. Her paradoxical resignation and passionate resistance—her emotionalism—seem more authentic than the urbane gentility of the two 'educated' young girls.

Between the Edwardian period in which Duncan wrote and the Second World War—after which the majority of the stories collected here were first published—there is a remarkable lacuna in Canadian short fiction. (Even Ethel Wilson, the writer who follows Barry in this anthology, did not begin publishing until 1937.) This long gap was in part created by the colonial status of literature in Canada, which was particularly hazardous for the short-story genre. With the Depression, the publishing industry more or less collapsed: few collections of stories by women or men appeared. The remaining work in this volume was written after 1944. Most of these writers are still producing fiction, and what they share and what distinguishes them is less generational than temperamental. Yet writers of Wilson's, and even Laurence's, generation portray women with an objectivity and compassion that suggest gratitude for having won their own fight for independence. Younger women, perhaps more shocked at the intransigence of social structures and mental attitudes, tend to resent the battles for autonomy and authority that must still be waged—anger is often at the core of their work.

Ethel Wilson began her career late (publishing her first novel in 1947 at the age of fifty-nine). *Mrs Golightly and Other Stories* (1961) collects the work of several decades. In 'Mrs Golightly and the First Convention' she portrays the archetypal middle-class housewife, not cynically or dismissively but with wit and generosity. Mrs Golightly (the irony of that name!) is a totally ingenuous, apologetic soul whose self-effacement and earnestness are manipulated by the surrounding sanitized commercial world. Joyce Marshall's 'So Many Have Died' portrays ninety-one-year-old Georgina Dinsborough—a former medical doctor and early pioneer of women's suffrage—on the day of her death. Using random memories, telephone conversations, and an encounter with a young man, Marshall has created a loving tribute to a powerful, complex woman who was forged by the challenges of this century.

Gabrielle Roy, as a Franco-Manitoban, stands slightly to the side of the Québécois tradition, writing evocatively of Montreal, the Prairies, and the North. In 'The Satellites' she tells of a dying Inuit woman, Deborah, who is transported 'south' for treatment in a white hospital. Roy enters the mind of her character and sees the world as she does—as a landscape of vital forms where trees are creatures. The story concerns discrepant values: death viewed through the eyes of the modern technological world ('white men cling to their lives'), and through the insights of a 'primitive' past, which allows the Inuit to face death with stoic dignity. This is an elegiac story, not simply because its subject is a dying woman, but because the wisdom of an ancient culture is seen to be violated. Anne Hébert's early works show an absorption with entrapment and spiritual deprivation, which perhaps expressed the mood of

Québec in the 1940s, when it was still culturally colonized and dominated by Catholic traditionalism. In 'House on the Esplanade' —which evokes the traditions of French literature with its Flaubertian rigour of language and commitment to style—Stephanie Bichette, an archetypal Québec spinster, is as much a symbol as a person, a female sacrifice to the outmoded cult of patriarchy. This superbly controlled portrait of the wasted progeny of an empty tradition suggests Hébert's demand for a new order. Claire Martin composes a witty reply to a lover who demands that she write about the feminine desire to 'wertherize' men, an allusion to Goethe's pathological romantic, the young Werther. She turns his own game against him and exposes the changes men demand of women, which women accept as part of the price of love. At the end of the story, assuming the masculine role of moral teacher, she assures her lover that she will wait patiently for him to reach the level of self-recognition she has already achieved.

The English-Canadian short story tends to be realistic and to focus on the delineation of individual psychology. But a few writers have rebelled against the constraints of realism, turning instead to myth or symbol to probe other possible structures of reality. Sheila Watson's 'Antigone' retells the myth in a vernacular mode. Watson explores its psychological profundities and gives ironic resonance and dignity to her anecdote of contemporary desolation, interweaving the mythic and the modern strands so closely that the motive springs of the story are inextricable. The story is a desperate cry of woe in a world that offers no spiritual consolation. P.K. Page, in 'Unless the Eye Catch Fire . . .', follows the tradition of fantasy or speculative fiction (bringing to mind Isak Dinesen or Doris Lessing). A poet, she writes with a dazzling display of precise language, adjectival flourish, and wordplay as she imagines the world's end. The story opens with an extraordinary moment of altered vision, wonderfully familiar to readers of Page's poetry, in which the colour spectrum changes, rearranging the dimensions of space. Page brings the real and supra-real into conjunction, offering a stunning view of the literalist world's response to something it cannot understand intellectually. But her vision is joyous: 'The eye altering alters all.'

With the stories by Elizabeth Spencer and Mavis Gallant we enter the psychological territory of relationships that preoccupies modern women. Each story focuses on the evolution of a woman's attitude toward marriage and love. Spencer's 'I, Maureen', is about a conventional middle-class wife who accepts all the received definitions of her role, play-acts at fashioning the perfect domestic world, and lives a quiet double life until a psychological shock turns her 'inside out like a sleeve' and she becomes her other self—a total reversal of values that is incomprehensible to her husband (though not, perhaps, to other women). Gallant's 'The Moslem Wife' explores, with wise irony, the facts of a relationship over decades: physical need and revulsion, affection and fear, pride and guilt, admiration and resentment. Gallant encloses the experience of the Second World War within the brackets of the relationship, as if to assert that real life is lived in the pauses between dramatic events—just as her writing style implies that truth speaks in the spaces between words. Shirley Faessler's main character is a type—the irritating, loveable immigrant matriarch—who, in her most dramatic moment, reveals herself as a model of loyalty and love for her daughter. In 'The Rain Child' Margaret Laurence writes, from her experience of living in Africa, about the painful implications of being uprooted and of becoming a stranger in one's homeland. Her narrator, an aging woman alone, with a heart kneaded by loneliness, pride, and independence, understands that in overcoming the threat of vulnerability implicit in exposing oneself to another, she liberates herself.

The work of Alice Munro, Jane Rule, Audrey Thomas, and Margaret Atwood delineates another world—one that seems more stark than that of Laurence or Faessler, in which the need to be aware of, and note, the dynamics of power in relationships is all-important. Munro describes her experience of growing up female in small-town southwestern Ontario as one of feeling alienated, learning to be ultra-protective, ultra-secretive. Women, as she once put it, being the subject race, are survivors, tougher than men. In 'The Peace of Utrecht' she creates a world of women: the fierce, tragically egocentric mother, stubbornly feeding on her daughters; the timid spinster aunts steeped in the discretion and circumlocution that leads women to search every encounter for nuance and subtext; the sisters, resisting female rituals of emotionalism, yet pitted against each other. One sister saves herself at the cost of enormous guilt; the other, never having learned to demand a life for herself, is a victim. Jane Rule's post-modern story, 'Invention for Shelagh', written in the self-referential mode of writing about writing, celebrates the joy and pleasure of intimacy with women.

The form mirrors the struggle to 'climb up through process to make something', and is itself a statement of values—to come upon patterns rather than to impose them. The narrator, rejecting the female myth of immunity from failure—'If the world doesn't take you seriously to begin with, your failure in it can't be all that much of a disaster'—wants a re-invention: in the uncertain aftermath of exploded myths, we must begin again. This story is a moving appeal for solidarity among women: 'We all . . . need so much more of the world than anyone is willing to risk alone.' Audrey Thomas's 'If One Green Bottle . . .', an interior monologue, records the narrator's madly racing thoughts, fuelled by anger and pain, as she undergoes an abortion in an African clinic. No guilt or self-recrimination here: we learn nothing of the narrator's history. Thomas portrays instead the shocked sense of unreality experienced by an actor in a drama of pain and fear who directs her anger at false cultural assumptions: death, birth, pain, have always been presented to her as abstractions. Betrayed by her sense of immunity, she feels victimized by chance, biology, and the world of men. The story ends with a profound sense of desolation and confusion. Margaret Atwood's 'Polarities' is a disturbing portrait of growing spiritual debility. Louise, though ostensibly insane, renders an accurate account of the cultural malaise. Having worked out her own system, taking as 'real what the rest of us pretend is metaphorical', she wishes to 'complete the circle', to unite the fragments of individual existence, until she discovers that she herself is the circle. She becomes the victim of society, which cannot accommodate her wisdom.

The modern Québec authors included here—Bosco, Maheux-Forcier, Ouvrard, and Blais—write stories pervaded by a sense of anguish and a conviction of metaphysical absurdity. In 'The Old Woman's Lamentations on Yom Kippur' Monique Bosco writes a lyrical monologue from the perspective of a woman recording the horrors of aging with sardonic humour. Recalling her doctor's questions about her 'well-being', she watches the world unthread and waits only for her death. Louise Maheux-Forcier's 'Discretion' is taken from *En toutes lettres*, a collection of stories whose titles follow the letters of the alphabet. Here the author recreates the sinister world of the elusive Maude—a world where life is 'not for living but for hiding away'. Maheux-Forcier's style is lyrical, incantatory, symbolistic yet forceful, evoking the enigmatic evil that lurks at the core of Maud's world. (This world of adolescence—introverted, secretive, narcissistic, and violent—is not unfamiliar in Québec fiction.) Hélène Ouvrard, who has published many books on fine arts and crafts, writes of painting with the sophistication of a practitioner. In 'The Angel' she uses a painter's language of line and space to describe the psychologies of her characters. Judith, a nude model whose gift for abstraction from her physical body is a form of escapism, is brought disconcertingly and painfully to an awareness of her retreat by a woman who lives comfortably in the quotidian, corporeal world. Marie-Claire Blais, in 'The Forsaken', pares language to the bone in this apocalyptic story that has the resonance of parable or allegory. Her unnamed character lives in an ordinary world empty of calamity, in which there is nothing to dread. She envies those whom evil has not abandoned, since, in her comfortable world, she thinks she has no right to feel anguish. Like a refugee, with her life in a wheelbarrow, she simulates the flight of those who suffer in far-off countries and enters a clean landscape where she can imagine a new vision of a world to come. For this character guilt and evil are living concepts, though the religious structure that gives them meaning has been entirely emptied: God is an invisible cruelty. To a soul with this kind of moral earnestness, the comfortable vacuum we call normalcy causes a kind of spiritual dismemberment.

The short-story genre is remarkably strong in English Canada, and new writers are surfacing continually. In 'The day I sat with Jesus on the sundeck and a wind came up and blew my kimono open and He saw my breasts' Gloria Sawai writes a comic and surrealistic story about a Second Coming: a harrassed housewife, sorting her blue-moulded laundry in her suburban home in Moose Jaw, Saskatchewan, meets Jesus Christ. The anecdote, with its sexual innuendoes, seems a fantastic revenge against the fundamentalist father who has made sure his daughter was educated rigorously in 'the Word'. The meeting is described ingenuously —Jesus approaches across the prairie, robes flapping in the wind, and climbs onto her sundeck; out of their clumsy conversation a simple, human accord emerges.

The documentary narrative has been an important force in short fiction. In 'Obasan', a story that first appeared in *The Canadian Forum* and later provided the basis for her novel of the title, Joy Kogawa uses a complex structure, woven with memories, historical anecdotes, and photographs, to write a deeply poetic memoir of her own people. Visiting her aunt shortly after the death of her uncle, the narrator is confronted with her own clotted history of pain and stoic resignation. Her relatives were among the thousands of Japanese-Canadians dispossessed and interned as enemy aliens by the Canadian government in the Second World War. Rooting in the upstairs attic 'of humus and memory', she writes a poem of praise to all the old women embodied in Obasan who serve as guardians of 'life's infinite personal details'. The story does not assign blame, but expiates the bitter silence that seeks to bury injustice and in so doing destroys the possibility of love. Sandra Birdsell is a sophisticated stylist. 'The Wednesday Circle' is a sinister story written from the naïve perspective of an adolescent girl who is harrassed by the unwelcome attentions of the egg man, Mr Joy. Guilty, confused by her nascent sexuality, and filled with the superstitions of fundamentalist religion, the narrator is robbed of her illusions of security in the comforting world of the mothers who survive their own suffering by hiding behind a web of invective and illusion. The story is a bitter exposé of the desperate lives of people who live in the endless, small prairie towns scattered along the gun-metal highways. The subject of Edna Alford's 'Tuesday, Wednesday, Thursday' is similar to that of Monique Bosco's 'The Old Woman's Lamentations on Yom Kippur'. Alford writes a brutal portrait of the disintegration of mind and body in old age. Arla, the narrator, an attendant in an old-age home, ministers to the bodies of the women, which demand attention though their spirits are oblivious. Her repugnance and indifference fade only when she recognizes herself in the cracked mirror of the tragic Mrs Langland, who resists her with an oppressive, enigmatic silence. Aritha van Herk's 'Never Sisters' is a monologue in which a sibling tries to penetrate the enigma of her older sister—an inextricable part of the fabric of her own life—who has nevertheless been inaccessible. In a deeply sensual portrait of her sister's fragility, she rehearses her own childish need and resentment, and, from the perspective of maturity, begins to identify with her sister's stoicism and loneliness. Dionne Brand records the life history of a woman in five brief poetic vignettes. Her fertile and exuberant prose draws its energy from the landscape and environment of her Caribbean past. The woman, in painful isolation, fantasizing escape—becoming like sand and changing places with the ocean 'sitting in its fat-legged deepness'—is set against the man who visits. Egocentric and indifferent, he is little more than a brutal sound that violates her life. Brand's images—the vegetation that looks from a distance 'like women with great bushy hair, embracing'—complement the power and elegiac tone of this story. The author is compassionate: both men and women are victims of their history.

As the editor of this volume I found it deeply satisfying to read and collect stories by Canadian women, and to present the varieties of language, background, and experience upon which they draw. This book, I hope, is a testament to their vision and their art. My dilemma in arriving at the selection has been that of all editors: coping with the constraints of space. I have included those writers who have established reputations in the genre through a substantial body of work, and, where this is not the case, writers whose work suggests new directions. Many fine writers are not represented here: May Agnes Fleming, Rosanna Leprohon, Marjorie Pickthall, Mazo de la Roche; and among contemporary writers: Nicole Brossard, Marian Engel, Madeleine Ferron, Margaret Gibson, Phyllis Gotlieb, Katherine Govier, Beth Harvor, Isabel Huggan, Gwendolyn MacEwen, Bharati Mukherjee, Helen Weinzweig, Adele Wiseman, and many others. The length of the list testifies to the vitality of the short story in Canada. New writers are appearing continually, as any reading of *Fireweed: A Feminist Quarterly* and *La Vie En Rose* confirms. Other anthologies will be necessary to keep pace with this remarkable energy.

I wish to thank Marie-Claire Blais, who wrote a new story specially for this collection; her agent, Louise Myette, who offered invaluable advice on Québec writers; and Barbara Godard, whose conversations on the difficulties of research in women's writing were very helpful. I would like especially to thank Richard Teleky, who was more collaborator than publisher's editor and shared this project from the beginning.

Toronto, June 1984 ROSEMARY SULLIVAN

ISABELLA VALANCY CRAWFORD

Extradited

'Oh, Sam! back so soon? Well, I'm glad.'

She had her arms round his neck. She curved serpent-wise in his clasp to get her eyes on his eye.

'How's mammy?' she asked, in a slight panic, 'not worse, is she?'

'Better,' returned Sam; he pushed her away mechanically, and glanced round the rude room with its touches of refinement: the stop organ against the wall of unplastered logs, the primitive hearth, its floor of hewn planks.

'Oh yes! Baby!' she exclaimed, 'you missed him; he's asleep on our bed; I'll fetch him.'

He caught her apron string, still staring round the apartment.

'Where's Joe, Bess? I don't see him round.'

Bessie crimsoned petulantly.

'You can think of the hired man first before me and Baby!'

'Baby's a sort of fixed fact. A hired man, ain't,' said Sam, slowly. 'Mebbe Joe's at the barn!'

'Maybe he is, and maybe he isn't,' retorted Bessie sharply. 'I didn't marry Samuel O'Dwyer to have a hired man set before me and my child, and I won't stand it—so there!'

'You needn't to,' said Sam, smiling. He was an Irish Canadian; a rich smack of brogue adorned his tongue; a kindly graciousness of eye made a plain face almost captivating, while the proud and melancholy Celtic fire and intentness of his glance gave dignity to his expression. The lips were curved in a humorous smile, but round them were deeply graven heroic and Spartan lines.

'Sure, darlin', isn't it you an' the boy are the pulses of my heart?' he said, smiling. 'Sure Joe can wait. I was sort of wonderin' at not seein' him—that's all. Say, I'll unhitch the horses. They've done fifteen miles o' mud holes an' corduroy since noon, an' then we'll have supper. I could 'most eat my boots, so hurry up, woman darlin', or maybe it's the boy I'll be aitin', or the bit of a dog your daddy sent to him. Hear the baste howlin' like a banshee out yonder.'

'It's one of Cricket's last year's pups,' cried Bessie, running to the waggon. 'Wonder Father spared him; he thinks a sight of her pups. My! ain't he a beauty; won't baby just love him!'

She carried the yelping youngster into the house, while Sam took the horses to the barn, a primitive edifice of rough logs, standing in a bleak chaos of burned stumps, for 'O'Dwyer's Clearing' was but two years old, and had the rage of its clearing fires on it yet. The uncouth eaves were fine crimson on one side, from the sunset; on the other a delicate, spiritual silver, from the moon hanging above the cedar swamp; the rude doors stood open; a vigorous purple haze, shot with heavy bars of crimson light, filled the interior; a 'Whip-Poor-Will' chanted from a distant tree, like a muezzin from a minaret; the tired horses whinnied at a whiff of fresh clover, and rubbed noses in sedate congratulation. Sam looked at the ground a moment, reflectively, and then shouted:

'Hullo, Joe!'

'Hullo, Sam!'

By this time Sam was stooping over the Waggon-tongue, his rugged face in the shadow, too intent on straps and buckles to glance up.

'Back all right, you see, Joe,' he remarked. 'How's things gettin' along?'

'Sublimely,' said Joe, coming to his assistance. 'I got the south corner cut—we've only to draw it tomorrow.'

'I never seen the beat of you at hard work,' remarked Sam. 'A slight young chap like you, too. It's just the spirit of you! But you mustn't outdo the strength that is in you for all that. I'm no slave-driver; I don't want your heart's blood. Sure, I've had your sweat two long years—an' the place shows it—it's had your sense an' sinews, so it had. I'll never forget it to you, Joe.'

Joe's tanned, nervous face was shaded by the flap of his limp straw hat. He looked piercingly at Sam, as the released horses walked decorously into the barn.

'Go to your supper, Sam,' he said. 'I'll bed them. I venture to say you're pretty sharp-set; go in.'

'I'll lend a hand first,' returned Sam. He followed the other into the barn.

'It's got dark in here suddenly,' remarked Joe. 'I'll get the lantern.'

'Don't,' said Sam, slowly. 'There's something to be spoke about betwixt you an' me, Joe, an' I'd as lieve say it in the dark; let the lantern be—I'd as lieve say it in the dark.'

'A thousand dollars!'

Bessie rose on her elbow and looked at her sleeping husband. Slumber brought the iron to the surface instead of melting it, and his face became sterner and more resolute in its repose. Its owner was not a man to be trifled with, she admitted as she gazed, and watching him she shivered slightly in the mournful moonlight. Many of her exceedingly respectable virtues were composed mainly of two or three minor vices: her conjugal love was a compound of vanity and jealousy; her maternal affection an agreement of rapacity and animal instinct. In giving her a child, nature had developed the she eagle in her breast. She was full of impotent, unrecognized impulses to prey on all things in her child's behalf. By training and habit she was honest, but her mind was becoming active with the ingenuity of self-cheatry. She held a quiet contempt for her husband, the unlearned man who had won the pretty schoolmistress; and, hedged in by the prim fence of routine knowledge and imperfect education, she despised the large crude movements of the untrained intellect, and the primitive power of the strong and lofty soul. He muttered uneasily as she slipped out of bed. The electric chill of the moonlight did not affect her spirit—she was not vulnerable to these hints and petitions of nature. She crept carefully into the great rude room, which was hall, parlor, and kitchen. The back log, which never died out, smouldered on the hearth. A block of moonlight fell like a slab of marble on the floor of loose planks which rattled faintly under her firm, bare foot. The wooden benches, the coarse table, the log walls, started through the gloom like bleak sentinels of the great Army of Privation. She looked at them without disgust, as she stole to the corner where her organ stood. She sang a silent little hymn of self-laudation.

'Some women would spend it on fine fallals for their backs or houses,' she thought. 'I won't. I'll bank every cent of it for baby. Money doubles in ten years. A thousand dollars will grow nicely in twenty—or I'll get Daddy to loan it out on farm mortgages.

I guess Sam will stare twenty years hence when he finds how rich I've got to be. I'm glad I know my duty as a parent—Sam would never see things as I do—and a thousand dollars is a sight of money.'

She groped on the organ for her paper portefolio, an elegant trifle Joe had sent to the city for, to delicately grace her last birthday; its scent of violets guided her. She took from it a paper and pencil, and standing in the moonlight scribbled a few lines. She dotted her 'i's' and crossed her 't's' with particularity, and was finnickin in her nice folding of the written sheet. Her cool cheeks kept their steady pink; her round eyes their untroubled calm; her chin bridled a little with spiritual pride, as she cautiously opened the outer door.

'It's my clear duty as a parent and a citizen,' she thought, with self-approval, 'the thousand dollars would not tempt me if my duty were not so plainly set before me; and the money will be in good hands. I'm not one to spend it in vain show. Money's a great evil to a weak and worldly mind, but I'm not one for vain show.'

She looked up at the sky from under the morning glories Joe had thoughtfully planted to make cool shadows for her rocker in the porch.

'It will rain to-morrow. So I'll not wash till Friday; I wonder will that pink print Sam fetched home turn out a fast colour; I'll make it up for Baby; he'll look too cunning for anything in it, with those coral sleeve links Joe gave him. I hope he won't cry, and wake Sam before I get back.'

He did not. As she had left him she found him on her return, a little snowy ball, curled up against his father's massive shoulder, the beautiful, black, baby head, thrust against the starting sinews of the man's bare and massive throat. When choice was possible Baby scrambled into the aura of the father—not of the mother. Sam stirred, started, and yawned.

'What's up, Bess?' he asked sleepily.

'I went to the well to draw fresh water,' she replied, folding her shawl neatly on the back of a chair. 'I was wakeful and thirsty—the night is so hot.'

'Guess that consarned pup worried you with his howlen',' he said. 'I don't hear him now—hope he won't get out of the barn—but that ain't probable—Joe shut him in, right enough; you should have sent me to the well, girl darlin', so you should.'

Bessie picked out a burr which she felt in the fringes of her shawl, and said nothing. She was strictly truthful, so far as the letter of truth went; she had gone to the well and had drawn a bucket of cool water from that shaft of solid shadow. What else she had accomplished she decidedly had no intention of confiding to Sam. She slipped into bed, took the baby on her arm, and kissed his pouting lips.

'God bless the darling,' she said with her pretty smile.

'Amen,' said Sam earnestly. 'God come betwixt every man's child an' harm.' Bessie dosed off placidly, the child on her arm. Sam lay staring at the moonlight, listening, thinking, and grandly sorrowing.

There was the unceasing sound of someone tossing feverishly on a creaking bedstead, the eternal sound of heavy sighs resolutely smothered.

'He ain't sleepin' well, ain't Joe,' thought Sam. 'Not even though he knows Bessie an' me is his friends, true as the day. Guess he ain't sleepin' at all, poor chap!'

'The consarned pup is gone,' remarked Sam, disgustedly, as he came in to breakfast. 'Guess he scrambled up to the hay gap and jumped out. Too bad!'

'He's safe enough,' said Joe. 'He probably ran for home. You will find him at your father's on your next visit, Mrs O'Dwyer. Dogs have the "homing" instinct as well as pigeons.'

'Yes, I guess he went back to pa,' said Bessie. Her colour rose, her eyes flashed. 'Do put baby down, Joe,' she said sharply, 'I don't want—that is, you are mussing his clean frock.'

Joe looked keenly at her.

'I understand,' he said, gently. He placed the child tenderly on the rude lounge, which yet was pretty like all Bessie's belongings, and walked to the open door.

'I think I'll straighten things a bit at the landing,' he said. 'Piner's booms burst yesterday and before the drive reaches here it's as well to see to the boats—those river drivers help themselves to canoes wherever they come across them.'

'Just as you say, Joe,' said Sam, gravely. 'I've never known your head or your heart at fault yet.'

Joe gave a long, wistful look of gratitude, and went out. He did not glance at Bessie, nor she at him.

'Bess, woman,' said Sam, 'what ails you at Joe?'

'You know well enough,' she said placidly. 'He's free to stay here; I don't deny he's working well; though that was his duty, and he was paid for it, but he shan't touch my child again. No parent who understood her duty would permit it; I know mine, I'm thankful to say.'

Her small rancors and spites were the 'Judas' doors' through which she most frequently betrayed herself. She had always faintly disliked Joe, before whom her shabby little school routine, her small affectations of intellectual superiority had shrivelled into siccous leaves. She would assert herself now against Sam's dearly-loved friend, she thought, jealously and with an approving conscience, and it was her plain duty to tear him out of that large and constant heart, she was pleased to feel.

Sam's face changed, in a breath, to a passionate pallor of skin; a proud and piercing gloom of anger darkened his blue eyes to black; he looked at her in wonder.

'What's all this, woman?' he demanded, slowly. 'But it's never your heart that's said it! Him that gave the sweat of his body and the work of his mind to help me make this home for you! Him that's saved my life more nor once at risk of his own young days! Him that's as close to my heart as my own brother! Tut, woman! It's never you would press the thorn in the breast of him into his heart's core. I won't demane myself with leavin' the thought to you, Bessie O'Dwyer!'

He struck his fist on the table; he stared levelly at her, defying her to lower herself in his eyes.

She smoothly repaired her error.

'I spoke in a hurry,' she said, lifting the baby's palm, and covering Sam's lips with its daintiness. 'I feel hurt he had so little confidence in me. I wish him well; you know that.'

Sam smiled under the fluttering of the child's palm upon his lips; he gave a sigh of relief. 'Be kind to him, Bessie darlin',' he said, 'Shure our own boy is born—but he isn't dead yet: the Lord stand betwixt the child an' harm! An' there is no tellin' when he, too, may need the kind word and the tender heart. Shure I'm sorry I took you up in arnest just now.'

'I spoke in a pet,' said Bessie gently. 'I remember, of course, all we owe to Joe—how could I forget it?'

'Forgettin's about the aisiest job in life,' said Sam, rising. 'Guess I'll help Joe at the landin'; he's downhearted, an' I won't lave him alone to his throuble.'

Bessie looked after him disapprovingly.

'Trouble indeed! I thought Sam had clearer ideas on such points. The notion of confounding trouble with rightdown sin and wickedness! Well, it's a good thing I know my duty. I wonder if Pa has any mortgage in his mind ready for that money? It must be a first mortgage; I won't risk any other—I know my responsibility as a mother better than that.'

'Why, man alive!'

Sam was astonished; for the first time in his experience of Joe, the latter was idle. He sat on a fallen tree, looking vacantly into the strong current below him.

'I'm floored, Sam,' he answered, without looking up, 'I've no grit left in me—not a grain.'

'Then it's the first time since I've known you,' said Sam, regarding him with wistful gravity. 'Don't let the sorrow master you, Joe.'

'You call it sorrow, Sam?'

'That's the blessed an' holy name for it now,' said Sam, with his lofty, simple seriousness, 'what ever it may have been afore. Hearten up, Joe! Shure you're as safe at O'Dwyer's Clearin', as if you were hid unther a hill. Rouse your heart, man alive! What's to fear?'

'Not much to fear, but a great deal to feel,' said Joe. 'Am I not stripped of my cloak to you—that's bitter.'

'The only differ is that I'm dead sure now of what I suspicioned right along,' said Sam. 'It's not in reason that a schollard an' a gentleman should bury himself on O'Dwyer's Clearin' for morenor two years, unless to sconce shame an' danger. Rouse your sowl, Joe! don't I owe half of all I have to your arm an' your larnin'? When this danger blows past I'll divide with you, an' you can make a fresh start in some sthrange counthry. South Americay's a grond place, they tell me; shure, I'll take Bessie an' the boy an' go with you. I've no kin nor kith of my own, an' next to her an' the child it is yourself is in the core of my heart. Kape the sorrow, Joe; it's the pardon of God on you, but lave the shame an' the fear go; you'll do the world's wonder yet, boy.'

Joe was about three-and-twenty, Sam in middle age. He placed his massive hand on the other's bare and throbbing head, and both looked silently at the dark and rapid river: Joe with a faint pulse of hope in his bruised and broken soul.

'Piner's logs'll get here about to-morrow,' said Sam at last, 'shure it's Bessie'll be in the twitteration, watchin' the hens an' geese from them mauraudtherin river drivers. I wish the pup hadn't got away; it's a good watch dog his mother is, an' likely he'd show her blood in him—the villain that he was to run away with himself, like that, but liberty's a swate toothful, so it is, to man or brute.'

The following day, Bessie having finished her ironing and baking with triumphant exactness, stood looking from the lovely vines of the porch, down the wild farm road. She was crystal-clean and fresh, and the child in her arms was like a damask rose in his turkey-red frock and white bib. A model young matron was Mrs O'Dwyer and looked it to the fine point of perfection, Sam thought, as he glanced back at her, pride and tenderness in his eyes. She was not looking after his retreating figure, but eagerly down the farm road, and, it seemed to Sam, she was listening intently. 'Mebbe she thinks the shouting of them river drivers is folks comin' up the road,' he thought, as he turned the clump of cedar bushes by the landing, and found Joe at work, patching a bark canoe. As usual he was labouring fiercely as men rush in battle, the sweat on his brow, his teeth set, his eyes fixed. Sam smiled reprovingly.

'Shure, it's all smashed up; you'll have her, Joe, again she's mended,' he remarked, 'more power to your elbow; but take it easy, man! You'll wear out soon enough.'

'I must work like the devil, or think,' said Joe, feverishly. 'Some day, Sam, I'll tell you all the treasures of life I threw from me, then you'll understand.'

'When a man understands by the road of the heart, where's the good of larnin' by the road of the ears?' said Sam, with the tenderest compassion; 'but I'll listen when it's your will to tell, never fear. Hark, now! don't I hear them rollickin' divvils of pike pole men shoutin' beyant the bend there?'

'Yes; Piner's logs must be pretty close,' answered Joe, looking up the river.

'They'll come down the rapids in style,' said Sam, throwing a chip on the current, 'the sthrame's swift as a swallow and strong as a giant with the rains.'

They worked in silence for a while, then Joe began to whistle softly. Sam smiled.

'That's right, Joe,' he said, 'there's nothing so bad that it mightn't be worse—there's hope ahead for you yet, never fear.'

A glimmer of some old joyous spirit sparkled in the young man's melancholy eyes, to fade instantly. 'It's past all that, dear old friend,' he said. As he spoke he glanced towards the cedar scrub between them and the house.

'Here comes Mrs O'Dwyer with the boy,' he said, 'and Sam, there are three men, strangers, with her.'

'Shanty bosses come to buy farm stuff,' said Sam. He turned on Joe with an air of sudden mastery.

'Away with you down the bank,' he said, 'Into the bush with you, an' don't come out until you hear me fire five shots in a string. Away with you!'

'Too late, Sam,' said the other, 'they have seen me.'

'What's all this, Bessie?'

Bessie wiped the baby's wet lips with her apron.

'These gentlemen asked to see you, Sam. I guess they want some farm stuff off us for Piner's Camp. So I brought them along.'

She looked placidly at her husband; the baby sprang in her arms eager to get to his friend Joe, whose red flannel shirt he found very attractive.

'Potatoes or flour?' asked Sam curtly, turning on the strangers.

'Well, it ain't neither,' said one of them—he laid his hand on Joe's wrist. 'It's this young gentleman we're after; he robbed his employer two years' back, and he's wanted back by Uncle Sam. That's about the size of it.'

There was nothing brutal in his look or speech; he knew he was not dealing with a hardened criminal: he even felt compassion for the wretched quarry he had in his talons.

'He's in Canada—on British soil; I dare you to touch him!' said Sam fiercely.

'We have his extradition papers right enough,' said one of the other detectives. 'Don't be so foolish as to resist the law, Mr O'Dwyer.'

'He shan't for me,' said Joe, quietly. He stood motionless while the detective snapped one manacle of the handcuffs on his wrist; the steel glittered like a band of fire in the sun.

The child leaped strongly in Bessie's arms, crowing with delight at the pretty brightness. She was a little off her guard, somewhat faint as she watched the deathly shame on the young man's face which had never turned on her or hers but with tenderness and goodwill. Her brain reeled a little, her hands felt weak.

Suddenly there was a shriek, a flash of red, a soft plunge in the water. Joe threw his arms open, dashing aside the detectives like straws.

'Don't hold me—let me save him!' he cried.

Sam could not swim; he stood on the bank holding Bessie, who screamed and struggled in convulsions of fright as she saw her child drowning. Joe rose in the current, fighting his way superbly towards the little red bundle whirling before him. One of the detectives covered him with a revolver.

'Try to escape and I'll shoot,' he called out, 'understand?'

Joe smiled. Escape to the opposite shore and leave Sam's child to drown? No; he had no idea of it. It was a terrible fight between the man and the river—and the man subdued it unto him. He turned back to shore, the child in his teeth, both arms—one with the shining hand-cuff on it—beating the hostile current with fine, steady strokes.

Another moment and he would be safe on shore, a captive and ashamed.

He spurned the yellow fringes of the current; he felt ground under his feet; he half rose to step on the bank. Then there rose a bewildering cry from Sam and the men watching him; he turned and saw his danger.

With one sublime effort he flung the child on the bank, and then with the force of a battering ram the first of Piner's logs crashed upon him. It reared against him like a living thing instinct with rage, and wallowing monster-like led its barky hordes down the rushing stream, rolling triumphantly over a bruised and shattered pigmy of creation, a man.

'Extradited, by ginger,' said one of the detectives, as the groaning logs rolled compactly together over the spot where Joe had gone down.

Before the men departed, Bessie, with the baby on her arm, in a nice clean frock, found opportunity to ask one of them a momentous question. 'Do you think, he being dead, that I shall get any of the reward promised for his arrest? Only for me sending that note to Pa tied round the pup's neck, you would never have found him away back here, you know.'

'I guess not,' replied the detective eyeing her thoughtfully. 'You're a smart woman, you are, but you won't get no reward all the same; pity, ain't it?'

'It's a shame,' she said, bursting into a passion of tears. 'It don't seem that there's any reward for doing one's duty; oh, it's a downright shame.'

'Best keep all this tol'ble shady from that man of yours,' said the detective, meditatively. 'He ain't got no idee of dooty to speak of, he ain't, and seein' he was powerful fond of that poor, brave, young chap as saved that remarkably fine infant in your arms, he might cut up rough. Some folks ain't got no notion of dooty, they ain't. You best keep dark, ma'am, on the inspiritin' subject of havin' done your dooty an' lost a thousand dollars reward.'

And Bessie followed his advice very carefully indeed, though she always had the private luxury of regarding herself as an unrewarded and unrecognized heroine of duty.

SUSIE FRANCES HARRISON

The Idyl of the Island

There lies mid-way between parallels 48 and 49 of latitude, and degrees 89 and 90 of longitude, in the northern hemisphere of the New World, serenely anchored on an ever-rippling and excited surface, an exquisitely lovely island. No tropical wonder of palm-treed stateliness, or hot tangle of gaudy bird and glowing creeper, can compare with it; no other northern isle, cool and green and refreshing to the eye like itself, can surpass it. It is not a large island. It is about half-a-mile long and quarter of a mile broad. It is an irregular oval in shape, and has two distinct and different sides. On the west side its grey limestone rises to the height of twenty feet straight out of the water. On the east side there occurs a gradual shelving of a sumach-fringed shore, that mingles finally with the ever-rippling water. For the waters in this northern country are never still. They are perpetually bubbling up and boiling over; seething and fuming and frothing and foaming and yet remaining so cool and clear that a quick fancy would discover thousands of banished fountains under that agitated and impatient surface. Both ends of the island are as much alike as its sides are dissimilar. They taper off almost to a distinct bladepoint of rock, in which a mere doll's flagstaff of a pine-tree grows; then comes a small detached rock, with a small evergreen on it, then a still smaller rock, with a tuft of grass, then a line of partially submerged stones, and so out to the deep yet ever-bubbling water. This island might seem just the size for two, and there were two on it on a certain July morning at five o'clock. One of these was a lady who lay at full length and fast asleep upon a most unique couch. These northern islands are in many places completely covered with a variety of yellowish-green moss, varying from a couple of inches to a foot and a half in thickness; and yielding to the pressure of the foot or the body as comfortably as a feather bed, if not more so, being elastic in nature. A large square of this had been cut up from some other part of the island and placed on the already moss-grown and cushioned ground, serving as a mattress, while two smaller pieces served as pillows. A sumach tree at the head of the improvised couch gave the necessary shade to the face of the sleeper, while a wild grapevine, after having run over and encircled with its moist green every stone and stem on the island, fulfilled its longing at length in a tumultuous possession of the sumach making a massive yet aerial patched green curtain or canopy to the fantastic bed, and ending seemingly in two tiny transparent spirals curling up to the sky.

If there were a fault in the structure it was that it was too clever, too well thought out, too rectangular, too much in fact like a bed. But it told certainly of a skilful pair of hands and of a beautiful mind and the union of art with nature perfectly suited the charms —contradictory yet consistent—of the occupant. For being anything but a beautiful woman she was still far from a plain one, which though no original mode of putting it does convey the actual impression she made upon a gentleman in a small boat who rowing past this island at the hour of five o'clock in the morning was so much struck with this curious sight, quite visible from the water below, that he was rude enough to stand up that he might see better. The lady was dressed in some dark blue stuff that evidently covered her all over and fitted tightly where it could be seen. A small linen collar, worn all night and therefore shorn of its usual freshness was round her neck, and she was tucked up from the waist under a Scotch woollen rug. Her hair, of a peculiar red-brown, was allowed to hang about her and was lovely; her mouth sad; her nose, rather too prominent; her complexion natural and healthy, but marred by freckles and moles, not many of either but undeniably scattered over the countenance. All told but her eyes which, if they proved to match with her hair, would atone for these other shortcomings. The gentleman sat down again and reflected.

'How still it is!' he said under his breath. 'Absolutely not a thing stirring. This is the time when the fish bite. I ought to be fishing I suppose. Going to be warm by-and-bye.'

It was indeed almost absolutely silent. The sun climbed higher but the lady slept on, and the gentleman gazed as if fascinated.

The only sound that broke the beautiful early morning silence was the occasional weird laugh of the loon. It came twice and then a third time. The sleeper stirred.

'If that thing out there cries again she will wake,' said the gentleman to himself. 'I must be off before that happens. But I *should* like to see her eyes. What a pretty picture it is!' Once more the loon gave its maniacal laugh and the lady started, sat bolt upright and wide awake. Her admirer had not time to retreat but he took his oars up and confronted her manfully. It was an awkward moment. He apologized. The lady listened very politely. Then she smiled.

'Most of the islands in this lake are owned by private people,' she said, 'who use them during the summer months for the purpose of camping out upon them. I should advise you, if you row about much here, to keep to the open water, unless you wish to be seriously handled by the fathers and mothers of families.'

'Thank you very much,' returned the gentleman, standing up in his boat, 'I assure you I intended no rudeness, but I have never seen so charming a summer couch before, and I was really fascinated by the—ah,—the picture you made. May I ask what you mean by "camping out"? Is it always done in this fashion?'

The lady stared. 'Have *you* never camped out?'

'Never in my life,' said the gentleman. 'I am an Englishman, staying at the hotel near the point for a day or two. I came out to see something of the country.'

'Then you should at least have camped out for a week or so. That is a genuine Canadian experience,' said the lady with a frankness which completely restored the equanimity of the Englishman.

'But how do you live?' he went on in a puzzled manner that caused the lady with the red-brown hair, still all hanging about her, much amusement.

'O, capitally! Upon fish and eggs, and gooseberry tarts, and home-made bread and French coffee. Just what you would get in town, and much better than you get at the hotel.'

'O, that would be easy!' the gentleman groaned. 'I eat my meals in a pitch-dark room, in deadly fear and horror of the regiments of flies that swarm in and settle on everything the minute one raises the green paper blinds.'

The lady nodded. 'I know. We tried it for two or three seasons, but we could not endure it; the whole thing, whitewash and all, is so trying, isn't it? So we bought this lovely island and bring our tent here and live *so* comfortably.' The gentleman did not reply at once. He was thinking that it was his place to say 'Good morning,' and go, although he would much have liked to remain a little longer. He hazarded the remark:

'Now, for instance, what are you going to breakfast on presently?'

The lady laughed lightly and shook her red-brown hair.

'First of all I have to make a fire.'

'Oh!'

'But that is not so very difficult.'

'How do you do it?'

'Would you like to know?'

'Very much indeed. I should like to see, if I may.'

The lady reflected a moment. 'I suppose you may, but if you do, you ought to help me, don't you think?' The gentleman much amused and greatly interested.

'Ah but you see, it is you I want to see make it. I am very useless you know at that sort of thing, still, if you will allow me, I will try my best. Am I to come ashore?'

'Certainly, if you are to be of any use.'

The lady jumped lightly off the pretty couch of moss and wound her plentiful hair round her head with one turn of her arm. Her dress was creased but well-fitting, her figure not plump enough for beauty but decidedly youthful. She watched her new friend moor his boat and ascend with one or two strides of his long legs up the side of the cliff that was not so steep. He took off his hat.

'I am at your service,' he said with a profound bow. The lady made him another, during which all her long hair fell about her again, at which they both laughed.

'What do we do first?' said he.

'O we find a lot of sticks and pieces of bark, mostly birch bark, and anything else that will burn—you may have to fell a tree while you are about it—and I'll show you how to place them properly between two walls of stones, put a match to them and there is our fire. Will you come with me?'

He assented of course, and they were soon busy in the interior of the little wood that grew up towards the centre of the island. I must digress here to say that the gentleman's name was Amherst. He was known to the world in latter life as Admiral Amherst, and he was a great friend of mine. When he related this story to me, he was very particular in describing the island as I have done—

indeed he carried a little chart about with him of it which he had made from memory, and he told me besides that he never forgot the peculiar beauty of that same little tract of wood. The early hour, the delicious morning air, the great moss-grown and brown decaying tree trunks, the white, clammy, ghostly, flower or fungus of the Indian Pipe at his feet, the masses of ferns, the elastic ground he trod upon, and the singular circumstance that he was alone in this exquisite spot with a woman he had never seen until five minutes previously, all combined to make an ineffaceable impression upon his mind. The lady showed herself proficient in the art of building a fire and attended by Amherst soon had a fine flame rising up from between the fortifications evidently piled by stronger hands than her own.

'What do we do now?' asked Amherst. 'I should suggest—a kettle.'

'Of course, that is the next step. If I give it to you, you might run and fill it, eh?'

'Delighted!' and away went Amherst. When he returned the lady was not to be seen. The place was shorn of its beauty, but he waited discreetly and patiently, putting the kettle on to boil in the meanwhile.

'It's very singular,' said he, 'how I came to be here. I wonder who are with her in her party; no one else appears to be up or about. That striped red and white thing is the tent, I see, over there. Ah! that's where she has gone, and now she beckons me! Oh! I'll go, but I don't want to meet the rest of them!'

But when he reached the tent, it was quite empty, save for rugs and wraps, boxes, etc., and the lady was laughingly holding out a loaf of bread in one hand and a paper package in the other.

'You will stay and breakfast with me?' 'What will you give me?' said Amherst, smiling. 'I can only give you eggs, boiled in the kettle, coffee and bread and butter. The fish haven't come in yet.'

'What can be nicer than eggs—especially when boiled in the kettle, that is, if you make the coffee first.'

'Certainly I do.'

'And it is really French coffee?'

'Really. Café des Gourmets, you know; we—I always use it—do not like any other.'

Amherst was fast falling in love. He told me that at this point his mind was quite made up that if it were possible he would remain in the neighbourhood a few days at least, in order to see more of this charming girl. She seemed to him to be about twenty-six or seven, and so frank, simple, and graceful, one could not have resisted liking her. Her hair and eyes were identical in colour and both were beautiful; her expression was arch and some of her gestures almost childish, but a certain dignity appeared at times and sat well upon her. Her hands were destitute of rings as Amherst soon discovered, and were fine and small though brown. While she made the coffee, Amherst threw himself down on the wonderful moss, the like of which he had never seen before and looked out over the water. An unmistakeable constraint had taken the place of the unaffected hilarity of the first ten minutes. A reaction had set in. Amherst could of course only answer to me in telling this for himself, but he divined at the time a change in his companion's manner as well.

'I hope you like your eggs,' she said presently.

'They are very nice, indeed, thank you,' rejoined Amherst.

'And I have made your coffee as you like it?'

'Perfectly, thank you. But you—you are not eating anything! Why is that?'

As he asked the question he turned quickly around, in order to rise that he might help her with the ponderous kettle that she was about lifting off the camp-fire, when a long strand of her hair again escaping from its coil blew directly across his face. Amherst uttered a radiant 'Oh!' and taking it to his lips forgot himself so far as to press kiss after kiss upon it. The lady stood as if transfixed and did not move, even when Amherst actually swept all her hair down over one arm and turning her face to his, pressed one long long kiss on her forehead.

The moment he had done this his senses returned and he stepped back in indignation with himself. But his companion was still apparently transfixed. Amherst looked at her in dismay. She did not seem to see him and had grown very pale. He touched her gently on the arm but she did not show that she felt the touch. He retreated a few paces and stood by himself, overcome with shame and contrition. What had he done? How should he ever atone for such an unwarrantable action? Had it been the outcome of any ordinary flirtation, he would have felt no such scruples, but the encounter, though short, had been one of singular idyllic charm until he had by his own rash act spoilt it. A few minutes passed thus in self contemplation appeared like an eternity. He must speak.

'If you would allow me—'

But the lady put out her left hand in deprecation as it were and he got no further. The silence was unendurable. Amherst took a step or two forward and perceived great tears rolling down her cheeks.

'Oh!' he began desperately, 'won't you allow me to say a word to tell you how very, very sorry I am, how grieved I am and always shall be? I never —I give you my word of honor—I never do those sort of things, have never done such a thing before! But I can't tell what it was, the place is so beautiful, and when all that lovely hair came sweeping past my face, I could not help doing as I did, it was so electrical! Any man would have done the same. I know that sounds like a miserable, cowardly excuse, but it is true, perfectly true.' The lady seemed to struggle to appear calm and with a great effort she turned her face towards Amherst.

'I know one man,' she said, in a voice choked with sobs, 'who would not have done it.'

Amherst started. 'I am sorrier than ever, believe me. I might have known you were engaged, or had a lover—one so charming'—

'It is not that,' said the lady. 'I am married.' She was still struggling with her emotion.

Amherst recoiled. He was torn with conflicting thoughts. What if he had been seen giving that involuntary salute? He might have ruined her peace for ever. Who would believe in the truth of any possible explanation?

'I will leave you at once,' he said stiffly; 'there is nothing more to be said.'

'Oh! you will reproach me now!' said his companion, wiping her eyes as the tears came afresh.

'I will try not to,' said Amherst; 'but you could so easily have told me; I do not think it was—quite—fair.' Yet he could not be altogether angry with the partner of his thoughtlessness, nor could he be entirely cold. Her beautiful eyes, her despairing attitude would haunt him he knew for many a day. She had ceased weeping and stood quietly awaiting his departure. Amherst felt all the force of a strong and novel passion sweep along his frame as he looked at her. Was she happy, was she a loved and loving wife? Somehow the conviction forced itself upon him that she was not. Yet he could not ask her, it must remain her secret.

Amherst looked at his watch. It aroused her.

'What is the time?' she said lifting her head for the first time since he had kissed her.

'Ten minutes past six,' Amherst replied.

'You must go' she said, with an effort at self-control. 'I shall have much to do presently.'

He cast one look about and approached her.

'Will you forgive me'—he began in a tone of repression, then with another mighty and involuntary movement he caught her hands and pressed them to his breast. 'My God,' he exclaimed, 'how I should have loved you!'

A moment after he flung her hands away and strode down the cliff, unfastened his boat and rowed away in the direction of the hotel as fast as he could. Rounding a sharp rock that hid what lay beyond it, he nearly succeeded in overturning another boat like his own, in which sat a gentleman of middle age, stout and pleasant and mild of countenance. The bottom of the boat was full of fish. Amherst made an incoherent apology, to which the gentleman answered with a good-natured laugh, insisting that the fault was his own. He would have liked to enter into conversation with Amherst, but my friend was only anxious to escape from the place altogether and forget his recent adventure in the hurry of departure from the hotel. Three days after he embarked at Quebec for England, and never revisited Canada. But he never married and never forgot the woman whom he always asserted he might have truly and passionately loved. He was about twenty-eight when that happened and perfectly heart-whole. Why—I used to say to him, why did you not learn her name and that of her husband? Perhaps she is a widow now, perhaps you made as great an impression upon her mind and affections as she did upon yours.

But my friend Admiral Amherst, as the world knew him, was a strange, irrational creature in many ways, and none of these ideas would he ever entertain. That the comfortable gentleman in the boat was her husband he never doubted; more it was impossible to divine. But the cool northern isle, with its dark fringe of pines; its wonderful moss, its fragrant and dewy ferns, its graceful sumachs, just putting on their scarlet-lipped leaves, the morning stillness broken only by the faint unearthly cry of the melancholy loon, the spar-dyked cliffs of limestone, and the fantastic couch, with its too lovely occupant, never faded from his memory and remained to the last as realities which indeed they have become likewise to me, through the intensity with which they were described to me.

SARA JEANNETTE DUNCAN

A Mother in India

I

There were times when we had to go without puddings to pay John's uniform bills, and always I did the facings myself with a cloth-ball to save getting new ones. I would have polished his sword, too, if I had been allowed; I adored his sword. And once, I remember, we painted and varnished our own dog-cart, and very smart it looked, to save fifty rupees. We had nothing but our pay—John had his company when we were married, but what is that?—and life was made up of small knowing economies, much more amusing in recollection than in practice. We were sodden poor, and that is a fact, poor and conscientious, which was worse. A big fat spider of a money-lender came one day into the veranda and tempted us—we lived in a hut, but it had a veranda—and John threatened to report him to the police. Poor when everybody else had enough to live in the open-handed Indian fashion, that was what made it so hard; we were alone in our sordid little ways. When the expectation of Cecily came to us we made out to be delighted, knowing that the whole station pitied us, and when Cecily came herself, with a swamping burst of expense, we kept up the pretense splendidly. She was peevish, poor little thing, and she threatened convulsions from the beginning, but we both knew that it was abnormal not to love her a great deal, more than life, immediately and increasingly; and we applied ourselves honestly to do it, with the thermometer at a hundred and two, and the nurse leaving at the end of a fortnight because she discovered that I had only six of everything for the table. To find out a husband's virtues, you must marry a poor man. The regiment was under-officered as usual, and John had to take parade at daylight quite three times a week; but he walked up and down the veranda with Cecily constantly till two in the morning, when a little coolness came. I usually lay awake the rest of the night in fear that a scorpion would drop from the ceiling on her. Nevertheless, we were of excellent mind toward Cecily; we were in such terror, not so much of failing in our duty toward her as toward the ideal standard of mankind. We were very anxious indeed not to come short. To be found too small for one's place in nature would have been odious. We would talk about her for an hour at a time, even when John's charger was threatening glanders and I could see his mind perpetually wandering to the stable. I would say to John that she had brought a new element into our lives—she had indeed!—and John would reply, 'I know what you mean,' and go on to prophesy that she would 'bind us together'. We didn't need binding together; we were more to each other, there in the desolation of that arid frontier outpost, than most husbands and wives; but it seemed a proper and hopeful thing to believe, so we believed it. Of course, the real experience would have come, we weren't monsters; but fate curtailed the opportunity. She was just five weeks old when the doctor told us that we must either pack her home immediately or lose her, and the very next day John went down with enteric. So Cecily was sent to England with a sergeant's wife who had lost her twins, and I settled down under the direction of a native doctor, to fight for my husband's life, without ice or proper food, or sickroom comforts of any sort. Ah! Fort Samila, with the sun glaring up from the sand!—however, it is a long time ago now. I trusted the baby willingly to Mrs Berry and to Providence, and did not fret; my capacity for worry, I suppose, was completely absorbed. Mrs Berry's letter, describing the child's improvement on the voyage and safe arrival came, I remember, the day on which John was allowed his first solid mouthful; it had been a long siege. 'Poor little wretch!' he said when I read it aloud; and after that Cecily became an episode.

She had gone to my husband's people; it was the best arrangement. We were lucky that it was possible; so many children had to be sent to strangers and hirelings. Since an unfortunate infant must be brought into the world and set adrift, the haven of its grandmother and its Aunt Emma and its Aunt Alice certainly seemed providential. I had absolutely no cause for anxiety, as I often told people, wondering that I did not feel a little all the same. Nothing, I knew, could exceed the conscientious devotion of all three Farnham ladies to the child. She would appear upon their somewhat barren horizon as a new and interesting duty, and the small additional income she also represented would be almost nominal compensation for the care she would receive. They were excellent persons of the kind that talk about matins and vespers, and attend both. They helped little charities and gave little teas, and wrote little notes, and made deprecating allowance for the eccentricities of their titled or moneyed acquaintances. They were the subdued, smiling, unimaginatively dressed women on a small definite income that you meet at every rectory garden-party in the country, a little snobbish, a little priggish, wholly conventional, but apart from these weaknesses, sound and simple and dignified, managing their two small servants with a display of the most exact traditions, and keeping a somewhat vague and belated but constant eye upon the doings of their country as chronicled in a biweekly paper. They were all immensely interested in royalty, and would read paragraphs aloud to each other about how the Princess Beatrice or the Princess Maud had opened a fancy bazaar, looking remarkably well in plain gray poplin trimmed with Irish lace—an industry which, as is well known, the Royal Family has set its heart upon rehabilitating. Upon which Mrs Farnham's comment invariably would be, 'How thoughtful of them, dear!' and Alice would usually say, 'Well, if I were a princess, I should like something nicer than plain gray poplin.' Alice, being the youngest, was not always expected to think before she spoke. Alice painted in water-colours, but Emma was supposed to have the most common sense.

They took turns in writing to us with the greatest regularity about Cecily; only once, I think, did they miss the weekly mail, and that was when she threatened diphtheria and they thought we had better be kept in ignorance. The kind and affectionate terms of these letters never altered except with the facts they described—teething, creeping, measles, cheeks growing round and rosy, all were conveyed in the same smooth, pat, and proper phrases, so absolutely empty of any glimpse of the child's personality that after the first few months it was like reading about a somewhat uninteresting infant in a book. I was sure Cecily was not uninteresting, but her chroniclers were. We used to wade through the long, thin sheets and saw how much more satisfactory it would be when Cecily could write to us herself. Meanwhile we noted her weekly progress with much the feeling one would have about a far-away little bit of property that was giving no trouble and coming on exceedingly well. We would take possession of Cecily at our convenience; till then, it was gratifying to hear of our unearned increment in dear little dimples and sweet little curls.

She was nearly four when I saw her again. We were home on three months' leave; John had just got his first brevet for doing something which he does not allow me to talk about in the Black Mountain country; and we were fearfully pleased with ourselves. I remember that excitement lasted well up to Port Said. As far as the Canal, Cecily was only one of the pleasures and interests we were going home to: John's majority was the thing that really gave savor to life. But the first faint line of Europe brought my child to my horizon; and all the rest of the way she kept her place, holding out her little arms to me, beckoning me on. Her four motherless years brought compunction to my heart and tears to my eyes; she should have all the compensation that could be. I suddenly realized how ready I was—how ready!—to have her back. I rebelled fiercely against John's decision that we must not take her with us on our return to the frontier; privately, I resolved to dispute it, and, if necessary, I saw myself abducting the child—my own child. My days and nights as the ship crept on were full of a long ache to possess her; the defrauded tenderness of the last four years rose up in me and sometimes caught at my throat. I could think and talk and dream of nothing else. John indulged me as much as was reasonable, and only once betrayed by a yawn that the subject was not for him endlessly absorbing. Then I cried and he apologized. 'You know,' he said, 'it isn't exactly the same thing. I'm not her mother.' At which I dried my tears and expanded, proud and pacified. I was her mother!

Then the rainy little station and Alice, all-embracing in a damp waterproof, and the drive in the fly, and John's mother at the gate and a necessary pause while I kissed John's mother. Dear thing, she wanted to hold our hands and look into our faces and tell us how little we had changed for all our hardships; and on the way to the house she actually stopped to point out some alterations in the flower-borders. At last the drawing-room door and the smiling housemaid turning the handle and the unforgettable picture of a little girl, a little girl unlike anything we had imagined, starting bravely to trot across the room with the little speech that had been taught her. Half-way she came; I suppose our regards were too fixed, too absorbed, for there she stopped with a wail of terror at the strange faces, and ran straight back to the outstretched arms of her Aunt Emma. The most natural thing in the world, no doubt. I walked over to a chair opposite with my hand-bag and umbrella and sat down—a spectator, aloof and silent. Aunt Emma fondled and quieted the child, apologizing for her to me, coaxing her to look up, but the little figure still shook with sobs, hiding its face in the bosom that it knew. I smiled politely, like any other stranger, at Emma's deprecations, and sat impassive, looking at my alleged baby breaking her heart at the sight of her mother. It is not amusing even now to remember the anger that I felt. I did not touch her or speak to her; I simply sat observing my alien possession, in the frock I had not made and the sash I had not chosen, being coaxed and kissed and protected and petted by its Aunt Emma. Presently I asked to be taken to my room, and there I locked myself in for two atrocious hours. Just once my heart beat high, when a tiny knock came and a timid, docile little voice said that tea was ready. But I heard the rustle of a skirt, and guessed the directing angel in Aunt Emma, and responded, 'Thank you, dear, run away and say that I am coming,' with a pleasant visitor's inflection which I was able to sustain for the rest of the afternoon.

'She goes to bed at seven,' said Emma.

'Oh, does she?' said I. 'A very good hour, I should think.'

'She sleeps in my room,' said Mrs Farnham.

'We give her mutton broth very often, but seldom stock soup,' said Aunt Emma. 'Mamma thinks it is too stimulating.'

'Indeed?' said I, to all of it.

They took me up to see her in her crib, and pointed out, as she lay asleep, that though she had 'a general look' of me, her features were distinctively Farnham.

'Won't you kiss her?' asked Alice. 'You haven't kissed her yet, and she is used to so much affection.'

'I don't think I could take such an advantage of her,' I said.

They looked at each other, and Mrs Farnham said that I was plainly worn out. I mustn't sit up to prayers.

If I had been given anything like reasonable time I might have made a fight for it, but four weeks—it took a month each way in those days—was too absurdly little; I could do nothing. But I would not stay at mamma's. It was more than I would ask of myself, that daily disappointment under the mask of gratified discovery, for long.

I spent an approving, unnatural week, in my farcical character, bridling my resentment and hiding my mortification with pretty phrases; and then I went up to town and drowned my sorrows in the summer sales. I took John with me. I may have been Cecily's mother in theory, but I was John's wife in fact.

We went back to the frontier, and the regiment saw a lot of service. That meant medals and fun for my husband, but economy and anxiety for me, though I managed to be allowed as close to the firing line as any woman.

Once the Colonel's wife and I, sitting in Fort Samila, actually heard the rifles of a punitive expedition cracking on the other side of the river—that was a bad moment. My man came in after fifteen hours' fighting, and went sound asleep, sitting before his food with his knife and fork in his hands. But service makes heavy demands besides those on your wife's nerves. We had saved two thousand rupees, I remember, against another run home, and it all went like powder, in the Mirzai expedition; and the run home diminished to a month in a boarding-house in the hills.

Meanwhile, however, we had begun to correspond with our daughter, in large round words of one syllable, behind which, of course, was plain the patient guiding hand of Aunt Emma. One could hear Aunt Emma suggesting what would be nice to say, trying to instil a little pale affection for the far-off papa and mamma. There was so little Cecily and so much Emma—of course, it could not be otherwise—that I used to take, I fear, but a perfunctory joy in these letters. When we went home again I stipulated absolutely that she was to write to us without any sort of supervision—the child was ten.

'But the spelling!' cried Aunt Emma, with lifted eyebrows.

'Her letters aren't exercises,' I was obliged to retort; 'she will do the best she can.'

We found her a docile little girl, with nice manners, a thoroughly unobjectionable child. I saw quite clearly that I could not have brought her up so well; indeed, there were moments when I fancied that Cecily, contrasting me with her aunts, wondered a little what my bringing up could have been like. With this reserve of criticism on Cecily's part, however, we got on very tolerably, largely because I found it impossible to assume any responsibility toward her, and in moments of doubt or discipline referred her to her aunts. We spent a pleasant summer with a little girl in the house whose interest in us was amusing, and whose outings it was gratifying to arrange; but when we went back, I had no desire to take her with us. I thought her very much better where she was.

•

Then came the period which is filled, in a subordinate degree, with Cecily's letters. I do not wish to claim more than I ought; they were not my only or even my principal interest in life. It was a long period; it lasted till she was twenty-one. John had had promotion in the meantime, and there was rather more money, but he had earned his second brevet with a bullet through one lung, and the doctors ordered our leave to be spent in South Africa. We had photographs, we knew she had grown tall and athletic and comely, and the letters were always very creditable. I had the unusual and qualified privilege of watching my daughter's development from ten to twenty-one, at a distance of four thousand miles, by means of the written word. I wrote myself as provocatively as possible; I sought for every string, but the vibration that came back across the seas to me was always other than the one I looked for, and sometimes there was none. Nevertheless, Mrs Farnham wrote me that Cecily very much valued my communications. Once when I had described an unusual excursion in a native state, I learned that she had read my letter aloud to the sewing circle. After that I abandoned description, and confined myself to such intimate personal details as no sewing circle could find amusing. The child's own letters were simply a mirror of the ideas of the Farnham ladies; that must have been so, it was not altogether my jaundiced eye. Alice and Emma and grandmamma paraded the pages in turn. I very early gave up hope of discoveries in my daughter, though as much of the original as I could detect was satisfactorily simple and sturdy. I found little things to criticize, of course, tendencies to correct; and by return post I criticized and corrected, but the distance and the deliberation seemed to touch my maxims with a kind of arid frivolity, and sometimes I tore them up. One quick, warm-blooded scolding would have been worth a sheaf of them. My studied little phrases could only inoculate her with a dislike for me without protecting her from anything under the sun.

However, I found she didn't dislike me, when John and I went home at last to bring her out. She received me with just a hint of kindness, perhaps, but on the whole very well.

II

John was recalled, of course, before the end of our furlough, which knocked various things on the head; but that is the sort of thing one learned to take with philosophy in any lengthened term of Her Majesty's service. Besides, there is usually sugar for the pill; and in this case it was a Staff command bigger than anything we expected for at least five years to come. The excitement of it when it was explained to her gave Cecily a charming colour. She took a good deal of interest in the General, her papa; I think she had an idea that his distinction would alleviate the situation in India, however it might present itself. She accepted that prospective situation calmly; it had been placed before her all her life. There would always be a time when she should go and live with papa and mamma in India, and so long as she was of an age to receive the idea with rebel tears she was assured that papa and mamma would give her a pony. The pony was no longer added to the prospect; it was absorbed no doubt in the general list of attractions calculated to reconcile a young lady to a parental roof with which she had no practical acquaintance. At all events, when I feared the embarrassment and dismay of a pathetic parting with darling grandmamma and the aunties, and the sweet cat and the dear vicar and all the other objects of affection, I found an agreeable unexpected philosophy.

I may add that while I anticipated such broken-hearted farewells I was quite prepared to take them easily. Time, I imagined, had brought philosophy to me also, equally agreeable and equally unexpected.

It was a Bombay ship, full of returning Anglo-Indians. I looked up and down the long saloon tables with a sense of relief and of solace; I was again among my own people. They belonged to Bengal and to Burma, to Madras and to the Punjab, but they were all my people. I could pick out a score that I knew in fact, and there were none that in imagination I didn't know. The look of wider seas and skies, the casual experienced glance, the touch of irony and of tolerance, how well I knew it and how well I liked it! Dear old England, sitting in our wake, seemed to hold by comparison a great many soft, unsophisticated people, immensely occupied about very particular trifles. How difficult it had been, all the summer, to be interested! These of my long acquaintance belonged to my country's Executive, acute, alert, with the marks of travail on them. Gladly I went in and out of the women's cabins and listened to the argot of the men; my own ruling, administering, soldiering little lot.

Cecily looked at them askance. To her the atmosphere was alien, and I perceived that gently and privately she registered objections. She cast a disapproving eye upon the wife of a Conservator of Forests, who scanned with interest a distant funnel and laid a small wager that it belonged to the Messageries Maritimes. She looked with a straightened lip at the crisply stepping women who walked the deck in short and rather shabby skirts with their hands in their jacket-pockets talking transfers and promotions; and having got up at six to make a water-colour sketch of the sunrise, she came to me in profound indignation to say that she had met a man in his pajamas; no doubt, poor wretch, on his way to be shaved. I was unable to convince her that he was not expected to visit the barber in all his clothes.

At the end of the third day she told me that she wished these people wouldn't talk to her; she didn't like them. I had turned in the hour we left the Channel and had not left my berth since, so possibly I was not in the most amiable mood to receive a douche of cold water. 'I must try to remember, dear,' I said, 'that you have been brought up altogether in the society of pussies and vicars and elderly ladies, and of course you miss them. But you must have a little patience. I shall be up tomorrow, if this beastly sea continues to go down; and then we will try to find somebody suitable to introduce to you.'

'Thank you, mamma,' said my daughter, without a ray of suspicion. Then she added consideringly, 'Aunt Emma and Aunt Alice do seem quite elderly ladies beside you, and yet you are older than either of them aren't you? I wonder how that is.'

It was so innocent, so admirable, that I laughed at my own expense; while Cecily, doing her hair, considered me gravely. 'I wish you would tell me why you laugh, mamma,' quoth she; 'you laugh so often.'

We had not to wait after all for my good offices of the next morning. Cecily came down at ten o'clock that night quite happy and excited; she had been talking to a bishop, such a dear bishop. The bishop had been showing her his collection of photographs, and she had promised to play the harmonium for him at the eleven-o'clock service in the morning. 'Bless me!' said I, 'is it Sunday?' It seemed she had got on very well indeed with the bishop, who knew the married sister, at Tunbridge, of her very greatest friend. Cecily herself did not know the married sister, but that didn't matter—it was a link. The bishop was charming. 'Well, my love,' said I—I was teaching myself to use these forms of address for fear she would feel an unkind lack of them, but it was difficult —'I am glad that somebody from my part of the world has impressed you favourably at last. I wish we had more bishops.'

'Oh, but my bishop doesn't belong to your part of the world,' responded my daughter sleepily. 'He is travelling for his health.'

It was the most unexpected and delightful thing to be packed into one's chair next morning by Dacres Tottenham. As I emerged from the music saloon after breakfast—Cecily had stayed below to look over her hymns and consider with her bishop the possibility of an anthem—Dacres's face was the first I saw; it simply illuminated, for me, that portion of the deck. I noticed with pleasure the quick toss of the cigar overboard as he recognized and bore down upon me. We were immense friends; John liked him too. He was one of those people who make a tremendous difference; in all our three hundred passengers there could be no one like him, certainly no one whom I could be more glad to see. We plunged at once into immediate personal affairs, we would get at the heart of them later. He gave his vivid word to everything he had seen and done; we laughed and exclaimed and were silent in a concert of admirable understanding. We were still unraveling, still demanding and explaining when the ship's bell began to ring for church, and almost simultaneously Cecily advanced toward us. She had a proper Sunday hat on, with flowers under the brim, and a church-going frock; she wore gloves and clasped a prayer-book. Most of the women who filed past to the summons of the bell were going down as they were, in cotton blouses and serge skirts, in tweed caps or anything, as to a kind of family prayers. I knew exactly how they would lean against the pillars of the saloon during the psalms. This young lady would be little less than a rebuke to them. I surveyed her approach; she positively walked as if it were Sunday.

'My dear,' I said, 'how *endimanchée* you look! The bishop will be very pleased with you. This gentleman is Mr Tottenham, who administers Her Majesty's pleasure in parts of India about Allahabad. My daughter, Dacres.' She was certainly looking very fresh, and her calm gray eyes had the repose in them that has never known itself to be disturbed about anything. I wondered whether she bowed so distantly also because it was Sunday, and then I remembered that Dacres was a young man, and that the Farnham ladies had probably taught her that it was right to be very distant with young men.

'It is almost eleven, mamma.'

'Yes, dear. I see you are going to church.'

'Are you not coming, mamma?'

I was well wrapped up in an extremely comfortable corner. I had *La Duchesse Bleue* uncut in my lap, and an agreeable person to talk to. I fear that in any case I should not have been inclined to attend the service, but there was something in my daughter's intonation that made me distinctly hostile to the idea. I am putting things down as they were, extenuating nothing.

'I think not, dear.'

'I've turned up two such nice seats.'

'Stay, Miss Farnham, and keep us in countenance,' said Dacres, with his charming smile. The smile displaced a look of discreet and amused observation. Dacres had an eye always for a situation, and this one was even newer to him than to me.

'No, no. She must run away and not bully her mamma,' I said. 'When she comes back we will see how much she remembers of the sermon;' and as the flat tinkle from the companion began to show signs of diminishing, Cecily, with one grieved glance, hastened down.

'You amazing lady!' said Dacres. 'A daughter—and such a tall daughter! I somehow never——'

'You knew we had one?'

'There was theory of that kind, I remember, about ten years ago. Since then—excuse me—I don't think you've mentioned her.'

'You talk as if she were a skeleton in the closet!'

'You *didn't* talk—as if she were.'

'I think she was, in a way, poor child. But the resurrection day hasn't confounded me as I deserved. She's a very good girl.'

'If you had asked me to pick out your daughter——'

'She would have been the last you would indicate! Quite so,' I said. 'She is like her father's people. I can't help that.'

'I shouldn't think you would if you could,' Dacres remarked absently; but the sea air, perhaps, enabled me to digest his thoughtlessness with a smile.

'No,' I said, 'I am just as well pleased. I think a resemblance to me would confuse me, often.'

There was a trace of scrutiny in Dacres's glance. 'Don't you find yourself in sympathy with her?' he asked.

'My dear boy, I have seen her just twice in twenty-one years! You see, I've always stuck to John.'

'But between mother and daughter—I may be old-fashioned, but I had an idea that there was an instinct that might be depended on.'

'I am depending on it,' I said, and let my eyes follow the little blue waves that chased past the handrail. 'We are making very good speed, aren't we? Thirty-five knots since last night at ten. Are you in the sweep?'

'I never bet on the way out—can't afford it. Am I old-fashioned?' he insisted.

'Probably. Men are very slow in changing their philosophy about women. I fancy their idea of the maternal relation is firmest fixed of all.'

'We see it a beatitude!' he cried.

'I know,' I said wearily, 'and you never modify the view.'

Dacres contemplated the portion of the deck that lay between us. His eyes were discreetly lowered, but I saw embarrassment and speculation and a hint of criticism in them.

'Tell me more about it,' said he.

'Oh, for heaven's sake don't be sympathetic!' I exclaimed. 'Lend me a little philosophy instead. There is nothing to tell. There she is and there I am, in the most intimate relation in the world, constituted when she is twenty-one and I am forty.' Dacres started slightly at the ominous word; so little do men realize that the women they like can ever pass out of the constated years of attraction. 'I find the young lady very tolerable, very creditable, very nice. I find the relation atrocious. There you have it. I would like to break the relation into pieces,' I went on recklessly, 'and throw it into the sea. Such things should be tempered to one. I should feel it much less if she occupied another cabin, and would consent to call me Elizabeth or Jane. It is not as if I had been her mother always. One grows fastidious at forty—new intimacies are only possible when on a basis of temperament——'

I paused; it seemed to me that I was making excuses, and I had not the least desire in the world to do that.

'How awfully rough on the girl!' said Dacres Tottenham.

'That consideration has also occurred to me,' I said candidly, 'though I have perhaps been even more struck by its converse.'

'You had no earthly business to be her mother,' said my friend, with irritation.

I shrugged my shoulders—what would you have done?—and opened *La Duchesse Bleue*.

III

Mrs Morgan, wife of a judge of the High Court of Bombay, and I sat amidships on the cool side in the Suez Canal. She was outlining 'Soiled Linen' in chain-stitch on a green canvas bag; I was admiring the Egyptian sands. 'How charming,' said I, 'is this solitary desert in the endless oasis we are compelled to cross!'

'Oasis in the desert, you mean,' said Mrs Morgan; 'I haven't noticed any, but I happened to look up this morning as I was putting on my stockings, and I saw through my port-hole the most lovely mirage.'

I had been at school with Mrs Morgan more than twenty years agone, but she had come to the special enjoyment of the dignities of life while I still liked doing things. Mrs Morgan was the kind of person to make one realize how distressing a medium is middle age. Contemplating her precipitous lap, to which conventional attitudes were certainly more becoming, I crossed my own knees with energy, and once more resolved to be young until I was old.

'How perfectly delightful for you to be taking Cecily out!' said Mrs Morgan placidly.

'Isn't it?' I responded, watching the gliding sands.

'But she was born in sixty-nine—that makes her twenty-one. Quite time, I should say.'

'Oh, we couldn't put it off any longer. I mean—her father has such a horror of early débuts. He simply would not hear of her coming before.'

'Doesn't want her to marry in India, I dare say—the only one,' purred Mrs Morgan.

'Oh, I don't know. It isn't such a bad place. I was brought out there to marry, and I married. I've found it very satisfactory.'

'You always did say exactly what you thought, Helena,' said Mrs Morgan excusingly.

'I haven't much patience with people who bring their daughters out to give them the chance they never would have in England, and then go about devoutly hoping they won't marry in India,' I said. 'I shall be very pleased if Cecily does as well as your girls have done.'

'Mary in the Indian Civil and Jessie in the Imperial Service Troops,' sighed Mrs Morgan complacently. 'And both, my dear, within a year. It *was* a blow.'

'Oh, it must have been!' I said civilly.

There was no use in bandying words with Emily Morgan.

'There is nothing in the world like the satisfaction and pleasure one takes in one's daughters,' Mrs Morgan went on limpidly. 'And one can be in such *close* sympathy with one's girls. I have never regretted having no sons.'

'Dear me, yes. To watch oneself growing up again—call back the lovely April of one's prime, etcetera—to read every thought and anticipate every wish—there is no more golden privilege in life, dear Emily. Such a direct and natural avenue for affection, such a wide field for interest!'

I paused, lost in the volume of my admirable sentiments.

'How beautifully you talk, Helena! I wish I had the gift.'

'It doesn't mean very much,' I said truthfully.

'Oh, I think it's everything! And how companionable a girl is! I quite envy you, this season, having Cecily constantly with you and taking her about everywhere. Something quite new for you, isn't it?'

'Absolutely,' said I; 'I am looking forward to it immensely. But it is likely she will make her own friends, don't you think?' I added anxiously.

'Hardly the first season. My girls didn't. I was practically their only intimate for months. Don't be afraid; you won't be obliged to go shares in Cecily with anybody for a good long while,' added Mrs Morgan kindly. 'I know just how you feel about *that*.'

The muddy water of the Ditch chafed up from under us against its banks with a smell that enabled me to hide the emotions Mrs Morgan evoked behind my handkerchief. The pale desert was pictorial with the drifting, deepening purple shadows of clouds, and in the midst a blue glimmer of the Bitter Lakes, with a white sail on them. A little frantic Arab boy ran alongside keeping pace with the ship. Except for the smell, it was like a dream, we moved so quietly; on, gently on and on between the ridgy clay banks and the rows of piles. Peace was on the ship; you could hear what the Fourth in his white ducks said to the quartermaster in his blue denims; you could count the strokes of the electric bell in the wheel-house; peace was on the ship as she pushed on, an ever-venturing, double-funneled impertinence, through the sands of the ages. My eyes wandered along a plank-line in the deck till they were arrested by a petticoat I knew, when they returned of their own accord. I seemed to be always seeing that petticoat.

'I think,' resumed Mrs Morgan, whose glance had wandered

in the same direction,'that Cecily is a very fine type of our English girls. With those dark gray eyes, a *little* prominent possibly, and that good colour—it's rather high now perhaps, but she will lose quite enough of it in India—and those regular features, she would make a splendid Britannia. Do you know, I fancy she must have a great deal of character. Has she?'

'Any amount. And all of it good,' I responded, with private dejection.

'No faults at all?' chaffed Mrs Morgan.

I shook my head. 'Nothing,' I said sadly, 'that I can put my finger on. But I hope to discover a few later. The sun may bring them out.'

'Like freckles. Well, you are a lucky woman. Mine had plenty, I assure you. Untidiness was no name for Jessie, and Mary—I'm *sorry* to say that Mary sometimes fibbed.'

'How lovable of her! Cecily's neatness is a painful example to me, and I don't believe she would tell a fib to save my life.'

'Tell me,' said Mrs Morgan, as the lunch-bell rang and she gathered her occupation into her work-basket, 'who is that talking to her?'

'Oh, an old friend,' I replied easily; 'Dacres Tottenham, a dear fellow, and most benevolent. He is trying on my behalf to reconcile her to the life she'll have to lead in India.'

'She won't need much reconciling, if she's like most girls,' observed Mrs Morgan, 'but he seems to be trying very hard.'

That was quite the way I took it—on my behalf—for several days. When people have understood you very adequately for ten years you do not expect them to boggle at any problem you may present at the end of the decade. I thought Dacres was moved by a fine sense of compassion. I thought that with his admirable perception he had put a finger on the little comedy of fruitfulness in my life that laughed so bitterly at the tragedy of the barren woman, and was attempting, by delicate manipulation, to make it easier. I really thought so. Then I observed that myself had preposterously deceived me, that it wasn't like that at all. When Mr Tottenham joined us, Cecily and me, I saw that he listened more than he talked, with an ear specially cocked to register any small irony which might appear in my remarks to my daughter. Naturally he registered more than there were, to make up perhaps for dear Cecily's obviously not registering any. I could see, too, that he was suspicious of any flavour of kindness; finally, to avoid the strictures of his upper lip, which really, dear fellow, began to bore me, I talked exclusively about the distant sails and the Red Sea littoral. When he no longer joined us as we sat or walked together, I perceived that his hostility was fixed and his *parti pris*. He was brimful of compassion, but it was all for Cecily, none for the situation or for me. (She would have marvelled, placidly, why he pitied her. I am glad I can say that.) The primitive man in him rose up as Pope of nature and excommunicated me as a creature recusant to her functions. Then deliberately Dacres undertook an office of consolation; and I fell to wondering, while Mrs Morgan spoke her convictions plainly out, how far an impulse of reparation for a misfortune with which he had nothing to do might carry a man.

I began to watch the affair with an interest which even to me seemed queer. It was not detached, but it was semi-detached, and, of course, on the side for which I seem, in this history, to be perpetually apologizing. With certain limitations it didn't matter an atom whom Cecily married. So that he was sound and decent, with reasonable prospects, her simple requirements and ours for her would be quite met. There was the ghost of a consolation in that; one needn't be anxious or exacting.

I could predict with a certain amount of confidence that in her first season she would probably receive three or four proposals, any one of which she might accept with as much propriety and satisfaction as any other one. For Cecily it was so simple; prearranged by nature like her digestion, one could not see any logical basis for difficulties. A nice upstanding sapper, a dashing Bengal Lancer—oh, I could think of half a dozen types that would answer excellently. She was the kind of young person, and that was the summing up of it, to marry a type and be typically happy. I hoped and expected that she would. But Dacres!

Dacres should exercise the greatest possible discretion. He was not a person who could throw the dice indifferently with fate. He could respond to so much, and he would inevitably, sooner or later, demand so much response! He was governed by a preposterously exacting temperament, and he wore his nerves outside. And what vision he had! How he explored the world he lived in and drew out of it all there was, all there was! I could see him in the years to come ranging alone the fields that were sweet and the horizons that lifted for him, and ever returning to pace the common dusty mortal road by the side of a purblind wife. On general principles, as a case to point at, it would be a conspicuous pity. Nor would it lack the aspect of a particular, a personal misfortune. Dacres was occupied in quite the natural normal degree with his charming self; he would pass his misery on, and who would deserve to escape it less than his mother-in-law?

I listened to Emily Morgan, who gleaned in the ship more information about Dacres Tottenham's people, pay, and prospects than I had ever acquired, and I kept an eye upon the pair which was, I flattered myself, quite maternal. I watched them without acute anxiety, deploring the threatening destiny, but hardly nearer to it than one is in the stalls to the stage. My moments of real concern for Dacres were mingled more with anger than with sorrow—it seemed inexcusable that he, with his infallible divining-rod for temperament, should be on the point of making such an ass of himself. Though I talk of the stage there was nothing at all dramatic to reward my attention, mine and Emily Morgan's. To my imagination, excited by its idea of what Dacres Tottenham's courtship ought to be, the attentions he paid to Cecily were most humdrum. He threw rings into buckets with her—she was good at that—and quoits upon the 'bull' board; he found her chair after the decks were swabbed in the morning and established her in it; he paced the deck with her at convenient times and seasons. They were humdrum, but they were constant and cumulative. Cecily took them with an even breath that perfectly matched. There was hardly anything, on her part, to note—a little discreet observation of his comings and goings, eyes scarcely lifted from her book, and later just a hint of proprietorship, as the evening she came up to me on deck, our first night in the Indian Ocean. I was lying in my long chair looking at the thick, low stars and thinking it was a long time since I had seen John.

'Dearest mamma, out here and nothing over your shoulders! You *are* imprudent. Where is your wrap? Mr Tottenham, will you please fetch mamma's wrap for her?'

'If mamma so instructs me,' he said audaciously.

'Do as Cecily tells you,' I laughed, and he went and did it, while I by the light of a quartermaster's lantern distinctly saw my daughter blush.

Another time, when Cecily came down to undress, she bent over me as I lay in the lower berth with unusual solicitude. I had been dozing, and I jumped.

'What is it, child?' I said. 'Is the ship on fire?'

'No, mamma, the ship is not on fire. There is nothing wrong. I'm so sorry I startled you. But Mr Tottenham has been telling me all about what you did for the soldiers the time plague broke out in the lines at Mian-Mir. I think it was splendid, mamma, and so does he.'

'Oh, *Lord!*' I groaned. 'Good night.'

IV

It remained in my mind, that little thing that Dacres had taken the trouble to tell my daughter; I thought about it a good deal. It seemed to me the most serious and convincing circumstance that had yet offered itself to my consideration. Dacres was no longer content to bring solace and support to the more appealing figure of the situation; he must set to work, bless him! to improve the situation itself. He must try to induce Miss Farnham, by telling her everything he could remember to my credit, to think as well of her mother as possible, in spite of the strange and secret blows which that mother might be supposed to sit up at night to deliver to her. Cecily thought very well of me already; indeed, with private reservations as to my manners and—no, *not* my morals, I believe I exceeded her expectations of what a perfectly new and untrained mother would be likely to prove. It was my theory that she found me all she could understand me to be. The maternal virtues of the outside were certainly mine; I put them on with care every morning and wore them with patience all day. Dacres, I assured myself, must have allowed his preconception to lead him absurdly by the nose not to see that the girl was satisfied, that my impatience, my impotence, did not at all make her miserable. Evidently, however, he had created our relations differently; evidently he had set himself to their amelioration. There was portent in it; things seemed to be closing in. I bit off a quarter of an inch of wooden pen-handle in considering whether or not I should mention it in my letter to John, and decided that it would be better just perhaps to drop a hint. Though I could not expect John to receive it with any sort of perturbation. Men are different; he would probably think Tottenham well enough able to look after himself.

I had embarked on my letter, there at the end of a corner-table of the saloon, when I saw Dacres saunter through. He wore a very conscious and elaborately purposeless air; and it jumped with my mood that he had nothing less than the crisis of his life in his pocket, and was looking for me. As he advanced toward me between the long tables doubt left me and alarm assailed me. 'I'm glad to find you in a quiet corner,' said he, seating himself, and confirmed my worst anticipations.

'I'm writing to John,' I said, and again applied myself to my pen-handle. It is a trick Cecily has since done her best in vain to cure me of.

'I am going to interrupt you,' he said. 'I have not had an opportunity of talking to you for some time.'

'I like that!' I exclaimed derisively.

'And I want to tell you that I am very much charmed with Cecily.'

'Well,' I said, 'I am not going to gratify you by saying anything against her.'

'You don't deserve her, you know.'

'I won't dispute that. But, if you don't mind—I'm not sure that I'll stand being abused, dear boy.'

'I quite see it isn't any use. Though one spoke with the tongues of men and of angels——'

'And had not charity,' I continued for him. 'Precisely. I won't go on, but your quotation is very apt.'

'I so bow down before her simplicity. It makes a wide and beautiful margin for the rest of her character. She is a girl Ruskin would have loved.'

'I wonder,' said I. 'He did seem fond of the simple type, didn't he?'

'Her mind is so clear, so transparent. The motive spring of everything she says and does is so direct. Don't you find you can most completely depend upon her?'

'Oh yes,' I said; 'certainly. I nearly always know what she is going to say before she says it, and under given circumstances I can tell precisely what she will do.'

'I fancy her sense of duty is very beautifully developed.'

'It is,' I said. 'There is hardly a day when I do not come in contact with it.'

'Well, that is surely a good thing. And I find that calm poise of hers very restful.'

'I would not have believed that so many virtues could reside in one young lady,' I said, taking refuge in flippancy, 'and to think that she should be my daughter!'

'As I believe you know, that seems to me rather a cruel stroke of destiny, Mrs Farnham.'

'Oh yes, I know! You have a constructive imagination, Dacres. You don't seem to see that the girl is protected by her limitations, like a tortoise. She lives within them quite secure and happy and content. How determined you are to be sorry for her!'

Mr Tottenham looked at the end of this lively exchange as though he sought for a polite way of conveying to me that I rather was the limited person. He looked as if he wished he could say things. The first of them would be, I saw, that he had quite a different conception of Cecily, that it was illuminated by many trifles, nuances of feeling and expression, which he had noticed in his talks with her whenever they had skirted the subject of her adoption by her mother. He knew her, he was longing to say, better than I did; when it would have been natural to reply that one could not hope to compete in such a direction with an intelligent young man, and we should at once have been upon delicate and difficult ground. So it was as well perhaps that he kept silence until he said, as he had come prepared to say, 'Well, I want to put that beyond a doubt—her happiness—if I'm good enough. I want her, please, and I only hope that she will be half as willing to come as you are likely to be to let her go.'

It was a shock when it came, plump, like that; and I was horrified to feel how completely every other consideration was lost for the instant in the immense relief that it prefigured. To be my whole complete self again, without the feeling that a fraction of me was masquerading about in Cecily! To be freed at once, or almost, from an exacting condition and an impossible ideal! 'Oh!' I exclaimed, and my eyes positively filled. 'You *are* good, Dacres, but I couldn't let you do that.'

His undisguised stare brought me back to a sense of the proportion of things. I saw that in the combination of influences that had brought Mr Tottenham to the point of proposing to marry my daughter consideration for me, if it had a place, would be fantastic. Inwardly I laughed at the egotism of raw nerves that had conjured it up, even for an instant, as a reason for gratitude. The situation was not so peculiar, not so interesting, as that. But I answered his stare with a smile; what I had said might very well stand.

'Do you imagine,' he said, seeing that I did not mean to amplify it, 'that I want to marry her out of any sort of *good*ness?'

'Benevolence is your weakness, Dacres.'

'I see. You think one's motive is to withdraw her from a relation which ought to be the most natural in the world, but which is, in her particular and painful case, the most equivocal.'

'Well, come,' I remonstrated. 'You have dropped one or two things, you know, in the heat of your indignation, not badly calculated to give one that idea. The eloquent statement you have just made, for instance—it carries all the patness of old conviction. How often have you rehearsed it?'

I am a fairly long-suffering person, but I began to feel a little annoyed with my would-be son-in-law. If the relation were achieved it would give him no prescriptive right to bully me; and we were still in very early anticipation of that.

'Ah!' he said disarmingly. 'Don't let us quarrel. I'm sorry you think that; because it isn't likely to bring your favour to my project, and I want you friendly and helpful. Oh, confound it!' he exclaimed, with sudden temper. 'You ought to be. I don't understand this aloofness. I half suspect it's pose. You undervalue Cecily—well, you have no business to undervalue me. You know me better than anybody in the world. Now are you going to help me to marry your daughter?'

'I don't think so,' I said slowly, after a moment's silence, which he sat through like a mutinous schoolboy. 'I might tell you that I don't care a button whom you marry, but that would not be true. I do care more or less. As you say, I know you pretty well. I'd a little rather you didn't make a mess of it; and if you must I should distinctly prefer not to have the spectacle under my nose for the rest of my life. I can't hinder you, but I won't help you.'

'And what possesses you to imagine that in marrying Cecily I should make a mess of it? Shouldn't your first consideration be whether *she* would?'

'Perhaps it should, but, you see, it isn't. Cecily would be happy with anybody who made her comfortable. You would ask a good deal more than that, you know.'

Dacres, at this, took me up promptly. Life, he said, the heart of life, had particularly little to say to temperament. By the heart of life I suppose he meant married love. He explained that its roots asked other sustenance, and that it throve best of all on simple elemental goodness. So long as a man sought in women mere casual companionship, perhaps the most exquisite thing to be experienced was the stimulus of some spiritual feminine counterpart; but when he desired of one woman that she should be always and intimately with him, the background of his life, the mother of his children, he was better advised to avoid nerves and sensibilities, and try for the repose of the common—the uncommon—domestic virtues. Ah, he said, they were sweet, like lavender. (Already, I told him, he smelled the housekeeper's linen-chest.) But I did not interrupt him much; I couldn't, he was too absorbed. To temperamental pairing, he declared, the century owed its breed of decadents. I asked him if he had ever really recognized one; and he retorted that if he hadn't he didn't wish to make a beginning in his own family. In a quarter of an hour he repudiated the theories of a lifetime, a gratifying triumph for simple elemental goodness. Having denied the value of the subtler pretensions to charm in woman as you marry her, he went artlessly on to endow Cecily with as many of them as could possibly be desirable. He actually persuaded himself to say that it was lovely to see the reflections of life in her tranquil spirit; and when I looked at him incredulously he grew angry, and hinted that Cecily's sensitiveness to reflections and other things might be a trifle beyond her mother's ken. 'She responds instantly, intimately, to the beautiful everywhere,' he declared.

'Aren't the opportunities of life on board ship rather limited to demonstrate that?' I inquired. 'I know—you mean sunsets. Cecily is very fond of sunsets. She is always asking me to come and look at them.'

'I was thinking of last night's sunset,' he confessed. 'We looked at it together.'

'What did she say?' I asked idly.

'Nothing very much. That's just the point. Another girl would have raved and gushed.'

'Oh, well, Cecily never does that,' I responded. 'Nevertheless she is a very ordinary human instrument. I hope I shall have no temptation ten years hence to remind you that I warned you of her quality.'

'I wish, not in the least for my own profit, for I am well convinced already, but simply to win your cordiality and your approval—never did an unexceptional wooer receive such niggard encouragement!—I wish there were some sort of test for her quality. I would be proud to stand by it, and you would be convinced. I can't find words to describe my objection to your state of mind.'

The thing seemed to me to be a foregone conclusion. I saw it accomplished, with all its possibilities of disastrous commonplace. I saw all that I have here taken the trouble to foreshadow. So far as I was concerned, Dacres's burden would add itself to my philosophies, *voilà tout*. I should always be a little uncomfortable about it, because it had been taken from my back; but it would not be a matter for the wringing of hands. And yet—the hatefulness of the mistake! Dacres's bold talk of a test made no suggestion. Should my invention be more fertile? I thought of something.

'You have said nothing to her yet?' I asked.

'Nothing. I don't think she suspects for a moment. She treats me as if no such fell design were possible. I'm none too confident, you know,' he added, with a longer face.

'We go straight to Agra. Could you come to Agra?'

'Ideal!' he cried. 'The memory of Mumtaz! The garden of the Taj! I've always wanted to love under the same moon as Shah Jehan. How thoughtful of you!'

'You must spend a few days with us in Agra,' I continued. 'And as you say, it is the very place to shrine your happiness, if it comes to pass there.'

'Well, I am glad to have extracted a word of kindness from you at last,' said Dacres, as the stewards came to lay the table. 'But I wish,' he added regretfully, 'you could have thought of a test.'

V

Four days later we were in Agra. A time there was when the name would have been the key of dreams to me; now it stood for John's headquarters. I was rejoiced to think I would look again upon the Taj; and the prospect of living with it was a real enchantment; but I pondered most the kind of house that would be provided for the General Commanding the District, how many the dining-room would seat, and whether it would have a roof of thatch or of corrugated iron—I prayed against corrugated iron. I confess these my preoccupations. I was forty, and at forty the practical considerations of life hold their own even against domes of marble, world-renowned, and set about with gardens where the bulbul sings to the rose. I smiled across the years at the raptures of my first vision of the place at twenty-one, just Cecily's age. Would I now sit under Arjamand's cypresses till two o'clock in the morning to see the wonder of her tomb at a particular angle of the moon? Would I climb one of her tall white ministering minarets to see anything whatever? I very greatly feared that I would not. Alas for the aging of sentiment, of interest! Keep your touch with life and your seat in the saddle as long as you will, the world is no new toy at forty. But Cecily was twenty-one, Cecily who sat stolidly finishing her lunch while Dacres Tottenham talked about Akbar and his philosophy. 'The sort of man,' he said, 'that Carlyle might have smoked a pipe with.'

'But surely,' said Cecily reflectively, 'tobacco was not discovered in England then. Akbar came to the throne in 1526.'

'Nor Carlyle either for that matter,' I hastened to observe. 'Nevertheless, I think Mr Tottenham's proposition must stand.'

'Thanks, Mrs Farnham,' said Dacres. 'But imagine Miss Farnham's remembering Akbar's date! I'm sure you didn't!'

'Let us hope she doesn't know too much about him,' I cried gaily, 'or there will be nothing to tell!'

'Oh, really and truly very little!' said Cecily, 'but as soon as we heard papa would be stationed here Aunt Emma made me read up about those old Moguls and people. I think I remember the dynasty. Baber, wasn't he the first? and then Humayon, and after him Akbar, and then Jehangir, and then Shah Jehan. But I've forgotten every date but Akbar's'

She smiled her smile of brilliant health and even spirits as she made the damaging admission, and she was so good to look at, sitting there simple and wholesome and fresh, peeling her banana with her well-shaped fingers, that we swallowed the dynasty as it were whole, and smiled back upon her. John, I may say, was extremely pleased with Cecily; he said she was a very satisfactory human accomplishment. One would have thought, positively, the way he plumed himself over his handsome daughter, that he alone was responsible for her. But John, having received his family, straightway set off with his Staff on a tour of inspection, and thereby takes himself out of this history. I sometimes think that if he had stayed—but there has never been the lightest recrimination between us about it, and I am not going to hint one now.

'Did you read,' asked Dacres, 'what he and the Court poet wrote over the entrance gate to the big mosque at Fattehpur-Sikri? It's rather nice. "The world is a looking-glass, wherein the image has come and is gone—take as thine own nothing more than what thou lookest upon." '

My daughter's thoughtful gaze was, of course, fixed upon the speaker, and in his own glance I saw a sudden ray of consciousness; but Cecily transferred her eyes to the opposite wall, deeply considering, and while Dacres and I smiled across the table, I saw that she had perceived no reason for blushing. It was a singularly narrow escape.

'No,' she said, 'I didn't; what a curious proverb for an emperor to make! He couldn't possibly have been able to see all his possessions at once.'

'If you have finished,' Dacres addressed her, 'do let me show you what your plain and immediate duty is to the garden. The garden waits for you—all the roses expectant——'

'Why, there isn't one!' cried Cecily, pinning on her hat. It was pleasing, and just a trifle pathetic, the way he hurried her out of the scope of any little dart; he would not have her even within range of amused observation. Would he continue, I wondered vaguely, as, with my elbows on the table, I tore into strips the lemon-leaf that floated in my finger-bowl—would he continue, through life, to shelter her from his other clever friends as now he attempted to shelter her from her mother? In that case he would have to domicile her, poor dear, behind the curtain, like the native ladies—a good price to pay for a protection of which, bless her heart! she would be all unaware. I had quite stopped bemoaning the affair; perhaps the comments of my husband, who treated it with broad approval and satisfaction, did something to soothe my sensibilities. At all events, I had gradually come to occupy a high fatalistic ground toward the pair. If it was written upon their foreheads that they should marry, the inscription was none of mine; and, of course, it was true, as John had indignantly stated, that Dacres might do very much worse. One's interest in Dacres Tottenham's problematical future had in no way diminished; but the young man was so positive, so full of intention, so disinclined to discussion—he had not reopened the subject since that morning in the saloon of the Caledonia—that one's feeling about it rather took the attenuated form of a shrug. I am afraid, too, that the pleasurable excitement of such an impending event had a little supervened; even at forty there is no disallowing the natural interests of one's sex. As I sat there pulling my lemon-leaf to pieces, I should not have been surprised or in the least put about if the two had returned radiant from the lawn to demand my blessing. As to the test of quality that I had obligingly invented for Dacres on the spur of the moment without his knowledge or connivance, it had some time ago faded into what he apprehended it to be—a mere idyllic opportunity, a charming background, a frame for his project, of prettier sentiment than the funnels and the handrails of a ship.

Mr Tottenham had ten days to spend with us. He knew the place well; it belonged to the province to whose service he was dedicated, and he claimed with impressive authority the privilege of showing it to Cecily by degrees—the Hall of Audience today, the Jessamine Tower tomorrow, the tomb of Akbar another, and the Deserted City yet another day. We arranged the expeditions in conference, Dacres insisting only upon the order of them, which I saw was to be cumulative, with the Taj at the very end, on the night precisely of the full of the moon, with a better chance of roses. I had no special views, but Cecily contributed some; that we should do the Hall of Audience in the morning, so as not to interfere with the club tennis in the afternoon, that we should bicycle to Akbar's tomb and take a cold luncheon—if we were sure there would be no snakes—to the Deserted City, to all of which Dacres gave loyal assent. I endorsed everything; I was the encouraging chorus, only stipulating that my number should be swelled from day to day by the addition of such persons as I should approve. Cecily, for instance, wanted to invite the Bakewells because we had come out in the same ship with them; but I could not endure the Bakewells, and it seemed to me that our having made the voyage with them was the best possible reason for declining to lay eyes on them for the rest of our natural lives. 'Mamma has such strong prejudices,' Cecily remarked, as she reluctantly gave up the idea; and I waited to see whether the graceless Tottenham would unmurmuringly take down the Bakewells. How strong must be the sentiment that turns a man into a boa-constrictor without a pang of transmigration! But no, this time he was faithful to the principles of his pre-Cecilian existence. 'They are rather Boojums,' he declared. 'You would think so, too, if you knew them better. It is that kind of excellent person that makes the real burden of India.' I could have patted him on the back.

Thanks to the rest of the chorus, which proved abundantly available, I was no immediate witness to Cecily's introduction to the glorious fragments which sustain in Agra the memory of the Moguls. I may as well say that I arranged with care that if anybody must be standing by when Dacres disclosed them, it should not be I. If Cecily had squinted, I should have been sorry, but I would have found in it no personal humiliation. There were other imperfections of vision, however, for which I felt responsible and ashamed; and with Dacres, though the situation, Heaven knows, was none of my seeking, I had a little the feeling of a dealer who offers a defective *bibelot* to a connoisseur. My charming daughter—I was fifty times congratulated upon her appearance and her manners—had many excellent qualities and capacities which she never inherited from me; but she could see no more than the bulk, no further than the perspective; she could register exactly as much as a camera.

This was a curious thing, perhaps, to displease my maternal vanity, but it did; I had really rather she squinted; and when there was anything to look at I kept out of the way. I can not tell precisely, therefore, what the incidents were that contributed to make Mr Tottenham, on our return from these expeditions, so thoughtful, with a thoughtfulness which increased, toward the end of them, to a positive gravity. This would disappear during dinner under the influence of food and drink. He would talk nightly with new enthusiasm and fresh hope—or did I imagine it?—of the loveliness he had arranged to reveal on the following day. If again my imagination did not lead me astray, I fancied this occurred later and later in the course of the meal as the week went on; as if his state required more stimulus as time progressed. One evening, when I expected it to flag altogether, I had a whim to order champagne and observe the effect; but I am glad to say that I reproved myself, and refrained.

Cecily, meanwhile, was conducting herself in a manner which left nothing to be desired. If, as I sometimes thought, she took Dacres very much for granted, she took him calmly for granted; she seemed a prey to none of those fluttering uncertainties, those suspended judgments and elaborate indifferences which translate themselves so plainly in a young lady receiving addresses. She turned herself out very freshly and very well; she was always ready for everything, and I am sure that no glance of Dacres Tottenham's found aught but direct and decorous response. His society on these occasions gave her solid pleasure; so did the drive and the lunch; the satisfactions were apparently upon the same plane. She was aware of the plum, if I may be permitted a brusque but irresistible simile; and with her mouth open, her eyes modestly closed, and her head in a convenient position, she waited, placidly, until it should fall in. The Farnham ladies would have been delighted with the result of their labours in the sweet reason and eminent propriety of this attitude. Thinking of my idiotic sufferings when John began to fix himself upon my horizon, I pondered profoundly the power of nature in differentiation.

One evening, the last, I think, but one, I had occasion to go to my daughter's room, and found her writing in her commonplace-book. She had a commonplace-book, as well as a Where Is It? an engagement-book, an account-book, a diary, a Daily Sunshine, and others with purposes too various to remember. 'Dearest mamma,' she said, as I was departing, 'there is only one "p" in "opulence", isn't there?'

'Yes,' I replied, with my hand on the door-handle, and added curiously, for it was an odd word in Cecily's mouth, 'Why?'

She hardly hesitated. 'Oh,' she said, 'I am just writing down one or two things Mr Tottenham said about Agra before I forget them. They seemed so true.'

'He has a descriptive touch,' I remarked.

'I think he describes beautifully. Would you like to hear what he said today?'

'I would,' I replied, sincerely.

' "Agra," ' read this astonishing young lady, ' "is India's one pure idyl. Elsewhere she offers other things, foolish opulence, tawdry pageant, treachery of eunuchs and jealousies of harems, thefts of kings' jewels and barbaric retributions; but they are all actual, visualized, or part of a past that shows to the backward glance hardly more relief and vitality than a Persian painting" —I should like to see a Persian painting—"but here the immortal tombs and pleasure-houses rise out of colour delicate and subtle; the vision holds across three hundred years; the print of the court is still in the dust of the city." '

'Did you really let him go on like that?' I exclaimed. 'It has the license of a lecture!'

'I encouraged him to. Of course he didn't say it straight off. He said it naturally; he stopped now and then to cough. I didn't understand it all; but I think I have remembered every word.'

'You have a remarkable memory. I'm glad he stopped to cough. Is there any more?'

'One little bit. "Here the Moguls wrought their passions into marble, and held them up with great refrains from their religion, and set them about with gardens; and here they stand in the twilight of the glory of those kings and the noonday splendor of their own.'' '

'How clever of you!' I exclaimed. 'How wonderfully clever of you to remember!'

'I had to ask him to repeat one or two sentences. He didn't like that. But this is nothing. I used to learn pages letter-perfect for Aunt Emma. She was very particular. I think it is worth preserving, don't you?'

'Dear Cecily,' I responded, 'you have a frugal mind.'

There was nothing else to respond. I could not tell her just how practical I thought her, or how pathetic her little book.

VI

We drove together, after dinner, to the Taj. The moonlight lay in an empty splendor over the broad sandy road, with the acacias pricking up on each side of it and the gardens of the station bungalows stretching back into clusters of crisp shadows. It was an exquisite February night, very still. Nothing seemed abroad but two or three pariah dogs, upon vague and errant business, and the Executive Engineer going swiftly home from the club on his bicycle. Even the little shops of the bazaar were dark and empty; only here and there a light showed barred behind the carved balconies of the upper rooms, and there was hardly any tom-tomming. The last long slope of the road showed us the river curving to the left, through a silent white waste that stretched indefinitely into the moonlight on one side, and was crowned by Akbar's fort on the other. His long high line of turrets and battlements still guarded a hint of their evening rose, and dim and exquisite above them hovered the three dome-bubbles of the Pearl Mosque. It was a night of perfect illusion, and the illusion was mysterious, delicate, and faint. I sat silent as we rolled along, twenty years nearer to the original joy of things when John and I drove through the same old dream.

Dacres, too, seemed preoccupied; only Cecily was, as they say, herself. Cecily was really more than herself, she exhibited an unusual flow of spirits. She talked continually, she pointed out this and that, she asked who lived here and who lived there. At regular intervals of about four minutes she demanded if it wasn't simply too lovely. She sat straight up with her vigorous profile and her smart hat; and the silhouette of her personality sharply refused to mingle with the dust of any dynasty. She was a contrast, a protest; positively she was an indignity. 'Do lean back, dear child,' I exclaimed at last. 'You interfere with the landscape.'

She leaned back, but she went on interfering with it in terms of sincerest enthusiasm.

When we stopped at the great archway of entrance I begged to be left in the carriage. What else could one do, when the golden moment had come, but sit in the carriage and measure it? They climbed the broad stone steps together and passed under the lofty gravures into the garden, and I waited. I waited and remembered. I am not, as perhaps by this time is evident, a person of overwhelming sentiment, but I think the smile upon my lips was gentle. So plainly I could see, beyond the massive archway and across a score of years, all that they saw at that moment—Arjamand's garden, and the long straight tank of marble cleaving it full of sleeping water and the shadows of the marshalling cypresses; her wide dark garden of roses and of pomegranates, and at the end the Vision, marvelous, aerial, the soul of something—is it beauty? is it sorrow?—that great white pride of love in mourning such as only here in all the round of our little world lifts itself to the stars, the unpaintable, indescribable Taj Mahal. A gentle breath stole out with a scent of jessamine and such a memory! I closed my eyes and felt the warm luxury of a tear.

Thinking of the two in the garden, my mood was very kind, very conniving. How foolish after all were my cherry-stone theories of taste and temperament before that uncalculating thing which sways a world and builds a Taj Mahal! Was it probable that Arjamand and her Emperor had loved fastidiously, and yet how they had loved! I wandered away into consideration of the blind forces which move the world, in which comely young persons like my daughter Cecily had such a place; I speculated vaguely upon the value of the subtler gifts of sympathy and insight which seemed indeed, at that enveloping moment, to be mere flowers strewn upon the tide of deeper emotions. The garden sent me a fragrance of roses; the moon sailed higher and picked out the little kiosks set along the wall. It was a charming, charming thing to wait, there at the portal of the silvered, scented garden, for an idyl to come forth.

When they reappeared, Dacres and my daughter, they came

with casual steps and cheerful voices. They might have been a couple of tourists. The moonlight fell full upon them on the platform under the arch. It showed Dacres measuring with his stick the length of the Sanscrit letters which declared the stately texts, and Cecily's expression of polite, perfunctory interest. They looked up at the height above them; they looked back at the vision behind. Then they sauntered toward the carriage, he offering a formal hand to help her down the uncertain steps, she gracefully accepting it.

'You—you have not been long,' said I. 'I hope you didn't hurry on my account.'

'Miss Farnham found the marble a little cold under foot,' replied Dacres, putting Miss Farnham in.

'You see,' explained Cecily, 'I stupidly forgot to change into thicker soles. I have only my slippers. But, mamma, how lovely it is! Do let us come again in the daytime. I am dying to make a sketch of it.'

Mr Tottenham was to leave us on the following day. In the morning, after 'little breakfast', as we say in India, he sought me in the room I had set aside to be particularly my own.

Again I was writing to John, but this time I waited for precisely his interruption. I had got no further than 'My dearest husband,' and my pen-handle was a fringe.

'Another fine day,' I said, as if the old, old Indian joke could give him ease, poor man!

'Yes,' said he, 'we are having lovely weather.'

He had forgotten that it was a joke. Then he lapsed into silence while I renewed my attentions to my pen.

'I say,' he said at last, with so strained a look about his mouth that it was almost a contortion, 'I haven't done it, you know.'

'No,' I responded, cheerfully, 'and you're not going to. Is that it? Well!'

'Frankly——' said he.

'Dear me, yes! Anything else between you and me would be grotesque,' I interrupted, 'after all these years.'

'I don't think it would be a success,' he said, looking at me resolutely with his clear blue eyes, in which still lay, alas! the possibility of many delusions.

'No,' I said, 'I never did, you know. But the prospect had begun to impose upon me.'

'To say how right you were would seem, under the circumstances, the most hateful form of flattery.'

'Yes,' I said, 'I think I can dispense with your verbal endorsement.' I felt a little bitter. It was, of course, better that the connoisseur should have discovered the flaw before concluding the transaction; but although I had pointed it out myself I was not entirely pleased to have the article returned.

'I am infinitely ashamed that it should have taken me all these days—day after day and each contributory—to discover what you saw so easily and so completely.'

'You forget that I am her mother,' I could not resist the temptation of saying.

'Oh, for God's sake don't jeer! Please be absolutely direct, and tell me if you have reason to believe that to the extent of a thought, of a breath—to any extent at all—she cares.'

He was, I could see, very deeply moved; he had not arrived at this point without trouble and disorder not lightly to be put on or off. Yet I did not hurry to his relief, I was still possessed by a vague feeling of offense. I reflected that any mother would be, and I quite plumed myself upon my annoyance. It was so satisfactory, when one had a daughter, to know the sensations of even any mother. Nor was it soothing to remember that the young man's whole attitude toward Cecily had been based upon criticism of me, even though he sat before me whipped with his own lash. His temerity had been stupid and obstinate; I could not regret his punishment.

I kept him waiting long enough to think all this, and then I replied, 'I have not the least means of knowing.'

I can not say what he expected, but he squared his shoulders as if he had received a blow and might receive another. Then he looked at me with a flash of the old indignation. 'You are not near enough to her for that!' he exclaimed.

'I am not near enough to her for that.'

Silence fell between us. A crow perched upon an opened venetian and cawed lustily. For years afterward I never heard a crow caw without a sense of vain, distressing experiment. Dacres got up and began to walk about the room. I very soon put a stop to that. 'I can't talk to a pendulum,' I said, but I could not persuade him to sit down again.

'Candidly,' he said at length, 'do you think she would have me?'

'I regret to say that I think she would. But you would not dream of asking her.'

'Why not? She is a dear girl,' he responded, inconsequently.

'You could not possibly stand it.'

Then Mr Tottenham delivered himself of this remarkable phrase: 'I could stand it,' he said, 'as well as you can.'

There was far from being any joy in the irony with which I regarded him and under which I saw him gather up his resolution to go; nevertheless I did nothing to make it easy for him. I refrained from imparting my private conviction that Cecily would accept the first presentable substitute that appeared, although it was strong. I made no reference to my daughter's large fund of philosophy and small balance of sentiment. I did not even—though this was reprehensible—confess the test, the test of quality in these ten days with the marble archives of the Moguls, which I had almost wantonly suggested, which he had so unconsciously accepted, so disastrously applied. I gave him quite fifteen minutes of his bad quarter of an hour, and when it was over I wrote truthfully but furiously to John. . . .

That was ten years ago. We have since attained the shades of retirement, and our daughter is still with us when she is not with Aunt Emma and Aunt Alice—grandmamma has passed away. Mr Tottenham's dumb departure that day in February—it was the year John got his C.B.—was followed, I am thankful to say, by none of the symptoms of unrequited affection on Cecily's part. Not for ten minutes, or far as I was aware, was she the maid forlorn. I think her self-respect was of too robust a character, thanks to the Misses Farnham. Still less, of course, had she any reproaches to serve upon her mother, although for a long time I thought I detected—or was it my guilty conscience?—a spark of shrewdness in the glance she bent upon me when the talk was of Mr Tottenham and the probabilities of his return to Agra. So well did she sustain her experience, or so little did she feel it, that I believe the impression went abroad that Dacres had been sent disconsolate away. One astonishing conversation I had with her some six months later, which turned upon the point of a particularly desirable offer. She told me something then, without any sort of embarrassment, but quite lucidly and directly, that edified me much to hear. She said that while she was quite sure that Mr Tottenham thought of her only as a friend—she had never had the least reason for any other impression—he had done her a service for which she could not thank him enough—in showing her what a husband might be. He had given her a standard; it might be high, but it was unalterable. She didn't know whether she could describe it, but Mr Tottenham was different from the kind of man you seemed to meet in India. He had his own ways of looking at things, and he talked so well. He had given her an ideal, and she intended to profit by it. To know that men like Mr Tottenham existed, and to marry any other kind would be an act of folly which she did not intend to commit. No, Major the Hon. Hugh Taverel did not come near it—very far short, indeed! He had talked to her during the whole of dinner the night before about jackal-hunting with a bobbery pack—not at all an elevated mind. Yes, he might be a very good fellow, but as a companion for life she was sure he would not be at all suitable. She would wait.

And she has waited. I never thought she would, but she has. From time to time men have wished to take her from us, but the standard has been inexorable, and none of them have reached it. When Dacres married the charming American whom he caught like a butterfly upon her Eastern tour, Cecily sent them as a wedding present an alabaster model of the Taj, and I let her do it—the gift was so exquisitely appropriate. I suppose he never looks at it without being reminded that he didn't marry Miss Farnham, and I hope that he remembers that he owes it to Miss Farnham's mother. So much I think I might claim; it is really very little considering what it stands for. Cecily is permanently with us—I believe she considers herself an intimate. I am very reasonable about lending her to her aunts, but she takes no sort of advantage of my liberality; she says she knows her duty is at home. She is growing into a firm and solid English maiden lady, with a good colour and great decision of character. That she always had.

I point out to John, when she takes our crumpets away from us, that she gets it from him. I could never take away anybody's crumpets, merely because they were indigestible, least of all my own parents'. She has acquired a distinct affection for us, by some means best known to herself; but I should have no objection to that if she would not rearrange my bonnet-strings. That is a fond liberty to which I take exception; but it is one thing to take exception and another to express it.

Our daughter is with us, permanently with us. She declares that she intends to be the prop of our declining years; she makes the statement often, and always as if it were humorous. Nevertheless I sometimes notice a spirit of inquiry, a note of investigation in her encounters with the opposite sex that suggests an expectation not yet extinct that another and perhaps a more appreciative Dacres Tottenham may flash across her field of vision—alas, how improbable! Myself I can not imagine why she should wish it; I have grown in my old age into a perfect horror of cultivated young men; but if such a person should by a miracle at any time appear, I think it is extremely improbable that I will interfere on his behalf.

ROBERTINE BARRY

La Gothe and Her Husband

Many weddings have I seen; not one did I find tempting;
Yet everywhere the human race seems bound to undertake
The step that runs the greatest risk of ending in mistake:
And everywhere the human race is also now repenting.
FABLE OF LA FONTAINE

'Such stifling weather! We're sure to have rain.'

'No sooner said than done. A great drop just fell on my nose. Heaven knows how drenched we're going to be!'

'Excellent reason to make haste and find shelter. This little path leads to the home of mère Madeloche, the nearest neighbour. Follow me—if we go quickly we can be there before the storm.'

This was during one July hot spell. The sun's scorching rays had been beating down so intensely, it seemed like the days of Phaeton, when he grazed the earth, venturing to set it ablaze. Oppressive and suffocating, the atmosphere made breathing a laborious effort. The very ground was feverish, thirsting for water, for refreshment, for dew; the plants, thickly coated with dust, had lost the green of spring and seemed to be withering before their time.

Suddenly the sky darkened and menacing clouds rose on the horizon. The cricket silenced his chirp in the grass, as did the bird his song in the wood. In the meadows the animals roused themselves from their torpor, and with their rough tongues lolling, panted—as if waiting anxiously for some strange occurrence. Out in the countryside, where the voices of animals are more commonly heard than the sounds of men, the hour before a storm is a solemn time. And when everything is hushed, insects, birds, when the breeze no longer murmurs in the leaves, a great silence falls, majestic and unsettling, like the reverent lull preceding creation's end, the disintegration of the elements.

All at once the storm broke, violent and terrible, like anger long-suppressed. The wind recovered its voice, but not a soft whisper of leaves in the boughs. Rising in long whistling sounds, it scourged those same shrubs that only moments before had been caressed by it: the grand master loves no more. The frail willows plead for mercy, bowed down and weeping, then submit, while the indomitable poplar arrogantly thrusts defiance at the clouds.

The storm was raging in all its fury by the time the two young girls, who had exchanged the few words above, managed to make their way, running, to a long, low, whitewashed house with a pointed roof and heavy shutters neatly fastened to the walls with leather hinges. An elderly woman, still erect despite her years, came to answer the urgent knocking of the two young strollers. She wore a dress of coarse fabric and sombre hue, and a white cap, with wide trimmings that only partially concealed her grey hair; an apron of blue and white chequered cotton completed her costume.

Mère Madeloche showed a broad smile of welcome upon recognizing Louise Bressoles, the daughter of a wealthy landowner from the village, whom she had known from infancy.

'Come in, come in, 'demoiselles,' said the good old woman. 'What a weather for Christen folks to be out in, when it's pouring like this!'

'It's tremendously beautiful,' said Madeline, pausing on the doorstep to observe the havoc being created by the storm. 'Who could have forseen such an upheaval a few moments ago? It has often been compared to the winds of passion . . .'

'Do come inside quickly,' cried Louise, 'you may philosophize at your leisure when you are safely under the hospitable roof of good mère Madeloche!

'Come in, come in, 'demoiselle, you're going to get your pretty dress all spoilt, an' you'll be as doused as a dinghy. This here's a storm that'll be real good for the crops and make barrels o' *patates,* for sure! Sit you down. We don't often have the pleasure of your company.'

'Thank you, mère Madeloche. You seem to be enjoying your usual good health. This is my cousin Madeline, whose mother—my aunt Renaud—you used to know before she went to live in Quebec city.'

'What's that you say—Madame Renaud? Such a nice little lady—so pleasant! She's one that had many kind ways, an' I rocked her in her cradle when she was ever so little. *Mon Dieu*—can it be that this here grown-up 'demoiselle is her daughter? That makes you feel old, for sure!'

'Nevertheless, mère, you are still hale and hearty, like a young woman of twenty.'

'These city 'demoiselles love to make their little jokes,' said the old woman, secretly flattered by the compliment. 'I'll be seventy years old come harvest time, an' since the deceased passed on, I'm not like before—my strength is going.'

While she spoke, the good woman had taken up her spindle full of flax and tucked the end of it into the waistband of her apron, whereupon the thread began to fly between her nimble fingers.

'What a lovely little spinning wheel! Oh, I would so much rather spin than drudge away at our everlasting embroidery,' exclaimed Madeline. 'But what is that you are doing now, mère Madeloche?' she added, as the old woman ran her thread over small steel pins with pointed ends that were bent back at the top.

'I'm filling up the bobbin so's it's even from top to bottom; if I didn't wind the thread around the teeth of the blades, the bobbin, d'you see, would only fill up on one side.'

'And this big screw on the end of the spinning wheel?'

'That there, 'demoiselle, is the prop that makes sure the thread don't get too thick or too thin; when the spinning wheel gobbles too much, I tighten her or loosen her, just as I need. The loop—that little wheel there at the end of the bobbin—it's where you take the thread so it turns the big wheel. An' this here, where I put my foot, that's the treadle that makes everything go. An' this little wooden bowl 'tached to the pin here, that's called the dish; see there, it's still got some water in it, for wetting down the warp from time to time.'

'Most interesting, mère Madeloche. And what do you call the little reel there at your side?'

'Why, a winder my dear, a winder for the spindleful, after it's all spun out. Hey, *mon Sauveur*, how times change, eh! In my day a girl—let alone grown-up 'demoiselles—wouldn't have no chance to get married if she didn't know nothing about how to spin proper.'

The room in which the young girls found themselves renewing their acquaintance with mère Madeloche was a spacious chamber that made up the main body of the dwelling and served as sitting-room, dining-room, bedroom, and kitchen, all at the same time. Picture, if you will, whitewashed walls, and a ceiling with broad cross-beams; long poles attached crosswise to the beams for drying laundry; a long table of white pine; a bed in one corner, covered with a brightly-coloured patchwork quilt and surrounded by snow-white curtains, and at its head a phial of holy water attached to a woollen cord that hung from a nail. Near the bed, a large chest—a favourite seat for lovers—a few rustic chairs, and you have before you, almost without exception, the standard interior of our farmers' homes.

Holding the place of honour, in plain view, on a square of painted paper or a coloured page from a magazine, hangs the cross, black, simple, as severe as the event in commemorates. Beside the cross, a huge palm branch, still draped with the red, white, and blue paper flowers that adorned it on Palm Sunday.

On the smouldering coals of the soot-covered hearth a pot of potatoes simmered for the evening meal. The hutch displayed rows of blue earthenware crockery, gleaming like fine china. By the door, on a low bench, two oblong pails—frequent visitors to the well near the vegetable garden behind the house. The room was filled with the aroma of hearth-baked bread, and of the pine boughs used for sweeping the floor, whose balmy forest fragrance still lingered in the air . . .

Here everything has an air of homely simplicity, in keeping with the rough ways and naive ingenuousness of our country *habitants.*

Rain continued to beat furiously against the panes; through the ill-fitting windows, water seeped onto the floor.

'Do you think the storm will last long, mère?'

'No, young 'demoiselle, it's brightening up a bit over towards the sou' west; but we'll get some tricky weather this week, 'cause Sunday past, the gospel-side of the altar was shut. Hey there—la Gothe! Come bring these 'demoiselles some milk an' cream. It's all I can offer you, but I give it with an open heart.'

At mère Madeloche's call, a heavy tread could be heard as the woman called la Gothe began to descend the ladder from the loft. A strapping young woman of about thirty years of age, she was plump and jolly-looking. She approached, greeting them in an awkward manner, but laughing good-naturedly at the friendly questions put to her by Louise, whose servant she had been for many years.

'So, you are staying here with your grandmother now, la Gothe?

I imagine it is much less tiring for you than being out in service?'

'Oh—I'm pledged again, only this time it'll be for a good long spell,' replied la Gothe, exhibiting a row of great broad teeth.

Madeline threw a questioning glance at her friend, as if to say, 'What does she mean?'

'Are you going to marry again?' asked Louise, thus translating La Gothe's quaint expression for the benefit of the city girl.

'Yes, an' more fool her!' muttered the old grandmother, 'as if she didn't get beatings aplenty with her old one.'

'Ah well, it's wrote all over a woman that she's always for getting married.'

'Were you not very happy with your first husband, my poor woman?'

The old woman took it upon herself to reply: 'Well, he sure never hid from her what he was, 'demoiselle. Père Duque, her dead husband, he'd already put two other women into their graves with his cruelties and miseries; we told her time an' again, but she wouldn't listen to nobody an' married him anyway, despite God and the saints.'

'Hey, old lady—if not me, it would of been another!'

'But surely,' exclaimed Madeline, 'you were not obliged to sacrifice yourself for someone else?'

'It was my fate,' replied la Gothe, with a shrug of her shoulders.

The last word had been spoken.

Why is it that fatalism is so deeply engrained in our country folk? Destiny—that is the great answer to everything. It terminates all discussion and is the consolation of everyone. Misfortune befalls? The means of preventing it are never spoken of, nor is thought taken to avoid it in future. Everything is simply accounted for by saying, 'It was fated.' Fruitless tc oppose any dangerous endeavour; if fate permits, the person involved will emerge unscathed; otherwise, nothing can rescue him from peril—his destiny needs must be accomplished.

And who is to say that they are entirely mistaken? Regardless of the conflict between fatalism and our innate sense that we have total freedom in all our actions, who can declare that the latter is always victorious? Some events occur quite apart from our will, foreseen throughout eternity, and their outcome can never be thwarted by vain human precautions.

While the young widow talked, she covered the table with a linen cloth, the pride of the French-Canadian housewife, of a coarse fabric it is true, but sparkling white. Then, shuffling out to the dairy, she soon returned with two large bowls of fine fresh milk, topped with tempting rich cream; and lifting the lid of the bread bin, she brought forth an enormous loaf, crusty and golden, which she sliced into thick chunks for the young girls.

'Eat your bit of lunch, pretty 'demoiselles,' and taking up her knitting, she settled herself in her chair.

'Yes,' she continued, as if this stormy hour had revived all her memories of turbulent times, 'there are some terrible wicked men! An' I'm sure one that knows it! Many's the time mine gave me black and blue arms—an' every other part of me. He slaughtered me with his beatings; many's the time he'd pound my head against the wall an' lock me up in a big chest, an' wouldn't give me nothing to eat. *Sainte bénite!* A woman can take a heap of suffering without it kills her. I can tell about it now, when it's all over an' done with . . .'

'Besides that, he was jealous like a pigeon-cock,' added the grandmother.

'I sure got him going—I sure did!' replied la Gothe, and a wild gleam flashed in her pale eyes.

Her whole being trembled with mute rage as she recalled her past sufferings. This creature, so placid a moment before, now assumed a vicious expression; her nostrils quivered, as if she were in the grip of a powerful emotion; the lips that had smiled so sweetly now curled, and her long knitting needles clacked furiously in her tense fingers. Not the years, not even death had made her forget, so cruel had been her trials. The wounds rankled still from having been under the yoke of that harsh durance.

'Might he have been under the influence of strong drink, and not always responsible for his actions?' asked Louise, who felt a vague need to excuse such vile brutality.

'No,' came the firm reply from la Gothe. 'I'd of gladly given him every penny I could lay hands on, if he'd only stayed drunk, 'cause he was always better with me when he had a skinful. But, y'know, I think meanness and the pleasure of tormenting me kep' him away from the drink, seeing that I could always get clear of him at such times—an' he never wanted me to be farther away than the end of his arm.'

'How many years did this ill-treatment last?'

'Eight years, 'demoiselle, eight years of all the time waiting on him, working for him, an' taking every kind of cruelty from him. A long time of it, mother of God, a long time of it! Well—you don't die from it, that's all you can say. He's the one that died first, eh, all of a sudden an' without no time to ask God's blessing—or anyone else's. He was sitting in the big chair by the hearth an' he bent down for a coal to light his pipe—an' he never got up again. By the time Toinette, his daughter from his first marriage, spied him there, his hands an' feet—with all respect—were just like lumps of ice, an' not so much as an eyelid moving. They sent quick, quick for the priest. An' then, when the good father came to give the extra-munction, that old busybody Jacques Bonsens had to go to the door an' say that the deceased was dead an' gone. An' M. l'curé, he said, "Poor wretch, why did you tell me that?"—an' turned 'round an' went back the way he came. He might at least have confessed him.'

'How could he have confessed him, if he was dead?'

'But 'demoiselle, you're so educated, don't you know that as soon as the priest leaves his vestry to see a man that's just died, he has power to bring him to life, so's he can hear his confession? Only, you mustn't tell the priest he's dead, 'cause then he can't do nothing about it.'

'Have you ever been afraid of your dead husband?' enquired Madeline, whose curiosity and interest had been aroused by this strange tale.

'No!' she replied with passion. 'Whoever was keeping him there—where he was on the other side—was hangin' on to him good, I can tell you. . . . M. l'curé wanted me to have masses said for him, but I knew him better than he did, an' I knew that the deceased was so pig-headed he'd serve his time without help from nobody, 'specially from me.'

The rain had ceased to fall. A few clouds, chased by the wind, scurried here and there across the sky, but the sun, now radiant and refreshed from her bath, gaily sent a last kiss to earth from the end of the horizon, before retiring for the night.

Madeline had another question. 'Were you at home when your husband died?'

'No, I was down scrubbing clothes by the little stream. When they came an' told me, it was quite a blow, for sure! But—I can tell you,' added la Gothe, suddenly recovering her great foolish grin, 'it was the last one he ever gave me!'

Translated by Patricia Sillers

ETHEL WILSON

Mrs Golightly and the First Convention

Mrs Golightly was a shy woman. She lived in Vancouver. Her husband, Tommy Golightly, was not shy. He was personable and easy to like. He was a consulting engineer who was consulted a great deal by engineering firms, construction firms, logging firms in particular, any firm that seemed to have problems connected with traction. When he was not being consulted he played golf, tennis, or bridge according to whether the season was spring, summer, autumn, or winter. Any time that was left over he spent with his wife and three small children of whom he was very fond. When he was with them, it seemed that that was what he liked best. He was a very extroverted sort of man, easy and likeable, and his little wife was so shy that it just was not fair. But what can you do?

At the period of which I write, Conventions had not begun to take their now-accepted place in life on the North American continent. I am speaking of conventions with a capital C. Conventions with a small c have, of course, always been with us, but not as conspicuously now as formerly. In those days, when a man said rather importantly I am going to a Convention, someone was quite liable to ask What is a Convention? Everyone seemed to think that they must be a good thing, which of course they are. We now take them for granted.

Now Mr Golightly was admirably adapted to going to Conventions. His memory for names and faces was good; he liked people, both in crowds and separately; he collected acquaintances who rapidly became friends. Everyone liked him.

One day he came home and said to his wife, How would you like a trip to California?

Mrs Golightly gave a little gasp. Her face lighted up and she said, Oh Tom. . . !

There's a Western and Middle Western Convention meeting at Del Monte the first week of March, and you and I are going down said Mr Golightly.

Mrs Golightly's face clouded and she said in quite a different tone and with great alarm, Oh Tom. . . !

Well what? said her husband.

Mrs Golightly began the sort of hesitation that so easily overcame her. Well, Tom, she said, I'd have to get a hat, and I suppose a suit and a dinner dress, and Emmeline isn't very good to leave with the children and you know I'm no good with crowds and people, I never know what to say and—

Well, *get* a new hat, said her husband, get one of those hats I see women wearing with long quills on. And *get* a new dress. Get *twenty* new dresses. And Emmeline's *fine* with the children and what you need's a change and I'm the only one in my profession invited from British Columbia. You get a hat with the longest feather in town and a nice dinner dress! Mr Golightly looked fondly at his wife and saw with new eyes that she appeared anxious and not quite as pretty as she sometimes was. He kissed her and she promised that she would get the new hat, but he did not know how terrified she was of the Convention and all the crowds of people, and that she suffered at the very thought of going. She could get along all right at home, but small talk with strangers—oh poor Mrs Golightly. These things certainly are not fair. However, she got the dress, and a new hat with the longest quill in town. She spent a long time at the hairdresser's; and how pretty she looked and how disturbed she felt! I'll break the quill every time I get into the car, Tom, she said.

Non-*sense*, said her husband, and they set off in the car for California.

Mrs Golightly travelled in an old knitted suit and a felt hat well pulled down on her head in observance of a theory which she had inherited from her mother that you must never wear good clothes when travelling. The night before arriving at Del Monte a car passing them at high speed sideswiped them ever so little, but the small damage and fuss that resulted from that delayed them a good deal. The result was that they got late to bed that night, slept little, rose early, and had to do three hundred miles before lunch. Mrs Golightly began to feel very tired in spite of some mounting excitement, but this did not make her forget to ask her husband to stop at the outskirts of Del Monte so that she could take her new hat out of the bag and put it on. Mr Golightly was delighted with the way his wife was joining in the spirit of the thing. Good girl, he said, which pleased her, and neither of them noticed that nothing looked right about Mrs Golightly except her hat, and even smart hats, worn under those circumstances, look wrong.

How impressive it was to Mrs Golightly, supported by her hat, to approach the portals of the fashionable Del Monte Hotel. Large cars reclined in rows, some sparkling, some dimmed by a film of dust, all of them costly. Radiant men and women, expensively dressed (the inheritors of the earth evidently) strolled about without a care in the world, or basked on the patio, scrutinizing new arrivals with experienced eyes. Mrs Golightly had already felt something formidably buoyant in the air of California, accustomed as she was to the mild, soft, and (to tell the truth) sometimes deliciously drowsy air of the British Columbia coast. The air she breathed in California somehow alarmed her. Creatures customarily breathing this air must, she thought, by nature, be buoyant, self-confident—all the things that Mrs Golightly was not. Flowers bloomed, trees threw their shade, birds cleft the air, blue shone the sky, and Mrs Golightly, dazzled, knocked her hat crooked as she got out of the car, and she caught the long quill on the door. She felt it snick. Oh, she thought, my darling quill!

No sooner had they alighted from their car, which was seized on all sides by hotel minions of great competence, than her husband was surrounded by prosperous men who said, Well Tom! And how's the boy! Say Tom this is great! And Tom turned from side to side greeting, expansive, the most popular man in view. Mrs Golightly had no idea that Tom had so many business friends that loved him dearly. And then with one accord these prosperous men turned their kindly attention to Mrs Golightly. It overwhelmed her but it really warmed her heart to feel that they were all so pleased that she had come, and that she had come so far, and although she felt shy, travel-worn and tired, she tried to do her best and her face shone sweetly with a desire to please.

Now, said the biggest of the men, the boys are waiting for you Tom. Up in one three three. Yes in one three three. And Mrs Golightly I want you to meet Mrs Allyman of the Ladies' Committee. Mrs Allyman meet Mrs Tom Golightly from British Columbia. Will you just register her please, we've planned a good time for the ladies, Tom . . . we'll take good care of Tom, Mrs Golightly. And Mr Golightly said, But my wife . . . and then a lot of people streamed in, and Tom and the other men said, Well, well, *well,* so here's Ed! Say Ed . . . the words streamed past Mrs Golightly and Tom was lost to her view.

A lump that felt large came in her throat because she was so shy and Tom was not to be seen, but Mrs Allyman was very kind and propelled her over to a group of ladies and said, Oh this is the lady from British Columbia, the name is Golightly isn't it? Mrs Golightly I want you to meet Mrs Finkel and Mrs Connelly and Mrs Magnus and pardon me I didn't catch the name Mrs Sloper from Colorado. Oh there's the President's wife Mrs Bagg. Well Mrs Bagg did you locate Mr Bagg after all, no doubt he's in one three three. Mrs Golightly I'd like to have you meet Mrs Bagg and Mrs Simmons, Mrs Bagg, Mrs Finkel, Mrs Bagg, and Mrs Sloper, Mrs Bagg. Mrs Golightly is all the way from British Columbia, I think that's where you come from Mrs Golightly? Mrs Allyman, speaking continually, seemed to say all this in one breath. By the time that Mrs Golightly's vision had cleared (although she felt rather dizzy) she saw that all these ladies were chic, and that they wore hats with very long quills, longer even than hers, which made her feel much more secure. However, her exhilaration was passing, she realized that she was quite tired, and she said, smiling sweetly, I *think* I'd better find my room. The hubbub in the hotel rotunda increased and increased.

When she reached her room she found that Tom had sent the bags up, and she thought she would unpack, and lie down for a bit to get rested, and then go down and have a quiet lunch. Perhaps she would see Tom somewhere. But first she went over to the window and looked out upon the incredible radiance of blue and green and gold, and the shine of the ethereal air. She looked at the great oak trees and the graceful mimosa trees and she thought, After I've tidied up and had some lunch I'll just go and sit under one of those beautiful mimosa trees and drink in this . . . this largesse of air and scent and beauty. Mrs Golightly had never seen anything like it. The bright air dazzled her, and made her sad and gay. Just then the telephone rang. A man's strong and purposeful voice said, Pardon me, but may I speak to Tom?

Oh I'm sorry, said Mrs Golightly, Tom's not here.

Can you tell me where I can get him? asked the voice very urgently.

I'm so sorry . . . faltered Mrs Golightly.

Sorry to troub . . . said the voice and the telephone clicked off.

There. The convention had invaded the bedroom, the azure sky, and the drifting grace of the mimosa tree outside the bedroom window.

I think, said Mrs Golightly to herself, if I had a bath it would freshen me, I'm beginning to have a headache. She went into the bathroom and gazed with pleasure on its paleness and coolness and shiningness, on the lavish array of towels, and an uneven picture entered and left her mind of the bathroom at home, full, it seemed to her, of the essentials for cleaning and dosing a father and mother and three small children, non-stop. The peace! The peace of it! She lay in the hot water regarding idly and alternately the soap which floated agreeably upon the water, and the window through which she saw blue sky of an astonishing azure.

The telephone rang.

Is that Mrs Goodman? purred a voice.

No, no, not Mrs Goodman, said Mrs Golightly, wrapped in a towel.

I'm *so* sorry, purred the voice.

Mrs Golightly got thankfully into the bath and turned on some more hot water.

The telephone rang.

She scrambled out, Hello, hello?

There's a wire at the desk for Mr Golightly, said a voice, shall we send it up?

Oh dear, oh dear, said Mrs Golightly wrapped in a towel, well . . . not yet . . . not for half an hour.

Okay, said the voice.

She got back into the bath. She closed her eyes in disturbed and recovered bliss.

The telephone rang.

Hello, hello, said Mrs Golightly plaintively, wrapped in a very damp towel.

Is that Mrs Golightly? said a kind voice.

Yes, oh yes, agreed Mrs Golightly.

Well, this is Mrs Porter speaking and we'd be pleased if you'd join Mrs Bagg and Mrs Wilkins and me in the Tap Room and meet some of the ladies and have a little drink before lunch.

Oh thank you, thank you, that will just be lovely, I'd love to, said Mrs Golightly. Away went the sky, away went the birds, away went the bath, and away went the mimosa tree.

Well, that will be lovely, said Mrs Porter, in about half-an-hour?

Oh thank you, thank you, that will be lovely . . . ! said Mrs Golightly, repeating herself considerably.

She put on her new grey flannel suit which was only slightly rumpled, and straightened the tip of her quill as best she could. She patted her rather aching forehead with cold water and felt somewhat refreshed. She paid particular and delicate attention to her face, and left her room looking and feeling quite pretty but agitated.

When she got down to the Tap Room everyone was having Old-Fashioneds and a little woman in grey came up and said, Pardon me but are you Mrs Golightly from British Columbia? Mrs Golightly, I'd like to have you meet Mrs Bagg (our President's wife) and Mrs Gillingham from St Louis, Mrs Wilkins from Pasadena, Mrs Golightly, Mrs Finkel and—pardon me?—Mrs Connelly and Mrs Allyman of Los Angeles.

Mrs Golightly felt confused, but she smiled at each lady in turn, saying How do you do, but neglected to remember or repeat their names because she was so inexperienced. She slipped into a chair and a waiter brought her an Old-Fashioned. She then looked round and tried hard to memorize the ladies, nearly all of whom had stylish hats with tall quills on. Mrs Bagg very smart. Mrs Wilkins with pince-nez. Little Mrs Porter in grey. Mrs Simmons, Mrs Connelly, and Mrs Finkel in short fur capes. Mrs Finkel was lovely, of a gorgeous pale beauty. Mrs Golightly sipped her Old-Fashioned and tried to feel very gay indeed. She and Mrs Connelly who came from Chicago found that each had three small children, and before they had finished talking, a waiter brought another Old-Fashioned. Then Mrs Connelly had to speak to a lady on her other side, and Mrs Golightly turned to the lady on her left. This lady was not talking to anyone but was quietly sipping her Old-Fashioned. By this time Mrs Golightly was feeling unusually bold and responsible, and quite like a woman of the world. She thought to herself, Come now, everyone is being so lovely and trying to make everyone feel at home, and I must try too.

So she said to the strange lady, I don't think we met, did we?

My name is Mrs Golightly and I come from British Columbia. And the lady said, I'm pleased to meet you. I'm Mrs Gampish and I come from Toledo, Ohio. And Mrs Golightly said, Oh isn't this a beautiful hotel and wouldn't you like to see the gardens, and then somehow everyone was moving.

When Mrs Golightly got up she felt as free as air, but as if she was stepping a little high. When they reached the luncheon table there must have been about a hundred ladies and of course everyone was talking. Mrs Golightly was seated between two perfectly charming people, Mrs Carillo from Little Rock, Arkansas, and Mrs Clark from Phoenix, Arizona. They both said what a cute English accent she had and she had to tell them because she was so truthful that she had never been to England. It was a little hard to talk as there was an orchestra and Mrs Golightly and Mrs Carillo and Mrs Clark were seated just below the saxophones. Mrs Golightly couldn't quite make out whether she had no headache at all, or the worst headache of her life. This is lovely, she thought as she smiled back at her shouting companions, but how nice it will be to go upstairs and lie down. Just for half an hour after lunch, before I go and sit under the mimosa tree.

But when the luncheon was over, Mrs Wilkins clapped her hands and said, Now Ladies, cars are waiting at the door and we'll assemble in the lobby for the drive. And Mrs Golightly said, Oh hadn't I better run upstairs and see whether my husband . . . But Mrs Wilkins said again, Now Ladies! So they all gathered in the lobby, and for one moment, one moment, Mrs Golightly was still.

Oh, she thought, I feel awful, and I am so sleepy, and I feel a little queer. But she soon started smiling again, and they all got into motor-cars.

She got into a nice car with some other ladies whom she did not know. They all had tall quills on their hats which made it awkward. Mrs Golightly was the smallest and sat in the middle. She turned from side to side with great politeness. Flick, flick went the quills, smiting against each other. Well, we'd better introduce ourselves, she thought. But the lady on her right had already explained that she was Mrs Johnson from Seattle, so she turned to her left and said to the other stranger, Do tell me your name? I'm Mrs Golightly and I come from British Columbia.

The other lady said a little stiffly, Well, I'm Mrs Gampish and I come from Toledo, Ohio, and Mrs Golightly felt awful and said, Oh Mrs Gampish, how stupid of me, we met in the Tap Room, of course! So *many* people!—Oh, it's quite all right, said Mrs Gampish rather coldly. But she and Mrs Johnson soon found that their husbands both had gastric ulcers and so they had a very very interesting conversation. Mrs Golightly did not join in because she had nothing to offer in the way of an ulcer, as she and Tom and the children never seemed to be ill and the ladies did not appear to need sympathy. She dodged this way and that behind Mrs Gampish and Mrs Johnson, interfering with their quills, and peering at gleaming Spanish villas enfolded in green, blazing masses of flowers, a crash and white spume of breakers, a twisted Monterey pine—they all rushed dazzling past the car windows—villas, pines, ocean, and all. If I were courageous or even tactful, thought Mrs Golightly, I could ask to sit beside the window where I want to be, and these ladies could talk in comfort (the talk had moved from ulcers to their sons' fraternities) which is what they wish, but she knew that she was not skilful in such matters, and it would not do. Oh, she yearned, if I could ever be a woman of the world and achieve these simple matters!

Then all the cars stopped at a place called Point Lobos, and everybody got out.

Mrs Golightly sped swiftly alone toward the cliffs. She stood on a high rock overlooking the vast ocean, and the wind roared and whistled about her. She took off her hat as the whistling, beating broken quill seemed to impede her. She looked down and could hardly believe the beauty that lay below her. Green ocean crashed and broke in towering spray on splintered rocky islets, on the cliffs where she stood, and into swirling, sucking, rock-bound bays and caves. In the translucent green waves played joyous bands of seals, so joyous that they filled her with rapture. Bellowing seals clambered upon the rocks, but the din of wind and ocean drowned their bellowing. The entrancement of sea and sky and wind and the strong playing bodies of the seals so transported Mrs Golightly that she forgot to think, Oh I must tell the children, and how Tom would love this! She was one with the rapture of that beautiful unexpected moment. She felt someone beside her and turned. There was Mrs Carillo with a shining face. They shouted at each other, laughing with joy, but could not hear each other, and stood arm in arm braced against the wind, looking down at the playing bands of seals.

As the party assembled again, Mrs Golightly stepped aside and waited for Mrs Gampish and Mrs Johnson to get in first. Then she got in, and sat down beside the window. Conversation about Point Lobos and the seals became general, and Mrs Johnson, who was in the middle, found herself turning from side to side, bending and catching her quill. They then became quiet, and the drive home was peaceful. I shall never forget, thought Mrs Golightly, as the landscape and seascape flashed past her rather tired eyes, the glory of Point Lobos, and the strong bodies of the seals playing in the translucent water. Whatever happens to me on earth, I shall never never forget it.

When she arrived at the hotel she discovered that she was nearly dead with excitement and noise and fatigue and when Tom came in she said, because she was so simple and ignorant, Oh darling, can we have dinner somewhere quietly tonight, I must tell you about all those seals. And Tom looked quite shocked, and he said, Seals? But darling, aren't you having a good time? I was just talking to Mr Bagg and he tells me that you made a great hit with his wife. This is a Convention you know, he said reprovingly, and you can't do *that* kind of thing! Seals indeed! Where's your program? Yes, Ladies' Dinner in the Jacobean Room, and I'll be at the Men's. And Mrs Golightly said, Oh Tom. . . . Yes, of course, I know, how stupid of me. . . . I'm having the *loveliest* time, Tom, and we had the *loveliest* drive, and now I'm really going to have a proper bath and a rest before I dress. And Tom said, *Fine*! But can I have the bathroom first because . . . and then the telephone rang and Tom said Yes? Yes, Al, what's that? In the Tap Room? In fifteen minutes? Make it twenty Al, I want to bath and change. Okay Al. . . . That was Al, dear. I'll have to hurry but you have a good rest. And then the telephone rang and it was Mrs Wilkins and she said, Oh Mrs Golightly will you join Mrs Porter and me and some of the ladies in my room one seven five for cocktails at six o'clock. I do hope it won't rush you. One seven five. Oh that will be lovely.—Oh, yes, that will be lovely, said Mrs Golightly. She put her hands to her face and then she took out her blue dinner dress and began pressing it, and away went the bath and away went the rest and away went the mimosa tree. And Tom came out of the bathroom and said, Why ever aren't you lying down. That's the trouble with you, you never will rest! Well so long darling, have a good time. And he went, and she finished pressing her dress and put it on.

The next time Mrs Golightly saw Tom was downstairs in the hotel lobby as she waited with some of the other ladies to go into the ladies' dinner. Tom was in the middle of a group of men who walked down the centre of the lobby. They walked almost rolling with grandeur or something down the lobby, owning it, sufficient unto themselves, laughing together at their own private jokes and unaware of anyone else. But Mr Golightly's eyes fell on his wife. He saw how pretty she looked and was delighted with her. He checked the flow of men down the lobby and stepped forward and said, Terry I want you to meet Mr Flanagan, Bill this is my wife. And a lively and powerful small man seized Mrs Golightly's hand and held it and looked admiringly at her and said, Well, Mrs Golightly, I certainly am pleased to meet you. I've just got Tom here to promise that you and he will come and stay with Mrs Flanagan and me this fall when the shooting's good up at our little place in Oregon—now, no argument, it's all settled, you're coming! What a genial host! It would be a pleasure to stay with Mr Flanagan.

Tom beamed in a pleased way, and Mrs Golightly's face sparkled with pleasure. Oh Mr Flanagan, she said, how kind! Tom and I will just *love* to come. (Never a word or thought about What shall we do with the children—just We'd love to come.) So *that's* settled, said Mr Flanagan breezily and the flow of men down the hotel lobby was resumed.

At dinner Mrs Golightly sat beside a nice woman from San Francisco called Mrs de Kay who had once lived in Toronto so of course they had a lot in common. Before dinner everyone had had one or two Old-Fashioneds, and as the mists cleared a bit, Mrs Golightly had recognized Mrs Bagg, Mrs Connelly, dear Mrs Carillo, and beautiful Mrs Finkel. How lovely was Mrs Finkel sitting in blonde serenity amidst the hubbub, in silence looking around her with happy gentle gaze. You could never forget Mrs Finkel. Her face, her person, her repose, her shadowed eyes invited scrutiny. You gazed with admiration and sweetly she accepted your admiration. While all around her were vivacious, Mrs Finkel sat still. But now Mrs Finkel and Mrs Carillo were far down the table and Mrs Golightly conversed with Mrs de Kay as one woman of the world to another. How well I'm coming along! she thought, and felt puffed up.

During the sweet course she became hot with shame! She had not spoken a word to the lady on her left who wore a red velvet dress. She turned in a gushing way and said to the lady in the red dress who, she realized, was not speaking to anyone at the moment. Isn't this a delightful dinner! We haven't had a chance of a word with each other, have we, and I don't believe we've met, but I'm Mrs Golightly from British Columbia.

The lady in the red cut-velvet dress turned towards Mrs Golightly and said clearly, I am Mrs Gampish, and I come from Toledo, Ohio. Their eyes met.

Mrs Golightly remained silent. Blushes flamed over her. She thought, This is, no doubt, some dreadful dream from which I shall soon awake. And still the chatter and clatter and music went on. Mrs Golightly could not think of anything to say. Mrs Gampish continued to eat her dessert. Mrs Golightly attempted to smile in a society way, but it was no good, and she couldn't say a thing.

After dinner there was bridge and what do you suppose? Mrs Golightly was set to play with Mrs Magnus and Mrs Finkel and Mrs Gampish. Trembling a little, she stood up.

I think I will go to bed, she said. She could not bear to think of Mrs Gampish being compelled to play bridge with her.

No, *I* shall go to bed, said Mrs Gampish.

No, do let me go to bed, cried Mrs Golightly, I simply insist on going to bed.

And *I* insist on going to bed too, said Mrs Gampish firmly, in any case I have a headache. Mrs Magnus and Mrs Finkel looked on in amazement.

No, no, I shall go to bed, said Mrs Golightly in distress.

No, *I* shall go to bed, said Mrs Gampish. It was very absurd.

Mrs Bagg hurried up. Everything all set here? she said in a hostess voice.

Mrs Gampish and Mrs Golightly said, speaking together, I am going to bed.

Oh, don't *both* go to bed, pleaded Mrs Bagg, unaware of any special feeling. If one of you must go to bed, do please one of you stay, and I will make the fourth.

Mrs Golightly considered and acted quickly. If Mrs Gampish *really* wants to go to bed, she said, timidly but with effect, I will stay . . . a slight headache . . . she said bravely fluttering her fingers and batting her eyelashes which were rather long.

Mrs Gampish did not argue any more. She said good night to the ladies and left.

Oh do excuse me a minute, said Mrs Golightly, flickering her eyelashes, and she caught Mrs Gampish at the elevator. Mrs Gampish looked at her with distaste.

I want to tell you, Mrs Gampish, said Mrs Golightly with true humility, and speaking very low, that I have never been to a Convention before, and I want to confess to you my stupidity. I am not really rude, only stupid and so shy although I have three children that I am truly in a whirl. Will you be able ever to forgive me? . . . It would be very kind of you if you feel that you could. Oh, please do try.

There was a silence between them as the elevators came and went. Then Mrs Gampish gave a wan smile.

You are too earnest, my child, she said. (Oh how good you are! breathed Mrs Golightly.) I wouldn't myself know one person in this whole Convention—except Mrs Finkel and no one could forget her, continued Mrs Gampish, and I never knew you each time you told me who you were *until* you told me, so you needn't have worried. If you want to know why I'm going to bed, it's because I don't like bridge and anyway, I *do* have a headache.

Oh I'm so glad you *really* have a headache, no I mean I'm so sorry, and I think you're perfectly sweet, Mrs Gampish, and if ever you come to Canada . . . and she saw the faintly amused smile of Mrs Gampish going up in the elevator. Well I never, she said, but she felt happier.

She turned and there was Tom hurrying past. Oh Tom, she called. He stopped.

Having a good time darling? he said in a hurry. D'you want to come to the meeting at Salt Lake City next year? and he smiled at her encouragingly.

Oh Tom, she said, I'd adore it! (What a changed life. Del Monte, Mr Flanagan's shooting lodge, Salt Lake City, all in a minute, you might say.)

Well, well! said Tom in surprise and vanished.

On the way to her bedroom that night Mrs Golightly met Mr Flanagan walking very slowly down the hall.

How do you do Mr Flanagan! said Mrs Golightly gaily. She felt that he was already her host at his shooting lodge.

Mr Flanagan stopped and looked at her seriously as from a great distance. It was obvious that he did not know her. How do you do, he said very carefully and with a glazed expression. Did we meet or did we meet. In any case, how do you do. And he continued walking with the utmost care down the corridor.

Oh . . . , said Mrs Golightly, her eyes wide open, . . . oh . . . . It was probable that Mr Flanagan invited everyone to the shooting lodge. The shooting lodge began to vanish like smoke.

When she entered the bedroom she saw that in her hurry before dinner she had not put her hat away. The quill was twice bent, and it dangled. She took scissors and cut it short. There, she thought, caressing and smoothing the feather, it looks all right, doesn't it? She had felt for a moment very low, disintegrated, but now as she sat on the bed in her blue dinner dress she thought, Mr Flanagan isn't a bit afraid to be him and Mrs Gampish isn't a bit afraid to be her and now I'm not a bit afraid to be me . . . at least, not much. As she looked down, smoothing her little short feather, a dreamy smile came on her face. Seals swam through the green waters of her mind. Mrs Finkel passed and repassed in careless loveliness. Mrs Gampish said austerely, Too earnest, my child, too earnest. The ghost of the mimosa tree drifted, drifted. Salt Lake City, she thought fondly . . . and then . . . where? . . . anticipation . . . a delicious fear . . . an unfamiliar pleasure.

Mrs Golightly was moving out of the class for beginners. She is much more skilful now (How agile and confiding are her eyelashes!) and when her husband says, There's going to be a Convention in Mexico City (or Chilliwack or Trois Rivières), she says with delight, Oh *Tom* . . . !

GABRIELLE ROY

The Satellites

In the transparent night of the Arctic summer, beside a little lake far away in the immense naked land, glimmered the fire lit to guide the seaplane that was expected at any moment. Stocky shadows all around fed the flames with handfuls of reindeer moss torn from the soil.

Nearby, at the end of a plank fastened to two empty oil-drums and placed on the water to serve as a gangway, there were a few cabins, one of them faintly illuminated. A little farther away were seven or eight other rickety houses, quite enough, in these parts, to constitute a village. From all sides rose the lament of the always famished dogs which no one ever heard any more.

Near the fire the men chatted calmly. They spoke in that smooth and gentle Eskimo voice with its occasional rises, a voice much like the summer night and punctuated only by brief bursts of laughter about everything and nothing. With them such laughter was very often just a way of concluding a sentence, providing a full stop, perhaps a sort of commentary on fate.

They had begun to make little wagers among themselves. They wagered that the seaplane was going to come, that it would not come, that it had set out but would never arrive, and even that it had not set out at all.

Fort Chimo had spoken, however. The radio had told them to be in readiness; the seaplane would stop on its way back from Frobisher Bay that evening to pick up the patient. The patient was Deborah, and it was for her that light had been left in the hut.

The men went on wagering for their own entertainment. For instance, they said that Deborah would have died before the seaplane arrived, as the Eskimos used to die in former times, without fuss. Or the seaplane would carry her a long way off and no one would ever see her again, living or dead. They wagered also that she would return by the road of the sky cured and looking twenty years younger. At this notion they all laughed heartily, especially Jonathan, Deborah's husband, as if he were once more the butt of the joking of his wedding night. They even went so far as to wager that the white men might soon find a remedy against death. No one would die any more. They would live forever—multitudes of old people. At this prospect they fell silent, but impressed even so. There were about ten of them around the fire: old men like Isaac, Deborah's father, reared in the old harsh way; middle-aged men like Jonathan, divided between two influences, the ancient and the modern; and finally young men, more erect of body than their elders, slimmer too, and these were definitely inclined towards the life of today.

Old Isaac, standing slightly to one side, perpetually rolling a round pebble between his fingers, said that nothing now was as it had been in the old days.

'In the old days,' he declared with pride, 'no one would have taken all this trouble to prevent a woman from dying when her hour had come. Nor even a man, for that matter. What sense is it,' he asked, 'to prevent at such great expense someone from dying today who in any event is going to die tomorrow? What is the sense of it?'

No one knew what the sense of it was, so they began to search for it together with touching good will.

Isaac, for his part, continued to gaze attentively at the fire. His eyes filled with memories, and what seemed a sort of compassion mingled with hardness. They knew then what he was going to speak of and even the youngest moved closer, for the subject was fascinating.

'That night you know of,' the old man began, 'was not as cold as some have said. It was a seasonal night, that's all. Nor did we abandon the Old One on the pack-ice as they have also said. We spoke to her first. We said good-bye to her. In short, we behaved as good sons should. We wrapped her in caribou skins. We even left her one that was brand new. Find me any white men,' he asked all in general, 'who would do as much for one of their old people, for all their fine words. We didn't abandon her,' he repeated with a curious stubbornness.

'And isn't it true,' asked one of the young men, 'that you left her something to eat?'

'Yes,' said Benjamin, Isaac's younger brother. 'We left her something to eat—a big piece of fresh seal-meat.'

'That's right,' said Isaac with a sort of disdain, head high, 'but to my thinking she didn't eat.'

'How could we know?' said one of the men. 'She might have wished to hold on for a day, perhaps two . . . to watch for . . . .'

'Not to my thinking,' Isaac repeated. 'She could no longer walk alone. She could scarcely swallow. She was almost blind. Why would she want to hold on for a few days more? And why do they all want to hold on now?'

They were silent, looking at the flames. There was in their eyes a sort of beauty about the death of the Old One in the shadow, wind, and silence; they were still not sure how it had come to pass, whether by water, by the cold, or from shock.

'Didn't they at least find something? The new skin, perhaps?' asked one of the young Eskimos.

'No,' said Isaac. 'Not a trace. The Old One had departed as she came into the world. There wouldn't even have been a scrap of her to bury.'

Jonathan rose then and announced that he would go to see whether Deborah needed anything.

He stood for a moment on the doorsill, looking at a human form that lay stretched upon two old automobile seats placed end to end.

'Are you there?'

'I'm here,' she said weakly.

'You're not worse?'

'I'm not worse.'

'Be patient,' said Jonathan then and went at once to rejoin the others around the fire.

What else could she do but be patient? Emaciated and short of breath, she had been lying there for weeks, victim of a swiftly progressing illness. She was only forty-two, and yet she considered this old enough to die. From the moment one was no longer good for anything, one was always old enough for death.

But then their pastor, the Reverend Hugh Paterson, had passed that way last week. Seated on the ground near Deborah's 'bed', he had begged her not to let herself die.

'Come, Deborah! At least make an effort!'

Feeble as she was, she had managed to draw from herself something like a grieving laugh.

'What, don't want . . . but when the body isn't good any more . . .'

'But yours *is* still good—strong and sturdy. You're too young to leave life. Come, a little courage!'

Courage? She was willing, but what was the use? How did you manage to stop death once it was on its way? Was there a means?

There was a means, and it was very simple: arrange for the seaplane to come. Deborah would be put on board. She would be taken to a hospital in the South. And there, almost certainly, she would be cured.

Of all this she chiefly retained a word that for her held magic: South. She had dreamed of it, just as the people of the South—if she had known this, her astonishment would have been boundless—dream of the North at times. Simply for the pleasure of the journey, to see at last what this famous South was like, she might have made up her mind. But she was too weary now.

'As long as there is life,' the pastor continued, 'we must hope, we must try to hold on to it.'

Deborah then turned her head towards the pastor to examine him in her turn, at length. She had already observed that the white men cling to their lives more than the Eskimos.

'Why?' she asked. 'Is it because your lives are better than ours?'

This very simple question seemed to plunge into utter perplexity a man who until then had been able to answer some very perplexing questions.

'It is true,' he replied, 'that the white men fear dying more than you Eskimos do, but why this is so I would find it hard to say. It is very strange when you think of it, for we haven't learned to live in peace with one another or, for that matter, with ourselves. We haven't learned what is most essential, yet it's true that we are bent upon living longer and longer.'

The illogic of this drew from Deborah another rather sad little laugh.

Still, the pastor pointed out a short time later, charity and mutual love had made great progress among the Eskimos since they had accepted the Word.

She knew then that he was going to refer once more to that old story of the grandmother abandoned on the pack-ice—a story he had had from them and had later reworked to his own liking and recalled to them on every occasion; he had even made it the theme of his principal sermon, drawing from it the conclusion that the Eskimos of today were more compassionate than those of past times.

It wasn't that there was no truth in the story as he recounted it, for there was. But he omitted certain illuminating details, for instance that the grandmother had asked to be left on the pack-ice because she could not manage to keep up with the others; she had asked it with her eyes, if not in words. At any rate, this is what her sons had believed they read in her gaze, and why should they have been mistaken?

For several minutes Jonathan, who had returned to the cabin, listened to Deborah thinking aloud and repeating the words of encouragement the pastor had addressed to her before he left.

'The plane still isn't here,' said Jonathan. 'It may come any minute. How are you?'

She said she was not too bad.

'Good,' he said then, and added that he would go and wait with the others.

Next it was Deborah's daughter-in-law, who came from the neighbouring cabin and stopped for a moment on the threshold.

'Do you need anything?'

'No, nothing. Thanks just the same, Mary.'

Alone once more, Deborah dragged herself to the door and leaned her weary back against the frame, her face raised towards the sky. Thus she too would see the arrival of this famous seaplane that was coming to save her.

What had eventually decided her was not the love of life as such. Simply to live did not mean at all that much to her. No, what had decided her was the wish to recover the years that were past. To walk for hours after the men, laden with bundles, over the broken soil of the tundra, camp here, hunt there, fish a little farther long, build fires, mend the clothes—it was this good life she wanted to have once more.

'I don't see why you shouldn't recover sufficiently to do what you used to do,' the pastor had somewhat imprudently promised her.

She had believed him. Had he not spoken the truth so many times before? For instance, when he said that he loved his children of Iguvik with all his heart. This was certainly true, for to remain here one must either become rich or love; and the pastor had not become rich.

He said also that times were changing and that there was good in all these changes. Today the government took better care of its Eskimo children. It spent a great deal of money on them. And the Eskimos themselves had greatly changed.

'You wouldn't any longer—admit it, Deborah—abandon the Old One to the cold and the night.'

This, it was true, might never happen again. In a sense this was precisely what was troubling Deborah. For what would they do now with their poor old people? They would look after them, this was understood, but for what purpose?

She had reached the point now of searching her mind to find imaginary solutions to hypothetical or possible evils, without the least idea, as yet, that it is through this door that sorrow enters a life.

'Good,' she had agreed finally. 'Get your plane to come.'

Just when she had reached that stage in her reflections Jonathan came running.

'We can hear a noise behind the clouds. It must be the seaplane.'

Immediately afterwards, the noise swelled and drowned out his voice. The dogs joined in. There was an indescribable din, a huge splash in the water, then almost silence again.

The cabin of the seaplane opened. The nurse descended first, a tiny bit of a woman with a decided air.

'Where is the patient?' she asked.

She was holding an electric lamp with a handle as long as a rifle, directing its powerful rays all around. From the night emerged objects which seemed to amaze even the Eskimos, who had never beheld them before in this unusual light: for example, the old washbasin Jonathan had found a little while ago, which had remained stranded ever since on the mossy ground without the arrival or outflow of any water but rain; sometimes, when enough had gathered, Jonathan took it into his head when he passed to wash his hands. There were also hundreds of discarded rusted oil-drums; scrap-iron of every sort; and, between two posts, some laundry hung up to dry.

Behind the nurse came the Reverend Hugh Paterson and the pilot. They all walked down the gangway, the young woman in the lead. With white men this wasn't surprising, it was quite often the woman who commanded.

They arrived at the shack. They took Deborah from between skins and old gnawed blankets and thrust aside almost everything that was hers to wrap her in new clean whiteness. They loaded her upon a sort of plank, despite her protests. Only yesterday, after all, she had got up to prepare meals for her household. They ignored everything she said and hoisted her aboard as if she were a parcel. They then climbed in themselves, slammed the doors, and rose into the air. A moment or so later there was no more trace of them.

Below, returned to the fire, the stupefied men did not quite know what to say about all this. At last they went back to wagering among themselves—what else was there to do? She would not return; she would perhaps return.

'Not to my thinking,' cut in Isaac. 'Not with the wind there is this evening.'

II

With daybreak Deborah began to see her country. They had tried to keep her lying down, but she had resisted and been granted permission finally to sit up, and now she could see her strange and enormous country from one end to the other. What had she ever been able to see of it before today, always more or less on the move across the barren expanse? It is true. But in winter, pricked and blinded by the winds and the snow, in summer by the mosquitoes, burdened in all weather up to the forehead with bundles, and always preoccupied with something that must be done—hunting, fishing, meals? Only today, at last, she was discovering it. She found it beautiful, much better even than she would have believed from the scraps she had had till then in her head.

She herself, now that the nurse had washed, combed and tidied her, was far from plain. She possessed, in any case, the lively and readily sparkling eyes of her race; but hers, as well—perhaps because of some melancholy of spirit—lingered upon everything they encounterd with loving insistence. What astonished and even fascinated her was the lakes—their often peculiar shapes, their unbelievable profusion. Yet she must have known these little lakes, almost all of them stoppered with no visible communication between them, from wandering and toiling entire days with Jonathan in their maze, packs on back, seeking a dry path, skirting this one, turning back on their steps, searching elsewhere—but always ahead of them, hollowed in the rock, there would be yet another basin brimming with water. Yet nothing, perhaps, had more appeal for her now than this curious region she had always found so difficult.

The movement and stir of the journey had done her good, had revived her, unless it was the medicine the nurse had given her. Nothing escaped her watchful attention. In the desert of water and rock stretching far into the distance, she recognized the fur-trading post where they used to trade, the people of her village, and of other villages too. How small it was, scarcely bigger than a die laid on the empty land, the post that since their birth had dominated almost all their journeys, on foot, by sleigh, by kayak—the goal, so to speak, of their lives. There was just time to catch sight of it beside an immense river flowing towards the ocean, with nothing else around it but clouds, and then you could see it no longer.

As she passed, she had taken time even so to say good-day in her heart to the factor, a widower whose life there alone, cut off from his own kind, seemed even to the Eskimos most pitiable.

In the distance she could distinguish the meeting, seemingly quite gentle, of earth and sea. Often, however, in Deborah's country, these two forces met as enemies, amidst piled-up ice, with blows and tumult, as in a savage struggle.

On the other side were the mountains. She contemplated them at length and saw finally just what they were like—old, round mountains, worn away by time. She saw their colours and their summits, how they ended and how they stood one beside the other along the horizon, like an endless encampment of tents of almost equal height. Perhaps really to see mountains one must have the good fortune, as she had at this moment, to be seated calmly in the clouds.

At this thought Deborah's sick face brightened with something very like a gentle desire to laugh.

At Fort Chimo she had to change planes and take a much larger one departing for the South.

While she was waiting, wrapped in a blanket on a stretcher, left by herself for a moment in the midst of cans and bales of all sorts, she noticed something fascinating on the edge of the runway a short distance away. This was a species of small creatures that bowed with the wind, quivering almost without cessation. Doubtless these were what she had heard called trees. She had heard that they came from the South, in an incalculable number first, and very tall when they set out. It was also said that, little by little, as they climbed towards the cold, their ranks dwindled; the survivors, like exhausted humans who had undergone too severe a test, stooped and sagged and could scarcely hold themselves erect.

Deborah glanced quickly around to make sure no one was there to prevent her doing as she wished. She was still feeling very well, probably because of her good medicine, and she had an irresistible impulse to take a closer look at those tiny trees in a row along the tarmac. With some difficulty she managed to extricate herself from the blanket and began to walk towards the midget birches. She tried to unroll their fragile leaves, whose very touch told her they were living things that left a little of their moisture in the hollow of her hand. Then stealthily, as if she were committing a robbery, she filled her pockets quickly with the little leaves. These would be for the children of Iguvik when she returned, so that they would have some notion of the foliage of a tree.

After several hours' flight, when the aircraft came out of the clouds and dipped close to earth, it was the white men's country that she began to discover. Luckily she had seen those first spindly trees; otherwise would she ever have believed her eyes when tall spruce trees and the first big maples appeared. Even from high in the air it was clear that these were creatures of surprising vitality, with numerous branches, some of them reaching higher than the rooftops. Yet all the houses here seemed at least as big as the factor's imposing residence in Deborah's country. In addition, they had windows on all their surfaces, so that they appeared to be looking from every side at once. There must be firewood here in abundance, since there was no fear of losing heat through all those openings.

Deborah began to wonder why, when their pastor was trying to show them the happiness of a future life, he had not simply described this green land unfolding pleasantly in the sun, all ablaze with the lights cast by windows, roofs, and steeples. Handsome animals seemed also to share in life's sweetness here; they could be seen browsing in very green grass or simply lying in the sun with nothing to do but switch their tails.

As companions among the animals, the Eskimos had only their dogs, and their life now seemed to her very cruel. It was perhaps by contrasting their lean-flanked huskies with these pampered beasts, which even from a distance looked plump and placid, that she began to grasp the impassable distance between the North and the South.

For as long as it was visible, she could not take her eyes from a little white horse that was standing at the end of a meadow beside water—probably in the wind too, to refresh himself. Such a pretty little animal—but for what could anything so slender and delicate be used?

The plane lost more altitude and a great many other details appeared. For instance those walls that cut the land into slices of all shapes and dimensions—what were they?

She was told that they were fences, something in the nature of a marker, a boundary used to separate the fields.

Separate! Cut!

Suddenly she was almost eager to be on her way back to her own people so she could share with them such an extraordinary piece of news. Just think, down there they've actually come to the point of cutting up the land into little pieces surrounded by strands of iron or planks.

'Planks!' they would say. 'Planks wasted like that!'

They perhaps wouldn't believe her, the only one of them who had ever gone to the South.

Now the aircraft was searching out a place to touch down, and Deborah's eyes could not capture all the unexpected things offered. At length the nurse came over to find out what so amazed her patient. There was nothing, however, in the least out of the ordinary. It was simply the approaches to a little city like hundreds in the country, with houses surrounded by massed roses and phlox—here a swing where children played at rising and falling, there a swimming pool into which people plunged; finally great beds of multicoloured flowers and also trees, some with fine white bark, others with foliage as pliant as hair. What would Deborah have felt if she could have understood that, to people living farther in the South, the gracious land beneath her was still the North, with its harsh climate and unrewarding soil?

Suddenly she was afraid, however, and overwhelmed by the sense that the earth was coming straight up to meet her. She clung to the seat. Rising into the air had seemed quite natural. Returning to earth was alarming. She closed her eyes. So it had been no use trying to escape from her death in the North. It had come on ahead to wait for her in the South.

At last she opened her eyes and saw to her great astonishment that the plane had landed without her knowledge and was now rolling quietly. Smiling with embarrassment, she glanced quickly at the other passengers, as if to discover whether she had been caught out in her fear.

She felt stiff with emotion and fatigue. The good medicine no longer seemed to be working well. Once more she was taken in hand, but now she had no strength to resist. And what was the use, anyway? She was beginning to realize that she had been placed in powerful hands and these hands were already so intent upon curing her that now there was no time or thought for anything else.

She was put once more upon a stretcher; then inside a vehicle that set off at great speed. Other vehicles passed or overtook them. Their occupants, as they glanced towards Deborah, seemed to her to look preoccupied and dispirited, and she wondered whether some crushing event had occurred here today.

But when she looked towards the horizon she felt a sudden, very quiet delight. Travelling along the rim of the sky were several small black sleighs on wheels, attached to one another and drawn by a larger sleigh that gave forth smoke, and from time to time brief peculiar cries, as if they were summoning people to leave what they were doing and come on board. Deborah felt a sort of summons from far back in her life, from her first years. All the children in the world are perhaps summoned in this way; in the north by dog sleighs and here, probably, by this other sort of sleigh.

'It's a train,' she was told. 'Nothing but a train.'

She raised her head and let her eyes follow to the curve of the horizon the magic sleigh, which glided without bounds or jolts, as if there was a road for it along the sky that was as smooth as the air. The team seemingly went of its own accord without strokes of the whip on its spine and without any fatigue. Perhaps to Deborah it looked as if the team went only where it wished.

Later, when she was asked whether there were anything that

would particularly please her, her eyes would shine and she would invariably answer, 'Train. Deborah very much like to ride in train.'

III

After a week of examination, sometimes in the dark with the aid of a powerful roaring machine and at other times in floods of blinding light, she received a visit from the government in the person of an interpreter, who sat down unceremoniously beside the fine bed Deborah occupied all by herself in the hospital.

'Well now,' said the government, 'you have a tumour, a nasty lump that's eating you up inside. It must be removed. Do you give your consent?'

Deborah scarcely hesitated. Always the knife had seemed to her the best way to eradicate evil when that was indicated.

'Cut,' she decided, and went off, perfectly calm, almost without fear, to the operation.

Soon afterwards she seemed to be recovering. She was to be seen, in a long dressing-gown lent by the hospital but shod in her mukluks, wandering persistently about the corridors, without asking anything of anyone, until she had found the way out to the garden. It was planted with a few handsome trees. From the windows above they could watch her as she moved with her still slightly shuffling steps along the gravel walks. She approached one of the maples warily, rather as one might a living creature, so as not to startle it. She stretched forth her hand and touched it delicately with her fingertips. It was as if she were trying to tame it. Then she looked at it with delight, listening to it rustle. Finally she put her arm around its trunk and, leaning her cheek there, stood motionless, contemplating the great mass of leaves high in the sky as the wind stirred them gently.

She also made friends among humans. First, among her own people. There was a fair number of them in the hospital, several of whom could once have been considered neighbours, since they all lived only three or four hundred miles from each other; at times, no doubt, by some accident of stopping-point or itinerary—small groups of travellers going towards or away from the trading-post—they had passed very close to one another; perhaps engulfed in blizzards, they had missed one another only by a hair. So their meeting at last today seemed to them a miracle. They visited back and forth continually, always with great signs of delight.

Among the whites she also made friends, and of these several died. When she saw that they were no better off than the Eskimos, that they were attacked by the same bodily afflictions, she felt amazement, first, and later almost as much grief for them as for the sick Eskimos. Then the vague hope she had maintained till then, though half hiding it from herself—that the white men would eventually manage to stretch life out forever—was extinguished once for all. Because she had almost come to believe this for a moment, she now found the truth harder to bear.

Happily she still had two excellent distractions to help her pass the time. First the shower. From the moment she first discovered this seemingly inexhaustible fountain of hot water and soap, it became with her a sort of passion. Perhaps this passion always existed in a latent state, frustrated for centuries among all those of her race. For close to a half-hour at a time, without noticing that people came now and then to try to turn the door-knob, Deborah would soap and then rinse the magnificent dark hair that draped her like a shawl to her knees.

When she returned to her bed, she would brush and brush it with the idea, perhaps, of making it shine like the gentle glow of the seal-oil lamp in the little snow-house of old, the memory of which had suddenly returned to her. After this, she would go back and wash her hair again.

'You'll end by rubbing so hard it will fall out,' the Sister reprimanded her gently.

Deborah's little smile was at once timid and a shade mischievous. For it was the poor Sister, actually, who was rather short of hair.

Her second and almost equally unbridled passion was for smoking cigarettes. When she was not busy tending her hair, she was almost always to be found squatting in the middle of her bed as if it were the ground,shrouded in heavy smoke. Her expression would then be a little less melancholy. It was as if all this smoke managed to obscure, at least slightly, the thought that was now trying to present itself at every instant to Deborah's mind. After the manner of her people, she had thus managed to take from civilization two things that seemed almost incompatible: soap for cleanliness and clarity, tobacco to blur the thoughts and soil the fingers.

The Sister reproached her one day. This was a nun who had been delegated for a long time to visit the sick Eskimos. She knew their language.

'Really, Deborah, I don't understand you.'

Deborah's big astonished eyes seemed to say: Well, do I understand you? But no matter, I love you anyway.

'On the one hand,' the Sister continued, 'you are cleanliness itself, forever washing yourself. On the other hand, you scatter cigarette ashes almost everywhere, you dirty everything. You're like an old bush camp all by yourself. What can this do for you, all this smoke?'

It didn't perhaps do very much. Just gave her some little fragments of dream, pictures she had believed lost. But still it brought the great savage and distant North to some extent into this skimpy room. That was what it did.

One day, through the smoke, Deborah managed to recover almost everything she had ever possessed. The camp appeared before her half-closed eyes. It was all there, down to the wash-basin Jonathan had salvaged after the departure of the troops, which might be full of water at this very moment, down to her washing that no one perhaps had thought of bringing in. She saw the narrow walkway joined to the empty oil-drums, rising and falling with the slight movements of the water, like a creature that breathed; she saw her shack, its door wide open, and all around the pure and naked sky. She felt upon her cheeks what might have been drops of lukewarm rain. She put her fingers to her face and gathered a tear, which she examined with amazement and a trace of shame. What was this now? Except for those drawn from her by the extreme cold or, in summer, by the smoke from the fires lit to drive away the mosquitoes, she had no recollection of ever shedding tears.

In her surprise, the tears for a moment stopped flowing. Then they resumed in a storm. So that she would at least not be seen or heard, she hid herself under the sheet.

Quite often after that, she was found in a motionless little round heap in the middle of the bed.

The Sister began almost to plead with her, 'Smoke, Deborah, or go and wash your lovely hair.'

But this did not mean very much to her now. However, they discovered her from time to time eating oranges, with tears streaming down her face. She had thought of saving those she was given in her drawer or under the mattress to take to the children of her country. Until the day when the smell warned the nurse.

'Now look, Deborah. Oranges don't keep indefinitely.'

'Ah!'

Her face showed that this was a very cruel disappointment. So there was no hope of trying to take them back with her. Well in that case, she would do her best to eat them. However, her heart was not in it. She looked as if she were eating the most bitter of fruit. Many of the fine good things of the South lost interest in her eyes as soon as she learned they could not bear the journey. It was as if she were now refusing to become attached to them. Perhaps she even held it obscurely against them.

From then on she grew sadder from day to day. The idea seemed to have come to her that like the oranges, like the tender leaves on the branches of the trees, like the flowers plucked from the garden, she herself would not last long enough to make the journey back to her country.

She stopped washing herself. She no longer sat leafing through magazines while giving the impression that she was reading the text here and there. She gave up everything except the little cloud of blue smoke in which she enclosed herself more often than ever now, as if inside a precarious wall that defined her modest place in the world.

Then one day the government came back to her again and said, 'So you're as lonesome as that! Come, this isn't reasonable, Deborah.'

So that's what it was—lonesomeness. She had needed to be surrounded with attention, showered with oranges and visits, loved as never before and treated like a queen to know lonesomeness. What a curious illness it was!

'Yes, it must be that I'm lonesome,' Deborah admitted.

'You think about your own country all the time, eh?'

'Yes, I do.'

'Well, in that case,' said the government, 'we're going to let you go. Of course it would have been better for you to stay with us a little longer. Your illness may return. We don't know yet whether it's been rooted out completely and for good. But if you're dying of lonesomeness. . . .'

So she could go if she wanted to. She wouldn't be kept against her will. She had permission? She was free?

Tears flowed from the dark eyes, and this was stranger than

ever. For now they did not come from the pain of lonesomeness but because this pain had been removed.

IV

Once more she saw the tender aspect of the world with its trees, all laden these days with gold, and its pleasant valleys in which rivers, winding from one island of greenness to another, seemed to be visiting each in turn.

But she loved the earth beneath her more when there were no longer any trees. Most appealing of all to her were the arid knolls and bald hummocks of the naked land, between which gleaned the icy water of solitary lakes. So many, many lakes, and so remote as well that very few of them have been given a name. Her eyes devoured this singular network of water and rock where she had so often roamed in former days with Jonathan, packs on her back, sometimes with a child in her womb, her face so bathed in sweat that she could scarcely see before her, and now this period of her life seemed to have been of moving tenderness. So one had to go very far in order to judge one's life, and it was perhaps on its most arduous days that the best memories were being prepared.

She remained seated this time, too, to make the crossing of the sky, though she could no longer manage to hold her head erect.

For rather a long time the land disappeared from their sight. Even Deborah closed her eyes and dozed a little, while they were in the clouds, and there was nothing to look at but their masses of snow—very soft snow, it was true, but a little too similar to everlasting pack-ice.

Suddenly she sat up. Her eyes, so heavy with fatigue, blazed with interest. Below, once again, was the big river flowing towards the sea, with the little fur-trading post beside it, alone in the infinite barren land.

Now she was nearly home. Almost at once, in fact, she recognized the place in the world which belonged to her and to which she belonged; and finding it again, returning from so far away, must have seemed to her a sort of miracle, for the worn face, so long spiritless, was suddenly radiant.

The seaplane was about to touch water. The various objects of the camp grew closer. There was the wash-basin, which was beginning to fill with moss and rust; there were the discarded oil-drums and, where her washing had been, some skins that had been cleaned and stretched to dry in the sun. And there was Jonathan.

He was standing beside the lake, in almost the same spot where he had watched her leave and in almost the same attitude. With the years he had become a heavy little man, almost as broad as he was high. His head thrown up and his neck drawn back between his shoulders, he followed the movement of the seaplane in the bright sun. Deborah could even distinguish the thick fringe of his hair and the handsome dark colour of his skin. She herself had had time in the hospital to become as pale and ugly as a white woman. At one point he raised his hands above his head. Perhaps in greeting. But it looked, quite truthfully, as if he were saying. to the aircraft, 'Hi there, be a bit careful.' Then, without waiting any longer, he went into the cabin. This was perhaps to tidy up a little, at least to conceal the worst of the litter that had lain strewn about for weeks. Even though this meant that they had to go and fetch him to help carry Deborah, at least to lend a hand at the reception of his own wife. And not until then did he let it be clear that he knew who was arriving.

After the event, at least for some time, he seemed fairly pleased to see her back. He even went one day to a lake that was very hard to reach, eight knolls away, and caught her a fine fish with delicate flesh. She scarcely touched it; everything disagreed with her nowadays. He spent some time tinkering with the two automobile seats she used as a bed and finally attached them together so they no longer parted at every moment, leaving a space into which she slipped.

But when he saw that despite all this attention Deborah was still without appetite, nauseated by odours, as if she no longer knew what an Eskimo house was like—hadn't she gone as far as to ask him to remove some animal guts that were only a week old?—and that she lay stretched out in her corner just as before, he lost patience and went to complain to the other men.

'She shouldn't have gone,' he said and then, in the same level tone, 'She shouldn't have come back either.'

'That was my thinking, as I told you,' Isaac reminded him. 'When it's time to die, one doesn't make all this fuss. One dies.'

But Jonathan was irritable these days, and although the old man had essentially just supported his own argument, he turned on him suddenly.

'You're a fine one to talk, old man,' he said. 'Here you are, seventy years old, fat and well fed. What do you do to deserve that? Nothing. You live on the government with your pension. You have nothing to do but you have all you need: your lard, your flour, your tobacco, your sugar, your tea . . . .'

'It's not the same thing,' Isaac defended himself. 'I at least still have my strength. I don't need anyone to help me walk or do what I want to do.'

'Even so, you don't do anything either from morning till night but you still have your lard, your flour, your sugar . . . .'

More than anything, perhaps, the tedium of the enumeration wearied Isaac. He departed, grumbling, to seek refuge in the shack. It was impossible to have peace anywhere now. He sat down in a corner on a wooden crate that bore on one side the warning, *This side up*, and on the other, *Haut*. He looked all around him for something with which to busy himself. It was true that for quite some time he had done nothing. But what was there to do? Hunt? There were no more caribou to speak of. Fish then, perhaps? Yes, but from the moment one had the old-age pension and was no longer pressed from behind, what was the use of all that trouble? Something broke in man, perhaps, when he received without giving as much in return. The perplexed old man, sitting on his crate, looked as if he were glimpsing a little of the misfortune that had befallen the population of the North, not long ago so industrious. He shook himself and picked up an old fishing net which he began to examine to see whether it was worth the trouble of mending.

He caught the eye of his daughter, who had been lying in her own little corner watching him think.

To tell the truth, he scarcely recognized her since she had been in the South. This was not only because she had grown thin and pale. Even the expression of her face seemed to him completely changed. One might have said that she no longer thought quite as they did now, or even that they could not quite guess what she was thinking.

'Do you want me to tell you?' he said. 'I should go off of my own accord and put myself on the pack-ice as we put the Old One in the good time.'

He mused a little.

'It was a beautiful cold night. There were spirits in white tunics dancing and circling all around the sky.'

He was becoming more and more fond of remembering that time.

'Since the wind was from the right direction,' he said, 'the ice must have gone very quickly. It certainly didn't take long. The ice broke loose with a little snap. Then off with it! It was far away.'

In contrast to what he had always said until now, that the Old One had totally disappeared, he now maintained that she must have been preserved by the frost.

'The cold is good and compassionate,' he claimed.

And he began to describe the Old One as he now pictured her, intact, seated in the centre of her column of ice—a tiny white island on the raging black sea—turning and turning continually at the end of the world in the last free waters of the earth, just like those satellites of today, those curious objects, he said, that they were going to hang high in the air so that they would never come down again.

'That's what she has become,' he said dreamily. 'I'd stake my life on it. A satellite.'

He lowered his gaze once more to Deborah's emaciated face, which was marked with suffering and anxieties of the spirit that one did not often find in the old days on Eskimo faces. But it was true that in the old days one did not often see Eskimos grown thin and pale. They had died before that.

Isaac grumbled on, 'Ha, that's all nonsense! Eh, my poor Deborah? What do you think? When do we show more kindness to people? When we keep them from dying? Or when we help them just a little? . . . Eh?'

V

Then, with the first snows, the Reverend Hugh Paterson chanced to pass that way again on his early-winter rounds. The voices of the dogs were heard resounding sharply in air that had been scoured by the already icy winds. A few moments later in came the pastor, a long lean silhouette beside the Eskimos, most of them round and short. He seated himself on the corner of one of the old automobile seats that weather and perhaps ocean-salt had pitted. He had often wondered how they could have reached this place, by what curious journey, who or what could have brought them—the sea, a plane, or perhaps some old trapper on his back?

'So, my poor Deborah,' he said. 'You're no better?'

He met the gaze of soft and sorrowful eyes that seemed to reproach him for preventing death from striking in its hour.

Dying, Deborah appeared to be thinking, is easier the first time than the second. Who knows, it may even become harder the longer it is deferred.

Sad enough to make one weep and yet in their depths still a little mocking, doubtless from force of habit, Deborah's great dark eyes seemed to appeal for understanding across the silence.

And then, as if he understood perfectly, he stretched out his hands to join Deborah's together, and then draw them towards him, keeping them pressed between his own.

'My poor child, all you have learned, loved, and understood in these few more months you've lived is yours forever. Nothing can take any of it from you. Even a single additional step in life and you are enhanced forever.'

The dark eyes reflected. They seemed to grasp these fine words and take them into herself to keep for the day when she might make something from them. Does one ever know with thoughts?

'Still, you ought to have stayed in the hospital where you'd have been better looked after,' he said without logic but with tender affection.

'Why want so much to look after?' she asked and, powerless to understand, sank into a sort of silent misery.

It was this that disconcerted her most among civilized people, this terrible determination, even when death was close and certain, to defy it still. This absurd preference also, when they must finally die, that it should be in a bed.

'Dear Mr Paterson,' she said, 'Deborah much prefers for dying to be here than there.'

'Who's talking about dying?' Once again he tried to deceive her with false lightness.

Then he remembered to give her the little present of drugs that the government had entrusted to him for her. The government was very concerned about her, he said, and would be anxious to hear whether the operation had been a complete success.

'Say thank you,' she said simply.

Finally the pastor went on to point out that death was not an evil. In fact it was death now, and no longer life, that he described as the best friend of human beings. It was the deliverance from all our ills. At last one was free. We departed with shoulders, hands, and hearts finally unburdened.

These were fine things to hear, though seemingly quite the opposite to what he had said when he had been encouraging Deborah to live. They were none the less convincing in their fashion. Even Deborah knew now that one ought to say those things that best fitted the affair of the moment, otherwise there would be nothing left to say, it would no longer be worth the trouble of opening one's mouth, and no one would ever speak again.

'Deborah would like to be free right away,' she said.

'Deborah will perhaps not have very long to wait,' he replied tenderly, as if this were his wish for her. 'A few steps more, a little patience still, and she will be in complete happiness.'

Happiness. Another incomprehensible expression. If happiness simply lived somewhere on earth, where was that? When she arrived in the South, she had been able to believe it might be here in the midst of favour and wealth. But soon she had come to feel that there was even less happiness here than in her home. Now, she never stopped puzzling about this.

'When all's said and done,' the pastor was forced to admit, 'we can encounter happiness in all its radiance only on the other side of life.'

She agreed wholeheartedly, her eyes eager, as if hungry for the unknown. And for what else could she hunger now?

'On that side,' he said again, 'all that has been obscure to us will be understood. Clarity will reign. No one will lack again for anything.'

VI

The nights are long in that latitude, as winter approaches, even for those who sleep well. For Deborah they were interminable. Her short life, which had been devoured by needs that left little time for thinking, was coming to an end, paradoxically, in an infinity of time in which there was nothing else to do. So it seemed as if her short life were being prolonged for some reason that Deborah was trying to comprehend.

She lay resting on the automobile seats while the others around her, wrapped in whatever old blankets they still possessed, slept directly on the floor.

The air in the hut was fouled, both by the unpleasant odour her diseased body was beginning to give off and by the Eskimos' own odour of oil and fish, which she now found sickening. With the coming of winter they had reached the point, in this rickety shack which the fierce cold obliged them to keep tightly closed, of restricting one another cruelly. One could cough, spit, turn over, and everyone would stir, cough, turn over.

Deborah had taken it into her head to try to picture that place after death, so different from life, where no one would lack again for anything. She needed all her confidence in the pastor to have faith in such words. For at the present time she lacked almost everything. What she most lacked, moreover, was all she had so recently learned to know, those comforts of life in the South: hot water and soap, the clear and abundant light, always ready to flash on, of electricity; a little space all to herself; but especially, perhaps, that sort of friendliness—or show of friendliness—between people in the South. She had thought this uncalled-for, but now, even though still not entirely convinced it was real affection, she would have liked to feel its warmth around her.

As she now saw it, the better life became, the more needs it satisfied and the more new needs arose. So that it seemed to her quite unlikely that there ever could be a life or a place where one would lack for nothing.

The others around her too were, on her account, in want and deprivation, Isaac of the warm blanket he had 'lent' her—just for a time and not for the whole winter—and Jonathan of love, for to Deborah love had become torture.

The nights therefore were increasingly long and uncomfortable for them all.

Outside the complaining of the dogs would diminish for a moment only to swell again. In the old days she had not heard this. It existed, inevitable as the frost that overtakes the water or as the click of the trap on a prey. It existed, that was all. Now she heard it continually and the sound harassed her. Couldn't they give the dogs just once enough to eat? Jonathan looked at her sidelong. Was she crazy? Satisfy the dogs? You might as well try to satisfy the animals of the tundra, the whole of famished creation.

She came close to suffocating one evening in the tightly closed cabin. Who would have believed that in this frigid land, so full of wind, she would find herself wishing, more than anything in the world, for a single breath of fresh air. It was in the South too, with its wide-open windows, that she had acquired this taste for the movement of air in the house. If only, this night again, they could have left the door open just a crack. But the others were freezing. While she was burning.

More and more, also, she was impatient to be on that other side of life where no one would be sad any more. And for what else now could she be impatient?

She threw off her blankets, and took the warmest and spread it over old Isaac, who lay curled up on the floor. He had coughed a good deal latterly, though without yet making up his mind to ask her for his blanket. She put on her mukluks and pulled open the door. The cutting air seemed to strengthen her.

The night was clear and cold. Snow had fallen. In this fresh but shallow snow Deborah left very clean imprints of her steps.

So it was that they were able to follow next day the journey she had made.

She had first struggled painfully to the top of the nearest knoll. To hear the beating of the surf? Or because she remembered climbing up there often with other children to try to glimpse the ocean, which was not very far away? Whatever her reason had been, she went on. To the next hummock, then to yet another. Moving from knoll to knoll, she finally reached the pack-ice.

There before her eyes, probably revealed to her in the pale glimmer from the snow, lay the most broken terrain on earth, an uneven buckling expanse of ice-floes, roughly hinged to one another.

No doubt the wind on that tormented coast had been blowing with utmost fury.

Yet she had entered it. Here and there, on the crust of snow a few more tracks could be picked out. They showed that Deborah had fallen on several occasions and that at last she had crawled more than she had walked. The tracks continued a little farther. They were to be found right to the edge of the open water.

When they examined the contour of the pack-ice from the ocean side, they saw that a portion of it had recently broken loose.

But though they peered long and searchingly through the dark and tumultuous landscape of black water, it was useless; they could distinguish nothing within it that bore any relation to a human shape. Or hear anything but the shrieking of the wind.

Translated by Joyce Marshall

JOYCE MARSHALL

So Many Have Died

On that day, her last, Georgiana Dinsborough was three months into her ninety-first year. She was a marvel. Everyone told her so and, though the reiteration grew tiresome, Georgiana herself acknowledged that in many ways she was. Marvellously lucky, at least, for how much of her reasonably steady health and mental clearness she owed to nature, how much to the habit, so long part of her, of weeding out any hint of frailty or contradiction, she didn't know. (As if it were possible even to think of untangling what you'd brought to life—no doubt squawling from the weight of it in that big farm-bedroom in the Eastern Townships—from what life and you yourself had made of what you'd brought.) She'd continued in practice till she was 80; her patients hadn't wanted her to retire and she had felt loyal to them, the grandchildren in many cases (even the male grandchildren) of those young women who had come timidly or in fierce feminist solidarity to the office she'd opened with her friend Mary Balsam in the living-room of this very flat. Loyal above all to her profession; anything so strenuously fought for acquired rights, couldn't be put aside the moment you began to feel a little tired. For ten years she'd taken no new patients and might have continued in that way, the attrition of death and dispersal slowly lightening the load, if she hadn't felt that quite new wish to have some time for herself, time to ask questions and find answers, evaluate her life. Wasn't that what you were supposed to do when you were very old? With the honesty she'd always required of herself, she'd wondered whether her decision wasn't a shade suspect, much like her Grandfather Dinsborough's announcement when he was 80 and crippled with arthritis, that deer were too beautiful to kill so he'd never hunt again. But if it was softness to want to go out proud, under her own steam, why not? She might even deserve it. So she booked passage for England and stayed away for six months, looked up old friends and family connections, learned about leisure in new places. When she returned, her office equipment had been sold, files stored in the basement, she was retired. It was as painless as such a thing could ever be.

She found that she rather liked this part of her life, as she'd liked all the other parts. (Liked it at least on her good days. Lying in bed, waiting for the telephone to ring, she was sure this would be one of the best. No aches, not even a twinge in her bad hip, broken in a fall three years ago. Sun washed through the room. Spring, that treacherous season, was coming in cool and bright —and very slow.) Despite urgings to move to a more compact apartment, she'd stayed on in the long duplex flat in Notre Dame de Grâce where her entire adult life had been lived—with Mary Balsam first, then briefly with her mother, for almost 50 years alone. She went to concerts, read, watched television, could count on at least one visit a week with some member of her large family connection. A varied lot, which provided stimulation and just enough irritation to keep her feeling alive. From time to time she considered her life (or, as it sometimes seemed, her life came back to consider her) though more as pure memory, she had to admit, than as material for questions she must answer. Perhaps once you've decided, as she had at eighteen, to be an agnostic, there were no questions, the notions of God and immortality having been packed away, to be taken out if ever only after you've ceased to breathe. She laughed at the thought of breathing her last, with relief if her final illness was painful (and she would fight, she knew that, even unconscious she'd fight) only to be roused at once by a voice—from where?—'Well now, Georgiana Lilian, about that deferred matter of My existence?' Her mind supplied the capital and she laughed again, for God had spoken in Grandfather Dinsborough's voice, coming clear and intimidating across 70 years.

She was still laughing when the phone gave its first warning ding. (Good. Now she'd be able to get up.) Who would it be today? Though she supposed they'd arranged some schedule, she'd never cracked it. Her lying alone all those hours with her hip broken had alarmed them—and God knows it had alarmed her—so she played along with their concern (and with their wariness of her that drove them to subterfuge) by pretending not to notice that, except on Tuesdays and Fridays when her charwoman came, there was always a call at just this time, when she was awake but not yet in her bath.

'Hi, Aunt George.' The tiny voice identified herself as Phyllis, granddaughter of Raymond, her youngest brother, a skinny little creature who'd recently put on the trappings of rebellion—cascades of muffling hair, ragged trousers, a vocabulary her mother found distressing—and though this child wasn't one of the coterie of fussers, Georgiana said exactly what she'd planned when she picked up the phone, 'Your great—no, *great* great grandfather just spoke to me out of a cloud like God.'

'Aunt George, you're kidding.' No humour. That was the real trouble with the young, the thing, at least, that worried her. It made conversation so patchy. The older lot, like Nora, her mother, could share the occasional joke, if you sneaked it in on them, though even they seemed to think your bones had become so brittle real laughter might break them. (Were we the last of the belly-laughers? It seems to me that we were always laughing and I miss it. How Charles and I could laugh. And after all these years, she wanted him. My God, it never ends, she thought, with astonishment, with delight.) 'What did he say, Aunt George?' Phyllis was asking.

'Some rot about my soul. He was a sadly limited old man. Godlike. Ruling unto the third and fourth generation. With some success till he encountered me.' Now why do I tell her this, she wondered and said briskly, 'Well, time's a-wasting. What can I do for you this fine May morning?'

'How's about lunch, Aunt George? I could pick you up, Mother says she'll let me have her car so if you like we can—'

'Out of the question, alas. Unless you want to eat here—no, that won't do either. Place will be a shambles. Got a man coming to take down double windows, put up screens.'

'Oh,' said Phyllis.

'Is it so urgent? Won't some other day do?'

'No you see I'm going to Europe next week and Mother's laid on all sorts of dentists and—' ('Breathe, child,' said Georgiana.) 'Oh sorry, I—I'd like very much to see you, Aunt George I'm proud of you. No-one else in our group has a relative like you. Your generation made a lot of mistakes but *you* didn't chicken out, not about everything. Aunt George I'm going *away*, I want to talk to you, you might even be able to tell me some things.'

Touched by this longest, if rambling, speech she'd ever heard from the child, intrigued too, novelty wasn't all that abundant nowadays, 'Well, come then,' Georgiana said. 'I'm charmed to hear I give you prestige with your group. Come at four. Fellow should be through and I'll be ready for a break.'

'Oh thanks,' said Phyllis. 'I'll turn you over to Mother, she wants to—'

'But hasn't that been settled,' said Georgiana, 'that I'm still breathing and in one piece?' and hung up laughing.

Nora rang back at once. Georgiana had just started the slow vertebra by vertebra stretching that preceded the foot and ankle exercises that enabled her to walk so well. With a cane, of course, but well. (Steve, her doctor-nephew, had feared she'd never walk. 'We'll see about that,' she'd said.)

'Phyllis hung up.' At 55 Nora still had almost the light, breathy voice of her youth. 'I wanted to talk to you too, Aunt George.'

'Then talk,' said Georgiana, 'while I get on with my exercises.' When she'd lain in the dark in frightening pain, she'd sobbed for three people—her mother, Charles and Nora. (Before she'd begun to inch that eternity down the hall to the point, just inside her bedroom door, where she could jiggle the phone from its stand. She'd learned then, she believed, what death would be like—an empty calling and help so far down the hall no inching could reach it.) The choice of names had startled her and she'd felt uneasy with her once-favourite niece since then. That was one of the risks in loving seldom. There was too much space in you, roots grew deep. For a few years she and Nora had seemed equal, almost contemporaries, and she, who confided seldom, had confided fully in Nora; even now the memory was humiliation. Rubbish, she thought, the girl probably doesn't remember. Though it might be amusing to try her out. You know, Nora, she could say, a moment ago I actually felt a stir of sexual longing for Charles.

'Aunt George,' Nora was saying sternly, 'Phyllis tells me you're going to be traipsing around after some man while he puts up screens.'

'Did I say that? I'll only traipse if it seems necessary. Since Antoine died and I've had to rely on agencies—But tell me,' she said, cutting off any impulse Nora might feel to come and supervise, as if even giving instructions was beyond you now. 'This European jaunt of Phyllis's. Isn't it a bit sudden?'

'She just sprang it on us. She's going with one of her girl friends.' And only eighteen, she wailed. And the way they dressed. Like fishermen. 'I want her to look in on my English relatives. Use them as a base. She won't hear of it.'

'Very wise,' said Georgiana. 'In your cousin Isabel's house, as I recall, there were plastic tulips and china dogs. And do you know? Each of those damn dogs had its snout pointing into the street.'

Nora laughed. 'Aunt George, you sure have a gift for putting people down. But when she comes . . . We tend to forget what it's like. How fragile they are. And you grew up in a tough school. She's gone a bit overboard about women's lib,' and before Georgiana could say, 'Well, good for her,' 'Don't try to influence her, Aunt George,' said Nora firmly.

'I couldn't. I didn't succeed with you, did I?'

'Well, in a way you did.' Nora paused, as if startled by her own words. 'You may not believe this but there's always been something whispering in my ear. I may break out yet, Aunt George.'

'No, not you, Nora,' said Georgiana. 'And look here. I believe I apologized at the time for any harm I might have done. I'll do so again if you insist.'

'Aunt George, it's marvellous the way you never change.' Why did she have to say that? What was so marvellous about continuing to be one's self? 'I've often wondered. Have you ever had doubts in your life? About anything?'

'*Doubts*? Oh Nora.'

At one time her life had been all doubt, she thought, after Nora had rung off and, with a final rotation of her ankles, she began to edge out of bed. (Whenever you became absorbed in a single thing, talking in this case, you forgot what a bag of recalcitrant bones you inhabited now. I have never felt more alive and yet it must take me 30 seconds to sit, then pull myself to my feet. Someone—Yeats?—put it well—*this caricature, decrepit age, that has been tied to me as to a dog's tail*. This *thing*. This hindrance. A tin can rattling behind. Never me.) Doubts, Nora? she repeated as she clumped down to the bathroom, the day's first steps so balky, feet like shovels, and set about preparing her bath. Doubt she'd be admitted to medicine at McGill, doubts she'd get through the course—discrimination could go to almost any length; you're damn right I grew up in a tough school—doubts she'd be allowed to intern, that patients would come. Doubt of herself. She might make some early disastrous error in diagnosis; she'd never be permitted another. But the War came—it would always be that to her, 'the War', the word a gong, sounding only once. What a society, she thought with an old, undiminished rage—it had to murder its men before it could value its women. And a few years later she was appointed examining physician to some of the Protestant schools. One of those who read of her death next day remembered her from that time: A stumpy alarming figure who spoke disparagingly of her tonsils and gave her a note to take home, which 'home', being somewhat harum scarum, ignored. She'd been puzzled at the doctor's being a lady, such a comically dressed lady—ankle-length skirt, frogged jacket hugging ample hips. Now she wondered whether the poor dear was impervious to her own appearance or couldn't afford to buy clothes. The suit in question, which gave Georgiana years of wear, had been a hand-me-down from her mother. And people seemed to like women doctors to be dowdy. Though Mary was always elegant, hard not to be with those delicate bones and perfect Grecian head.

Georgiana smiled, remembering the day during their second year when they'd marched down to St James Street and sold their long hair to a wig-maker; the proceeds bought them a skeleton. (A screen lifted to show her the two of them running through a Montreal snowstorm, hats loose on their shorn heads.) What a furor that created, my little Phyllis. Sniggers from the male students, our mothers sobbing, Grandfather Dinsborough quoting St Paul. (She eased onto the little stool in the tub, built by a handyman nephew at just the right, most comfortable height.) Imagine that little snip informing me coolly that we made mistakes. As if we had the time or the energy to be perfect. Still it was real rebellion and, if you don't understand, that's because we succeeded. Fun too; such vigour came from being an outsider. Though thank God for Mary, soft and boneless and tiny, but tough as the best steel. (Could she have managed alone? She'd often wondered.) One of the 'mistakes', she supposed, was in not demanding sexual equality. But the child has no idea how vulnerable we were. Morally we had to be impeccable and only odd around the edges. In one of their 'serious talks'—they'd had a great many in their little room at the residence; no chaperoned cocoa-parties or mountain sleigh-rides or dances for them (and don't think we didn't sometimes wish there were; it's part of being human to want everything)—she and Mary had renounced all thought of marriage, superfluously perhaps, since only the rarest of men, they knew, could take both their persons and their professions. And the two were indivisible, no question about that. (Laugh if you like, Phyllis. Call us pathetic, childish. It was so.)

Her graduation picture, when it turned up among her mother's things, had showed a round face, which she remembered as being rosy, good eyes and a cheerful mouth. Perhaps men's eyes had followed her and she hadn't known. Charles had said they must have, that she was one of the sexiest bits of goods he'd ever seen. Charles. Moving slowly, washing her old body, she could see him, though his face slid away in a dark smudge, leaving only his hands, rather small, always slightly cupped. She was 42, a useful and fairly happy woman but dry, she knew, a little too gruff and hearty. (They all read Huxley and Lawrence, knew the signs.) Two days, she thought—meeting at a medical convention, first kiss, first fondling, bedding down. Now, she'd told herself—belatedly, the harm done, looking with some amazement at her undergarments strewn about the hotel-room floor—she could risk this sort of thing. Discretion proved easy, privacy so much a matter of finances; she'd simply bought the building and moved her mother, who'd just come to live with her, into the upper flat. No-one had guessed the connection that had continued so happily for twenty years.

Tamped down so long, she should have been impossible to rouse. But she'd known the ecstasies of any twenty-year-old. (How Charles would laugh at my trying to be poetic. It was wild and vigorous, heady as good wine.) The storms too, passions of jealous weeping when he stayed away too long, humiliation at what seemed to her servitude, less to Charles than to claims unleashed in her own body. This only for the first years till she realized that he was as bound to her as she to him. So that now she chiefly remembered their laughter. And when he died, suddenly of a stroke two days after they'd been together, it hadn't seemed to matter that her grief couldn't be public, that though there was a black-clad widow at the funeral, it wasn't she. (She'd had no wish to be present while Charles's body, washed by those lovely unmeaning words, was committed to the ground. Bad enough to have to see it done to parents, brothers, sister, friends. I am not resigned, she thought. I have never grown used to it. Death is the final obscenity, sooner or later taking almost every one of those I fought to keep. The first time a child she had delivered died under her care—only three years separating the birth-bellow, tiny gasp—she and Mary had got drunk in the kitchen. Or at least Georgiana had got drunk for she had dim recollections of Mary helping her to bed. So only Mary had heard words she'd never repeated to anyone else, only Mary knew the despair that underlay her life. The battle is lost in advance yet I fight. I fight because it's lost.)

She'd have shrieked and moaned at Charles's funeral; just as well she could grieve in her own way and in private. Her love hadn't been public either and perhaps the better and stronger for that.

This she'd tried to tell Nora, that it wasn't loss necessarily to be barred from dailiness; it could be gain. If you had enough in yourself, enough to bring and to go back to. And Nora hadn't. Perhaps everyone had a right to one mistake, Nora had certainly been hers. She'd felt so alone with Charles gone and Nora the only child of Raymond, her favourite brother, whom she'd watched for eighteen years as he coughed up lungs that had drunk mustard gas at Ypres. A rangy girl, not pretty but with something open and quirky about her, 27 years old and still fighting to escape from her twittery Limey mother. Georgiana had helped set her up in a studio and, when Jérôme came along, encouraged that. Nora had been almost too apt a pupil; it was her nature to say yes. Georgiana hadn't realized she was saying yes, not to painting as a career (though she had talent), not to Jérôme as a lover (though she'd loved him) but to the admired (blind) aunt who talked to her and listened and made that absurd mistake of thinking she saw her ideas going forward in another. (She was the vanguard; Nora, the inheritor, would go farther, more freely.) And then tearfully, messily (at 35) the girl tossed everything away for a 'normal', very wealthy marriage with a man a little younger than herself, apologizing to Georgiana as if the last years had been a college course and she had failed. It had been the apology Georgiana had found hardest to forgive . . . 'It's your life,' she'd said. 'You must live it. If you want to marry whoever-it-is, go ahead and marry him.' And now there was Phyllis, cosseted child of Nora's middle years, who'd 'gone a bit overboard' about women's lib (as well she might, given the example of her parents, Nora having assumed all her husband's opinions as swiftly as she'd once assumed Georgiana's) and wanted to see her mother's ancient aunt. When was the last time, Georgiana wondered, when anyone wanted to see me in that sense. People share with me now, give generously, kindly. No-one takes.

Well, well, she thought, out of her bath and dressed. She'd trained herself to think along the edge of her mind so she wouldn't have to look too clearly at her body as she prepared it for the day. She'd been stocky, breasts and buttocks like rocks. (Built like a duck, they'd said at home.) Her breasts had emptied, everything else—hips, abdomen, thighs—slipped down till she became pear-shaped, then emptied in their turn. (*This caricature,* she thought. It isn't me but I'm *in* it.) Well, better think of something more cheerful such as what poor little Phyllis wanted. If the child was actually curious about the past—could she be? None of the young were—Georgiana would simply tell her about it. Trying not to sound like a character. She'd slipped rather on the phone. It was so easy; people trapped you with shrieks of 'how marvellous', as if it were a miracle anyone so old could speak, let alone arrange words in sentences that ran coherently. So you performed. It was diverting at the time but shaming later. I didn't live so long just to become a stereotype peppery old lady. I'm very complex. I'm Georgiana.

At nine she was in the kitchen, eating the bowl of hot Roman Meal that had fueled each of her days for 50 years. The man to do the windows was due at 9.30; she'd told the agency she wouldn't let him in if he arrived one minute before. She'd lit her first cigarette and poured coffee when Paul Thomas, her upstairs tenant, knocked and came in to leave his key. On family orders she'd consented to leave the door into the shared back vestibule unlocked; the day she broke her hip, Paul and her nephew Steve had had to smash it down. She'd been semi-delirious by then; the sounds and their faces above her had fitted into some black dream of rending and threatened attack. 'Go away,' she'd screamed. 'I'm not ready for you yet.' Since then, her tenants, a working couple in their thirties, wandered in rather often, always with an excuse, to bring something, ask something. Of the two she preferred Paul. He had more life and, with her, sometimes dropped the over-heartiness she knew was a defence. Not today. He looked tired and agitated.

'Great morning, Dr Din.'

Georgiana agreed that it was, agreed that it would be fine to have the double windows off .She could leave his key on the table, he said, and if he got home before his wife, he'd pop in and get it.

'Is Cynthia quite up to par?' she asked. 'I've wondered.'

'Oh—well—she took a long time getting round after that London flu.' Georgiana nodded. She'd had it too, had fought (successfully) against going to the hospital, had got even with Steve's insistence on a practical nurse by sharing the woman with Cynthia. 'Needs some sun and rest,' Paul said. 'You know Cynthia. She won't ever give in, won't leave the floor without wax or a dish in the sink.'

Georgiana was about to suggest he tell the girl to drop in—just the worried look (so known) on Paul's face. He seemed honestly to love that pinched, terribly house-proud little woman. 'I forgot,' she said, delighted. 'Forgot I wasn't still a practising physician.' She was going to add that she'd never felt more alive but to Paul, looking down at her froglike form and the face, firm and rosy once, now putty-coloured, creased and re-creased as if someone had gone at it too vigorously with a sewing-machine—no, that wouldn't do. No need to make a fool of yourself. So she merely laughed. 'Been laughing like a maniac all morning. Losing my marbles no doubt.'

'Dr Din, you're not losing a thing, ' Paul said. 'Not only that. You're a living doll. If I were 60 years older, you'd be afraid to leave your door unlocked.'

'God spare me from a 95-year-old lover,' she said and they parted laughing. (He remembered this later with pleasure and pain, for he'd been fond of the old girl. 'She was so gay this morning,' he kept saying to Phyllis when he came in at five and found her coping so well for such a youngster.)

Georgiana had lit her second cigarette when the phone rang; she reached for it (phones in every room were another concession to the family)—Stella Farnham, not yet 80 but of all the people she knew now the closest in age. (One by one they toppled off the edge and left her the oldest.) Damn, she thought, outraged, barely hearing Stella as she twittered something about thinking of the old days (as if that fluttery idiot had been present in the real old days), sick suddenly, as happened every now and then, from the force of all those steady, single deaths. Her friends. Her kind. The other early graduates in medicine, the pioneers with her in the women's suffrage movement (before they turned it over to the French where it belonged). How good and tolerant they'd been with each other, even those earnest souls who'd muddled prohibition of liquor with women's rights. Well, they'd all been odd in one way or another, but freed and strengthened by that. And every one of them had aged better than poor Stella, keeping enough of themselves to serve as reminders of how they'd once moved and looked. (She'd tell Phyllis this, so someone would know, what friends they'd been, how none of them had become senile; worked hard and widely, their minds had simply given out when the time came. Mary, dying of cancer at 55, had been perfectly intact. Die, Mary, she'd thought, looking down at that bit of bone and waste. Stop fighting, Mary. But Mary couldn't and Georgiana had continued to help for as long as she must. And I still don't know why, why it has to be or what it means. This I was supposed to discover in my last years. This is one of the questions I put off asking.) Thank God, she needn't participate in another death—except one, but then the choice (at what point to withdraw and let the body die) would be Steve's. Thank God, she repeated, listening to Stella's voice, as she was forced to now that it was rising, lamenting that her son had done this and her daughter the other, or rather not done this and the other, for they were neglectful, wouldn't—

'Then tell them so,' said Georgiana, who'd delivered both these children; the boy had been magnificent, lungs like bellows. 'Aren't you a grown woman and their mother?'

'George, if I were only like you,' Stella wailed.

'Well, why aren't you for mercy's sake? Stella, I braced you during your pregnancies. I prevailed on you to nurse when you didn't want to. I tried to put starch into you. I'm an old woman now. I'm retired. You're on your own.'

The doorbell rang. Georgiana excused herself, saying she'd call back. (A lie. She didn't intend to.) She reached for her cane, put her other hand palm-down on the table and pulled herself to her feet, then started the slow journey down the hall of this very stretched-out flat. (The hall she used to take at a run when the ring meant Charles; she could almost feel that other woman rising out of her bones and rushing forward. They're dead, she thought. Everyone who meant anything. There's no-one who remembers what I remember. Damn. I didn't ask to be the survivor. It should have been someone stronger. Mary.)

'You were supposed to come to the back door,' she told the young man from the agency. He muttered something, looking down. 'Français?' He shook his head. 'Too bad. I used to speak it pretty well, with a lousy accent. Like the Spanish cow, as the French say.' He didn't answer. One of those battened-down young people clearly. Just what I need. About 25, she judged, and with the green waxy look of malnutrition. Like so many of the young. Phyllis too. You'd swear Nora had never heard of vitamins. 'Well, don't just stand there,' she said, shooing him towards the kitchen.

'The strange thing about being old,' she told his back as she stumped after him, 'is that though your flesh goes, you don't get lighter. You get heavier. A paradox.'

He was silent, just walked straight through to the kitchen and stood with his back against the farther door.

'See here,' she said. 'I won't have anyone in my house if I can't be human with him. You want your money, I suppose?'

'Yes,' he said and did seem finally to look at her, at least move his eyes in her direction. He was pale in every respect, especially so about the mouth. Even his eyes and wispy hair were pale.

'Very well then,' she said, 'in future speak when you're spoken to,' and told him in what part of the cellar he'd find the screens and the hose, how to line the screens against the fence while he washed them. 'Sort them by rooms. My old valued handyman and friend pencilled it on in French. You can read French?' He said he could.

He was slow, she saw as she watched from the window, smoking another cigarette with some warmed-up coffee, trying to salvage this day that had started so well. Till the dead began to walk. (Be still, be still, she told them. I did what I could.) Look around you, Georgiana. Don't be a damned crybaby. The sky was that high, very dark blue of spring. Soon there'd be crocuses—Paul had moved the patch so she could see them from her window. Later they'd discuss colours and he'd fill the tiny yard with petunias. (Something's eating Paul. I must manage to learn what, must still serve. But I'm fussy and old; I snapped at foolish Stella. But Paul has life. Now watch it, Georgiana. Was it ever your right to decide who was worth your effort and who wasn't?) The young man was spraying the screens, making great pools of slop and walking through them. Naming his actions to himself as she had done during those humiliating months of learning to walk again. Once headed in a particular direction, he continued in that way, no matter how muddy, made no free movements, never improvised. He finished, disconnected the hose and turned back to the house. She heard him scrape each foot on the stoop. Then he came in and stood silent in front of her.

'I'm a retired physician, not a member of the narcotics squad,' she said. 'Are you on drugs?'

He did actually smile then, just a swift tuck of the lips.

'You think that's the first thing we old people think of. Well, not this old person. Call me an interfering old party if you wish but I'm used to taking care of people, sometimes when they'd just as soon I didn't. It's hard to hide things from me. You look what my mother used to call mingy. Never did understand that word. A composite perhaps of miserable and mangy. Have you been ill?'

'No,' he said, 'I haven't,' then, 'Which floor'll I start on?' A shallow breather, the voice using only the upper segment of the lungs.

'Upstairs,' she told him and handed him Paul's key, indicated the pail and cloths, told him where to stack the double windows when he'd scrubbed them. 'Your lunch will be ready on the dot of twelve. Here on this table . . . Did you say something?'

'I go out to lunch.'

'Not from this house you don't. You're going to eat properly for once. No French fries. No Coca Cola.'

'I'd rather you didn't go to too much trouble.' Curiously educated expression.

'I'll go to exactly as much trouble as it requires,' she said, wanting to see that little smile again and thinking that, just briefly, she did so. 'Ha—now I know why the lower part of your face is so white. You used to have a beard.'

'What if I did?' He should have looked at her then but did not.

'Why are you so defensive? I suppose the agency made you shave it. Well, they're damned idiots. I'm accustomed to facial hair. My own father and grandfather had beards—finer and bushier beards than you could grow.'

Her mood lifted. She felt suddenly gay as a girl as she listened to his steps on the stairs and over her head, the pauses. In some ways old age was an adolescence, though a less painful one—hers had been hideous; no other part of her life had touched it for sheer darkness. The feeling of looseness, of belonging nowhere, not even with her own body. (That she might tell Phyllis too; from now on everything has to be better.) The gaieties of old age were like the rare gaieties of adolescence, same sense of spinning off towards some wonderful country that was waiting to receive you if you could only find the way. But now you knew there was no such country and no way, and treasured and drank the joy. There was a dark side too. Like the pubescent you were very conscious of your effect on others. Had to be, knowing they watched you for weakness, ready to take over. Still, life is wonderful, she told Phyllis, told the young man upstairs. If I could just prove it to you. (The dead would say so too. Every one of them. I assure you. There was a young man once who died of what we used to call blood poisoning. With his last bit of strength, he sat bolt upright, staring ahead. His mother thought he'd seen one of God's angels, perhaps the old man himself. But he was looking at me and in the instant before the light went out, there was rage in those eyes—rage and appeal. Having seen that even once, you *know*. It is precious just to be, in a body that will function, and to have senses—even though barely, and with tremendous struggle, as I have them. Don't ask why. It is.)

She'd have to start to fix the young man's lunch—he'd so quickly (though oddly) become an individual that she'd forgotten to ask his name—at half past eleven, was almost late because Nora called again.

'Aunt George, I felt I should warn you. I hope you won't mind. Phyllis has become awfully curious about your sex life.'

'Don't be a solemn ninny, Nora. I'm flattered. It's such ages since anyone's thought I might have had one.'

'She wonders if you were all lesbians. As a defence against chauvinist pigs.' She sighed. 'She's threatening to take that way herself. As a means of consciousness-raising or whatever they call it.'

'Is she indeed? Seems a strange thing to discuss with one's mother. And don't say that you and she discuss everything. I don't believe it. . . . As a matter of fact, several of my friends were —some by nature, others from fear. I think it was the latter with Mary.'

'Aunt Mary Balsam? But she was so—womanly.'

'Your father certainly thought so. I've always believed they'd have married, even though she was a good seven years older, if poor silly Raymond could have brought himself to let her continue in practice. But the War came and, as you know, he met your mother in England.' She became aware of her gabbling voice and Nora's silence. 'You didn't know this?'

'No. No, I never even—So that's why she was always so good to me. . . . Aunt George, are you sure?'

'Oh yes. She told me herself.' She'd gone in to get Mary to fit her for a diaphragm and Mary had made that wry joke about not needing that sort of thing herself. And I was shocked, though I should have seen it in the wind when Mother came to live with me after Father died and Mary moved in with Irene Sanders. But was she happy? How after all these years could it be of any importance or even interest to know whether Mary was happy? She said she was, though all I could think was that it must be sad to turn and find only a similar body, another self. And did I say the right things, so full of myself that day, myself and Charles? A scene in a doctor's examining room, two women talking—neither the room nor the furnishings nor the women (one now only a clumsy bag of bones, the other dust I may have washed from my hand or face) to be found anywhere now—yet I feel I could reach back, change the words. 'What did you say, Nora?'

'That I'd rather you didn't tell Phyllis, Aunt George.'

'Or about Charles? Or,' she couldn't help adding, 'Jérôme?' Silence. That had made the Westmount matron jump. 'He still sends me cards at Christmas. Did you know? Always with a funny note. I do like a man with humour.' Whoever-it-is had none.

'No, you never mentioned—it's not that I'm ashamed—but her own mother—'

'Really, Nora. I'm surprised at your thinking I'd give you away. But as for my life and my friends' lives, if the child asks, I'll tell her. No-one knows, you see. I thought of writing a book, even made a great many notes. But I couldn't. It seemed so—with none of them here to—'

'Yes—I see.' Abruptly, in a softened voice, she asked whether the man had come about the windows and was he doing a satisfactory—?

'Yes, he's a pretty good worker,' Georgiana said. 'And a bit of a challenge besides . . . Oh why should I have to explain?' for Nora was trying to get her to do just that. 'Really you're the world's most exasperating—a different sort of life . . . society. Have you any idea how unusual that is at my—'

'Aunt George, come and have dinner with us next week.' ('Thank God,' she kept saying later to Phyllis and Paul, 'it was the last thing I said to her. She'd been baiting me, as she could, cruel almost, and then, I don't know, being *old*. Thank God I didn't lose my temper.' They had a hard time silencing her. She kept thrusting Phyllis away, almost with hatred, and talking about people they didn't know.) 'I'll call,' she said now, 'and make it more—I'm going to be miserably lonely without Phyllis, Aunt George.'

Damn, Georgiana thought, rubbing angry tears from her eyes, trying to remember what it was she—Oh yes, casserole, put it in the oven. She'd slipped. With Nora of all people. Awkward having to sift each word. Out of character. Why shouldn't she be allowed to say that it was interesting, fun even, to have someone new about the house? Or mourn her friends? Without being found pitiable. Think of something else. So Phyllis was interested in her sexual habits. Well, well. Where had she put those notes? Several bulky folders. The child might like to see them. Georgiana, you old fool, don't go thinking you've found your inheritor so late in the day. Though wouldn't it be a wonderful revenge on whoever-it-is if Phyllis should turn out to be the woman Nora had only played at being? My heir straight from darling Raymond. The baby she'd held in her arms in the big farm kitchen, only hours after his birth. God, she was slow. Slower than a month ago? Washing and tearing greens for salad took so long, even putting bread and knife on the board and groping in the fridge for butter. She set a place and was about to fetch the tea-cart, which she'd ask the lad to wheel into the living-room, when impulsively she put a second set of cutlery on the table for herself.

At five past twelve he came downstairs—a spot of independence in this that she approved of—walked into the kitchen and stood with his back to her, washing his hands at the sink.

'Clean towel to your right,' she told him. 'I forgot to mention another rule of this house. I eat with the help.'

He stiffened. She saw it in his back under the thin t-shirt. This was wrong. An intrusion. Unfortunately phrased too. But she'd have to go through with it now, could scarcely let him put her out of her own kitchen.

'I must ask you to humour me,' she said. 'I enjoy company.'

'You're the boss.' He dried his hands and came to sit in the chair she indicated, sat rather far back from the table, arms hanging at his sides. That nothing face, merely young, but with three tension-cracks across the forehead. Georgiana served him, hands slow but steady, planning what she would say.

'You a native Montrealer?' she asked finally.

'Yes.' She waited, looking at him. 'Yes, I am.'

'I was born on a farm near Compton. In the Townships, as you may have noticed from my speech—if you're familiar with that twangy drawl we have. It was wholly English in those days. And now it's all—or almost all—French. Our farm and most of the neighbouring farms.'

'Anything wrong with that?'

'Wrong? Of course not. Mercy, you *are* defensive.' This was the way with the untalkative. Chatter on with seeming lack of aim while they listened or not, to give yourself space to make certain observations. 'But it was a rather special society. Loyalists. In our case from Massachusetts. My grandfather's grandfather, who was what the French would call our first ancestor, had been a whaling captain sailing out of New Bedford. So, even landlocked, we were always within sight of the sea.' She belched loudly. 'Damn,' she said and continued. 'I wasn't impressed when I was young, all that leaning on the past. It was so hard to escape from, young ladies from such families just didn't become doctors. And now it's gone, something unique. Everything is unique though, wouldn't you agree? And every ending sad. I haven't been back since my father died. The younger of my brothers was to be the farmer but he was a casualty of the War, barely alive for eighteen years. So we sold the place. I've seen people change but I haven't wanted to see the house and the land changed, above all not the land. Is that strange, do you think?'

He didn't reply though she was sure he'd been listening, even that at one point—when?—she'd touched him. Her antenna still served. She felt exhilarated.

'Damned casserole needs salt,' she said. 'Here. It's sea-salt. I remember how mad I felt when I learned that even though I was the eldest I couldn't inherit the farm. I told my brother, the older of the two, a male chauvinist aged six, that I'd be a vet then, look after other people's stock. He said girls couldn't do that either so I said—I was eight years old and chewing a stalk of timothy, funny to remember that—"Very well, I'll be a people's doctor." And so it all began. And you cannot imagine the furor—' But this the young man didn't like to hear, that there was anything their imagination couldn't compass. 'I am garrulous,' she said.

He mumbled.

'What was that?'

He spoke for the first time clearly. 'I said I wouldn't know. Not knowing you and how much you usually run on.'

She laughed. 'As a matter of fact, I don't, as a rule. But you've hardly eaten.' He took up a forkful and she waited for him to swallow, take up a second. 'Why are you doing this kind of work? Don't say it's for the money—or bread as you undoubtedly call it. Surprised I know the term?'

She saw him trying to think of an answer, some sarcasm. He was in a mean mood but didn't know how to let it out. He shrugged finally as if the problem defeated him.

'You speak well,' she said, 'when you speak. Have good table manners. Are you educated?'

'Depends.'

'On what I mean by educated? Good answer.' She shot in a key question. 'Are you married?'

'No.' A lie, she suspected, the word spoken so much too swiftly, less tonelessly.

Ah, she thought, I can still do it, and asked him to fill the kettle for their tea.

'Unless you'd prefer coffee?'

'Tea's fine,' he said and she told him where to find the canister, how much to measure into the pot.

'Can't help giving directions,' she said. 'Been doing it all my life.'

'Guess I'm in no position to complain.'

'I'd find you insolent,' Georgiana said, 'if I didn't know you were unhappy. And now you'll think that's none of my business.' No answer, though she thought again, that his back tightened. 'Well, you may be right. Or so I'd have thought once, since you haven't come to me for help. But I haven't time any more for fine distinctions and niceties. And maybe you haven't either.'

He took the cups and saucers from the counter and put them with the tea-pot beside her. He was sweating, she saw, just a few drops along his upper lip. 'Got any honey?'

'Any—? Oh, honey. For our tea. Excellent idea. Should be a jar towards the back of that second shelf. Good strong buckwheat honey with a bite to it, kind I grew up on.'

He brought it to the table and she spooned some into their cups.

'Like it?'

'It's okay.'

She provided another space by telling him of the wide fields of buckwheat, deep coral and scented—vigorous and coarse and beautiful as the strong things always are; perhaps she'd never had a taste for delicacy (Charles had not been a delicate lover) —and found that the memory and the link with Charles gave her immense pleasure. She longed to see buckwheat in flower again. In fact, must see it. She'd ask someone—Nora—no, one of the others, so the excursion wouldn't involve the presence of whoever-it-is.

'You have a strange effect on me,' she told the young man. 'Or I'm having it on myself. I keep going back. Like thinking about chewing timothy a moment ago. Be telling you next what I was wearing.' And wondered whether she should just continue to go where her mind took her. He so clearly didn't want to open out to some ancient stranger. (Remember what he sees when he looks at you. Something held together with sticks.) No-one had said she need do anything about him. Why not just go on rambling, silly old bag of bones, till the meal was over?

'Got a great-niece coming in later,' she said. 'Wants to quiz me about sex. How's that for irony, eh? What should I tell her?' He said nothing, gulped his tea, no doubt relieved that her attention had wandered. 'Come, you must have some suggestions. Take this. Her mother's afraid she'll become a lesbian to—what was the phrase?—raise her consciousness. How could two young women bouncing awkwardly about in bed raise one another's consciousness? What does that mean even?' It was no use. She saw him trying to deal with this, face working, but, poor young devil, he was too barricaded within himself to come out and consider other people. (I owe him more than this. Owe it to him and to my life. This *will* be a good day. I'll make it so. I'll be useful. I'm not pitiable, damn you, Nora. I'm Georgiana. A very good doctor.) 'Look here, let's be done with this,' she said in the gruff offhand voice she'd always used for such matters. 'You've come to the end of something, haven't you? That's where I reached you before. Endings. And it's chewing at your gut. Admit it. It's not shameful.'

He breathed sawingly. 'Suppose I have. Suppose it is. Isn't it my gut?'

'Not entirely,' said Georgiana. 'When you walked into my house and my life, I think it became partly my gut. Talk. It will be a release. You don't know me. I'll never confront you with it. And I'm not a psychiatrist, except of a rough and ready sort. There can be only one kind of ending at your age. Which of you broke it off? She? Or you?'

He gave that little tuck of the lip that with him might pass for a smile—or was perhaps only a tic, defensive.

'*She* did, eh?' she hazarded.

'What if she did?' Sweat formed again on his upper lip. 'She had good reason to perhaps.'

'She had good reason to perhaps. What sort of answer is that?'

'It's her life,' he said, 'and if she wants to—'

'Are you telling me you didn't fight? Not at all?' He looked at her, emptily but from somewhere very deep inside. 'Obviously she means a lot to you or you wouldn't be walking around like a zombie without her. It's got into your muscles, every movement you make. Aren't you going to fight even now? It may not be too late. Women like strength. They always have and I don't fancy that just because they want to be more independent means they've changed all that—'

'I don't want to talk about it,' he said. 'I came here to do the windows. I'm the help. You said that. I don't have to—' Trembling, he laid his saucer on the plate, then the cup. They clattered.

'Oh leave those, for God's sake. I'll take care of them. Go on about your windows, you poor foolish—'

She snatched the dishes and started to the sink, so swiftly and impetuously that she forgot to hoist herself, forgot her cane, took an unassisted step or two. 'Don't you know that nothing on God's green earth has been got without fighting? Do you imagine for an instant that I didn't fight? I fought all the way for every inch. I'm an old woman and I still know more about fighting—fighting for breath, fighting for strength—' (My God, here I go being a character again. As if life were ever that simple. This particular fighter feared death as few can have feared it. Fighting when you know you're going to lose, especially when, that's what I must tell them, Phyllis too. But is it enough? Enough to give from a long life?)

She had started to speak again when something exploded in her head. She fell, heavily on all fours, as horses do. Good God, it's a stroke, she thought, so that's how, like a blow—'Thank God, you're here. My hand's cut from the—but don't worry about—just help me turn so I can—'

She had half turned on her own when her eyes looked into his. He was stooping over her with the cane. 'You hit me,' she said. 'Oh you silly, silly. Well, just give me a hand and—'

'Let's see you fight now, old know-it-all. Just like her. Just like all of—' He struck again.

'No,' she said. 'No. You don't want to—you can't possibly—' She had averted her face but now, dangerous as she knew this was, she looked back, trying to catch his eye, hold him. 'Your whole life—think of that—your whole life, you foolish, foolish—' The cane whistled down, found its mark, she couldn't move quickly enough. Blood spurted from her cheek. 'But I'll be responsible.' Did she say or only think these words? 'And I'm not supposed to—not me—not destroy—'

'Why did you keep bugging me? Why did you? I didn't ask for your damn—' He was crying now, sobbing aloud. 'Oh I didn't want to. You're not a bad old—Fuck you, I didn't want to.'

The blows came down and down, rhythmically. Georgiana could no longer speak but even in her mind she did not call on any of the names of her life. She fought as she must, would continue to do till pain wiped out her world. Her nose was broken. She was blind. She had never felt more alive.

CLAIRE MARTIN

Letter to Werther

You say to me, my love, 'Write something about this compulsion women have to do everything in their power to change the men they love.'

And you have the nerve to say this without a qualm. If that isn't like a man! Exactly like a man. You say it with a meaningful little look, for fear I won't understand that you're speaking for my benefit.

I know perfectly well that you have me in mind. What I want to know is just how I'm trying to change you. The answer comes as something of a shock: 'You're trying to wertherize me.'

Forgive me for wanting to laugh. I mean, of the men I've been in love with, you're by far the most wertherizing. Come to think of it, you're the only one. Yes, absolutely. If I were to tell you that I love you because of that—and in spite of it—would you be angry?

Of course you would. And when I tell you all the wertherizing things about yourself, you'll curse me. Go ahead. Today I feel like being in the right. A justifiable urge that you ought to understand. It's definitely my turn, dear antagonist, or rather—how shall I put it?—dear monopolizer.

First of all there's what you refer to, with a rueful smile, as your old-fashioned neurasthenia. Unless I'm very much mistaken, that's a real give-away. There's your despair, your bitterness, what I'd describe in general terms as your denial. And second—but by no means last—there's what you call your unfitness for life. And if you don't mind my adding that this unfitness sometimes amounts to a death-wish, I think it all adds up to a complete give-away. Let me say in passing, and just as a reminder, there's no better way to let a woman know that you don't care to live for her. Incidentally, I'm aware that it's not on my account, but on your own, that you might wish to die. It's not what I want for you. I too would die, I'd die gladly for you, if it would be any help to you. No one is in a better position to understand you than I am. So much for the morbid part.

Fortunately that isn't the whole story. Werther has his good points. Charming, exceptional points. There's the fact that you're so affectionate. And since (knowing yourself and despising yourself, you dread nothing so much as wertherization) you've given me fair warning that you're set against taking advantage of your affections, I believe you're genuinely affectionate. That, my love, is much more old-fashioned than your neurasthenia. One could live a whole lifetime without once meeting a truly affectionate lover. There are, of course, a few individuals who show vestiges, or traces, of the real thing. But the authentic features of the thing itself are less likely to be seen than a bowler hat. And anyway, what we often take for signs of affection are merely camouflage for lust. Which only leads to a terrific urge to quit the scene. Whereas with you . . . But on that score I swear you're worth your weight in gold. I swear it, trusting you won't have the bad taste to try and discover whether this opinion is peculiar to me alone.

There's your femininity. Men nowadays—terrified of seeming effeminate—wear their virility like a badge. And virility, in its pure form, that is, in the he-man, is just plain atrocious—uncouth, brutish. It's barbarism. Men and women are such strangers, they're so dissimilar, that unless they borrow from one another love is impossible. Once in a while they manage to come together, that's what I think. However, I'm talking about love, not biology. Yes, there is, thank God, your femininity. You won't mind if I don't pursue this, lest I appear too virile.

You accuse me of wanting to change you. But you're the guilty one. You're too humble, too complicated. And you don't love me enough. That's all there is to it. You can't believe that I could love you as you are. That's why I say you're too humble. Instead of reasoning logically that I ought to change you for once and for all, which is to say, for someone else who'd be everything I'm looking for, you choose to think that I'd rather indulge myself in the evil delights of trying to remould you into that other person. How horribly complicated.

You don't love me enough. And you have a guilty conscience about it. You're frightened by the intensity of my love. You're petrified that I'll pressure you, rush you, until you end up feeling as I do. That really scares you. My superior sentiments, if I may say so, leave you so nonplussed that you can't even be sure I don't have the power to bring you up to my level. If this were still the age of potions and witchcraft you'd be a nervous wreck. Never fear. What I still care most about in our love is your friendship. When I say that you don't love me enough, I'm not blaming—I'm explaining.

With any luck this paragraph will prove that you're Werther in everything but love. You're a Werther who loves his Charlotte, that's all. Or maybe Charlotte is part of yourself. One can't be different from others in every respect. And each person loves himself best.

To conclude this little discussion, I'll run through briefly, and without malice, the changes you've demanded of me. And you can cut me into little pieces before I'll take back that word 'demanded'. Physical changes, changes in direction, even career changes. You meddle outrageously in my life, and you do it with utter nonchalance. Do I complain? No. Because I know it's part of the price women have to pay for love. To transform themselves entirely, each time, without complaint. Luckily, most attack the physical side. One wants us to wear our hair long and straight, the other wants it short and curly. Or one of two other combinations. This one wants us thin, that one wants us plump. Too much make-up, not enough; jewels, or none. We're expected to tan our fair skin and bleach our dark hair. It's as if the ideal woman—the one you'd be really crazy about—is one who is not us, but someone we might have been if we were only more repressed, more pliable, more capable of being ground down. There are times when we simply don't know which transformations to make next. And people believe that if a woman does nothing to alter her appearance it's because she has no one to love her. Either that, or she's incredibly faithful. Take a woman for what she is? Never. That would make your successors too memorable.

And I want to wertherize you! Come now. I'm far too busy changing myself.

Listen, dear boy, do you want some good advice? Accept yourself for what you are. When you've managed to get that far you'll find that I've been there for ages, that I'm there, waiting for you. And my love for you is so strong that I promise never to try to de-wertherize you.

Translated by Patricia Sillers

ANNE HÉBERT

The House on the Esplanade

Stephanie de Bichette was a curious little creature with frail limbs that seemed badly put together. Only her starched collarette kept her head from falling over on her shoulder; it was too heavy for her long, slender neck. If the head of Stephanie de Bichette looked so heavy, it was because all the pomp of her aristocratic ancestors was symbolized in her coiffure, a high up-swept style, with padded curls arranged in rows on her narrow cranium, an architectural achievement in symmetrical silvery blobs.

Mademoiselle de Bichette had passed, without transition period, without adolescence, from the short frocks of her childhood to this everlasting ash-grey dress, trimmed at neck and wrists with a swirl of lilac braiding. She owned two parasols with carved ivory handles—one lilac and the other ash-grey. When she went out driving in the carriage she chose her parasol according to the weather, and everyone in the little town could tell the weather by the colour of Mademoiselle de Bichette's parasol. The lilac one appeared on days of brilliant sunshine, the ash-grey one whenever it was slightly cloudy. In winter, and when it rained, Stephanie simply never went out at all.

I have spoken at length about her parasols because they were the outward and visible signs of a well-regulated life, a perfect edifice of regularity. Unchanging routine surrounded and supported this innocent old creature. The slightest crack in this extraordinary construction, the least change in this stern programme would have been enough to make Mademoiselle de Bichette seriously ill.

Fortunately, she had never had to change her maid. Geraldine served and cared for her mistress with every evidence of complete respect for tradition. The whole life of Stephanie de Bichette was a tradition, or rather a series of traditions, for apart from the tradition of the well-known parasols and the complicated coiffure, there was the ritual of getting up, of going to bed, of lace-making, of mealtimes, and so on.

Stephanie Hortense Sophie de Bichette lived facing the Esplanade, in a grey stone house dating back to the days of the French occupation. You know the sort of house *that* implies—a tall, narrow edifice with a pointed roof and several rows of high windows, where the ones at the top look no bigger than swallows' nests, a house with two or three large attics that most old maids would have delighted in. But, believe it or not, Mademoiselle de Bichette never climbed up to her attics to sentimentalize over souvenirs, to caress treasured old belongings, or to plan meticulous orgies of housecleaning amid the smell of yellowing paper and musty air that even the best-kept attics seem to possess.

No, she occupied the very heart of the house, scarcely one room on each floor. On the fourth story, only Geraldine's room remained open, among the rooms of all the former servants. It was part of the family tradition to close off rooms that were no longer used. One after another, bedroom after bedroom had been condemned: the room where the little brothers had died of scarlet fever, when Stephanie was only ten years old; the bedroom of their mother, who had passed away soon after her two children; the room of Irénée, the elder brother who had been killed in an accident, out hunting; the room of the elder sister, Desneiges, who had entered the Ursuline convent; then the bedroom of Monsieur de Bichette, the father, who had succumbed to a long illness; to say nothing of the room belonging to Charles, the only surviving brother, which had been closed ever since his marriage.

The ritual was always the same: once the occupant of the room had departed for the cemetery, the convent, or the adventure of matrimony, Geraldine would tidy everything away, carefully leaving each piece of furniture exactly in place; then she would draw the shutters, put dust-covers on the arm-chairs, and lock the door for good. No one ever set foot in that room again. One more member of the family was finally disposed of.

Geraldine took a distinct pleasure in this solemn, unvarying rite, just as a gravedigger may take pride in a neat row of graves, with well-kept mounds and smoothly raked grass above them. Sometimes she remembered that one day she would have to close Mademoiselle Stephanie's room, too, and live on for a while, the only living creature among all the dead. She looked forward to that moment, not with horror, but with pleasant anticipation, as a rest and a reward. After so many years of housework in that great house, all its rooms would be fixed at last in order, for all eternity. Mildew and dust could take possession then; Geraldine would have no more cleaning to do then. The rooms of the dead are not 'done up'.

This was not the calculation of a lazy woman. Geraldine dreamed of the last door closed and the last key turned in the lock just as the harvester dreams of the last sheaf of corn, or the needlewoman of the last stitch in her embroidery. It would be the crowning achievement of her long life, the goal of her destiny.

It was strange that the old servant reckoned two living people among the dead: Mademoiselle Desneiges, the nun, and Monsieur Charles, a married man and the father of a family. They had both left the family roof, that was enough for Geraldine to class them as non-existent. The heavy door of the cloister had closed forever on one, while Charles, by marrying a common little seamstress from the Lower Town, had so grieved his father that the old house and all it contained had been left to Stephanie. Charles came to see his sister every evening, but Geraldine never spoke a word to him. For her, Stephanie was the whole of the de Bichette family.

On the third floor, all the bedrooms were closed, with the exception of Mademoiselle de Bichette's. On the second, only the small blue boudoir lived on, a life of dimness and disuse. On the first floor, an immense drawing-room stretched from front to back, cluttered with furniture of different periods, each piece bristling with fussy, elaborate knick-knacks. The ground-floor doors were always open, with high, carved portals to the vestibule, the parlour, the dining-room. In the basement was the old-fashioned kitchen, uncomfortable and always damp. Geraldine was the cook as well as the maid-of-all-work, but was never addressed as such.

If her mistress lived by tradition until it became a religion, Geraldine, too had her tradition, the collecting of bright-coloured buttons. Her black skirt and her white apron never changed, but she used her imagination in trimming her blouses. Red buttons sparkled on blue blouses, yellow ones on green, and so on, not to mention buttons in gold and silver and crystal. In the attic, she had discovered great chests of ancient garments which she stripped, shamelessly, of their trimmings. Apart from this innocent craze for buttons, the big woman with the ruddy complexion made no objection to touring the wine cellar every evening before going to bed, as the last of her duties, conscientiously and even devotedly performed. But where she excelled, was in the observance of tradition where her mistress was concerned.

Every morning, at seven o'clock in summer and eight in winter, she climbed the three flights of stairs and knocked at the bedroom door. . . . Two taps, two firm, decided taps, no more, no less. This was the signal for the ceremonial to begin.

Geraldine opened the bed curtains, then the window curtains, and finally the shutters. Her ageing mistress preferred to sleep in complete darkness, requiring several thicknesses of material and polished wood between herself and the wicked witchcraft of the night. She was afraid of the first rays of sunlight as well, not knowing what to do about them, since they might easily wake you long before the proper time for getting up.

Then Geraldine would return to the passage to fetch a kind of wagon equipped with everything Stephanie might need for the first few hours of the day. Two white pills in a glass of water, coffee and toast, toothbrush and toothpowder, a copper bathtub, white towels, white, starched underwear. Also a feather duster, a broom, a dust-pan . . . all that she used for tidying up the room. This wagon was as wide as a single bed, four feet wide, with three shelves. Geraldine had made it herself out of old packing cases.

When Stephanie's breakfast was finished, the maid would bathe, dress, and powder her mistress, then do her hair. Stephanie allowed her to do everything, silent, inert, trusting. After that, there was sometimes a moment of painful indecision, an anguished knot in the brain of Mademoiselle de Bichette, when Geraldine leaned over to look out of the window, examining the sky and frowning as she declared:

'I really don't know what sort of weather we're going to have today.'

Then the old lady would stare at her maid with such forlorn eyes that Geraldine would say, hurriedly:

'It's going to rain. You're not going to be able to go out this morning. I'll let the coachman know.'

Stephanie would grow calm again after that, but she would not be entirely herself until Geraldine had settled her carefully in the blue drawing-room, on her high-backed chair of finely carved wood, near the window, her half-finished lace on her knee and her crochet hook in her hand. Only then would the idea take firm root in her brain:

'It's going to rain. I can't go out. . . . All I have to do is to handle this hook and this thread as my mother taught me to do when I was seven years old. . . . If it had been a fine day, it would have been different, I would have gone out in the carriage. There are only two realities in the world . . . only two realities I can rely on . . . and close my eyes, deep inside them: the reality of going out in the carriage, the reality of making my lace. . . . How lost and strange I am when Geraldine cannot tell what the weather is going to do, and I am left in suspense with no solid ground beneath my feet. . . . It just *wracks* my brain! Oh! Not to have to think about it, to let myself be carried away by one or the other of these my only two sure and certain realities going out for a drive or sitting here, making my lace. . . .'

Even if the day turned out fine in the end, Geraldine never said so. It would have been too much of a shock for her mistress. Imagine what confusion in such a patterned existence if someone had suddenly announced a change, after she had firmly established herself for the day in the reality of lace-making, and dared to tell her she had taken the wrong road? She could never again have believed in any reality at all.

Since her childhood, Mademoiselle de Bichette had been making lace doilies of different sizes, which Geraldine used in many different ways. These doilies flowed from her fingers at the steady rate of four per week, small pieces of white lace that resembled each other like peas in a pod. They were everywhere in the house—five or six on the piano, seven or eight on all the tables, as many as ten on every arm-chair, one or two on all the smaller chairs. Every knick-knack rested on a piece of delicate openwork, so that the furniture all seemed powdered with snowflakes, enlarged as if under a microscope.

In winter, and in summer, on the days when Geraldine had decided the weather was not fit for going out, Mademoiselle de Bichette would crochet all the morning, in her blue boudoir, sitting up so straight and still that she scarcely seemed real, her feet resting on a stool covered by something that was strangely like the work the old lady held in her hands.

At five minutes to twelve, Geraldine would announce:

'Mademoiselle Stephanie's luncheon is served.'

At the mention of her name, the old lady would rise at once; the ritual phrase had touched a switch somewhere within her, so that without effort, without thinking, without even understanding, she would put herself slowly and ceremoniously in motion, descend the staircase and take her place at the table.

If Stephanie did go out, she invariably returned home at a quarter to twelve, so she had ample time to receive the announcement that luncheon was served with the necessary calm.

The outings of Mademoiselle de Bichette were governed by just as incredible a routine. She came out on the sidewalk with tiny steps, her frail little body bending under the weight of that enormous pile of scaffolded curls. Geraldine helped her mistress into the carriage, the coachman whipped up his horse, and the victoria started on its slow, quiet drive, invariably the same, through the streets of the little town. The horse knew the road by heart, so the coachman seized the opportunity for a short nap, his cap pulled down over his eyes, his legs stretched out, his hands folded on his stomach. He always waked up in time, as if by magic, when the drive came to an end, crying out and stretching himself, with a jolly air of surprise:

'Well, well, Mamzelle, here we are back again!'

Just as if the old fellow, when he went to sleep as the drive started, had not been quite sure he would come back when he awoke, or if his return would be to the country of the living!

Mademoiselle de Bichette would disappear into the house, on Geraldine's arm; the coachman would unharness the horse and put the carriage away; and it was all over. With regret, the townsfolk watched the disintegration of this strange conveyance, like a ghostly apparition cutting through the clear morning light . . . the ancient nag, pulling an antique carriage, with a sleeping coachman and a tiny figure like a mummy, swathed in ash-grey and lilac.

After luncheon, Geraldine would lead her mistress into the long drawing-room on the first floor, where, without ever laying her crochet aside, Stephanie would receive a few callers, and the maid would serve dandelion wine and madeleines.

The old lady never left her chair, forcing herself to hold her head high, though her neck felt as if it were breaking under the weight of her monumental coiffure. Sometimes, this constant, painful effort was betrayed by a twitch of the lips, the only change of expression that callers could ever distinguish upon that small, powdered face. Then Stephanie would ask: 'How is Madame your mother?' in a voice so white and colourless that it might have come from one of the closed rooms, where, according to the gossips of the town, some of the original inhabitants still lived on.

This phrase of Stephanie's had to do for greeting, for farewell, for conversation; indeed, it had to do for everything, for the wine was sour and the madeleines stale and hard as stones. The callers were all so aged and unsteady that the most utter stranger would have had the tact never to ask that preposterous question, but Mademoiselle de Bichette knew no other formula, and in any case, she attached no importance whatever to the words she was saying. If she finished a lace doily while her callers were present, she simply let it fall at her feet, like a pebble into a pool, and began another identical piece of lace. The visiting ladies never stayed very long, and Stephanie seemed to notice their departure as little as she did their presence.

At a quarter past six, Geraldine would announce that Monsieur Charles was waiting below. The programme of the day was ticking on like the machanism of a good Swiss watch, and the invisible wheels of Mademoiselle de Bichette responded perfectly, warning the limbs of this strange little creature that they must immediately convey her to the ground floor.

Her brother would kiss her brow and smile, rubbing his stubby-fingered hands together and remarking:

'Um-phm! It feels good in the house.'

Then he would hang his overcoat up on a hall stand, while Geraldine followed his every movement with her look of triumphant disdain. With her arms crossed upon her swelling chest, she doubtless thought she looked like the statue of the Commendatore, bound on revenge. She would cast a glance of scorn on the threadbare coat, as if to say:

'Well, what did you expect? Monsieur Charles *would* get married to a chit of a girl from the Lower Town, so naturally, his father cut him off, and I locked up his room as if he were dead. If Mademoiselle Stephanie wants him here every evening, it's her own business, but *I'm* going to let him know that I'm *glad* he was thrown out, if I *am* only the servant. I know he's poor, and that's his punishment for disobeying his father. He comes here because there isn't enough to eat at home. So he gobbles up our dinners and carries away on his nasty skin a bit of the warmth from our fires. . . . The good-for-nothing!'

If it were true that Charles had only one decent meal a day, it was astonishing that he was not at all thin. He was even fat, very fat, flabby and yellow-complexioned, with a bald head and a shiny face, colourless lips and almost colourless eyes. Geraldine said he had eyes like a codfish and his clothes always smelt of stale grease. Apart from that, she could not forgive a de Bichette for forgetting his table manners.

'To think that his slut of a wife has made him lose all he ever learned in decent society. . . . You wouldn't believe it possible,' she would grumble to herself.

As dinner-time drew near, Charles became more and more noisily jolly. He never stopped rubbing his hands together; he got up, sat down, got up again, went from window to door and back a dozen times, while Stephanie's eyes ignored him. Then the brother and sister took their places, one at each end of the long table in the dining-room. There was no gas chandelier in this room, so it seemed even longer and darker, lit only by two tall candles in silver candlesticks. The corners of the room disappeared into the dimness, and the shadows of the brother and sister danced like black flames on the curiously carved oak panelling of the walls.

Every evening, the atmosphere of this dining-room seemed more impressive to Charles. Perhaps he felt unseen forms hiding in the darkness, invisible spectators of this singular repast; perhaps he feared to find the ghosts that haunted the bedrooms above, to see them take their places at the huge dining-table, where an old creature presided, small as a cat, white as the table-linen, who seemed already to be living in the uneasy world of phantoms.

As soon as Stephanie's brother had swallowed a few mouthfuls of soup, his good humour fell away, lifeless, utterly destroyed. When he entered the house, the smell of cooking would stimulate him, would intoxicate him with its marvellous promise, but now that the promise was kept, the man became gloomy again. Through his own bitter thoughts, he stared at the lace cloth, the heavy silverware, the fine china, and at this sister of his, who was still alive, in spite of her look of belonging to some other world. What mysterious thread was keeping Stephanie here on earth? To look at her, you would have thought the slightest breath might carry her away, yet there she was, still alive.

Geraldine came and went around the table and her sharp eyes seemed to plumb the very depths of the man's thoughts. The brother sat there, knowing himself watched and understood, telling himself, in his embarrassment, that his sister would have joined her ancestors long ago had it not been for this fiendish servant, who by some diabolical process had contrived to keep the dying thing alive in her father's mansion, simply in order to enjoy as long as possible the spectacle of his own failure. In what dread 'No Man's Land' of the spirit had the old witch made a pact with Monsieur de Bichette—and with Satan himself? Geraldine had inherited all the father's anger against his son, and faithful to that anger as if to a sacred promise, she was constantly reminding Charles of the curse that lay heavy upon him. At that moment he raised his head, resenting the eyes he felt fixed upon his every movement, but Geraldine was no longer there, Charles could hear the tinkle of her keys, in the passage between the staircase and the kitchen. He shuddered, for he knew very well which keys she carried at her waist. No cupboard, no inhabited room possessed a key. It chilled his heart strangely to know that the key of his room was there, along with those of the rooms of the dead. It scared him. Then he took hold of himself again and muttered:

'This damned house! . . . Enough to drive a man crazy to sit here night after night with two cracked old fools of women. . . . The wine must have gone to my head.'

But Stephanie had just got up from the table, and Charles followed her as usual.

The evening began like all the rest. Stephanie took up her lace again, while her brother walked to and fro in the long drawing-room, his hands behind his back.

And so, night after night, in complete silence, without a single word exchanged between brother and sister, the time passed until the old clock chimed ten. Then Charles, having laid up a store of warmth for the night, kissed his sister's brow, slipped on his overcoat, and with his hands in his pockets, made for Ireland Street, walking slowly along, like an idle fellow accustomed to musing as he walked.

The man followed his shadow as it flickered on the walls. The same thoughts were turning and twisting in his brain; he was used to them, as a man gets used to animals he tends every day. He knew them too well to be surprised by them; he had stopped looking at them straight in the face; they passed to and fro behind his pale eyes without ever changing his passive stare.

As he came near his own home, Charles thought of his wife. He was going back to her, in no hurry, but with a certain feeling of security, as if to a piece of property he knew belonged to him.

Suddenly, he noticed that he was nearly there. Two low houses, identical twins in misery and poverty, stood waiting for him, their tumbledown grey 'stoops' jutting out to meet the sidewalk. He rented rooms on the second floor of one of these houses.

He climbed the stairs, lit a candle and went into the bedroom. A hoarse, veiled voice, a well-known voice, that could still charm him in spite of himself, said wearily:

'That you Charles?'

He set the candle on the night table. The woman shaded her eyes with her hand. He sat down on the foot of the bed.

'How's your sister?'

'Just the same.'

This question, this reply, as on every other night, fell heavily into a dull silence. Beneath the words was stirring in the shadows the real meaning, unexpressed:

'Do you think your sister will last much longer?'

''Fraid so. . . . She's still hanging on. . . .'

At that moment, in the house on the Esplanade, Stephanie de Bichette was crossing her tiny cold hands on her breast and abandoning to the great empty gulf of night the small emptiness that was herself, ridiculous as an old fashion plate and dry as a pressed fig.

And Geraldine lay awake, dreaming that death had closed the last door in the old house.

Translated by Morna Scott Stoddart

P.K. PAGE

Unless the Eye Catch Fire...

Unless the eye catch fire
The God will not be seen . . .

—THEODORE ROSZAK,
Where the Wasteland Ends

Wednesday, September 17.

The day began normally enough. The quails, cockaded as antique foot soldiers, arrived while I was having breakfast. The males black-faced, white-necklaced, cinnamon-crowned, with short, sharp, dark plumes. Square bibs, Payne's grey; belly and sides with a pattern of small stitches. Reassuring, the flock of them. They tell me the macadamization of the world is not complete.

A sudden alarm, and as if they had one brain among them, they were gone in a rush—a sideways ascending Niagara—shutting out the light, obscuring the sky and exposing a rectangle of lawn, unexpectedly emerald. How bright the berries on the cotoneaster. Random leaves on the cherry twirled like gold spinners. The garden was high-keyed, vivid, locked in aspic.

Without warning, and as if I were looking down the tube of a kaleidoscope, the merest shake occurred—moiréed the garden—rectified itself. Or, more precisely, as if a range-finder through which I had been sighting, found of itself a more accurate focus. Sharpened, in fact, to an excoriating exactness.

And then the colours changed. Shifted to a higher octave—a *bright spectrum*. Each colour with its own *light*, its own *shape*. The leaves of the trees, the berries, the grasses—as if shedding successive films—disclosed layer after layer of hidden perfections. And upon these rapidly changing surfaces the 'range-finder'—to really play hob with metaphor!—sharpened its small invisible blades.

I don't know how to describe the intensity and speed of focus of this gratuitous zoom lens through which I stared, or the swift and dizzying adjustments within me. I became a 'sleeping top', perfectly centred, perfectly—sighted. The colours vibrated beyond the visible range of the spectrum. Yet I saw them. With some matching eye. Whole galaxies of them, blazing and glowing, flowing in rivulets, gushing in fountains—volatile, mercurial, and making lack-luster and off-key the colours of the rainbow.

I had no time or inclination to wonder, intellectualize. My mind seemed astonishingly clear and quite still. Like a crystal. A burning glass.

And then the range-finder sharpened once again. To alter space.

The lawn, the bushes, the trees—still super-brilliant—were no longer *there*. *There*, in fact, had ceased to exist. They were now, of all places in the world, *here*. Right in the centre of my being. Occupying an immense inner space. Part of me. Mine. Except the whole idea of ownership was beside the point. As true to say I was theirs as they mine. I and they were here; they and I, there. (*There, here* . . . odd . . . but for an irrelevant, inconsequential 't' which comes and goes, the words are the same.)

As suddenly as the world had altered, it returned to normal. I looked at my watch. A ridiculous mechanical habit. As I had no idea when the experience began it was impossible to know how long it had lasted. What had seemed eternity couldn't have been more than a minute or so. My coffee was still steaming in its mug.

The garden, through the window, was as it had always been. Yet not as it had always been. Less. Like listening to mono after hearing stereo. But with a far greater loss of dimension. A grievous loss.

I rubbed my eyes. Wondered, not without alarm, if this was the onset of some disease of the retina—glaucoma or some cellular change in the eye itself—superlatively packaged, fatally sweet as the marzipan cherry I ate as a child and *knew* was poison.

If it *is* a disease, the symptoms will recur. It will happen again.

Tuesday, September 23.

It *has* happened again.

Tonight, taking Dexter for his late walk, I looked up at the crocheted tangle of boughs against the sky. Dark silhouetes against the lesser dark, but beating now with an extraordinary black brilliance. The golden glints in obsidian or the lurking embers in black opals are the nearest I can come to describing them. But it's a false description, emphasizing as it does, the wrong end of the scale. This was a *dark spectrum*. As if the starry heavens were translated into densities of black—black Mars, black Saturn, black Jupiter; or a master jeweller had crossed his jewels with jet and set them to burn and wink in the branches and twigs of oaks whose leaves shone luminous—a leafy Milky Way—fired by black chlorophyll.

Dexter stopped as dead as I. Transfixed. His thick honey-coloured coat and amber eyes glowing with their own intense brightness, suggested yet another spectrum. A *spectrum of light*. He was a constellated dog, shining, supra-real, against the foot-hills and mountain ranges of midnight.

I am reminded now, as I write, of a collection of lepidoptera in Brazil—one entire wall covered with butterflies, creatures of day-light—enormous or tiny—blue, orange, black. Strong-coloured. And on the opposite wall their anti-selves—pale night flyers spanning such a range of silver and white and lightest snuff-colour that once one entered their spectral scale there was no end to the subtleties and delicate nuances. But I didn't think like this then. All thought, all comparisons were prevented by the startling infinities of darkness and light.

Then, as before, the additional shake occurred and the two spectrums moved swiftly from without to within. As if two equal and complementary circles centred inside me—or I in them. How explain that I not only *saw* but actually *was* the two spectrums? (I underline a simple, but in this case, exactly appropriate anagram.)

Then the range-finder lost its focus and the world, once again, was back to normal. Dexter, a pale, blurred blob, bounded about within the field of my peripheral vision, going on with his doggy interests just as if a moment before he had not been frozen in his tracks, a dog entranced.

I am no longer concerned about my eyesight. Wonder only if we are both mad, Dexter and I? Angelically mad, sharing hallucinations of epiphany. *Folie à deux?*

Friday, October 3.

It's hard to account for my secrecy, for I *have* been secretive. As if the cat had my tongue. It's not that I don't long to talk about the colours but I can't risk the wrong response—(as Gaby once said of a companion after a faultless performance of *Giselle*: 'If she had criticised the least detail of it, I'd have hit her!').

Once or twice I've gone so far as to say, 'I had the most extraordinary experience the other day . . .' hoping to find some look or phrase, some answering, 'So did I.' None has been forthcoming.

I can't forget the beauty. Can't get it out of my head. Startling, unearthly, indescribable. Infuriatingly indescribable. A glimpse of—somewhere else. Somewhere alive, miraculous, newly-made yet timeless. And more important still—significant, luminous, with a meaning of which I was part. Except that I—the I who is writing this—did not exist; was flooded out, dissolved in that immensity where subject and object are one.

I have to make a deliberate effort now not to live my life in terms of it; not to sit, immobilized, awaiting the shake that heralds a new world. Awaiting the transfiguration.

Luckily the necessities of life keep me busy. But upstream of my actions, behind a kind of plate glass, some part of me waits, listens, maintains a total attention.

Tuesday, October 7.

Things are moving very fast.

Some nights ago my eye was caught by a news item. 'Trucker Blames Colours,' went the headline. Reading on: 'R.T. Ballantyne, driver for Island Trucks, failed to stop on a red light at the intersection of Fernhill and Spender. Questioned by traffic police, Ballantyne replied: "I didn't see it, that's all. There was this shake, then all these colours suddenly in the trees. Real bright ones I'd never seen before. I guess they must have blinded me." A breathalizer test proved negative.' Full stop.

I had an overpowering desire to talk to R.T. Ballantyne. Even looked him up in the telephone book. Not listed. I debated reaching him through Island Trucks in the morning.

Hoping for some mention of the story, I switched on the local radio station, caught the announcer mid-sentence:

'. . . to come to the studio and talk to us. So far no one has been able to describe just what the "new" colours are, but perhaps Ruby Howard can. Ruby, you say you actually *saw* "new" colours?'

What might have been a flat, rather ordinary female voice was sharpened by wonder. 'I was out in the garden, putting it to bed, you might say, getting it ready for winter. The hydrangeas are dried out—you know the way they go. Soft beiges and greys. And I was thinking maybe I should cut them back, when there was this—shake, like—and there they were shining. Pink. And blue. But not like they are in life. Different. Brighter. With little lights like . . .'

The announcer's voice cut in, 'You say ''not like they are in life''. D'you think this wasn't life? I mean, do you think maybe you were dreaming?'

'Oh, no,' answered my good Mrs Howard, positive, clear, totally unrattled. 'Oh, no, I wasn't *dreaming*. Not *dreaming*- . . . Why—*this* is more like dreaming.' She was quiet a moment and then, in a matter-of-fact voice, 'I can't expect you to believe it,' she said. 'Why should you? I wouldn't believe it myself if I hadn't seen it.' Her voice expressed a kind of compassion as if she was really sorry for the announcer.

I picked up the telephone book for the second time, looked up the number of the station. I had decided to tell Mrs Howard what I had seen. I dialled, got a busy signal, depressed the bar and waited, cradle in hand. I dialled again. And again.

Later.

J. just phoned. Curious how she and I play the same game over and over.

J: Were you watching Channel 8?

Me: No, I . . .

J: An interview. With a lunatic. One who sees colours and flashing lights.

Me: Tell me about it.

J: He was a logger—a high-rigger—not that that has anything to do with it. He's retired now and lives in an apartment and has a window-box with geraniums. This morning the flowers were like neon, he said, flashing and shining . . . *Hon*estly!

Me: Perhaps he saw something you can't . . .

J: (*Amused*) I might have known you'd take his side. Seriously, what *could* he have seen?

Me: Flashing and shining—as he said.

J: But they couldn't. Not geraniums. And you know it as well as I do. *Hon*estly, Babe . . . (She is the only person left who calls me the name my mother called me.) Why are you always so perverse?

I felt faithless. I put down the receiver, as if I had not borne witness to my God.

October 22.

Floods of letters to the papers. Endless interviews on radio and TV. Pros, cons, inevitable spoofs.

One develops an eye for authenticity. It's as easy to spot as sunlight. However they may vary in detail, true accounts of the colours have an unmistakable common factor—a common factor as difficult to convey as sweetness to those who know only salt. True accounts are inarticulate, diffuse, unlikely—impossible.

It's recently crossed my mind that there may be some relationship between having seen the colours and their actual manifestation—something as improbable as *the more one sees them the more they are able to be seen*. Perhaps they are always there in some normally invisible part of the electro-magnetic spectrum and only become visible to certain people at certain times. A combination of circumstances or some subtle refinement in the organ of sight. And then—from quantity to quality perhaps, like water to ice—a whole community changes, is able to see, catches fire.

For example, it was seven days between the first time I saw the colours and the second. During that time there were no reports to the media. But once the reports began, the time between lessened appreciably *for me*. Not proof, of course, but worth noting. And I can't help wondering why some people see the colours and others don't. Do some of us have extra vision? Are some so conditioned that they're virtually blind to what's there before their very noses? Is it a question of more, or less?

Reports come in from farther and farther afield; from all walks of life. I think now there is no portion of the inhabited globe without 'shake freaks' and no acceptable reason for the sightings. Often, only one member of a family will testify to the heightened vision. In my own small circle, I am the only witness—or so I think. I feel curiously hypocritical as I listen to my friends denouncing the 'shakers'. Drugs, they say. Irrational—possibly dangerous. Although no sinister incidents have occurred yet—just some mild shake-baiting here and there—one is uneasily reminded of Salem.

Scientists pronounce us hallucinated or mistaken, pointing out that so far there is no hard evidence, no objective proof. That means, I suppose, no photographs, no spectroscopic measurement—if such is possible. Interestingly, seismographs show very minor earthquake tremors—showers of them, like shooting stars in August. Pundits claim 'shake fever'—as it has come to be called—is a variant on flying saucer fever and that it will subside in its own time. Beneficent physiologists suggest we are suffering (why is it *always* suffering, never enjoying?) a distorted form of *ocular spectrum* or after-image. (An after-image of what?) Psychologists disagree among themselves. All in all, it is not surprising that some of us prefer to keep our experiences to ourselves.

January 9.

Something new has occurred. Something impossible. Disturbing. So disturbing, in fact, that according to rumour it is already being taken with the utmost seriousness at the highest levels. TV, press and radio—with good reason—talk of little else.

What seemingly began as a mild winter has assumed sinister overtones. Farmers in southern Alberta are claiming the earth is unnaturally hot to the touch. Golfers at Harrison complain that the soles of their feet burn. Here on the coast, we notice it less. Benign winters are our specialty.

Already we don't lack for explanations as to why the earth could not be hotter than usual, nor why it is naturally 'unnaturally' hot. Vague notes of reassurance creep into the speeches of public men. They may be unable to explain the issue, but they can no longer ignore it.

To confuse matters further, reports on temperatures seem curiously inconsistent. What information we get comes mainly from self-appointed 'earth touchers'. And now that the least thing can fire an argument, their conflicting readings lead often enough to inflammatory debate.

For myself, I can detect no change at all in my own garden.

Thursday . . . ?

There is no longer any doubt. The temperature of the earth's surface *is* increasing.

It is unnerving, horrible, to go out and feel the ground like some great beast, warm, beneath one's feet. As if another presence —vast, invisible—attends one. Dexter, too, is perplexed. He barks at the earth with the same indignation and, I suppose, fear, with which he barks at the first rumblings of earth-quake.

Air temperatures, curiously, don't increase proportionately—or so we're told. It doesn't make sense, but at the moment nothing makes sense. Countless explanations have been offered. Elaborate explanations. None adequate. The fact that the air temperature remains temperate despite the higher ground heat must, I think, be helping to keep panic down. Even so, these are times of great tension.

Hard to understand these two unexplained—unrelated?—phenomena: the first capable of dividing families; the second menacing us all. We are like animals trapped in a burning building.

Later.

J. just phoned. Terrified. Why don't I move in with her, she urges. After all she has the space and we have known each other forty years. (Hard to believe when I don't feel even forty!) She can't bear it—the loneliness.

Poor J. Always so protected, insulated by her money. And her charm. What one didn't provide, the other did . . . diversions, services, attention.

What do I think is responsible for the heat, she asks. But it turns out she means who. Her personal theory is that the 'shake-freaks' are causing it—involuntarily, perhaps, but the two are surely linked.

'How could they possibly cause it?' I enquire. 'By what reach of the imagination . . . ?'

'Search *me*!' she protests. 'How on earth should *I* know?' And the sound of the dated slang makes me really laugh.

But suddenly she is close to tears. 'How can you *laugh*?' she calls. 'This is nightmare. Nightmare!'

Dear J. I wish I could help but the only comfort I could offer would terrify her still more.

September.

Summer calmed us down. If the earth was hot, well, summers *are* hot. And we were simply having an abnormally hot one.

Now that it is fall—the season of cool nights, light frosts—and the earth like a feverish child remains worryingly hot, won't cool down, apprehension mounts.

At last we are given official readings. For months the authorities have assured us with irrefutable logic that the temperature of the earth could not be increasing. Now, without any apparent period of indecision or confusion, they are warning us with equal conviction and accurate statistical documentation that it has, in fact, increased. Something anyone with a pocket-handkerchief of lawn has known for some time.

Weather stations, science faculties, astronomical observatories all over the world, are measuring and reporting. Intricate computerized tables are quoted. Special departments of government have been set up. We speak now of a new Triassic Age—the Neo-Triassic—and of the accelerated melting of the ice caps. But we are elaborately assured that this could not, repeat not, occur in our lifetime.

Interpreters and analysts flourish. The media are filled with theories and explanations. The increased temperature has been attributed to impersonal agencies such as bacteria from outer space; a thinning of the earth's atmosphere; a build-up of carbon-dioxide in the air; some axial irregularity; a change in the earth's core (geologists are reported to have begun test borings). No theory is too far-fetched to have its supporters. And because man likes a scapegoat, blame has been laid upon NASA, atomic physicists, politicians, the occupants of flying saucers and finally upon mankind at large—improvident, greedy mankind—whose polluted, strike-ridden world is endangered now by the fabled flames of hell.

We are also informed that Nostradamus, the Bible, and Jeane Dixon have all foreseen our plight. A new paperback, *Let Edgar*

Casey Tell You Why sold out in a matter of days. Attendance at churches has doubled. Cults proliferate. Yet even in this atmosphere, we, the 'shake freaks', are considered lunatic fringe. Oddmen out. In certain quarters I believe we are seriously held responsible for the escalating heat, so J. is not alone. There have now been one or two nasty incidents. It is not surprising that even the most vocal among us have grown less willing to talk. I am glad to have kept silent. As a woman living alone, the less I draw attention to myself the better.

Our lives are greatly altered by this overhanging sense of doom. It is already hard to buy certain commodities. Dairy products are in very short supply. On the other hand, the market is flooded with citrus fruits. We are threatened with severe shortages for the future. The authorities are resisting rationing but it will have to come if only to prevent artificial shortages resulting from hoarding.

Luckily the colours are an almost daily event. I see them now, as it were, with my entire being. It is as if all my cells respond to their brilliance and become light too. At such times I feel I might shine in the dark.

No idea of the date.

It is evening and I am tired but I am so far behind in my notes I want to get something down. Events have moved too fast for me.

Gardens, parks, every tillable inch of soil have been appropriated for food crops. As an able, if aging body, with an acre of land and some knowledge of gardening, I have been made responsible for soy-beans—small trifoliate plants rich with the promise of protein. Neat rows of them cover what were once my vegetable garden, flower beds, and lawn.

Young men from the Department of Agriculture came last month, bull-dozed, cultivated, planted. Efficient, noisy desecrators of my twenty years of landscaping. Dexter barked at them from the moment they appeared and I admit I would have shared his indignation had the water shortage not already created its own desolation.

As a government gardener I'm a member of a new privileged class. I have watering and driving permits and coupons for gasoline and boots—an indication of what is to come. So far there has been no clothes rationing.

Daily instructions—when to water and how much, details of

mulching, spraying—reach me from the government radio station to which I tune first thing in the morning. It also provides temperature readings, weather forecasts and the latest news releases on emergency measures, curfews, rationing, insulation. From the way things are going I think it will soon be our only station. I doubt that newspapers will be able to print much longer. In any event, I have already given them up. At first it was interesting to see how quickly drugs, pollution, education, Women's Lib., all became by-gone issues; and, initially, I was fascinated to see how we rationalized. Then I became bored. Then disheartened. Now I am too busy.

Evening

A call came from J. Will I come for Christmas?

Christmas! Extraordinary thought. Like a word from another language learned in my youth, now forgotten.

'I've still got some Heidsieck. We can get tight.'

The word takes me back to my teens. 'Like old times . . .'

'Yes.' She is eager. I hate to let her down. 'J., I can't. How could I get to you?'

'In your *car*, silly. *You* still have gas. You're the only one of us who has.' Do I detect a slight hint of accusation, as if I had acquired it illegally?

'But J., it's only for emergencies.'

'My God, Babe, d'you think *this* isn't an emergency?'

'J., dear . . .'

'*Please*, Babe,' she pleads. 'I'm so afraid. Of the looters. The eeriness. You must be afraid too. *Please!*'

I should have said, yes, that of course I was afraid. It's only natural to be afraid. Or, unable to say that, I should have made the soothing noises a mother makes to her child. Instead, 'There's no reason to be afraid, J.,' I said. It must have sounded insufferably pompous.

'No reason!' She was exasperated with me. 'I'd have thought there was every reason.'

She will phone again. In the night perhaps when she can't sleep. Poor J. She feels so alone. She *is* so alone. And so idle. I don't suppose it's occurred to her yet that telephones will soon go. That a whole way of life is vanishing completely.

It's different for me. I have the soy-beans which keep me busy all the daylight hours. And Dexter. And above all I have the colours and with them the knowledge that there are others, other people, whose sensibilities I share. We are invisibly, inviolably related to one another as the components of a molecule. I say 'we'. Perhaps I should speak only for myself, yet I feel as sure of these others as if they had spoken. Like the quails, we share one brain—no, I think it is one heart—between us. How do I know this? How *do* I know? I know by knowing. We are less alarmed by the increasing heat than those who have not seen the colours. I can't explain why. But seeing the colours seems to change one—just as certain diagnostic procedures cure the complaint they are attempting to diagnose.

In all honesty I admit to having had moments when this sense of community was not enough, when I have had a great longing for my own kind—for so have I come to think of these others—in the way one has a great longing for someone one loves. Their presence in the world is not enough. One must see them. Touch them. Speak with them.

But lately that longing has lessened. All longing, in fact. And fear. Even my once great dread that I might cease to see the colours has vanished. It is as if through seeing them I have learned to see them. Have learned to be ready to see—passive; not striving to see—active. It keeps me very wide awake. Transparent even. Still.

The colours come daily now. Dizzying. Transforming. Life-giving. My sometimes back-breaking toil in the garden is lightened, made full of wonder, by the incredible colours shooting in the manner of children's sparklers from the plants themselves and from my own work-worn hands. I hadn't realized that I too am part of this vibrating luminescence.

Later.

I have no idea how long it is since I abandoned these notes. Without seasons to measure its passing, without normal activities—preparations for festivals, occasional outings—time feels longer, shorter or—more curious still—simultaneous, undifferentiated. Future and past fused in the present. Linearity broken.

I had intended to write regularly, but the soy-beans keep me busy pretty well all day and by evening I'm usually ready for bed. I'm sorry however to have missed recording the day-by-day changes. They were more or less minor at first. But once the heat began its deadly escalation, the world as we have known it—'our world'—had you been able to put it alongside 'this world'—would have seemed almost entirely different.

No one, I think, could have foreseen the speed with which everything has broken down. For instance, the elaborate plans made to maintain transportation became useless in a matter of months. Private traffic was first curtailed, then forbidden. If a man from another planet had looked in on us, he would have been astonished to see us trapped who were apparently free.

The big changes only really began after the first panic evacuations from cities. Insulated by concrete, sewer pipes and underground parkades, high density areas responded slowly to the increasing temperatures. But once the heat penetrated their insulations, Gehennas were created overnight and whole populations fled in hysterical exodus, jamming highways in their futile attempts to escape.

Prior to this the government had not publicly acknowledged a crisis situation. They had taken certain precautions, brought in temporary measures to ease shortages and dealt with new developments on an *ad hoc* basis. Endeavoured to play it cool. Or so it seemed. Now they levelled with us. It was obvious that they must have been planning for months, only awaiting the right psychological moment to take everything over. That moment had clearly come. What we had previously thought of as a free world ended. We could no longer eat, drink, move without permits or coupons. This was full-scale emergency.

Yet nothing proceeds logically. Plans are made only to be remade to accommodate new and totally unexpected developments. The heat, unpatterned as disseminated sclerosis, attacks first here, then there. Areas of high temperature suddenly and inexplicably cool off—or vice versa. Agronomists are doing everything possible to keep crops coming—taking advantage of hot-house conditions to force two crops where one had grown before—frantically playing a kind of agricultural roulette, gambling on the length of time a specific region might continue to grow temperate-zone produce.

Mails have long since stopped. And newspapers. And telephones. As a member of a new privileged class, I have been equipped with a two-way radio and a permit to drive on government business. Schools have of course closed. An attempt was made for a time to provide lessons over TV. Thankfully the looting and rioting seem over. Those desperate gangs of angry citizens who for some time made life additionally difficult, have now disappeared. We seem at last to understand that we are all in this together.

Life is very simple without electricity. I get up with the light and go to bed as darkness falls. My food supply is still substantial and because of the soy-bean crop I am all right for water. Dexter has adapted well to his new life. He is outdoors less than he used to be and has switched to a mainly vegetable diet without too much difficulty.

Evening.

This morning a new order over the radio. All of us with special driving privileges were asked to report to our zone garage to have our tires treated with heat resistant plastic.

I had not been into town for months. I felt rather as one does on returning home from hospital—that the world is unexpectedly large, with voluminous airy spaces. This was exaggerated perhaps by the fact that our whole zone had been given over to soybeans. Everywhere the same rows of green plants—small pods already formed—march across gardens and boulevards. I was glad to see the climate prove so favourable. But there was little else to make me rejoice as I drove through ominously deserted streets, paint blistering and peeling on fences and houses, while overhead a haze of dust, now always with us, created a green sun.

The prolonged heat has made bleak the little park opposite the garage. A rocky little park, once all mosses and rhododendrons, it is bare now, and brown. I was seeing the day as everyone saw it. Untransmuted.

As I stepped out of my car to speak to the attendant I cursed that I had not brought my insulators. The burning tarmac made me shift rapidly from foot to foot. Anyone from another planet would have wondered at this extraordinary quirk of earthlings. But my feet were forgotten as my eyes alighted a second time on the park across the way. I had never before seen so dazzling and variegated a display of colours. How could there be such prismed brilliance in the range of greys and browns? It was as if the perceiving organ—wherever it is—sensitized by earlier experience, was now correctly tuned for this further perception.

The process was as before: the merest shake and the whole park was 'rainbow, rainbow, rainbow'. A further shake brought the park from *there* to *here*. Interior. But this time the interior space had increased. Doubled. By a kind of instant knowledge that rid me of all doubt, I knew that the garage attendant was seeing it to. *We saw the colours.*

Then, with that slight shift of focus, as if a gelatinous film had moved briefly across my sight, everything slipped back.

I really looked at the attendant for the first time. He was a skinny young man standing up naked inside a pair of loose striped overalls cut off at the knee, *sidney* embroidered in red over his left breast pocket. He was blonde, small-boned, with nothing about him to stick in the memory except his clear eyes which at that moment bore an expression of total comprehension.

'You . . .' we began together and laughed.

'Have you seen them before?' I asked. But it was rather as one would say 'how do you do'—not so much a question as a salutation.

We looked at each other for a long time, as if committing each other to memory.

'Do you know anyone else?' I said.

'One or two. Three, actually. Do you?'

I shook my head. 'You are the first. Is it . . . is it . . . always like that?'

'You mean . . . ?' he gestured towards his heart.

I nodded.

'Yes,' he said. 'Yes, it is.'

There didn't seem anything more to talk about. Your right hand hasn't much to say to your left, or one eye to the other. There was comfort in the experience, if comfort is the word, which it isn't. More as if an old faculty had been extended. Or a new one activated.

Sidney put my car on the hoist and sprayed its tires.

Some time later.

I have not seen Sidney again. Two weeks ago when I went back he was not there and as of yesterday, cars have become obsolete. Not that we will use that word publicly. The official word is *suspended*.

Strange to be idle after months of hard labour. A lull only before the boys from the Department of Agriculture come back to prepare the land again. I am pleased that the soy-beans are harvested, that I was able to nurse them along to maturity despite the scorching sun, the intermittent plagues and the problems with water. Often the pressure was too low to turn the sprinklers and I would stand, hour after hour, hose in hand, trying to get the most use from the tiny trickle spilling from the nozzle.

Sometimes my heart turns over as I look through the kitchen window and see the plants shrivelled and grotesque, the baked earth scored by a web of fine cracks like the glaze on a plate subjected to too high an oven. Then it comes to me in a flash that of course, the beans are gone, the harvest is over.

The world is uncannily quiet. I don't think anyone had any idea of how much noise even distant traffic made until we were without it. It is rare indeed for vehicles other than Government mini-cars to be seen on the streets. And there are fewer and fewer pedestrians. Those who do venture out, move on their thick insulators with the slow gait of rocking-horses. Surreal and alien, they heighten rather than lessen one's sense of isolation. For one *is* isolated. We have grown used to the sight of helicopters like large dragon-flies hovering overhead—addressing us through their P.A. systems, dropping supplies—welcome but impersonal.

Dexter is my only physical contact. He is delighted to have me inside again. The heat is too great for him in the garden and as, officially, he no longer exists, we only go out under cover of dark.

The order to destroy pets, when it came, indicated more clearly than anything that had gone before, that the government had abandoned hope. In an animal-loving culture, only direct necessity could validate such an order. It fell upon us like a heavy pall.

When the Government truck stopped by for Dexter, I reported him dead. Now that the welfare of so many depends upon our cooperation with authority, law-breaking is a serious offence. But I am not uneasy about breaking this law. As long as he remains healthy and happy, Dexter and I will share our dwindling provisions.

No need to be an ecologist or dependent on non-existant media to know all life is dying and the very atmosphere of our planet is changing radically. Already no birds sing in the hideous hot dawns as the sun, rising through a haze of dust, sheds its curious bronze-green light on a brown world. The trees that once gave us shade stand leafless now in an infernal winter. Yet, as if in the masts and riggings of ships, St Elmo's fire flickers and shines in their high branches, and bioplasmic pyrotechnics light the dying soy-beans. I am reminded of how the ghostly form of a limb remains attached to the body from which it has been amputated. And I can't help thinking of all the people who don't see the colours, the practical earth-touchers with only their blunt senses to inform them. I wonder about J. and if, since we last talked, she has perhaps been able to see the colours too. But I think not. After so many years of friendship, surely I would be able to sense her, had she broken through.

Evening . . . ?

The heat has increased greatly in the last few weeks—in a quantum leap. This has resulted immediately in two things: a steady rising of the sea level throughout the world—with panic reactions and mild flooding in coastal areas; and, at last, a noticeably higher air temperature. It is causing great physical discomfort.

It was against this probability that the authorities provided us with insulator spray. Like giant cans of pressurized shaving cream. I have shut all rooms but the kitchen and by concentrating my insulating zeal on this one small area, we have managed to keep fairly cool. The word is relative, of course. The radio has stopped giving temperature readings and I have no thermometer. I have filled all cracks and crannies with the foaming plastic, even applied a layer to the exterior wall. There are no baths, of course, and no cold drinks. On the other hand I've abandoned clothes and given Dexter a shave and a haircut. Myself as well. We are a fine pair. Hairless and naked.

When the world state of emergency was declared we didn't need to be told that science had given up. The official line had been that the process would reverse itself as inexplicably as it had begun. The official policy—to hold out as long as possible. With this in mind, task forces worked day and night on survival strategy. On the municipal level, which is all I really knew about, everything that could be centralized was. Telephone exchanges, hydro plants, radio stations became centres around which vital activities took place. Research teams investigated the effects of heat on water mains, sewer pipes, electrical wiring; work crews were employed to prevent, protect or even destroy incipient causes of fire, flood and asphyxiation.

For some time now the city has been zoned. In each zone a large building has been selected, stocked with food, medical supplies and insulating materials. We have been provided with zone maps and an instruction sheet telling us to stay where we are until ordered to move to what is euphemistically called our 'home'. When ordered, we are to load our cars with whatever we still have of provisions and medicines and drive off *at once*. Helicopters have already dropped kits with enough gasoline for the trip and a small packet, somewhat surprisingly labelled 'emergency rations' which contains one cyanide capsule—grim reminder that all may not go as the planners plan. We have been asked to mark our maps, in advance, with the shortest route from our house to our 'home', so that in a crisis we will know what we are doing. These instructions are repeated *ad nauseam* over the radio, along with hearty assurances that everything is under control and that there is no cause for alarm. The Government station is now all that remains of our multi-media. When it is not broadcasting instructions, its mainly pre-recorded tapes sound inanely complacent and repetitive. Evacuation Day, as we have been told again and again, will be announced by whistle blast. Anyone who runs out of food before that or who is in need of medical aid is to use the special gas ration and go 'home' at once.

As a long-time preserver of fruits and vegetables, I hope to hold out until E. Day. When that time comes it will be a sign that broadcasts are no longer possible, that contact can no longer be maintained between the various areas of the community, that the process will not reverse itself in time and that, in fact, our world is well on the way to becoming—oh, wonder of the modern kitchen—a self-cleaning oven.

Spring, Summer, Winter, Fall.
What season is it after all?

I sense the hours by some inner clock. I have applied so many layers of insulating spray that almost no heat comes through from outside. But we have to have air and the small window I have left exposed acts like a furnace. Yet through it I see the dazzling colours; sense my fellow-men.

Noon.

The sun is hidden directly overhead. The world is topaz. I see it through the minute eye of my window. I, the perceiving organ that peers through the house's only aperture. We are one, the house and I—parts of some vibrating sensitive organism in which Dexter plays his differentiated but integral role. The light enters us, dissolves us. We are the golden motes in the jewel.

Midnight.

The sun is directly below. Beneath the burning soles of my arching feet it shines, a globe on fire. Its rays penetrate the earth. Upward beaming, they support and sustain us. We are held aloft, a perfectly balanced ball in the jet of a golden fountain. Light, dancing, infinitely upheld.

Who knows how much later.

I have just 'buried' Dexter.

This morning I realized this hot little cell was no longer a possible place for a dog.

I had saved one can of dog food against this day. As I opened it Dexter's eyes swivelled in the direction of so unexpected and delicious a smell. He struggled to his feet, joyous, animated. The old Dexter. I was almost persuaded to delay, to wait and see if the heat subsided. What if tomorrow we awakened to rain? But something in me, stronger than this wavering self, carried on with its purpose.

He sat up, begging, expectant.

I slipped the meat out of the can.

'You're going to have a really good dinner,' I said, but as my voice was unsteady, I stopped.

I scooped a generous portion of the meat into his dish and placed it on the floor. He was excited, and as always when excited about food, he was curiously ceremonial, unhurried—approaching his dish and backing away from it, only to approach it again at a slightly different angle. As if the exact position was of the greatest importance. It was one of his most amusing and endearing characteristics. I let him eat his meal in his own leisurely and appreciative manner and then, as I have done so many times before, I fed him his final *bon bouche* by hand. The cyanide pill, provided by a beneficient government for me, went down in a gulp.

I hadn't expected it to be so sudden. Life and death so close. His small frame convulsed violently, then collapsed. Simultaneously, as if synchronized, the familiar 'shake' occurred in my vision. Dexter glowed brightly, whitely, like phosphorus. In that dazzling, light-filled moment he was no longer a small dead dog lying there. I could have thought him a lion, my sense of scale had so altered. His beautiful body blinded me with its fires.

With the second 'shake' his consciousness must have entered mine for I felt a surge in my heart as if his loyalty and love had flooded it. And like a kind of ground bass, I was aware of scents and sounds I had not known before. Then a great peace filled me—an immense space, light and sweet—and I realized that this was death. Dexter's death.

But how describe what is beyond description?

As the fires emanating from his slight frame died down, glowed weakly, residually, I put on my insulators and carried his body into the now fever-hot garden. I laid him on what had been at one time an azalea bed. I was unable to dig a grave in the baked earth or to cover him with leaves. But there are no predators now to pick the flesh from his bones. Only the heat which will, in time, desiccate it.

I returned to the house, opening the door as little as possible to prevent the barbs and briars of burning air from entering with me. I sealed the door from inside with foam sealer.

The smell of the canned dog food permeated the kitchen. It rang in my nostrils. Olfactory chimes, lingering, delicious. I was intensely aware of Dexter. Dexter immanent. I contained him as simply as a dish contains water. But the simile is not exact. For I missed his physical presence. One relies on the physical more than I had known. My hands sought palpable contact. The flesh forgets slowly.

Idly, abstractedly, I turned on the radio. I seldom do now as the batteries are low and they are my last. Also, there is little incentive. Broadcasts are intermittent and I've heard the old tapes over and over.

But the government station was on the air. I tuned with extreme care and placed my ear close to the speaker. A voice, faint, broken by static, sounded like that of the Prime Minister.

'. . . all human beings can do, your government has done for you.' (Surely not a political speech *now*?) 'But we have failed. Failed to hold back the heat. Failed to protect ourselves against it; to protect you against it. It is with profound grief that I send this farewell message to you all.' I realized that this, too, had been pre-recorded, reserved for the final broadcast. 'Even now, let us not give up hope . . . '

And then, blasting through the speech, monstrously loud in the stone-silent world, the screech of the whistle summoning us 'home'. I could no longer hear the P.M.'s words.

I began automatically, obediently, to collect my few remaining foodstuffs, reaching for a can of raspberries, the last of the crop to have grown in my garden when the dawns were dewy and cool and noon sun fell upon us like golden pollen. My hand stopped in mid-air.

I would not go 'home'.

The whistle shrilled for a very long time. A curious great steam-driven cry—man's last. Weird that our final utterance should be this anguished inhuman wail.

The end.

Now that it is virtually too late, I regret not having kept a daily record. Now that the part of me that writes has become nearly absorbed, I feel obliged to do the best I can.

I am down to the last of my food and water. Have lived on little for some days—weeks, perhaps. How can one measure passing time? Eternal time grows like a tree, its roots in my heart. If I lie on my back I see winds moving in its high branches and a chorus of birds is singing in its leaves. The song is sweeter than any music I have ever heard.

My kitchen is as strange as I am myself. Its walls bulge with many layers of spray. It is without geometry. Like the inside of an eccentric styrofoam coconut. Yet, with some inner eye, I see its intricate mathematical structure. It is as ordered and no more random than an atom.

My face is unrecognizable in the mirror. Wisps of short damp hair. Enormous eyes. I swim in their irises. Could I drown in the pits of their pupils?

Through my tiny window when I raise the blind, a dead world shines. Sometimes dust storms fill the air with myriad particles burning bright and white as the lion body of Dexter. Sometimes great clouds swirl, like those from which saints receive revelations.

The colours are almost constant now. There are times when, light-headed, I dance a dizzying dance, feel part of that whirling incandescent matter—what I might once have called inorganic matter!

On still days the blameless air, bright as a glistening wing, hangs over us, hangs its extraordinary beneficence over us.

We are together now, united, indissoluble. Bonded.

Because there is no expectation, there is no frustration.

Because there is nothing we can have, there is nothing we can want.

We are hungry of course. Have cramps and weakness. But they are as if in *another body*. *Our* body is inviolate. Inviolable.

We share one heart.

We are one with the starry heavens and our bodies are stars.

Inner and outer are the same. A continuum. The water in the locks is level. We move to a higher water. A high sea.

A ship could pass through.

SHEILA WATSON

Antigone

My father ruled a kingdom on the right bank of the river. He ruled it with a firm hand and a stout heart though he was often more troubled than Moses, who was simply trying to bring a stubborn and moody people under God's yoke. My father ruled men who thought they were gods or the instruments of gods or, at very least, god-afflicted and god-pursued. He ruled Atlas who held up the sky, and Hermes who went on endless messages, and Helen who'd been hatched from an egg, and Pan the gardener, and Kallisto the bear, and too many others to mention by name. Yet my father had no thunderbolt, no trident, no helmet of darkness. His subjects were delivered bound into his hands. He merely watched over them as the hundred-handed ones watched over the dethroned Titans so that they wouldn't bother Hellas again.

Despite the care which my father took to maintain an atmosphere of sober common sense in his whole establishment, there were occasional outbursts of self-indulgence which he could not control. For instance, I have seen Helen walking naked down the narrow cement path under the chestnut trees for no better reason, I suppose, than that the day was hot and the white flowers themselves lay naked and expectant in the sunlight. And I have seen Atlas forget the sky while he sat eating the dirt which held him up. These were things which I was not supposed to see.

If my father had been as sensible through and through as he was thought to be, he would have packed me off to boarding school when I was old enough to be disciplined by men. Instead he kept me at home with my two cousins who, except for the accident of birth, might as well have been my sisters. Today I imagine people concerned with our welfare would take such an environment into account. At the time I speak of most people thought us fortunate

—especially the girls whose father's affairs had come to an unhappy issue. I don't like to revive old scandal and I wouldn't except to deny it; but it takes only a few impertinent newcomers in any community to force open cupboards which have been decently sealed by time. However, my father was so busy setting his kingdom to rights that he let weeds grow up in his own garden.

As I said, if my father had had all his wits about him he would have sent me to boarding school—and Antigone and Ismene too. I might have fallen in love with the headmaster's daughter and Antigone might have learned that no human being can be right always. She might have found out besides that from the seeds of eternal justice grow madder flowers than any which Pan grew in the gardens of my father's kingdom.

Between the kingdom which my father ruled and the wilderness flows a river. It is this river which I am crossing now. Antigone is with me.

How often can we cross the same river, Antigone asks.

Her persistence annoys me. Besides, Heraklitos made nonsense of her question years ago. He saw a river too—the Inachos, the Kephissos, the Lethaios. The name doesn't matter. He said: See how quickly the water flows. However agile a man is, however nimbly he swims, or runs, or flies, the water slips away before him. See, even as he sets down his foot the water is displaced by the stream which crowds along in the shadow of its flight.

But after all, Antigone says, one must admit that it is the same kind of water. The oolichans run in it as they ran last year and the year before. The gulls cry above the same banks. Boats drift towards the Delta and circle back against the current to gather up the catch.

At any rate, I tell her, we're standing on a new bridge. We are standing so high that the smell of mud and river weeds passes under us out to the straits. The unbroken curve of the bridge protects the eye from details of river life. The bridge is foolproof as a clinic's passport to happiness.

The old bridge still spans the river, but the cat-walk with its cracks and knot-holes, with its gap between planking and handrail has been torn down. The centre arch still grinds open to let boats up and down the river, but a child can no longer be walked on it or swung out on it beyond the water-gauge at the very centre of the flood.

I've known men who scorned any kind of bridge, Antigone says. Men have walked into the water, she says, or, impatient, have jumped from the bridge into the river below.

But these, I say, didn't really want to cross the river. They went Persephone's way, cradled in the current's arms, down the long halls under the pink feet of the gulls, under the booms and tow-lines, under the soft bellies of the fish.

Antigone looks at me.

There's no coming back, she says, if one goes far enough.

I know she's going to speak of her own misery and I won't listen. Only a god has the right to say: Look what I suffer. Only a god should say: What more ought I to have done for you that I have not done?

Once in winter, she says, a man walked over the river.

Taking advantage of nature, I remind her, since the river had never frozen before.

Yet he escaped from the penitentiary, she says. He escaped from the guards walking round the walls or standing with their guns in the sentry-boxes at the four corners of the enclosure. He escaped.

Not without risk, I say. He had to test the strength of the ice himself. Yet safer perhaps than if he had crossed by the old bridge where he might have slipped through a knot-hole or tumbled out through the railing.

He did escape, she persists, and lived forever on the far side of the river in the Alaska tea and bulrushes. For where, she asks, can a man go farther than to the outermost edge of the world?

The habitable world, as I've said, is on the right bank of the river. Here is the market with its market stalls—the coops of hens, the long-tongued geese, the haltered calf, the bearded goat, the shoving pigs, and the empty bodies of cows and sheep and rabbits hanging on iron hooks. My father's kingdom provides asylum in the suburbs. Near it are the convent, the churches, and the penitentiary. Above these on the hill the cemetery looks down on the people and on the river itself.

It is a world spread flat, tipped up into the sky so that men and women bend forward, walking as men walk when they board a ship at high tide. This is the world I feel with my feet. It is the world I see with my eyes.

I remember standing once with Antigone and Ismene in the square just outside the gates of my father's kingdom. Here from a bust set high on a cairn the stone eyes of Simon Fraser look from his stone face over the river that he found.

It is the head that counts, Ismene said.

It's no better than an urn, Antigone said, one of the urns we see when we climb to the cemetery above.

And all I could think was that I didn't want an urn, only a flat green grave with a chain about it.

A chain won't keep out the dogs, Antigone said.

But his soul could swing on it, Ismene said, like a bird blown on a branch in the wind.

And I remember Antigone's saying: The cat drags its belly on the ground and the rat sharpens its tooth in the ivy.

I should have loved Ismene, but I didn't. It was Antigone I loved. I should have loved Ismene because, although she walked the flat world with us, she managed somehow to see it round.

The earth is an oblate spheroid, she'd say. And I knew that she saw it there before her comprehensible and whole like a tangerine spiked through and held in place while it rotated on the axis of one of Nurse's steel sock needles. The earth was a tangerine and she saw the skin peeled off and the world parcelled out into neat segments, each segment sweet and fragrant in its own skin.

It's the head that counts, she said.

In her own head she made diagrams to live by, cut and fashioned after the eternal patterns spied out by Plato as he rummaged about in the sewing basket of the gods.

I should have loved Ismene. She would live now in some prefabricated and perfect chrysolite by some paradigm which made love round and whole. She would simply live and leave destruction in the purgatorial ditches outside her own walled paradise.

Antigone is different. She sees the world flat as I do and feels it tip beneath her feet. She has walked in the market and seen the living animals penned and the dead hanging stiff on their hooks. Yet she defies what she sees with a defiance which is almost denial. Like Atlas she tries to keep the vaulted sky from crushing the flat earth. Like Hermes she brings a message that there is life if one can escape to it in the brush and bulrushes in some dim Hades beyond the river. It is defiance not belief and I tell her that this time we walk the bridge to a walled cave where we can deny death no longer.

Yet she asks her question still. And standing there I tell her that Heraklitos has made nonsense of her question. I should have loved

Ismene for she would have taught me what Plato meant when he said in all earnest that the union of the soul with the body is in no way better than dissolution. I expect that she understood things which Antigone is too proud to see.

I turn away from her and flatten my elbows on the high wall of the bridge. I look back at my father's kingdom. I see the terraces rolling down from the red-brick buildings with their barred windows. I remember hands shaking the bars and hear fingers tearing up paper and stuffing it through the meshes. Diktynna, mother of nets and high leaping fear. O Artemis, mistress of wild beasts and wild men.

The inmates are beginning to come out on the screened verandas. They pace up and down in straight lines or stand silent like figures which appear at the same time each day from some depths inside a clock.

On the upper terrace Pan the gardener is shifting sprinklers with a hooked stick. His face is shadowed by the brim of his hat. He moves as economically as an animal between the beds of lobelia and geranium. It is high noon.

Antigone has cut out a piece of sod and has scooped out a grave. The body lies in a coffin in the shade of the magnolia tree. Antigone and I are standing. Ismene is sitting between two low angled branches of the monkey puzzle tree. Her lap is filled with daisies. She slits the stem of one daisy and pulls the stem of another through it. She is making a chain for her neck and a crown for her hair.

Antigone reaches for a branch of the magnolia. It is almost beyond her grip. The buds flame above her. She stands on a small fire of daisies which smoulder in the roots of the grass.

I see the magnolia buds. They brood above me, whiteness feathered on whiteness. I see Antigone's face turned to the light. I hear the living birds call to the sun. I speak private poetry to myself: Between four trumpeting angels at the four corners of the earth a bride stands before the altar in a gown as white as snow.

Yet I must have been speaking aloud because Antigone challenges me: You're mistaken. It's the winds the angels hold, the four winds of the earth. After the just are taken to paradise the winds will destroy the earth. It's a funeral, she says, not a wedding.

She looks towards the building.

Someone is coming down the path from the matron's house, she says.

I notice that she has pulled one of the magnolia blossoms from the branch. I take it from her. It is streaked with brown where her hands have bruised it. The sparrow which she has decided to bury lies on its back. Its feet are clenched tight against the feathers of its breast. I put the flower in the box with it.

Someone is coming down the path. She is wearing a blue cotton dress. Her cropped head is bent. She walks slowly carrying something in a napkin.

It's Kallisto the bear, I say. Let's hurry. What will my father say if he sees us talking to one of his patients?

If we live here with him, Antigone says, what can he expect? If he spends his life trying to tame people he can't complain if you behave as if they were tame. What would your father think, she says, if he saw us digging in the Institution lawn?

Pan comes closer. I glower at him. There's no use speaking to him. He's deaf and dumb.

Listen, I say to Antigone, my father's not unreasonable. Kallisto thinks she's a bear and he thinks he's a bear tamer, that's all. As for the lawn, I say quoting my father without conviction, a man must have order among his own if he is to keep order in the state.

Kallisto has come up to us. She is smiling and laughing to herself. She gives me her bundle.

Fish, she says.

I open the napkin.

Pink fish sandwiches, I say.

For the party, she says.

But it isn't a party, Antigone says. It's a funeral.

For the funeral breakfast, I say.

Ismene is twisting two chains of daisies into a rope. Pan has stopped pulling the sprinkler about. He is standing beside Ismene resting himself on his hooked stick. Kallisto squats down beside her. Ismene turns away, preoccupied, but she can't turn far because of Pan's legs.

Father said we never should
Play with madmen in the wood.

I look at Antigone.

It's my funeral, she says.

I go over to Ismene and gather up a handful of loose daisies from her lap. The sun reaches through the shadow of the magnolia tree.

It's my funeral, Antigone says. She moves possessively toward the body.

An ant is crawling into the bundle of sandwiches which I've put on the ground. A file of ants is marching on the sparrow's box.

I go over and drop daisies on the bird's stiff body. My voice speaks ritual words: Deliver me, O Lord, from everlasting death on this dreadful day. I tremble and am afraid.

The voice of a people comforts me. I look at Antigone. I look her in the eye.

It had better be a proper funeral then, I say.

Kallisto is crouched forward on her hands. Tears are running down her cheeks and she is licking them away with her tongue.

My voice rises again: I said in the midst of my days, I shall not see—

Antigone just stands there. She looks frightened, but her eyes defy me with their assertion.

It's my funeral, she says. It's my bird. I was the one who wanted to bury it.

She is looking for a reason. She will say something which sounds eternally right.

Things have to be buried, she says. They can't be left lying around anyhow for people to see.

Birds shouldn't die, I tell her. They have wings. Cats and rats haven't wings.

Stop crying, she says to Kallisto. It's only a bird.

It has a bride's flower in its hand, Kallisto says.

We shall rise again, I mutter, but we shall not all be changed.

Antigone does not seem to hear me.

Behold, I say in a voice she must hear, in a moment, in the twinkling of an eye, the trumpet shall sound.

Ismene turns to Kallisto and throws the daisy chain about her neck.

Shall a virgin forget her adorning or a bride the ornament of her breast?

Kallisto is lifting her arms towards the tree.

The bridegroom has come, she says, white as a fall of snow. He stands above me in a great ring of fire.

Antigone looks at me now.

Let's cover the bird up, she says. Your father will punish us all for making a disturbance.

He has on his garment, Kallisto says, and on his thigh is written King of Kings.

I look at the tree. If I could see with Kallisto's eyes I wouldn't be afraid of death, or punishment, or the penitentiary guards. I wouldn't be afraid of my father's belt or his honing strap or his bedroom slipper. I wouldn't be afraid of falling into the river through a knot-hole in the bridge.

But, as I look, I see the buds falling like burning lamps and I hear the sparrow twittering in its box: Woe, woe, woe because of the three trumpets which are yet to sound.

Kallisto is on her knees. She is growling like a bear. She lumbers over to the sandwiches and mauls them with her paw.

Ismene stands alone for Pan the gardener has gone.

Antigone is fitting a turf in place above the coffin. I go over and press the edge of the turf with my feet. Ismene has caught me by the hand.

Go away, Antigone says.

I see my father coming down the path. He has an attendant with him. In front of them walks Pan holding the sprinkler hook like a spear.

What are you doing here? my father asks.

Burying a bird, Antigone says.

Here? my father asks again.

Where else could I bury it? Antigone says.

My father looks at her.

This ground is public property, he says. No single person has any right to an inch of it.

I've taken six inches, Antigone says. Will you dig up the bird again?

Some of his subjects my father restrained since they were moved to throw themselves from high places or to tear one another to bits from jealousy or rage. Others who disturbed the public peace he taught to walk in the airing courts or to work in the kitchen or in the garden.

If men live at all, my father said, it is because discipline saves their life for them.

From Antigone he simply turned away.

ELIZABETH SPENCER

I, Maureen

On the sunny fall afternoon, I (Maureen) saw the girl sitting in the oval-shaped park near the St Lawrence River. She was sitting on green grass, bent lovingly, as though eternally, over her guitar. They are always like that, absorbed, hair falling past their faces, whether boys or girls: there seems little difference between them: they share the tender absorption of mother with child. The whole outside world regards them, forms a hushed circle about them.

I, Maureen, perceived this while driving by on an errand for Mr Massimo.

I used to live out there, on what in Montreal we call the Lakeshore. I did nothing right then, so returning to that scene is painful. I sought relief from the memories of five years ago by letting the girl with the guitar—bending to it, framed in grass, the blue river flowing by—redeem my memories, redeem me, I could only hope, also. Me, Maureen, stung with the identity of bad memories.

Everything any woman in her right mind could want—that was my life. Denis Partham's wife, and not even very pretty or classy: I never had anything resembling looks or background. I was a bit run-down looking, all my life. From the age of two, I looked run-down. People used to say right out to me: 'You've just had luck, that's all.' But Denis said the luck was his. He really thought that, for years and years. Until the day I thought he was dead. After that he had to face it that luck can run out, even for a Partham.

We had a house on the river and it was beautiful, right on the water. It was in Baie d'Urfé, one of the old townships, and you can describe it for yourself, if you so desire. There can be rugs of any texture, draperies of any fabric, paneling both painted and stained, shelves to put books in, cupboards to fill with china and linen. The choice of every upholstery sample or kitchen tile was a top-level decision; the struggle for perfection had a life-and-death quality about it. If my interest was not wholly taken up in all this, if I was play-acting, I did not know it. Are people when measuring and weighing and pondering names for a crown prince, serious? I was expecting the prince; that was why the Parthams gave us the house. Sure enough, the baby was a boy. Two years and another one arrived, a girl. (Isn't Nature great? She belongs to the Parthams.)

In the winter we had cocktails before dinner in a spacious room overlooking the frozen lake, watching the snow drift slowly down, seeing the skaters stroking outward. We had sherry between church services and Sunday lunch. Then the ice boats raced past, silent, fast as dreams.

Our children were beautiful, like children drawn with a pencil over and again in many attitudes, all pure, among many Canadian settings. Denis was handsome, a well-built man, younger than I, with dark hair and a strong, genuine smile. In his world, I was the only dowdy creature. Yet he loved me, heart and soul. And why? I used to sit in a big chair in a corner of the library hunched up like a crow, and wonder this. In summer I sat on the terraces, and there, too, I wondered.

All I knew was that aged twenty-five, a plain, single girl, I had come to the Parthams' big stone house high in Westmount with some friends. It was late, a gathering after a local play. A woman who worked at the library with me had a younger sister in the play and had asked me to come. One of the Parthams was in it, too, so we all got invited up for drinks. Somebody graciously learned that I was living way out in N.D.G., that area of the unnumbered middle class, and Denis, who had been talking to me about the library, offered to drive me home. When we reached the house, he turned off the motor, then the lights, and turning to me began to kiss me hungrily. He had fallen silent along the way, and I had felt he was going to do something like this. I simply judged that he was a rich boy out for more sexual experience, seeking it outside his own class, the way privileged people often do. Yet he was moved and excited way beyond the average: so I put him down as a boy with problems, and squirmed my way out of his arms and his Oldsmobile as best I could. Next day he telephoned me at the library, longing to see me again. He was that way from then on. He said he could never change. Through all our dates, then through season after season, year after year, I saw how his voice would take on a different note when he saw me, how his eyes would light up. I knew his touch, his sexual currents, his eager kisses, his talk, his thoughts, his tastes. At some point, we got married. But the marriage, I helplessly realized, had taken place already, in the moment he had seen me in the corner of one of the many Partham living rooms in their great stone house, me (Maureen), completely out of place. Before I knew it, he had enveloped me all over, encased me like a strong vine. My family could believe my good fortune no more than I could. It was too good to last, but it did; too good to be true, but it was. We had, in addition to the Lakeshore house at Baie d'Urfé, an apartment on Drummond Street in Montreal, servants, two cars, wonderful friends, a marvelous life.

Then, one summer day, it happened. It could never unhappen.

Denis was out sailing and in passing under a bridge, the metal mast of the boat struck a live wire. His hand was on the mast and the voltage knocked him down. When they brought him in they had rolled him onto the sail and were carrying him by four improvised corners, like somebody asleep in a hammock. His head was turned to one side. Everyone on our lawn and dock seemed to know from the minute the boat appeared, unexpectedly returned, that something terrible had happened. We crowded forward together, all the family and friends not sailing, left behind on the lawns to swim, sun, play, or talk, and though I was among the first, I felt just as one of them, not special. I saw his face turned to one side, looking (the eyes shut and the skin discoloured blue and red) like a face drowned through a rift in ice. I thought he was dead, and so did we all, even, I later learned, those who were carrying him. They laid him on the lawn and someone said: 'Stay back,' while another, running from the moment the boat touched the dock, was already at the telephone. But by that time there were arms around me, to hold me back from rushing to him. They encountered no forward force. I was in retreat already, running backward from the moment, into another world which had been waiting for me for some time. All they did was hasten me into it. My fierce sprinting backward plus the force of their normal human attention—that of trying to keep a wife from hurling herself with all the velocity of human passion toward her husband, so unexpectedly served up before her as (so it seemed) a corpse —outdid possibility. But we leave the earth with difficulty, and I wasn't up to that. I fell backward sprawling awkwardly; I lay observing the bluest of July skies in which white clouds had filled in giant areas at good distances from the sun. Sky, cloud, and sun completed me, while ambulances wailed and bore away whomever they would.

Denis did not die; he recovered nicely. All life resumed as before. A month later I made my first attempt at suicide.

It was finally to one of the psychiatrists I saw that I recounted how all of this had started, from a minor event, meaningless *to all but me*. (To me alone the world had spoken.)

I had been sunbathing on the pier a week or so before Denis's accident when two of the children whose parents owned a neighbouring property began to throw things into the water. I could see them—two skinny boys on the neighbouring pier—and know that while they pretended to be hurling rocks and bottles straight out into the lake, they were in reality curving them closer into land, striking near our docking area. I was thinking of getting up to shout at them when it happened. A bit of blue-green glass arching into the sun's rays, caught and trapped an angle of that light, refracting it to me. It struck, a match for lightning. My vision simply for a moment was by this brilliance extinguished; and in the plunge of darkness that ensued I could only see the glass rock reverse its course and speed toward me. It entered my truest self, my consciousness, reverberating with silent brilliance. From that point I date my new beginning. It was a nothing point, an illusion, but an illusion that had happened to me, if there is such a thing. . . .

'If there is such a thing,' the doctor repeated.

'If there is such a thing,' I said again, sounding, I knew, totally mad.

Doctors wait for something to be said that fits a pattern they have learned to be true, just as teachers wait for you to write English or French. If you wrote a new and unknown language they wouldn't know what to do with you—you would fail.

'It explains to me,' I went on, realizing I was taking the risk of being consigned to the asylum at Verdun for an indefinite period, 'why I ran backward instead of forward when I thought Denis was dead. I want my own world. I have been there once. I want to return. If I can't, I might as well be dead.'

'Your attempts to take your own life might be thought of as efforts to join your husband, whom you believed to have reached death,' the doctor suggested. He had a thick European accent, and an odd name, Miracorte. God knows where he was from.

I said nothing.

One day I left home. I had done this before but they had always come for me, tranquilized me, hospitalized me, removed things from me that might be handy ways of self-destruction, talked to me, loved me, nurtured me back to being what they wanted me to be—somebody, in other words, like themselves. This time they didn't come. A doctor came, a new one, younger than the first. He asked from the intercom system in the apartment building in East Montreal which I had fled to, taking the first furnished place I could find, whether he could see me. I let him in.

He was plain English-Canadian from Regina, named Johnson.

'Everyone is a little schizoid,' he said. They had told me that, told me and told me that. 'You choose the other side of the coin, the other side of yourself. You have to have it. If you don't have it, you will die. Don't you know that some people drink themselves into it, others hit drugs, some run off to the bush, some kill or steal or turn into religious freaks? You're a mild case, comparatively speaking. All you want is to be with it, calmly, like a lover.'

I was crying before I knew it, tears of relief. He was the first to consent to my line of feeling. Why had it been so hard, why were they all reluctant to do so? We allow people to mouth platitudes to us one after another, and agree to them blandly, knowing they aren't true, just because there's no bite to them, no danger. The truth is always dangerous, so in agreeing to what I felt, he was letting me in for danger. But it was all that was left to try.

'There's a bank account for you at this address.' He gave me the chequebook and the deposit slip. 'If you need more, call me. Your husband has agreed to this plan.'

I took the chequebook silently, but was vowing already that I would never use it. I was going to get a job.

The young doctor sat frowning, eyes on the floor.

'Denis feels awful,' I said, reading his thoughts aloud. 'This has made him suffer.'

'I didn't say that,' Dr Johnson said. 'It makes you suffer to stay with him. Maybe—well, maybe he can get through better without you than you can with him.'

From then on I was on my own, escaping into the mystery that is

East Montreal, a fish thrown barely alive back into water. Not that I had ever lived there. But to Westmount families who own houses in Baie d'Urfé, East Montreal presents even more of an opaque surface than N.D.G. It is thought to be French, and this is so, but it is also Greek, Italian, Oriental, and immigrant Jewish. I was poor, unattractive as ever; I ached for my children and the sound of Denis's voice, his love, everything I had known. I went through an agony of missing what I could have, all back, and whole as ever, just by picking up the phone, just by taking a taxi and saying, 'Take me home.'

But when I gave in (and I did give in every time the world clicked over and I saw things right side up instead of upside down), odd consequences resulted. I would call a number but strange voices out of unknown businesses or residences would answer, or someone among the Partham friends would say hello, and I would begin to talk about myself—me, *me*, ME—relating imagined insults, or telling stories that were only partly true, and though I knew I was doing this, though my mind stood by like a chance pedestrian at the scene of an accident, interested, but a little sickened, with other things to do, still my voice, never lacking for a word, went on. Once I took a taxi home with all my possessions loaded inside, but directed the driver to the wrong turning, overshot the mark and wound up at the wrong driveway. The people who came out the door knew me; oh, this was horrible; I crouched down out of sight and shouted, 'Go back, go back! Take me home!' (The meaning of home had shifted, the world had flipped once more.)

Again I came on the bus in the middle of a fine afternoon, calm and right within myself, to 'talk things over', sanely to prepare for my return to the family. I found no one there, the house open, the living room empty. I sat down to wait. At a still centre, waiting for loved ones' faces to appear through a radiance of outer sunlight, I stared too hard at nothing, closed my eyes and heard it from the beginning: a silent scream, waxing unbearably. I had come to put out my arms, to say, I have failed to love, but now I know this. I love you, I love you all. What was there in this to make the world shrink back, flee, recede, rock with agony to its fair horizons? I could bear it no longer, and so fled. I ran past one of them, one of the Partham women (my mother-in-law, sister-in-law, aunt-in-law, a cousin?—they look alike, all of them) coming in from the garden in her white work gloves with shears in hand, a flat of cut flowers on her arm. *She* must have screamed also, I saw her mouth make the picture of a scream, but that is unimportant except to her. For if she was Denis's mother she must have wanted to scream ever since I had first walked into her presence, hand in hand with Denis, and then there I was back again, crazy and fleeing with a bruised forehead all purple and gold (in my haste to reach them I had slammed into a door).

My journey back on one rattling bus after another, threading streets under an overcast sky, seemed longer than I could have imagined. I wondered then and since if I had dreamed that journey, if I would not presently wake up in the dark room where my resolution had taken place at 3 A.M. (the hour of weakness and resolve), if the whole matter of getting up, dressing, taking the taxi, were not all a dream of the soul's motion upon deciding, while I myself, like a chained dog, lay still held to sleep and darkness. On the other hand, I wondered whether I had made that same decision and that same trip not once or twice but twenty or thirty times, as though the split side of myself were carrying on a life it would not tell me about. Denis had a brother who was a physicist and used to talk about a 'black hole in space', where matter collapses of its own gravity, ceases to exist in any form that we know of as existence. Yet some existence must continue. Was this myself, turned inside-out like a sleeve, whirled counterclockwise to a vacuum point, when I disappeared would I (Maureen) know it? Confusion thickened in my head.

I thought I saw Denis at the end of a snowy street in East Montreal near Dorchester Boulevard, a child holding to either hand, and so sprang up my fantasy that they often came to watch silently from somewhere just to see me pass, but often as I thought I glimpsed them, I never hastened to close the distance and find the answer.

'You prefer the fantasy to the reality,' Dr Johnson said.

'What made me the way I am? Why have I caused all this?'

'Becoming is difficult.'

'Becoming what?'

'Your alter ego. Your other self.'

'You've said it a hundred times.'

'So what?'

'It makes no sense, my other self. None whatever.'

'You feel it's irrational?'

We both fell silent and looked down as if this self had fallen like an object between us on the floor.

'No one is wholly rational,' Dr Johnson said.

I still sat looking. Rational or not, could it live, poor thing? If I nudged it with my toe, would it move?

'Basically, you are happier now,' he told me.

'I am lonely,' I said. The words fell out, without my knowing it. Perhaps the self on the floor had spoken.

'You like it, or you wouldn't be,' he said at once.

I was surprised by this last remark and returned home with something like an inner smile. For the first time in months I thought of buying something new and pretty and I looked in shop windows along the way. I stopped in a drugstore and got a lipstick. That night I washed my hair. Sitting out on my balcony, watching the people drift by, smoking, the way I always like to do, I put a blanket over my still damp head, for it was only March, and the world was still iced, crusted in decaying snow. I sat like a squaw woman, but inside I felt a little stir of green feeling. I would be happy in this world I'd come to, not just an exile, a maverick that had jumped the fence. I would feel like a woman again.

A woman invisible, floating softly through a June day, I went to church when my daughter was confirmed. I sat far in the back in the dim church, St James on Bishop Street. Seeing her so beautiful, I felt exalted, meaning all the hymns, all the words. But as I was leaving I heard a murmuring behind me and my name spoken. Then a curate was chasing me, calling out my name. I knew him from the old days, didn't I? Wasn't he the one I'd asked to dinner and sherry and tea? He meant everything that was good; he wanted to grasp my hand and speak to me, about forgiveness, love, peace, the whole catalogue. But who stood back of him? Not the kingdom, the power, and the glory, but Parthams, Parthams, and Parthams. I ran like the wind. The air blew white in my face, white as my daughter's communion dress, white as a bridal veil. I stopped at last to gasp it down. No footsteps sounded from behind. I was safe once more. Running backward, I had broken records: forward, I'm unbeatable. This was the grim joke I told myself, skulking home.

'It was a big risk,' Dr Johnson warned me. 'How did you even know about the service?'

'A maid I used to have. She told me.'

'The trouble I've gone to. . . . Don't you realize they want to commit you? If they succeed, you may never get out again.'

'Nobody could keep me from seeing her,' I said. 'Not on that day.'

'To them you're a demon in the sacred place.' He was smiling, but I heard it solemnly. Maybe they were right.

Such, anyway, were my forays into enemy land.

But some were also made to me, in my new country. For I saw them, at times, and at others I thought I saw them, shadows at twilight on the edge of their forest, or real creatures venturing out and toward me; it was often impossible to tell which.

Carole Partham really came, graceful and hesitant, deerlike, and I let her come, perceiving that it was not curiosity or prying that brought her over, but an inner need to break away, to copy me, in some measure.

There she was one twilight, waiting in the pizza restaurant near my entrance. Carole was born a Partham, but her husband was Jim O'Brien, a broker. He was away in Europe, she said. Now's your big chance, she had doubtless told herself.

A smart-looking girl, up to the latest in clothes, a luxury woman, wearing suède with a lynx collar, tall brown rain boots, brushed brown hair.

'Come in,' I urged her, getting her out of that place where, dressed like that, she was making them nervous. 'I'm safe to be with. You can see my place.'

Then she was sitting, smoking, loosening her coat, eyes coasting about here and there, from floor to wall to ceiling. My apartment wasn't much to see. I would have set the dogs on her—dogs of my inner rages—if I hadn't seen her realness. Instead I saw it well: she was frightened. Happy or not? She didn't know. What does life mean? There was panic in the question, if you asked it often enough. She had no answer and her husband was away for quite some time.

'Come work here for a month,' I advised. 'You can get a job, or loaf, or think, or see what happens.'

But her eyes were restless; they stopped at closed drawers, probed at closet doors. Sex! Oh, certainly, I thought. Oh, naturally. I remember Jim O'Brien with his ready talk and his toothy grin flashing over an ever-present,ever-tilted tumbler of martini on the rocks, and the glitter and swagger in his stroll from guest to guest, his intimate flattering talk, and now I knew what I had thought all along: who would marry Jim O'Brien but a woman with a childhood terror still behind the door? And now she'd done it, how could she escape?

'Don't tell them where you are,' I advised. 'I can find a room for you maybe. Somewhere near if you want me to. You can see I've no space here.'

'Oh, I didn't want—'

'Just tell them you've gone away. What about Florida? You can say that.'

Helpless, the eyes roved.

'I've no one here,' I told her. 'No lover, no friend. I work in a photographer's studio. That's all there is to know. You'll see it at the corner. My boss is Mr Massimo. He owns it. There's nothing to know.'

After a long silence, she said, looking down at herself, 'These clothes are wrong.'

'Who cares? Just face it that nobody cares.'

'Nobody cares? Nobody *cares?* She kept repeating this. It was what she couldn't swallow, had got hung up on, I guess, all by herself. I had hit it by accident.

'I mean,' I said, 'nobody over *here* cares. Over there . . . I don't know about that.'

'Nobody . . . nobody. . . . ' Her voice now had gone flat. She got up to go, headed for the terrace window rather than the door, fell through the glass, stumbled over the terrace railing, her fashionable boots flailing the air, skirts sliding up to her neck. . . . But, no, this didn't happen. That wasn't the end of Carole. She went out the door, like anybody else.

She did move to the street for a time; I forget for how long. She brought plain old clothes and tied her head in a scarf. She worked some afternoons for a kind, arthritic Frenchman with white hair who ran a magazine shop. There was also the dark young man who stared down daily from a window four floors up; he descended to trail her home, offering to carry her grocery sack. How nice this tableau looked and how charming it would have been if only his I.Q. had been half-way average. He was once a doorman, I understood, but had kept falling asleep on his feet, like a horse.

She got drunk on resin-tasting wine one night in a Greek restaurant and lured eleven Greek waiters into a cheap hotel room. How sweet and eager and passionate they had seemed! They milled around—or so I was told—not knowing what to do. A humiliation to end all mental nymphomania: Carole escaped unmolested.

She had found a room with a woman whose mother had died and who baby-sat for pin money. On long evenings when she didn't baby-sit she told Carole the story of her life. Otherwise, Carole read, and drank, and told herself the story of her own life. She was happy in the butcher shop once and sat madonna-like with the butcher's cat purring in her lap, but the butcher's Spanish wife did not like her and kicked the cat to say so. Mr Massimo pondered about her. 'How did you know her?' he asked. 'She once knew my sister,' is all I answered.

Old clothes or not, Carole did one thing she didn't intend: she gave out the indefinable air of class. Surely, the street began to say, she was the forerunner of an 'in' group which would soon discover us and then we would all make money and turn into background to be glanced at. So some thought. But when I saw her, knowing better, I saw a host of other women—pretty, cared-for women—walking silently with her, rank on rank, women for whom nothing will ever quite add up. Every day, I guess, she wrote down her same old problems, in different combinations, and every day she got the same sum.

Suddenly, one day, she was before me. 'My month is up. It's been a wonderful experience.'

'I'm glad you thought so.'

We both sat smoking thoughtfully, occasionally glancing at each other. I knew her room had been rifled twice by thieves and that she could not sleep at night when the baby-sitter baby-sat. The faces of those Greek waiters would, I imagine, press on her memory forever. If the world is one, what was the great secret to make those faces accessible to her own self? The answer had escaped her.

'It's been a great experience,' she repeated, smiling brightly, her mouth like painted wood, like a wound.

A voice, another voice, in that same room is talking . . . Vinnie Partham and her husband Charles? It can't be.

'. . . I knew it was safe to see you again when Carole confessed that she had and you were all right. Carole's gone into social work, she got over her crisis whatever it was, and now we're thinking it's time you got through with yours, for you may not be able even to imagine how desolate Denis still is, Maureen. Can you, can you?

'We thought for a long time the problem was sexual but then we decided you were out to destroy us and then we thought your mental condition would make you incapable of anything at all by way of job or friends. But all our theories are wrong, I guess.'

On she goes, with Charles dozing in his chair after the manner of British detectives in the movies, who look dumb but are actually intelligent and wide awake, solving the perfect crime, the difference being that Charles really is both half-asleep and stupid and has never been known to solve anything at all. Vinnie knows it. The phrases have started looping out of her mouth like a backward spaghetti-eating process. Luminous cords reach up and twine with others, grow into patterns of thought. The patterns are dollar signs. I see them forming.

'With Denis having no heart for the estate affairs, what chance have Charles and I for the consideration he's always extended us? And if you think who, out of a perfect grab bag of women now getting interested, he might actually take it in his head to marry—'

Something dawns on me. Vinnie Partham is never going to stop talking!

I stare at her and stare, feeling cross-eyed with wonder and helpless and hypnotized, like someone watching a force in nature take its course. What can I do? She'll be there forever.

'I'm tired, Vinnie,' I tell her. 'I'm terribly tired.'

They melt away, her mouth is moving still. . . . Did I dream them? Do women still wear long beads? Can it really be they wanted me back for nothing but money? No, money is their name for something else. That chill place, that flaw in the world fabric, that rift in the Partham world about the size of Grand Canyon —they keep trying to fill it, trying to fill it, on and on, throwing everything in to fill it up. It was why Denis wanted me.

Oh, my poor children! Could they ever grow up to look like Aunt Vinnie and Uncle Charles?

At the thought of them, so impossibly beautiful, so possibly doomed, noises like cymbals crash in my ears, my eyes blur and stream. If my visitors were there I could not see them.

But they must be gone, I think, squinting around the room, if they were there at all. If they were ever alive at all . . . if they were ever anywhere.

Through all this, night was coming on; and summer—that, too, was coming on. Vinnie and Charles were dreams. But love is real.

I first saw Michel when he came to the photographer's shop for some application-size pictures. He was thin and ravaged, frowning, worried, *pressé*. I had learned to do routine requests as Mr Massino was often away taking wedding pictures or attending occasions such as christenings and retirements. Mr Massimo thrived on the events, which included fancy food and lots to drink and dressed-up women. It was when Michel and I got in the semi-dark of the photographing room together that I received his full impact. I stirred about among the electrical cords, the lamp stands; I wielded the heavy-headed camera into focus; I directed his chin to lift, then found him in the lenses, dark and straight. Indian blood? I snapped the shutter.

He said he was new in the neighbourhood, lived up the street, and would come back next day to see the proofs.

But I passed him again, not an hour later, on my way home. He was sitting outdoors at the pizza parlor talking volubly to the street cleaner who had stopped there for a beer. He saw me pass, go in my building, and I felt his regard in my senses.

Who was he? What would he do?

Something revolutionary was what I felt to be in his bones. Political? Then he would be making contacts and arguing for the liberation of the province.

I was wrong. No passion for Quebec but the rent of an empty barbershop was what had brought him there, one on the lower floor of a small building with a tree in front. He was going to put in one of those shops that sold hippie costumes, Indian shirts, long skirts, built-up shoes, some papier-mâché decorators' items, and some artwork. This would incidentally give him a chance to show some of his own artwork, which had failed to interest the uptown galleries. He was going to leave the barber chairs and mirrors, using them all as décor, props, for the things he sold.

He told me all this when he came to see the photographs. Mr Massimo had gone to a reunion of retired hockey players. Michel looked over the proofs and selected one. He wanted it enlarged, a glossy finish he could reproduce to make ads for his shop. He was telling me how in some detail and I thought that a little more would find him back in Mr Massimo's darkroom, doing it for himself.

'I hope your business works,' I said.

The day before, skirting about among the photographic equipment, we had entangled face to face among some electrical cords, which we had methodically to unplug and unwind to find release from a near embrace. Now, he turned from a scrutiny of his own face to a minute examination of my own.

'If you hope so, then you think it could. *Vous le croyez*, eh?'

'*Moi? J'en sais pas, moi.* What does it matter?'

His elbow skidded on the desk. His face beetled into my own. It was his eyes that were compelling, better than good, making an importance out of themselves, out of my opinions, out of me.

'Your thinking so . . . why, that's strong. You have power. *Vous êtes formidable.* That's it, madame. *C'est ça.*'

A tilt of the head, an inch or two more, and our mouths, once more, might have closed together. My own was dry and thirsty, it woke to tell me so.

He straightened, gathered up his pictures, and neatly withdrew. His step left the doorway empty. I filled the order blank carefully.

It had turned much warmer and after work now I sat on the balcony with the windows open behind me and what I had to call curtains even stirred a bit, a dreamy lift of white in a dusk-softened room. I was moved to put a Mozart record on. I remembered that Mozart had died a pauper and been carried by cart to the outskirts of Vienna in winter and dumped in a hole. To me, that made the music tenderer still. Michel! From the day I'd seen him a private tower had begun to rise about me; its walls were high and strong. I might gnaw toast and jam and gulp coffee standing in my closet-sized kitchen, wriggle into the same old skirt, blouse, sweater, and leather coat (now put away), and walk to work, a drab, square-set, middle-aged woman going past at an accustomed time, but, within myself, a princess came to life and she leaned from high-set window sills. Did Michel know, she kept on asking, as she studied the horizon and admired the blue sky.

He passed the shop twice, once for his enlargement, once to talk; he went by daily on the street. A stir went up about his footsteps. He would change us all. At the very least, I reasoned, he kept my mind off the divorce papers.

One night there was a shouting in the street and a clang of fire engines. I rushed to the balcony and saw where it was: Michel's, up on the corner. A moment later I heard his voice from the shadows, down in the street below, and I hurried to let him in, climbed back with him unseen, opened my door to him for the first time.

He had caught my hands, holding them together in his own, in a grasp warm with life. His explanations blundered out . . . coming back from somewhere, tired, smoking in bed, fell asleep, the stuff collected for the shop catching fire. 'But if they know I'm back, that I set the fire, then the shop will never open. Nobody saw me. Nobody. Will you let me stay? Will you?'

'Smoking in bed, that's crazy.'

'Correct.' He leaned wearily toward me, smiling, sallow cheekbone sharp against my cheek, then holding closer, his mouth searching, and mine searching, too, finding and holding. The will to have him there was present already: it was he who'd set the tower up, and furnished it, for this very thing, for his refuge. But for such enfoldment as we found, the binding of my thought was needed, the total silent agreement that a man and woman make, a matched pattern for love. The heart of his gamble was there. He won it.

Left alone while I worked, Michel sat in the corner and read all day.

'What do you do when you're not reading?' I would ask, coming in from work.

'Je pense.'

'A quoi?'

'A toi.'

'Tu pense à toi. Et tu le sais bien, toi.' I was putting down my bag, I was emptying my grocery sack, but always I was turning to him. And I was moving to him. And he to me.

There was talk on the street of the fire, how the whole house had almost caught, and about the strange absence of Michel, whose inflammable junk had caused it all, but for whom nobody had an address or a telephone number.

One day I came from work and the tower stood empty. I knew it before I opened the door; Michel was gone. Through empty space I moved at last to the balcony and there up the street a taxi was pulling up before the rooming house. Out stepped Michel, as though home from a long journey, even carrying a suitcase! For the first time, it seemed, he was discovering his charred quarters, calling out the building superintendent, raising a commotion on the steps for all to hear. Quarreling, shouting, and multiple stories—they went on till nightfall.

Michel tried, at least, to collect the insurance on damages to his property. I never knew for certain if it worked. He said that it did, but he seldom told the truth. It was not his nature. If the fire was accidental, he escaped without a damage suit. But if he did it on purpose, hoping for insurance money to buy a better class of junk, and counting in advance on me to shelter him, then he was a fool to take so much risk. But why begin to care? Liar, cheat, thief, and lover—he stays unchanged and unexplaining. We have never had it out, or made it up, or parted. The tower is dissolving as his presence fades from it, leaves as water drying from a fabric, thread by thread. It floats invisible, but at least undestroyed. I felt this even after his shop opened—even after a dark young girl with long hair and painted eyes came to work there.

He comes and goes. Summer is over. *C'est ça.*

To think the Parthams ever let go is a serious mistake.

I recall a winter night now, lost in driving snow. There is a madness of snow, snow everywhere, teeming, shifting, lofty as curtains in the dream of a mad opera composer, cosmic, yet intimate as a white thread caught in an eyelash. The buses stall on Côte des Neiges: there is a moaning impotence among them, clouds of exhaust and a dimming of their interior lights as they strain to ascend the long hill, but some already have given up and stand dull and bulky, like great animals in herd awaiting some imminent extinction. The passengers file from them. I toil upward from Sherbrooke through a deepening tunnel, going toward the hospital. My son's name has become the sound of my heart. The receptionist directs me to a certain floor.

I think of everyone inside as infinitely small because of the loftiness of the night outside, its mad whiteness, chaotic motion, insatiable teeming. The hospital is a toy with lights, set on the mountain, a bump like a sty. The night will go on forever, it seems to be saying; it will if it wants to and it wants to and it will. So I (human) am small beneath this lofty whim. Perhaps I think like this to minimize the dull yet painful edge of guilt. My son may die; I abandoned him years ago. Yet he wants to see me, and they have thought that he should be permitted to. And I have thought,

Why think it is good of them, nobody is that bad? and Why think it is good of me either, no mother is that cold? (But they might have been, and so might I.) Under realms of snow I progress at snail pace, at bug size, proving that great emotion lives in tiny hearts. On the floor, a passing aide, little as a sparrow, indicates the way. At the desk, a nurse, a white rabbit, peers at a note that has been left. Snow at the window, furious, boils. 'Mr Partham regrets he cannot be here. . . . You wish to see the boy? It's number ten.' Swollen feelings lift me down the corridor. I crack the door. 'Mother, is that you?' 'Yes.' 'I knew you'd come.' 'Of course, I came.' His hand, at last, is mine. It is the world.

Night after night I come, through blizzard, through ice and sleet, once in a silenced snow-bound city walking more than half the way into a wind with a $-40°$ wind chill against my face, ant-sized under the glitter of infinite distances, at home with the derision of stars. So I push my stubborn nightly way. 'You are sleepy,' says Mr Massimo at work. 'Why are you so sleepy lately?' I tell him nothing. I can't for yawning.

Bundled in my dark coat, in the shadowy corridor, I sometimes, when Parthams are present, doze. They walk around me, speak to one another, are aware of my presence but do not address it. Denis, once, appearing, stands directly before me; when I lift my head our eyes meet, and they speak and we know it, yes we do. But there is a wall clear as glass between us and if we should fling ourselves through it, it would smash and let us through. Still, we would hurtle past each other. For the glass has a trick in it, a layer at the centre seems to place us face to face but really angles us apart. He knows it, I know it. We have been shown the diagram. He nods and turns away.

Several times I see his wife. I recognize her by the newspaper photographs. She is quietly, expensively dressed, with soft shining hair, the one he should have married in the first place. I do not need the coat. Sitting there in the warm room, why do I wear it? The minute the Parthams leave, I shed it. Its dropping from me is real but a symbol also. I am in the room in the same moment.

We hardly talk at all, my son and I. We know everything there is to know already. I sense the hour, almost the minute, when his health begins to flow back again.

We are sitting together on a Saturday morning. Dawn has come to a clear spotless frozen sky. Smoke from the glittering city beneath us, laid out below the windows, turns white. It plumes upward in windless purity. I have been here through the night. We are talking. It is the last time; I know that, too. The needles have been withdrawn from his arms. Soon the morning routine of the hospital will begin to crackle along the hallway and some of it will enter here. I look around me and see what things the Parthams have filled the room with—elegant little transistor radios, sports books and magazines, a lovely tropical aquarium where brilliant fish laze fin and tail among the shells and water plants. Nothing has been spared. He is smiling. His nightmare with the long name—peritonitis—is over. His gaze is weak no longer, but has entered sunlight, is penetrating and can judge.

So much drops away from a sick person; ideas, personality, ambition, interests—all the important Partham baggage. When the pressures of the body turn eccentric and everything is wrong, then they find their secret selves. But once the Partham body returns, it's a sign of laziness not to look around, discriminate, find life 'interesting', activities 'meaningful'; it would be silly not to be a Partham since a Partham is what one so fortunately is. 'Can I come to find you when I get out of here?' my son begs. 'Can I, Mother?' 'Of course, of course, you can.' 'I promise to.' I am on my way, before the nurse comes with her thermometers or the elephantine gray wagon of trays lumbers in. I am into my coat again, retreating from the Partham gaze. But my insect heart in the unlikely shape of me, almost permanently bent, like a wind-blasted tree, by the awful humours of that phenomenal winter, is incandescent with inextinguishable joy. He will live, he will live. Nothing, nobody, can take that away. I stumble, slip, list, slide down frozen pavements, squeaking over surfaces of impacted snow. In the crystal truth of the day world, the night is done. He will live.

(His name? My son's name? I won't tell you.)

I wing, creep, crawl, hop—what you will—back into my world.

Denis, eventually, seeks me. He comes to find me. A third Partham. I see him at a street end.

He is gray; the winter has made everybody's skin too pale, except, I suppose, the habitual skiers who go up on peaks where the sun strikes. Denis used to ski, but not this year. There he is, gray at the street's end. All has been blown bare and lean by the awful winter. He is himself lean, clean, with gray overcoat and Persian lamb hat, darker gray trousers, brown, fur-lined gloves. 'Maureen? Can we go somewhere? Just have a coffee . . . talk a little?' We go to the 'bar-b-q' place. It's impersonal there, being on a busy corner; at the pizza restaurant they would want to know who Denis was, and why he'd come and do I have a new boy friend. Also Michel might pass by.

'He thinks you saved him,' Denis tells me. 'For all I know, it's true. But he thinks more than that. He's obsessed with you . . . can't talk of anything else at times. I don't know what to do, Maureen. He thinks you're a saint, something more than human. Your visits were only half-real to him. They were like—appearances, apparitions.' He stops, hesitant. It is the appealing, unsure Denis, absent, I imagine, for most of the time, that I see again as I saw him when we first met, seeking out my eyes, begging for something.

'It must be easy to disillusion him,' I say. 'You, of all people, could best do that.'

'Oh, he's heard all the facts. Not so much from me, mind you . . .'

From his grandmother, I think, and his grandfather and his aunts. Heard all those things he 'ought to know'.

'I didn't know you went there so often, sat for whole nights at a time, it seems.' He is speaking out of a deepening despair, floundering.

'But you saw me there.'

'I know, but I—'

'Didn't you know I loved him, too?'

'You loved—' At the mention of love, his face seems about to shatter into a number of different planes, a face in an abstract painting, torn against itself. 'To me your love was always defective. You—Maureen, when we were first married, I would think over and over, Now is forever; forever is now. Why did you destroy it all? It frightens me to think of you sitting, in the dark hours, with that boy. You could have pinched his life out like a match.'

'I wouldn't do that, Denis. I couldn't hurt what's hurt already.' I could have told him what light is like, as I had seen its illusion that day before his accident, how the jagged force tore into my smoothly surfaced vision. I had tried to tell him once; he thought I was raving. Later I smashed a set of his mother's china, and tore up a beautifully tiled wall with my nails, until they split and the blood ran down.

'I thought I had some force that would help him. That's not why I went but it's why I stayed.'

'It might not have worked,' Denis reflected. 'He might have died anyway.'

'Then you could have blamed me,' I pointed out. 'Then I could have been a witch, an evil spirit.'

'I don't know why you ever had to turn into a spirit at all! Just a woman, a wife, a mother, a human being—! That's all I ever wanted!'

'Believe me, Denis,' I said, *'I don't know either.'*

We'd had it out that way, about a million times. Making no real progress, returning to our old familiar dead end, our hovel, which, in a way, was the only home we had.

I was then inspired to say: 'It just may be, Denis, that if I'd never left, I could never have returned, and if I never had returned, it just may be that he would never have lived, he would have died, Denis, think of that, he would be dead.'

For a moment, I guess he did consider it. His face turned to mine, mouth parted. He slipped little by little into the idea, let himself submerge within it. I will say for Denis: at least, he did that. 'The doctors,' he said at last, 'they were terribly good, you know. The major credit,' he said, finishing his coffee, 'goes to them.'

'Undoubtedly,' I said. He had come to the surface, and turned back into a Partham again.

It had been a clear, still, frozen afternoon when we met, but holding just that soft touch of violet which said that winter would at last give over. Its grip was terrible, but a death grip no longer.

I tried to recall my old routine, to show my Partham side myself. 'I imagine he will find new interests, once he gets more active. He won't think so much about me. But, Denis, if he does want to hold on to something about me, can't you let him?'

'I wouldn't dream of stopping him. It's a matter of proportion, that's all.' He was pulling on his beautiful gloves. 'He's practically made a religion of you.'

As we were going out, I saw it all more clearly and began to laugh. 'Then that's your answer, Denis.'

'What is?'

'If I'm to be a "religion", then there are ways of handling me.

Confine me to one hour a week, on Sunday morning. . . I need never get out of bounds. Don't worry about him, Denis. He's a Partham, after all.'

'Maureen? You're bitter, aren't you? People *have* to live, even Parthams. Life *has* to go on.'

We were standing outside by then, at the intersection with my street. He wouldn't enter there, I thought; it was not in accord with his instincts to do so.

'I'm not bitter,' I said. 'I'm helpless.'

'It didn't have to be that way.'

It was like a final exchange; it had a certain ring. He leaned to touch my face, then drew back, moving quickly away, not looking behind.

And now I am waiting for the fourth visitor, my son. I think I will see him, at some street corner, seeking me, find him waiting for me in the pizza shop, hear a voice say, 'Mother? I promised you. . . .' And before I know it, I will have said his name. . . .

I am waiting still.

Mr Massimo, one day, leans at me over his portrait camera. 'I hear you were married to a wealthy man in Westmount,' he says.

'I am a princess in a silver tower,' I reply. 'Golden birds sing to me. I drift around in a long silk gown. What about you?'

'My father was Al Capone's brother. We rode around when young in a secondhand Rolls-Royce with a crest of the House of Savoia painted on the door. Then we got run out of Italy. The family took another name.' He is smiling at me. It is not the story that reaches me, true or false, but the outpouring sun of Italy.

'You'll get me fired,' I tell Michel.

'Come work for me,' he says. 'You can tell fortunes in the back. I'll make you rich.

He's using me again, working in collage—photography plus painting—he needs Mr Massimo's darkroom. I telephone him when Mr Massimo is gone and he comes to run a print through, or make an enlargement. When this phase passes, he will go again.

But he creates a picture before that, half-photo, half-drawing. He photographs my hands over a blood-red glass globe, lighted from within. I think the fortune-telling idea has given him the image. He makes the light strong; the veins of my hands stand out in great detail; the bones are almost X-ray visible. 'Let me wash my hands,' I say, because dirt shows under the nail tips. 'No, I like it that way, leave it.' So it stays. Watching Michel, I forget to feel anything else, and he is busy timing, setting, focusing. So the hands stay in place as my feelings rock with the sense of the light, and when he shuts it off, finished, we lock the shop up and go home together. Only the next day do I notice that my palm is burned so badly I have to bandage it and go for days in pain. Is the pain for Michel? Damn Michel! The pain is mine, active and virulent. It is mine alone.

The picture, with its background drawing of a woman in evening dress turned from a doorway, and its foreground of hands across a glowing glass, catches on. Michel has others in his package, but none is so popular as this one. He makes enlargements, sells them, makes others, sells those. They go out by the hundreds.

'What is it you carry? *Qu'est-ce que tu as*, Maureen?' Now he is after me, time and again, intense, vulpine, impossible, begging from doorways, brushing my shoulder as he passes in the dark. '*Qu'est-ce tu as?*'

'I don't know. *Que t'importe, toi?*'

Among his pictures, a U.S. distributor chooses this one, one of three. If I go to certain shops in New York where cheap exotic dress is sold, incense, and apartment decorations of the lowlier sort, bought for their grass-scented pads by homosexual pairs, or by students or young lovers, or by adventurous young people with litte taste for permanence, I will see that picture somewhere among them, speaking its silent language. I will look at my hands, see the splash of red that lingers. The world over, copies of it will eventually stick up out of garbage cans, or will be left in vacated apartments. Held to the wall by one thumb tack, it will hang above junk not thought to be worth moving. It celebrates life as fleeting as a dance.

Yet it was created, it happened, and that, in its smallness must pass for everything—must, in this instance, stand for all.

MAVIS GALLANT

The Moslem Wife

In the south of France, in the business room of a hotel quite near to the house where Katherine Mansfield (whom no one in this hotel had ever heard of) was writing 'The Daughters of the Late Colonel', Netta Asher's father announced that there would never be a man-made catastrophe in Europe again. The dead of that recent war, the doomed nonsense of the Russian Bolsheviks had finally knocked sense into European heads. What people wanted now was to get on with life. When he said 'life', he meant its commercial business.

Who would have contradicted Mr Asher? Certainly not Netta. She did not understand what he meant quite so well as his French solicitor seemed to, but she did listen with interest and respect, and then watched him signing papers that, she knew, concerned her for life. He was renewing the long lease her family held on the Hotel Prince Albert and Albion. Netta was then eleven. One hundred years should at least see her through the prime of life, said Mr Asher, only half jokingly, for of course he thought his seed was immortal.

Netta supposed she might easily live to be more than a hundred—at any rate, for years and years. She knew that her father did not want her to marry until she was twenty-six and that she was then supposed to have a pair of children, the elder a boy. Netta and her father and the French lawyer shook hands on the lease, and she was given her first glass of champagne. The date on the bottle was 1909, for the year of her birth. Netta bravely pronounced the wine delicious, but her father said she would know much better vintages before she was through.

Netta remembered the handshake but perhaps not the terms. When the lease had eighty-eight years to run, she married her first cousin, Jack Ross, which was not at all what her father had

had in mind. Nor would there be the useful pair of children—Jack couldn't abide them. Like Netta he came from a hotelkeeping family where the young were like blight. Netta had up to now never shown a scrap of maternal feeling over anything, but Mr Asher thought Jack might have made an amiable parent—a kind one, at least. She consoled Mr Asher on one count, by taking the hotel over in his lifetime. The hotel was, to Netta, a natural life; and so when Mr Asher, dying, said, 'She behaves as I wanted her to,' he was right as far as the drift of Netta's behaviour was concerned but wrong about its course.

The Ashers' hotel was not down on the seafront, though boats and sea could be had from the south-facing rooms.

Across a road nearly empty of traffic were handsome villas, and behind and to either side stood healthy olive trees and a large lemon grove. The hotel was painted a deep ochre with white trim. It had white awnings and green shutters and black iron balconies as lacquered and shiny as Chinese boxes. It possessed two tennis courts, a lily pond, a sheltered winter garden, a formal rose garden, and trees full of nightingales. In the summer dark, *belles-de-nuit* glowed pink, lemon, white, and after their evening watering they gave off a perfume that varied from plant to plant and seemed to match the petals' coloration. In May the nights were dense with stars and fireflies. From the rose garden one might have seen the twin pulse of cigarettes on a balcony, where Jack and Netta sat drinking a last brandy-and-soda before turning in. Most of the rooms were shuttered by then, for no traveller would have dreamed of being south except in winter. Jack and Netta and a few servants had the whole place to themselves. Netta would hire workmen and have the rooms that needed it repainted—the blue cardroom, and the red-walled bar, and the white dining room, where Victorian mirrors gave back glossy walls and blown curtains and nineteenth-century views of the Ligurian coast, the work of an Asher great-uncle. Everything upstairs and down was soaked and wiped and polished, and even the pictures were relentlessly washed with soft cloths and ordinary laundry soap. Netta also had the boiler overhauled and the linen mended and new monograms embroidered and the looking glasses resilvered and the shutters taken off their hinges and scraped and made spruce green again for next year's sun to fade, while Jack talked about decorators and expert gardeners and even wrote to some, and banged tennis balls against the large new garage. He also read books and translated poetry for its own sake and practiced playing the clarinet. He had studied music once, and still thought that an important life, a musical life, was there in the middle distance. One summer, just to see if he could, he translated pages of St John Perse, which were as blank as the garage wall to Netta, in any tongue.

Netta adored every minute of her life, and she thought Jack had a good life too, with nearly half the year for the pleasures that suited him. As soon as the grounds and rooms and cellar and roof had been put to rights, she and Jack packed and went travelling somewhere. Jack made the plans. He was never so cheerful as when buying Baedekers and dragging out their stickered trunks. But Netta was nothing of a traveller. She would have been glad to see the same sun rising out of the same sea from the window every day until she died. She loved Jack, and what she liked best after him was the hotel. It was a place where, once, people had come to die of tuberculosis, yet it held no trace or feeling of danger. When Netta walked with her workmen through sheeted summer rooms, hearing the cicadas and hearing Jack start, stop, start some deeply alien music (alien even when her memory automatically gave her a composer's name), she was reminded that here the dead had never been allowed to corrupt the living; the dead had been dressed for an outing and removed as soon as their first muscular stiffness relaxed. Some were wheeled out in chairs, sitting, and some reclined on portable cots, as if merely resting.

That is why there is no bad atmosphere here, she would say to herself. Death has been swept away, discarded. When the shutters are closed on a room, it is for sleep or for love. Netta could think this easily because neither she nor Jack was ever sick. They knew nothing about insomnia, and they made love every day of their lives—they had married in order to be able to.

Spring had been the season for dying in the old days. Invalids who had struggled through the dark comfort of winter took fright as the night receded. They felt without protection. Netta knew about this, and about the difference between darkness and brightness, but neither affected her. She was not afraid of death or of the dead—they were nothing but cold, heavy furniture. She could have tied jaws shut and weighted eyelids with native instinctiveness, as other women were born knowing the temperature for an infant's milk.

'There are no ghosts,' she could say, entering the room where her mother, then her father had died. 'If there were, I would know.'

Netta took it for granted, now she was married, that Jack felt as she did about light, dark, death, and love. They were as alike in some ways (none of them physical) as a couple of twins, spoke much the same language in the same accents, had the same jokes —mostly about other people—and had been together as much as their families would let them for most of their lives. Other men seemed dull to Netta—slower, perhaps, lacking the spoken shorthand she had with Jack. She never mentioned this. For one thing, both of them had the idea that, being English, one must not say too much. Born abroad, they worked hard at an Englishness that was innocently inaccurate, rooted mostly in attitudes. Their families had been innkeepers along this coast for a century, even before Dr James Henry Bennet had discovered 'the Genoese Rivieras'. In one of his guides to the region, a 'Mr Ross' is mentioned as a hotel owner who will accept English bank checks, and there is a 'Mr Asher', reliable purveyor of English groceries. The most trustworthy shipping agents in 1860 are the Montale brothers, converts to the Anglican Church, possessors of a British *laissez-passer* to Malta and Egypt. These families, by now plaited like hair, were connections of Netta's and Jack's and still in business from beyond Marseilles to Genoa. No wonder that other men bored her, and that each thought the other both familiar and unique. But of course they were unalike too. When once someone asked them, 'Are you related to Montale, the poet?' Netta answered, 'What poet?' and Jack said, 'I wish we were.'

There were no poets in the family. Apart from the great-uncle who had painted landscapes, the only person to try anything peculiar had been Jack, with his music. He had been allowed to study, up to a point; his father had been no good with hotels—had been a failure, in fact, bailed out four times by his cousins, and it had been thought, for a time, that Jack Ross might be a dunderhead too. Music might do him; he might not be fit for anything else.

Information of this kind about the meaning of failure had been gleaned by Netta years before, when she first became aware of her little cousin. Jack's father and mother—the commercial blunderers—had come to the Prince Albert and Albion to ride out a crisis. They were somewhere between undischarged bankruptcy and annihilation, but one was polite: Netta curtsied to her aunt and uncle. Her eyes were on Jack. She could not read yet, though she could sift and classify attitudes. She drew near him, sucking her lower lip, her hands behind her back. For the first time she was conscious of the beauty of another child. He was younger than Netta, imprisoned in a portable-fence arrangement in which he moved tirelessly, crabwise, hanging on a barrier he could easily have climbed. He was as fair as his Irish mother and sunburned a deep brown. His blue gaze was not a baby's—it was too challenging. He was naked except for shorts that were large and seemed about to fall down. The sunburn, the undress were because his mother was reckless and rather odd. Netta—whose mother was perfect—wore boots, stockings, a longsleeved frock, and a white sun hat. She heard the adults laugh and say that Jack looked like a prizefighter. She walked around his prison, staring, and the blue-eyed fighter stared back.

The Rosses stayed for a long time, while the family sent telegrams and tried to raise money for them. No one looked after Jack much. He would lie on a marble step of the staircase watching the hotel guests going into the cardroom or the dining room. One night, for a reason that remorse was to wipe out in a minute, Netta gave him such a savage kick (though he was not really in her way) that one of his legs remained paralyzed for a long time.

'*Why* did you do it?' her father asked her—this in the room where she was shut up on bread and water. Netta didn't know. She loved Jack, but who would believe it now? Jack learned to walk, then to run, and in time to ski and play tennis; but her lifelong gift to him was a loss of balance, a sudden lopsided bend of a knee. Jack's parents had meantime been given a small hotel to run at Bandol. Mr Asher, responsible for a bank loan, kept an eye on the place. He went often, in a hotel car with a chauffeur, Netta perched beside him. When, years later, the families found out that the devoted young cousins had become lovers, they separated them without saying much. Netta was too independent to be dealt with. Besides, her father did not want a rift; his wife had died, and he needed Netta. Jack, whose claim on music had been the subject of teasing until now, was suddenly sent to study in England. Netta saw that he was secretly dismayed. He wanted to be almost anything as long as it was impossible, and then only as an act of grace. Netta's father did think it was his duty to tell her that marriage was, at its best, a parched arrangement, intolerable without a flow of golden guineas and fresh blood. As cousins, Jack and Netta could not bring each other anything except stale money. Nothing stopped them: they were married four months after Jack became twenty-one. Netta heard someone remark at her wedding, 'She doesn't need a husband,' meaning perhaps the practical, matter-of-fact person she now seemed to be. She did have the dry, burned-out look of someone turned inward. Her dark eyes glowed out of a thin face. She had the shape of a girl of fourteen. Jack, who was large, and fair, and who might be stout at forty if he wasn't careful, looked exactly his age, and seemed quite ready to be married.

Netta could not understand why, loving Jack as she did, she did not look more like him. It had troubled her in the past when they did not think exactly the same thing at almost the same time. During the secret meetings of their long engagement she had noticed how even before a parting they were nearly apart—they had begun to 'unmesh', as she called it. Drinking a last drink, usually in the buffet of a railway station, she would see that Jack was somewhere else, thinking about the next-best thing to Netta. The next-best thing might only be a book he wanted to finish reading, but it was enough to make her feel exiled. He often told Netta, 'I'm not holding on to you. You're free,' because he thought it needed saying, and of course he wanted freedom for himself. But to Netta 'freedom' had a cold sound. Is that what I do want, she would wonder. Is that what I think he should offer? Their partings were often on the edge of parting forever, not just because Jack had said or done or thought the wrong thing but because between them they generated the high sexual tension that leads to quarrels. Barely ten minutes after agreeing that no one in the world could possibly know what they knew, one of them, either one, could curse the other out over something trivial. Yet they were, and remained, much in love, and when they were apart Netta sent him letters that were almost despairing with enchantment.

Jack answered, of course, but his letters were cautious. Her exploration of feeling was part of an unlimited capacity she seemed to have for passionate behaviour, so at odds with her appearance, which had been dry and sardonic even in childhood. Save for an erotic sentence or two near the end (which Netta read first) Jack's messages might have been meant for any girl cousin he particularly liked. Love was memory, and he was no good at the memory game; he needed Netta there. The instant he saw her he knew all he had missed. But Netta, by then, felt forgotten, and she came to each new meeting aggressive and hurt, afflicted with the physical signs of her doubts and injuries—cold sores, rashes, erratic periods, mysterious temperatures. If she tried to discuss it he would say, 'We aren't going over all that again, are we?' Where Netta was concerned he had settled for the established faith, but Netta, who had a wilder, more secret God, wanted a prayer a minute, not to speak of unending miracles and revelations.

When they finally married, both were relieved that the strain of partings and of tense disputes in railway stations would come to a stop. Each privately blamed the other for past violence, and both believed that once they could live openly, without interference, they would never have a disagreement again. Netta did not want Jack to regret the cold freedom he had vainly tried to offer her. He must have his liberty, and his music, and other people, and, oh, anything he wanted—whatever would stop him from saying he was ready to let her go free. The first thing Netta did was to make certain they had the best room in the hotel. She had never actually owned a room until now. The private apartments of her family had always been surrendered in a crisis: everyone had packed up and moved as beds were required. She and Jack were hopelessly untidy, because both had spent their early years moving down hotel corridors, trailing belts and raincoats, with tennis shoes hanging from knotted strings over their shoulders, their arms around books and sweaters and gray flannel bundles. Both had done lessons in the corners of lounges, with cups and glasses rattling, and other children running, and English voices louder than anything. Jack, who had been vaguely educated, remembered his boarding schools as places where one had a permanent bed. Netta chose for her marriage a south-facing room with a large balcony and an awning of dazzling white. It was furnished with lemonwood that had been brought to the Riviera by Russians for their own villas long before. To the lemonwood Netta's mother had added English chintzes; the result, in Netta's eyes, was not bizarre but charming. The room was deeply mirrored; when the shutters were closed on hot afternoons a play of light became as green as a forest on the walls, and as blue as seawater in the glass. A quality of suspension, of disbelief in gravity, now belonged to Netta. She became tidy, silent, less introspective, as watchful and as reflective as her bedroom mirrors. Jack stayed as he was, luckily; any alteration would have worried her, just as a change in an often-read story will trouble a small child. She was intensely, almost unnaturally happy.

One day she overheard an English doctor, whose wife played bridge every afternoon at the hotel, refer to her, to Netta, as 'the little Moslem wife'. It was said affectionately, for the doctor liked her. She wondered if he had seen through walls and had watched her picking up the clothing and the wet towels Jack left strewn like clues to his presence. The phrase was collected and passed from mouth to mouth in the idle English colony. Netta, the last person in the world deliberately to eavesdrop (she lacked that sort of interest in other people), was sharp of hearing where her marriage was concerned. She had a special antenna for Jack, for his shades of meaning, secret intentions, for his innocent contradictions. Perhaps 'Moslem wife' meant several things, and possibly it was plain to anyone with eyes that Jack, without meaning a bit of harm by it, had a way with women. Those he attracted were a puzzling lot, to Netta. She had already catalogued them—elegant elderly parties with tongues like carving knives; gentle, clever girls who flourished on the unattainable; untouchable-daughter types, canny about their virginity, wondering if Jack would be father enough to justify the sacrifice. There was still another kind—tough, sunburned, clad in dark colours—who made Netta think in the vocabulary of horoscopes. Her gem—diamonds. Her colour—black. Her language—worse than Netta's. She noticed that even when Jack had no real use for a women he never made it apparent; he adopted anyone who took a liking to him. He assumed—Netta thought—a tribal, paternal air that was curious in so young a man. The plot of attraction interested him, no matter how it turned out. He was like someone reading several novels at once, or like someone playing simultaneous chess.

Netta did not want her marriage to become a world of stone. She said nothing except, 'Listen, Jack, I've been at this hotel business longer than you have. It's wiser not to be too pally with the guests.' At Christmas the older women gave him boxes of expensive soap. 'They must think someone around here wants a good wash,' Netta remarked. Outside their fenced area of private jokes and private love was a landscape too open, too light-drenched, for serious talk. And then, when? Jack woke up quickly and early in the morning and smiled as naturally as children do. He knew where he was and the day of the week and the hour. The best moment of the day was the first cigarette. When something bloody happened, it was never before six in the evening. At night he had a dark look that went with a dark mood, sometimes. Netta would tell him that she could see a cruise ship floating on the black horizon like a piece of the Milky Way, and she would get that look for an answer. But it never lasted. His memory was too short to let him sulk, no matter what fragment of night had crossed his mind. She knew, having heard other couples all her life, that at least she and Jack never made the conjugal sounds that passed for conversation and that might as well have been bow-wow and quack quack.

If, by chance, Jack found himself drawn to another woman, if the tide of attraction suddenly ran the other way, then he would discover in himself a great need to talk to his wife. They sat out on their balcony for much of one long night and he told her about his Irish mother. His mother's eccentricity—'Vera's dottiness', where the family was concerned—had kept Jack from taking anything seriously. He had been afraid of pulling her mad attention in his direction. Countless times she had faked tuberculosis and cancer and announced her own imminent death. A telephone call from a hospital had once declared her lost in a car crash. 'It's a new life, a new life,' her husband had babbled, coming away from the phone. Jack saw his father then as beautiful. Women are beautiful when they fall in love, said Jack; sometimes the glow will last a few hours, sometimes even a day or two.

'You know,' said Jack, as if Netta knew, 'the look of amazement on a girl's face . . .'

Well, that same incandescence had suffused Jack's father when he thought his wife had died, and it continued to shine until a taxi deposited dotty Vera with her cheerful announcement that she had certainly brought off a successful April Fool. After Jack's father died she became violent. 'Getting away from her was a form of violence in me,' Jack said. 'But I did it.' That was why he was secretive; that was why he was independent. He had never wanted any woman to get her hands on his life.

Netta heard this out calmly. Where his own feelings were concerned she thought he was making them up as he went along. The garden smelled coolly of jasmine and mimosa. She wondered who his new girl was, and if he was likely to blurt out a name. But all he had been working up to was that his mother—mad, spoiled, devilish, whatever she was—would need to live with Jack and Netta, unless Netta agreed to giving her an income. An income would let her remain where she was—at the moment, in a Rudolf Steiner community in Switzerland, devoted to medieval gardening and to getting the best out of Goethe. Netta's father's training prevented even the thought of spending the money in such a manner.

'You won't regret all you've told me, will you?' she asked. She saw that the new situation would be her burden, her chain, her mean little joke sometimes. Jack scarcely hesitated before saying that where Netta mattered he could never regret anything. But what really interested him now was his mother.

'Lifts give her claustrophobia,' he said. 'She mustn't be higher than the second floor.' He sounded like a man bringing a legal concubine into his household, scrupulously anxious to give all his women equal rights. 'And I hope she will make friends,' he said. 'It won't be easy, at her age. One can't live without them.' He probably meant that he had none. Netta had been raised not to expect to have friends: you could not run a hotel and have scores of personal ties. She expected people to be polite and punctual and to mean what they said, and that was the end of it. Jack gave his friendship easily, but he expected considerable diversion in return.

Netta said dryly, 'If she plays bridge, she can play with Mrs Blackley.' This was the wife of the doctor who had first said 'Moslem wife.' He had come down here to the Riviera for his wife's health; the two belonged to a subcolony of flat-dwelling expatriates. His medical practice was limited to hypochondriacs and rheumatic patients. He had time on his hands: Netta often saw him in the hotel reading room, standing, leafing—he took pleasure in handling books. Netta, no reader, did not like touching a book unless it was new. The doctor had a trick of speech Jack loved to imitate: he would break up his words with an extra syllable, some words only, and at that not every time. 'It is all a matter of stu-hyle,' he said, for 'style', or, Jack's favourite, 'Oh, well, in the end it all comes down to su-hex.' 'Uh-hebb and flo-ho of hormones' was the way he once described the behaviour of saints—Netta had looked twice at him over that. He was a firm agnostic and the first person from whom Netta heard there existed a magical Dr Freud. When Netta's father had died of pneumonia, the doctor's 'I'm su-horry, Netta' had been so heartfelt she could not have wished it said another way.

His wife, Georgina, could lower her blood pressure or stop her heartbeat nearly at will. Netta sometimes wondered why Dr Blackley had brought her to a soft climate rather than to the man at Vienna he so admired. Georgina was well enough to play fierce bridge, with Jack and anyone good enough. Her husband usually came to fetch her at the end of the afternoon when the players stopped for tea. Once, because he was obliged to return at once to a patient who needed him, she said, 'Can't you be competent about anything?' Netta thought she understood, then, his resigned repetition of 'It's all su-hex.' 'Oh, don't explain. You bore me,' said his wife, turning her back.

Netta followed him out to his car. She wore an India shawl that had been her mother's. The wind blew her hair; she had to hold it back. She said, 'Why don't you kill her?'

'I am not a desperate person,' he said. He looked at Netta, she looking up at him because she had to look up to nearly everyone except children, and he said, 'I've wondered why we haven't been to bed.'

'Who?' said Netta. 'You and your wife? Oh. You mean me.' She was not offended, she just gave the shawl a brusque tug and said, 'Not a hope. Never with a guest,' though of course that was not the reason.

'You might have to, if the guest were a maharaja,' he said, to make it all harmless. 'I am told it is pu-hart of the courtesy they expect.'

'We don't get their trade,' said Netta. This had not stopped her liking the doctor. She pitied him, rather, because of his wife, and because he wasn't Jack and could not have Netta.

'I do love you,' said the doctor, deciding finally to sit down in his car. 'Ee-nee-ormously.' She watched him drive away as if she loved him too, and might never see him again. It never crossed her mind to mention any of this conversation to Jack.

That very spring, perhaps because of the doctor's words, the hotel did get some maharaja trade—three little sisters with ebony curls, men's eyebrows, large heads, and delicate hands and feet. They had four rooms, one for their governess. A chauffeur on permanent call lodged elsewhere. The governess, who was Dutch, had a perfect triangle of a nose and said 'whom' for 'who', pronouncing it 'whum'. The girls were to learn French, tennis, and swimming. The chauffeur arrived with a hairdresser, who cut their long hair; it lay on the governess's carpet, enough to fill a large pillow. Their toe- and fingernails were filed to points and looked like kitten's teeth. They came smiling down the marble staircase, carrying new tennis rackets, wearing blue linen skirts and navy blazers. Mrs Blackley glanced up from the bridge game as they went by the cardroom. She had been one of those opposed to their having lessons at the English Lawn Tennis Club, for reasons that were, to her, perfectly evident.

She said, loudly, 'They'll have to be in white.'

'End whay, pray?' cried the governess, pointing her triangle nose.

'They can't go on the courts except in white. It is a private club. Entirely white.'

'Whum do they all think they are?' the governess asked, prepared to stalk on. But the girls, with their newly cropped heads, and their vulnerable necks showing, caught the drift and refused to go.

'Whom indeed,' said Georgina Blackley, fiddling with her bridge hand and looking happy.

'My wife's seamstress could run up white frocks for them in a minute,' said Jack. Perhaps he did not dislike children all that much.

'Whom could,' muttered Georgina.

But it turned out that the governess was not allowed to choose their clothes, and so Jack gave the children lessons at the hotel. For six weeks they trotted around the courts looking angelic in blue, or hopelessly foreign, depending upon who saw them. Of course they fell in love with Jack, offering him a passionate loyalty they had nowhere else to place. Netta watched the transfer of this gentle, anxious gift. After they departed, Jack was bad-tempered for several evenings and then never spoke of them again; they, needless to say, had been dragged from him weeping.

When this happened the Rosses had been married nearly five years. Being childless but still very loving, they had trouble deciding which of the two would be the child. Netta overheard 'He's a darling, but she's a sergeant major and no mistake. And so *mean*.' She also heard 'He's a lazy bastard. He bullies her. She's a fool.' She searched her heart again about children. Was it Jack or had it been Netta who had first said no? The only child she had ever admired was Jack, and not as a child but as a fighter, defying her. She and Jack were not the sort to have animal children, and Jack's dotty mother would probably soon be child enough for any couple to handle. Jack still seemed to adopt, in a tribal sense of his, half the women who fell in love with him. The only woman who resisted adoption was Netta—still burned-out, still ardent, in a manner of speaking still fourteen. His mother had turned up meanwhile, getting down from a train wearing a sly air of enjoying her own jokes, just as she must have looked on the day of the April Fool. At first she was no great trouble, though she did complain about an ulcerated leg. After years of pretending, she at last had something real. Netta's policy of silence made Jack's mother confident. She began to make a mockery of his music: 'All that money gone for nothing!' Or else, 'The amount we wasted on schools! The hours he's thrown away with his nose in a book. All that reading—if at least it had got him somewhere.' Netta noticed that he spent more time playing bridge and chatting to cronies in the bar now. She thought hard, and decided not to make it her business. His mother had once been pretty; perhaps he still saw her that way. She came of a ramshackle family with a usable past; she spoke of the Ashers and the Rosses as if she had known them when they were tinkers. English residents who had a low but solid barrier with Jack and Netta were fences-down with his mad mother: they seemed to take her at her own word when it was about herself. She began then to behave like a superior sort of guest, inviting large parties to her table for meals, ordering special wines and dishes at inconvenient hours, standing endless rounds of drinks in the bar.

Netta told herself, Jack wants it this way. It is his home too. She began to live a life apart, leaving Jack to his mother. She sat wearing her own mother's shawl, hunched over a new, modern adding machine, punching out accounts. 'Funny couple,' she heard now. She frowned, smiling in her mind; none of these people knew what bound them, or how tied they were. She had the habit of dodging out of her mother-in-law's parties by saying, 'I've got such an awful lot to do.' It made them laugh, because they thought this was Netta's term for slave-driving the servants. They thought the staff did the work, and that Netta counted the profits and was too busy with bookkeeping to keep an eye on Jack—who now, at twenty-six, was as attractive as he ever would be.

A woman named Iris Cordier was one of Jack's mother's new friends. Tall, loud, in winter dully pale, she reminded Netta of a blond penguin. Her voice moved between a squeak and a moo, and was a mark of the distinguished literary family to which her father belonged. Her mother, a Frenchwoman, had been in and out of nursing homes for years. The Cordiers haunted the Riviera, with Iris looking after her parents and watching their diets. Now she lived in a flat somewhere in Roquebrune with the survivor of the pair—the mother, Netta believed. Iris paused and glanced in the business room where Mr Asher had signed the hundred-year lease. She was on her way to lunch—Jack's mother's guest, of course.

'I say, aren't you Miss Asher?'

'I was.' Iris, like Dr Blackley, was probably younger than she looked. Out of her own childhood Netta recalled a desperate adolescent Iris with middle-aged parents clamped like handcuffs on her life. 'How is your mother?' Netta had been about to say 'How is Mrs Cordier?' but it sounded servile.

'I didn't know you knew her.'

'I remember her well. Your father too. He was a nice person.'

'And still is,' said Iris, sharply. 'He lives with me, and he always will. French daughters don't abandon their parents.' No one had ever sounded more English to Netta. 'And your father and mother?'

'Both dead now. I'm married to Jack Ross.'

'Nobody told me,' said Iris, in a way that made Netta think, Good Lord, Iris too? Jack could not possibly seem like a patriarchal figure where she was concerned; perhaps this time the game was reversed and Iris played at being tribal and maternal. The idea of Jack, or of any man, flinging himself on that iron bosom made Netta smile. As if startled, Iris covered her mouth. She seemed to be frightened of smiling back.

Oh, well, and what of it, Iris too, said Netta to herself, suddenly turning back to her accounts. As it happened, Netta was mistaken (as she never would have been with a bill). That day Jack was meeting Iris for the first time.

The upshot of these errors and encounters was an invitation to Roquebrune to visit Iris's father. Jack's mother was ruthlessly excluded, even though Iris probably owed her a return engagement because of the lunch. Netta supposed that Iris had decided one had to get past Netta to reach Jack—an inexactness if ever there was one. Or perhaps it was Netta Iris wanted. In that case the error became a farce. Netta had almost no knowledge of private houses. She looked around at something that did not much interest her, for she hated to leave her own home, and saw Iris's father, apparently too old and shaky to get out of his armchair. He smiled and he nodded, meanwhile stroking an aging cat. He said to Netta, 'You resemble your mother. A sweet woman. Obliging and quiet. I used to tell her that I longed to live in her hotel and be looked after.'

Not by me, thought Netta.

Iris's amber bracelets rattled as she pushed and pulled everyone through introductions. Jack and Netta had been asked to meet a young American Netta had often seen in her own bar, and a couple named Sandy and Sandra Braunsweg, who turned out to be Anglo-Swiss and twins. Iris's long arms were around them as she cried to Netta, 'Don't you know these babies?' They were, like the Rosses, somewhere in their twenties. Jack looked on, blue-eyed, interested, smiling at everything new. Netta supposed that she was now seeing some of the rather hard-up snobbish—snobbish what? 'Intelligumhen-sia,' she imagined Dr Blackley supplying. Having arrived at a word, Netta was ready to go home; but they had only just arrived. The American turned to Netta. He looked bored, and astonished by it. He needs the word for 'bored', she decided. Then he can go home, too. The Riviera was no place for Americans. They could not sit all day waiting for mail and the daily papers and for the clock to show a respectable drinking time. They made the best of things when they were caught with a house they'd been rash enough to rent unseen. Netta often had them then *en pension* for meals: a hotel dining room was one way of meeting people. They paid a fee to use the tennis courts, and they liked the bar. Netta would notice then how Jack picked up any accent within hearing.

Jack was now being attentive to the old man, Iris's father. Though this was none of Mr Cordier's business, Jack said, 'My wife and I are first cousins, as well as second cousins twice over.'

'You don't look it.'

Everyone began to speak at once, and it was a minute or two before Netta heard Jack again. This time he said, 'We are from a family of great. . . .' It was lost. What now? Great innkeepers? Worriers? Skinflints? Whatever it was, old Mr Cordier kept nodding to show he approved.

'We don't see nearly enough of young men like you,' he said.

'True!' said Iris loudly. 'We live in a dreary world of ill women down here.' Netta thought this hard on the American, on Mr Cordier, and on the male Braunsweg twin, but none of them looked offended. 'I've got no time for women,' said Iris. She slapped down a glass of whiskey so that it splashed, and rapped on a table with her knuckles. 'Shall I tell you why? Because women don't tick over. They just simply don't tick over.' No one disputed this. Iris went on: women were underinformed. One could have virile conversations only with men. Women were attached to the past through fear, whereas men had a fearless sense of history. 'Men tick,' she said, glaring at Jack.

'I am not attached to a past,' said Netta, slowly. 'The past holds no attractions.' She was not used to general conversation. She thought that every word called for consideration and for an answer. 'Nothing could be worse than the way we children were dressed. And our mothers—the hard waves of their hair, the white lips. I think of those pale profiles and I wonder if those women were ever young.'

Poor Netta, who saw herself as profoundly English, spread consternation by being suddenly foreign and gassy. She talked the English of expatriate children, as if reading aloud. The twins looked shocked. But she had appealed to the American. He sat beside her on a scuffed velvet sofa. He was so large that she slid an inch or so in his direction when he sat down. He was Sandra Braunsweg's special friend: they had been in London together. He was trying to write.

'What do you mean?' said Netta. 'Write what?'

'Well—a novel, to start,' he said. His father had staked him to one year, then another. He mentioned all that Sandra had borne with, how she had actually kicked and punched him to keep him from being too American. He had embarrassed her to death in London by asking a waitress, 'Miss, where's the toilet?'

Netta said, 'Didn't you mind being corrected?'

'Oh, no. It was just friendly.'

Jack meanwhile was listening to Sandra telling about her English forebears and her English education. 'I had many years of undeniably excellent schooling,' she said. 'Mitten Todd.'

'What's that?' said Jack.

'It's near Bristol. I met excellent girls from Italy, Spain. I took *him* there to visit,' she said, generously including the American. 'I said, "Get a yellow necktie." He went straight out and bought one. I wore a little Schiaparelli. Bought in Geneva but still a real . . . A yellow jacket over a gray . . . Well, we arrived at my excellent old school, and even though the day was drizzly I said, "Put the top of the car back." He did so at once, and then he understood. The interior of the car harmonized perfectly with the yellow and gray.' The twins were orphaned. Iris was like a mother.

'When Mummy died we didn't know where to put all the Chippendale,' said Sandra, 'Iris took a lot of it.'

Netta thought, She is so silly. How can he respond? The girl's dimples and freckles and soft little hands were nothing Netta could have ever described: she had never in her life thought a word like 'pretty'. People were beautiful or they were not. Her happiness had always been great enough to allow for despair. She knew that some people thought Jack was happy and she was not.

'And what made you marry your young cousin?' the old man boomed at Netta. Perhaps his background allowed him to ask impertinent questions; he must have been doing so nearly forever. He stroked his cat; he was confident. He was spokesman for a roomful of wondering people.

'Jack was a moody child and I promised his mother I would look after him,' said Netta. In her hopelessly un-English way she believed she had said something funny.

At eleven o'clock the hotel car expected to fetch the Rosses was nowhere. They trudged home by moonlight. For the last hour of the evening Jack had been skewered on virile conversations, first with Iris, then with Sandra, to whom Netta had already given 'Chippendale' as a private name. It proved that Iris was right about concentrating on men and their ticking—Jack even thought Sandra rather pretty.

'Prettier than me?' said Netta, without the faintest idea what she meant, but aware she had said something stupid.

'Not so attractive,' said Jack. His slight limp returned straight out of childhood. *She* had caused his accident.

'But she's not always clear,' said Netta. 'Mitten Todd, for example.'

'Who're you talking about?'

'Who are *you*?'

'Iris, of course.'

As if they had suddenly quarrelled they fell silent. In silence they entered their room and prepared for bed. Jack poured a whiskey, walked on the clothes he had dropped, carried his drink to the bathroom. Through the half-shut door he called suddenly, 'Why did you say that asinine thing about promising to look after me?'

'It seemed so unlikely, I thought they'd laugh.' She had a glimpse of herself in the mirrors picking up his shed clothes.

He said, 'Well, is it true?'

She was quiet for such a long time that he came to see if she was still in the room. She said, 'No, your mother never said that or anything like it.'

'We shouldn't have gone to Roquebrune,' said Jack. 'I think those bloody people are going to be a nuisance. Iris wants her father to stay here, with the cat, while she goes to England for a month. How do we get out of that?'

'By saying no.'

'I'm rotten at no.'

'I told you not to be too pally with women,' she said, as a joke again, but jokes were her way of having floods of tears.

Before this had a chance to heal, Iris's father moved in, bringing his cat in a basket. He looked at his room and said, 'Medium large.' He looked at his bed and said, 'Reasonably long.' He was, in short, daft about measurements. When he took books out of the reading room, he was apt to return them with 'This volume contains about 70,000 words' written inside the back cover.

Netta had not wanted Iris's father, but Jack had said yes to it. She had not wanted the sick cat, but Jack had said yes to that too. The old man, who was lost without Iris, lived for his meals. He would appear at the shut doors of the dining room an hour too early, waiting for the menu to be typed and posted. In a voice that matched Iris's for carrying power, he read aloud, alone: 'Consommé. Good Lord, again? Is there a choice between the fish and the cutlet? I can't possibly eat all of that. A bit of salad and a boiled egg. That's all I could possibly want.' That was rubbish, because Mr Cordier ate the menu and more, and if there were two puddings, or a pudding and ice cream, he ate both and asked for pastry, fruit, and cheese to follow. One day, after Dr Blackley had attended him for faintness, Netta passed a message on to Iris, who had been back from England for a fortnight now but seemed in no hurry to take her father away.

'Keith Blackley thinks your father should go on a diet.'

'He can't,' said Iris. 'Our other doctor says dieting causes cancer.'

'You can't have heard that properly,' Netta said.

'It is like those silly people who smoke to keep their figures,' said Iris. 'Dieting.'

'Blackley hasn't said he should smoke, just that he should eat less of everything.'

'My father has never smoked in his life,' Iris cried. 'As for his diet, I weighed his food out for years. He's not here forever. I'll take him back as soon as he's had enough of hotels.'

He stayed for a long time, and the cat did too, and a nuisance they both were to the servants. When the cat was too ailing to walk, the old man carried it to a path behind the tennis courts and put it down on the gravel to die. Netta came out with the old man's tea on a tray (not done for everyone, but having him out of the way was a relief) and she saw the cat lying on its side, eyes wide, as if profoundly thinking. She saw unlicked dirt on its coat and ants exploring its paws. The old man sat in a garden chair, wearing a panama hat, his hands clasped on a stick. He called, 'Oh, Netta, take her away. I am too old to watch anything die. I know what she'll do,' he said, indifferently, his voice falling as she came near. 'Oh, I know that. Turn on her back and give a shriek. I've heard it often.'

Netta disburdened her tray onto a garden table and pulled the tray cloth under the cat. She was angered at the haste and indecency of the ants. 'It would be polite to leave her,' she said. 'She doesn't want to be watched.'

'I always sit here,' said the old man.

Jack, making for the courts with Chippendale, looked as if the sight of the two conversing amused him. Then he understood and scooped up the cat and tray cloth and went away with the cat over his shoulder. He laid it in the shade of a Judas tree, and within an hour it was dead. Iris's father said, 'I've got no one to talk to here. That's my trouble. That shroud was too small for my poor Polly. Ask my daughter to fetch me.'

Jack's mother said that night, 'I'm sure you wish that I had a devoted daughter to take me away too.' Because of the attention given the cat she seemed to feel she had not been nuisance enough. She had taken to saying, 'My leg is dying before I am,' and imploring Jack to preserve her leg, should it be amputated, and make certain it was buried with her. She wanted Jack to be close by at nearly any hour now, so that she could lean on him. After sitting for hours at bridge she had trouble climbing two flights of stairs; nothing would induce her to use the lift.

'Nothing ever came of your music,' she would say, leaning on him. 'Of course, you have a wife to distract you now. I needed a daughter. Every woman does.' Netta managed to trap her alone, and forced her to sit while she stood over her. Netta said, 'Look,

Aunt Vera, I forbid you, I absolutely forbid you, do you hear, to make a nurse of Jack, and I shall strangle you with my own hands if you go on saying nothing came of his music. You are not to say it in my hearing or out of it. Is that plain?'

Jack's mother got up to her room without assistance. About an hour later the gardener found her on a soft bed of wallflowers. 'An inch to the left and she'd have landed on a rake,' he said to Netta. She was still alive when Netta knelt down. In her fall she had crushed the plants, the yellow minted *girofleés de Nice*. Netta thought that she was now, at last, for the first time, inhaling one of the smells of death. Her aunt's arms and legs were turned and twisted; her skirt was pulled so that her swollen leg showed. It seemed that she had jumped carrying her walking stick—it lay across the path. She often slept in an armchair, afternoons, with one eye slightly open. She opened that eye now and, seeing she had Netta, said, 'My son.' Netta was thinking, I have never known her. And if I knew her, then it was Jack or myself I could not understand. Netta was afraid of giving orders, and of telling people not to touch her aunt before Dr Blackley could be summoned, because she knew that she had always been mistaken. Now Jack was there, propping his mother up, brushing leaves and earth out of her hair. Her head dropped on his shoulder. Netta thought from the sudden heaviness that her aunt had died, but she sighed and opened that one eye again, saying this time, 'Doctor?' Netta left everyone doing the wrong things to her dying—no, her murdered—aunt. She said quite calmly into a telephone, 'I'm afraid that my aunt must have jumped or fallen from the second floor.'

Jack found a letter on his mother's night table that began, 'Why blame Netta? I forgive.' At dawn he and Netta sat at a card table with yesterday's cigarettes still not cleaned out of the ashtray, and he did not ask what Netta had said or done that called for forgiveness. They kept pushing the letter back and forth. He would read it and then Netta would. It seemed natural for them to be silent. Jack had sat beside his mother for much of the night. Each of them then went to sleep for an hour, apart, in one of the empty rooms, just as they had done in the old days when their parents were juggling beds and guests and double and single quarters. By the time the doctor returned for his second visit Jack was neatly dressed and seemed wide awake. He sat in the bar drinking black coffee and reading a travel book of Evelyn Waugh's called *Labels*. Netta, who looked far more untidy and underslept, wondered if

Jack wished he might leave now, and sail from Monte Carlo on the Stella Polaris.

Dr Blackley said, 'Well, you are a dim pair. She is not in pu-hain, you know.' Netta supposed this was the roundabout way doctors have of announcing death, very like 'Her sufferings have ended.' But Jack, looking hard at the doctor, had heard another meaning. 'Jumped or fell,' said Dr Blackley. 'She neither fell nor jumped. She is up there enjoying a damned good thu-hing.'

Netta went out and through the lounge and up the marble steps. She sat down in the shaded room on the chair where Jack had spent most of the night. Her aunt did not look like anyone Netta knew, not even like Jack. She stared at the alien face and said, 'Aunt Vera, Keith Blackley says there is nothing really the matter. You must have made a mistake. Perhaps you fainted on the path, overcome by the scent of wallflowers. What would you like me to tell Jack?'

Jack's mother turned on her side and slowly, tenderly, raised herself on an elbow. 'Well, Netta,' she said, 'I daresay the fool is right. But as I've been given quite a lot of sleeping stuff, I'd as soon stay here for now.'

Netta said, 'Are you hungry?'

'I should very much like a ham sandwich on English bread, and about that much gin with a lump of ice.'

She began coming down for meals a few days later. They knew she had crept down the stairs and flung her walking stick over the path and let herself fall hard on a bed of wallflowers—had even plucked her skirt up for a bit of accuracy; but she was also someone returned from beyond the limits, from the other side of the wall. Once she said, 'It was like diving and suddenly realizing there was no water in the sea.' Again, 'It is not true that your life rushes before your eyes. You can see the flowers floating up to you. Even a short fall takes a long time.'

Everyone was deeply changed by this incident. The effect on the victim herself was that she got religion hard.

'We are all hopeless nonbelievers!' shouted Iris, drinking in the bar one afternoon. 'At least, I hope we are. But when I see you, Vera, I feel there might be something in religion. You look positively temperate.'

'I am allowed to love God, I hope,' said Jack's mother.

Jack never saw or heard his mother anymore. He leaned against the bar, reading. It was his favourite place. Even on the sunniest of afternoons he read by the red-shaded light. Netta was present only because she had supplies to check. Knowing she ought to keep out of this, she still said, 'Religion is more than love. It is supposed to tell you why you exist and what you are expected to do about it.'

'You have no religious feelings at all?' This was the only serious and almost the only friendly question Iris was ever to ask Netta.

'None,' said Netta. 'I'm running a business.'

'I love God as Jack used to love music,' said his mother. 'At least he said he did when we were paying for lessons.'

'Adam and Eve had God,' said Netta. 'They had nobody *but* God. A fat lot of good that did them.' This was as far as their dialectic went. Jack had not moved once except to turn pages. He read steadily but cautiously now, as if every author had a design on him. That was one effect of his mother's incident. The other was that he gave up bridge and went back to playing the clarinet. Iris hammered out an accompaniment on the upright piano in the old music room, mostly used for listening to radio broadcasts. She was the only person Netta had ever heard who could make Mozart sound like an Irish jig. Presently Iris began to say that it was time Jack gave a concert. Before this could turn into a crisis Iris changed her mind and said what he wanted was a holiday. Netta thought he needed something: he seemed to be exhausted by love, friendship, by being a husband, someone's son, by trying to make a world out of reading and sense out of life. A visit to England to meet some stimulating people, said Iris. To help Iris with her tiresome father during the journey. To visit art galleries and bookshops and go to concerts. To meet people. To talk.

This was a hot, troubled season, and many persons were planning journeys—not to meet other people but for fear of a war. The hotel had emptied out by the end of March. Netta, whose father had known there would never be another catastrophe, had her workmen come in, as usual. She could hear the radiators being drained and got ready for painting as she packed Jack's clothes. They had never been separated before. They kept telling each other that it was only for a short holiday—for three or four weeks. She was surprised at how neat marriage was, at how many years and feelings could be folded and put under a lid. Once, she went to the window so that he would not see her tears and think she was trying to blackmail him. Looking out, she noticed the American, Chippendale's lover, idly knocking a tennis ball against the garage, as Jack had done in the early summers of their life; he had come round to the hotel looking for a partner, but that season there were none. She suddenly knew to a certainty that if Jack were to die she would search the crowd of mourners for a man she could live with. She would not return from the funeral alone.

Grief and memory, yes, she said to herself, but what about three o'clock in the morning?

By June nearly everyone Netta knew had vanished, or, like the Blackleys, had started to pack. Netta had new tablecloths made, and ordered new white awnings, and two dozen rosebushes from the nursery at Cap Ferrat. The American came over every day and followed her from room to room, talking. He had nothing better to do. The Swiss twins were in England. His father, who had been backing his writing career until now, had suddenly changed his mind about it—now, when he needed money to get out of Europe. He had projects for living on his own, but they required a dose of funds. He wanted to open a restaurant on the Riviera where nothing but chicken pie would be served. Or else a vast and expensive café where people would pay to make their own sandwiches. He said that he was seeing the food of the future, but all that Netta could see was customers asking for their money back. He trapped her behind the bar and said he loved her; Netta made other women look like stuffed dolls. He could still remember the shock of meeting her, the attraction, the brilliant answer she had made to Iris about attachments to the past.

Netta let him rave until he asked for a loan. She laughed and wondered if it was for the chicken-pie restaurant. No—he wanted to get on a boat sailing from Cannes. She said, quite cheerfully, 'I can't be Venus and Barclays Bank. You have to choose.'

He said, 'Can't Venus ever turn up with a letter of credit?'

She shook her head. 'Not a hope.'

But when it was July and Jack hadn't come back, he cornered her again. Money wasn't in it now: his father had not only relented but had virtually ordered him home. He was about twenty-two, she guessed. He could still plead successfully for parental help and for indulgence from women. She said, no more than affectionately, 'I'm going to show you a very pretty room.'

A few days later Dr Blackley came alone to say goodbye.

'Are you really staying?' he asked.

'I am responsible for the last eighty-one years of this lease,' said Netta. 'I'm going to be thirty. It's a long tenure. Besides, I've got Jack's mother and she won't leave. Jack has a chance now to visit America. It doesn't sound sensible to me, but she writes encouraging him. She imagines him suddenly very rich and sending for her. I've discovered the limit of what you can feel about people. I've discovered something else,' she said abruptly. 'It is that sex and love have nothing in common. Only a coincidence, sometimes. You think the coincidence will go on and so you get married. I suppose that is what men are born knowing and women learn by accident.'

'I'm su-horry.'

'For God's sake, don't be. It's a relief.'

She had no feeling of guilt, only of amazement. Jack, as a memory, was in a restricted area—the tennis courts, the cardroom, the bar. She saw him at bridge with Mrs Blackley and pouring drinks for temporary friends. He crossed the lounge jauntily with a cluster of little dark-haired girls wearing blue. In the mirrored bedroom there was only Netta. Her dreams were cleansed of him. The looking glasses still held their blue-and-silver-water shadows, but they lost the habit of giving back the moods and gestures of a Moslem wife.

About five years after this, Netta wrote to Jack. The war had caught him in America, during the voyage his mother had so wanted him to have. His limp had kept him out of the Army. As his mother (now dead) might have put it, all that reading had finally got him somewhere: he had spent the last years putting out a two-pager on aspects of European culture—part of a scrupulous effort Britain was making for the West. That was nearly all Netta knew. A Belgian Red Cross official had arrived, apparently in Jack's name, to see if she was still alive. She sat in her father's business room, wearing a coat and a shawl because there was no way of heating any part of the hotel now, and she tried to get on with the letter she had been writing in her head, on and off, for many years.

'In June, 1940, we were evacuated,' she started, for the tenth or eleventh time. 'I was back by October. Italians had taken over the hotel. They used the mirror behind the bar for target practice.

Oddly enough it was not smashed. It is covered with spiderwebs, and the bullet hole is the spider. I had great trouble over Aunt Vera, who disappeared and was found finally in one of the attic rooms.

'The Italians made a pet of her. Took her picture. She enjoyed that. Everyone who became thin had a desire to be photographed, as if knowing they would use this intimidating evidence against those loved ones who had missed being starved. Guilt for life. After an initial period of hardship, during which she often had her picture taken at her request, the Italians brought food and looked after her, more than anyone. She was their mama. We were annexed territory and in time we had the same food as the Italians. The thin pictures of your mother are here on my desk.

'She buried her British passport and would never say where. Perhaps under the Judas tree with Mr Cordier's cat, Polly. She remained just as mad and just as spoiled, and that became dangerous when life stopped being ordinary. She complained about me to the Italians. At that time a complaint was a matter of prison and of death if it was made to the wrong person. Luckily for me, there was also the right person to take the message.

'A couple of years after that, the Germans and certain French took over and the Italians were shut up in another hotel without food or water, and some people risked their well-being to take water to them (for not everyone preferred the new situation, you can believe me). When she was dying I asked her if she had a message for one Italian officer who had made such a pet of her and she said, "No, why?" She died without a word for anybody. She was buried as "Rossini", because the Italians had changed people's names. She had said she was French, a Frenchwoman named Ross, and so some peculiar civil status was created for us—the two Mrs Rossinis.

'The records were topsy-turvy; it would have meant going to the Germans and explaining my dead aunt was British, and of course I thought I would not. The death certificate and permission to bury are for a Vera Rossini. I have them here on my desk for you with her pictures.

'You are probably wondering where I have found all this writing paper. The Germans left it behind. When we were being shelled I took what few books were left in the reading room down to what used to be the wine cellar and read by candlelight. You are probably wondering where the candles came from. A long story. I even have paint for the radiators, large buckets that have never been opened.

'I live in one room, my mother's old sitting room. The business room can be used but the files have gone. When the Italians were here your mother was their mother, but I was not their Moslem wife, although I still had respect for men. One yelled ''*Luce, luce*'', because your mother was showing a light. She said, ''Bugger you, you little toad.'' He said, ''Granny, I said '*luce*' not '*Duce*'.''

'Not long ago we crept out of our shelled homes, looking like cave dwellers. When you see the hotel again, it will be functioning. I shall have painted the radiators. Long shoots of bramble come in through the cardroom windows. There are drifts of leaves in the old music room and I saw scorpions and heard their rustling like the rustle of death. Everything that could have been looted has gone. Sheets, bedding, mattresses. The neighbours did quite a lot of that. At the risk of their lives. When the Italians were here we had rice and oil. Your mother, who was crazy, used to put out grains to feed the mice.

'When the Germans came we had to live under Vichy law, which meant each region lived on what it could produce. As ours produces nothing, we got quite thin again. Aunt Vera died plump. Do you know what it means when I say she used to complain about me?

'Send me some books. As long as they are in English. I am quite sick of the three other languages in which I've heard so many threats, such boasting, such a lot of lying.

'For a time I thought people would like to know how the Italians left and the Germans came in. It was like this: They came in with the first car moving slowly, flying the French flag. The highest-ranking French official in the region. Not a German. No, just a chap getting his job back. The Belgian Red Cross people were completely uninterested and warned me that no one would ever want to hear.

'I suppose that you already have the fiction of all this. The fiction must be different, oh very different, from Italians sobbing with homesickness in the night. The Germans were not real, they were specially got up for the events of the time. Sat in the white dining room, eating with whatever plates and spoons were not broken or looted, ate soups that were mostly water, were forbidden to complain. Only in retreat did they develop faces and I noticed then that some were terrified and many were old. A radio broadcast from some untouched area advised the local population not to attack them as they retreated, it would make wild animals of them. But they were attacked by some young boys shooting out of a window and eight hostages were taken, including the son of the man who cut the maharaja's daughters' black hair, and they were shot and left along the wall of a café on the more or less Italian side of the border. And the man who owned the café was killed too, but later, by civilians—he had given names to the Gestapo once, or perhaps it was something else. He got on the wrong side of the right side at the wrong time, and he was thrown down the deep gorge between the two frontiers.

'Up in one of the hill villages Germans stayed till no one was alive. I was at that time in the former wine cellar, reading books by candlelight.

'The Belgian Red Cross team found the skeleton of a German deserter in a cave and took back the helmet and skull to Knokke-le-Zoute as souvenirs.

'My war has ended. Our family held together almost from the Napoleonic adventures. It is shattered now. Sentiment does not keep families whole—only mutual pride and mutual money.'

This true story sounded so implausible that she decided never to send it. She wrote a sensible letter asking for sugar and rice and for new books; nothing must be older than 1940.

Jack answered at once: there were no new authors (he had been asking people). Sugar was unobtainable, and there were queues for rice. Shoes had been rationed. There were no women's stockings but lisle, and the famous American legs looked terrible. You could not find butter or meat or tinned pineapple. In restaurants, instead of butter you were given miniature golf balls of cream cheese. He supposed that all this must sound like small beer to Netta.

A notice arrived that a CARE package awaited her at the post office. It meant that Jack had added his name and his money to a mailing list. She refused to sign for it; then she changed her mind and discovered it was not from Jack but from the American she had once taken to such a pretty room. Jack did send rice and sugar and delicious coffee but he forgot about books. His letters followed; sometimes three arrived in a morning. She left them sealed for days. When she sat down to answer, all she could remember were implausible things.

Iris came back. She was the first. She had grown puffy in England—the result of drinking whatever alcohol she could get her hands on and grimly eating her sweets allowance: there would be that much less gin and chocolate for the Germans if ever they landed. She put her now wide bottom on a comfortable armchair—one of the few chairs the first wave of Italians had not burned with cigarettes or idly hacked at with daggers—and said Jack had been living with a woman in America and to spare the gossip had let her be known as his wife. Another Mrs Ross? When Netta discovered it was dimpled Chippendale, she laughed aloud.

'I've seen them,' said Iris. 'I mean I saw them together. King Charles and a spaniel. Jack wiped his feet on her.'

Netta's feelings were of lightness, relief. She would not have to tell Jack about the partisans hanging by the neck in the arches of the Place Masséna at Nice. When Iris had finished talking, Netta said, 'What about his music?'

'I don't know.'

'How can you not know something so important?'

'Jack had a good chance at things, but he made a mess of everything,' said Iris. 'My father is still living. Life really is too incredible for some of us.'

A dark girl of about twenty turned up soon after. Her costume, a gray dress buttoned to the neck, gave her the appearance of being in uniform. She unzipped a military-looking bag and cried, in an unplaceable accent, '*Ha*llo, *ha*llo, Mrs Ross? A few small gifts for you,' and unpacked a bottle of Haig, four tins of corned beef, a jar of honey, and six pairs of American nylon stockings, which Netta had never seen before, and were as good to have under a mattress as gold. Netta looked up at the tall girl.

'Remember? I was the middle sister. With,' she said gravely, 'the typical middle-sister problems.' She scarcely recalled Jack, her beloved. The memory of Netta had grown up with her. 'I remember you laughing,' she said, without loving that memory. She was a severe, tragic girl. 'You were the first adult I ever heard laughing. At night in bed I could hear it from your balcony. You sat smoking with, I suppose, your handsome husband. I used to laugh just to hear you.'

She had married an Iranian journalist. He had discovered that political prisoners in the United States were working under lamentable conditions in tin mines. President Truman had sent them there. People from all over the world planned to unite to get them out. The girl said she had been to Germany and to Austria, she had visited camps, they were all alike, and that was already the past, and the future was the prisoners in the tin mines.

Netta said, 'In what part of the country are these mines?'

The middle sister looked at her sadly and said, 'Is there more than one part?'

For the first time in years, Netta could see Jack clearly. They were silently sharing a joke; he had caught it too. She and the girl lunched in a corner of the battered dining room. The tables were scarred with initials. There were no tablecloths. One of the great-uncle's paintings still hung on a wall. It showed the Quai Laurenti, a country road alongside the sea. Netta, who had no use for the past, was discovering a past she could regret. Out of a dark, gentle silence—silence imposed by the impossibility of telling anything real—she counted the cracks in the walls. When silence failed she heard power saws ripping into olive trees and a lemon grove. With a sense of deliverance she understood that soon there would be nothing left to spoil. Her great-uncle's picture, which ought to have changed out of sympathetic magic, remained faithful. She regretted everything now, even the three anxious little girls in blue linen. Every calamitous season between then and now seemed to descend directly from Georgina Blackley's having said 'white' just to keep three children in their place. Clad in buttoned-up gray, the middle sister now picked at corned beef and said she had hated her father, her mother, her sisters, and most of all the Dutch governess.

'Where is she now?' said Netta.

'Dead, I hope.' This was from someone who had visited camps. Netta sat listening, her cheek on her hand. Death made death casual: she had always known. Neither the vanquished in their flight nor the victors returning to pick over rubble seemed half so vindictive as a tragic girl who had disliked her governess.

Dr Blackley came back looking positively cheerful. In those days men still liked soldiering. It made them feel young, if they needed to feel it, and it got them away from home. War made the break few men could make on their own. The doctor looked years younger, too, and very fit. His wife was not with him. She had survived everything, and the hardships she had undergone had completely restored her to health—which had made it easy for her husband to leave her. Actually, he had never gone back, except to wind up the matter.

'There are things about Georgina I respect and admire,' he said, as husbands will say from a distance. His war had been in Malta. He had come here, as soon as he could, to the shelled, gnawed, tarnished coast (as if he had not seen enough at Malta) to ask Netta to divorce Jack and to marry him, or live with him—anything she wanted, on any terms.

But she wanted nothing—at least, not from him.

'Well, one can't defeat a memory,' he said. 'I always thought it was mostly su-hex between the two of you.'

'So it was,' said Netta. 'So far as I remember.'

'Everyone noticed. You would vanish at odd hours. Dis-huppear.'

'Yes, we did.'

'You can't live on memories,' he objected. 'Though I respect you for being faithful, of course.'

'What you are talking about is something of which one has no specific memory,' said Netta. 'Only of seasons. Places. Rooms. It is as abstract to remember as to read about. That is why it is boring in talk except as a joke, and boring in books except for poetry.'

'You never read poetry.'

'I do now.'

'I guessed that,' he said.

'That lack of memory is why people are unfaithful, as it is so curiously called. When I see closed shutters I know there are lovers behind them. That is how the memory works. The rest is just convention and small talk.'

'Why lovers? Why not someone sleeping off the wine he had for lunch?'

'No. Lovers.'

'A middle-aged man cutting his toenails in the bathtub,' he said with unexpected feeling. 'Wearing bifocal lenses so that he can see his own feet.'

'No, lovers. Always.'

He said, 'Have you missed him?'

'Missed who?'

'Who the bloody hell are we talking about?'

'The Italian commander billeted here. He was not a guest. He was here by force. I was not breaking a rule. Without him I'd have perished in every way. He may be home with his wife now. Or in that fortress near Turin where he sent other men. Or dead.' She looked at the doctor and said, 'Well, what would you like me to do? Sit here and cry?'

'I can't imagine you with a brute.'

'I never said that.'

'Do you miss him still?'

'The absence of Jack was like a cancer which I am sure has taken root, and of which I am bound to die,' said Netta.

'You'll bu-hury us all,' he said, as doctors tell the condemned.

'I haven't said I won't.' She rose suddenly and straightened her skirt, as she used to do when hotel guests became pally. 'Conversation over,' it meant.

'Don't be too hard on Jack,' he said.

'I am hard on myself,' she replied.

After he had gone he sent her a parcel of books, printed on grayish paper, in warped wartime covers. All of the titles were, to Netta, unknown. There was *Fireman Flower* and *The Horse's Mouth* and *Four Quartets* and *The Stuff to Give the Troops* and *Better Than a Kick in the Pants* and *Put Out More Flags*. A note added that the next package would contain Henry Green and Dylan Thomas. She guessed he would not want to be thanked, but she did so anyway. At the end of her letter was 'Please remember, if you mind too much, that I said no to you once before.' Leaning on the bar, exactly as Jack used to, with a glass of the middle sister's drink at hand, she opened *Better Than a Kick in the Pants* and read, '. . . two Fascists came in, one of them tall and thin and tough looking; the other smaller, with only one arm and an empty sleeve pinned up to his shoulder. Both of them were quite young and wore black shirts.'

Oh, thought Netta, I am the only one who knows all this. No one will ever realize how much I know of the truth, the truth, the truth, and she put her head on her hands, her elbows on the scarred bar, and let the first tears of her after-war run down her wrists.

The last to return was the one who should have been first. Jack wrote that he was coming down from the north as far as Nice by bus. It was a common way of travelling and much cheaper than by train. Netta guessed that he was mildly hard up and that he had saved nothing from his war job. The bus came in at six, at the foot of the Place Masséna. There was a deep-blue late-afternoon sky and pale sunlight. She could hear birds from the public gardens nearby. The Place was as she had always seen it, like an elegant drawing room with a blue ceiling. It was nearly empty. Jack looked out on this sunlighted, handsome space and said, 'Well, I'll just leave my stuff at the bus office, for the moment' —perhaps noticing that Netta had not invited him anywhere. He placed his ticket on the counter, and she saw that he had not come from far away: he must have been moving south by stages. He carried an aura of London pub life; he had been in London for weeks.

A frowning man hurrying to wind things up so he could have his first drink of the evening said, 'The office is closing and we don't keep baggage here.'

'People used to be nice,' Jack said.

'Bus people?'

'Just people.'

She was hit by the sharp change in his accent. As for the way of speaking, which is something else again, he was like the heir to great estates back home after a Grand Tour. Perhaps the estates had run down in his absence. She slipped the frowning man a thousand francs, a new pastel-tinted bill, on which the face of a calm girl glowed like an opal. She said, 'We shan't be long.'

She set off over the Place, walking diagonally—Jack beside her, of course. He did not ask where they were headed, though he did make her smile by saying, 'Did you bring a car?', expecting one of the hotel cars to be parked nearby, perhaps with a driver to open the door; perhaps with cold chicken and wine in a hamper, too. He said, 'I'd forgotten about having to tip for every little thing.' He did not question his destination, which was no farther than a café at the far end of the square. What she felt at that instant was intense revulsion. She thought, I don't want him, and pushed away some invisible flying thing—a bat or a blown paper. He looked at her with surprise. He must have been wondering if hardship had taught Netta to talk in her mind.

This is it, the freedom he was always offering me, she said to herself, smiling up at the beautiful sky.

They moved slowly along the nearly empty square, pausing only when some worn-out Peugeot or an old bicycle, finding no other target, made a swing in their direction. Safely on the pavement, they walked under the arches where partisans had been hanged. It seemed to Netta the bodies had been taken down only a day or so before. Jack, who knew about this way of dying from hearsay, chose a café table nearly under a poor lad's bound, dangling feet.

'I had a woman next to me on the bus who kept a hedgehog all winter in a basketful of shavings,' he said. 'He can drink milk out of a wineglass.' He hesitated. 'I'm sorry about the books you asked for. I was sick of books by then. I was sick of rhetoric and culture and patriotic crap.'

'I suppose it is all very different over there,' said Netta.

'God, yes.'

He seemed to expect her to ask questions, so she said, 'What kind of clothes do they wear?'

'They wear quite a lot of plaids and tartans. They eat at peculiar hours. You'll see them eating strawberries and cream just when you're thinking of having a drink.'

She said, 'Did you visit the tin mines, where Truman sends his political prisoners?'

'*Tin* mines?' said Jack. 'No.'

'Remember the three little girls from the maharaja trade?'

Neither could quite hear what the other had to say. They were partially deaf to each other.

Netta continued softly, 'Now, as I understand it, she first brought an American to London, and then she took an Englishman to America.'

He had too much the habit of women, he was playing too close a game, to waste points saying, 'Who? What?'

'It was over as fast as it started,' he said. 'But then the war came and we were stuck. She became a friend,' he said. 'I'm quite fond of her'—which Netta translated as, 'It is a subterranean river that may yet come to light.' 'You wouldn't know her,' he said. 'She's very different now. I talked so much about the south, down here, she finally found some land going dirt cheap at Bandol. The mayor arranged for her to have an orchard next to her property, so she won't have neighbours. It hardly cost her anything. He said to her, "You're very pretty." '

'No one ever had a bargain in property because of a pretty face,' said Netta.

'Wasn't it lucky,' said Jack. He could no longer hear himself, let alone Netta. 'The war was unsettling, being in America. She minded not being active. Actually she was using the Swiss passport, which made it worse. Her brother was killed over Bremen. She needs security now. In a way it was sorcerer and apprentice between us, and she suddenly grew up. She'll be better off with a roof over her head. She writes a little now. Her poetry isn't bad,' he said, as if Netta had challenged its quality.

'Is she at Bandol now, writing poetry?'

'Well, no.' He laughed suddenly. 'There isn't a roof yet. And, you know, people don't sit writing that way. They just think they're going to.'

'Who has replaced you?' said Netta. 'Another sorcerer?'

'Oh, *he* . . . he looks like George II in a strong light. Or like Queen Anne. Queen Anne and Lady Mary, somebody called them.' Iris, that must have been. Queen Anne and Lady Mary wasn't bad—better than King Charles and his spaniel. She was beginning to enjoy his story. He saw it, and said lightly, 'I was too preoccupied with you to manage another life. I couldn't see myself going on and on away from you. I didn't want to grow middle-aged at odds with myself.'

But he had lost her; she was enjoying a reverie about Jack now, wearing one of those purple sunburns people acquire at golf. She saw him driving an open car, with large soft freckles on his purple skull. She saw his mistress's dog on the front seat and the dog's ears flying like pennants. The revulsion she felt did not lend distance but brought a dreamy reality closer still. He must be thirty-four now, she said to herself. A terrible age for a man who has never imagined thirty-four.

'Well, perhaps you have made a mess of it,' she said, quoting Iris.

'What mess? I'm here. *He*—'

'Queen Anne?'

'Yes, well, actually Gerald is his name; he wears nothing but brown. Brown suit, brown tie, brown shoes. I said, "*He* can't go to Mitten Todd. He won't match." '

'Harmonize,' she said.

'That's it. Harmonize with the—'

'What about Gerald's wife? I'm sure he has one.'

'Lucretia.'

'No, really?'

'On my honour. When I last saw them they were all together, talking.'

Netta was remembering what the middle sister had said about laughter on the balcony. She couldn't look at him. The merest crossing of glances made her start laughing rather wildly into her hands. The hysterical quality of her own laughter caught her in midair. What were they talking about? He hitched his chair nearer and dared to take her wrist.

'Tell me, now,' he said, as if they were to be two old confidence men getting their stories straight. 'What about you? Was there ever . . .' The glaze of laughter had not left his face and voice. She saw that he would make her his business, if she let him. Pulling back, she felt another clasp, through a wall of fog. She groped for this other, invisible hand, but it dissolved. It was a lost, indifferent hand; it no longer recognized her warmth. She understood: He is dead . . . Jack, closed to ghosts, deaf to their voices, was spared this. He would be spared everything, she saw. She envied him his imperviousness, his true unhysterical laughter.

Perhaps that's why I kicked him, she said. I was always jealous. Not of women. Of his short memory, his comfortable imagination. And I am going to be thirty-seven and I have a dark, an accurate, a deadly memory.

He still held her wrist and turned it another way, saying, 'Look, there's paint on it.'

'Oh, God, where is the waiter?' she cried, as if that were the one important thing. Jack looked his age, exactly. She looked like a burned-out child who had been told a ghost story. Desperately seeking the waiter, she turned to the café behind them and saw the last light of the long afternoon strike the mirror above the bar—a flash in a tunnel; hands juggling with fire. That unexpected play, at a remove, borne indoors, displayed to anyone who could stare without blinking, was a complete story. It was the brightness on the looking glass, the only part of a life, or a love, or a promise, that could never be concealed, changed, or corrupted.

Not a hope, she was trying to tell him. He could read her face now. She reminded herself, If I say it, I am free. I can finish painting the radiators in peace. I can read every book in the world. If I had relied on my memory for guidance, I would never have crept out of the wine cellar. Memory is what ought to prevent you from buying a dog after the first dog dies, but it never does. It should at least keep you from saying yes twice to the same person.

'I've always loved you,' he chose to announce—it really was an announcement, in a new voice that stated nothing except facts.

The dark, the ghosts, the candlelight, her tears on the scarred bar—*they* were real. And still, whether she wanted to see it or not, the light of imagination danced all over the square. She did not dare to turn again to the mirror, lest she confuse the two and forget which light was real. A pure white awning on a cross street seemed to her to be of indestructible beauty. The window it sheltered was hollowed with sadness and shadow. She said with the same deep sadness, 'I believe you.' The wave of revulsion receded, sucked back under another wave—a powerful adolescent craving for something simple, such as true love.

Her face did not show this. It was set in adolescent stubbornness, and this was one of their old, secret meetings when, sullen and hurt, she had to be coaxed into life as Jack wanted it lived. It was the same voyage, at the same rate of speed. The Place seemed to her to be full of invisible traffic—first a whisper of tires, then a faint, high screeching, then a steady roar. If Jack heard anything, it could be only the blood in the veins and his loud, happy thought. To a practical romantic like Jack, dying to get Netta to bed right away, what she was hearing was only the uh-hebb and flo-ho of hormones, as Dr Blackley said. She caught a look of amazement on his face: *Now* he knew what he had been deprived of. *Now* he remembered. It had been Netta, all along.

Their evening shadows accompanied them over the long square. 'I still have a car,' she remarked. 'But no petrol. There's a train.' She did keep on hearing a noise, as of heavy traffic rushing near and tearing away. Her own quiet voice carried across it, saying, 'Not a hope.' He must have heard that. Why, it was as loud as a shout. He held her arm lightly. He was as buoyant as morning. This *was* his morning—the first light on the mirror, the first cigarette. He pulled her into an archway where no one could see. What could I do, she asked her ghosts, but let my arm be held, my steps be guided?

Later, Jack said that the walk with Netta back across the Place Masséna was the happiest event of his life. Having no reliable counter-event to put in its place, she let the memory stand.

SHIRLEY FAESSLER

A Basket of Apples

This morning Pa had his operation. He said I was not to come for at least two or three days, but I slipped in anyway and took a look at him. He was asleep, and I was there only a minute before I was hustled out by a nurse.

'He looks terrible, nurse. Is he all right?'

She said he was fine. The operation was successful, there were no secondaries, instead of a bowel he would have a colostomy, and with care should last another—

Colostomy. The word had set up such a drumming in my ears that I can't be sure now whether she said another few years or another five years. Let's say she said five years. If I go home and report this to Ma she'll fall down in a dead faint. She doesn't even know he's had an operation. She thinks he's in the hospital for a rest, a check-up. Nor did we know—my brother, my sister, and I—that he'd been having a series of X-rays.

'It looks like an obstruction in the lower bowel,' he told us privately, 'and I'll have to go in the hospital for a few days to find out what it's all about. Don't say anything to Ma.'

'I have to go in the hospital,' he announced to Ma the morning he was going in.

She screamed.

'Just for a little rest, a check-up,' he went on, patient with her for once.

He's always hollering at her. He scolds her for a meal that isn't to his taste, finds fault with her housekeeping, gives her hell because her hair isn't combed in the morning and sends her back to the bedroom to tidy herself.

But Ma loves the old man. 'Sooner a harsh word from Pa than a kind one from anyone else,' she says.

'You're not to come and see me, you hear?' he cautioned her

the morning he left for the hospital. 'I'll phone you when I'm coming out.'

I don't want to make out that my pa's a beast. He's not. True, he never speaks an endearing word to her, never praises her. He loses patience with her, flies off the handle and shouts. But Ma's content. Poor man works like a horse, she says, and what pleasures does he have. 'So he hollers at me once in a while, I don't mind. God give him the strength to keep hollering at me, I won't repine.'

Night after night he joins his buddies in the back room of an ice-cream parlour on Augusta Avenue for a glass of wine, a game of klaberjass, pinochle, dominoes: she's happy he's enjoying himself. She blesses him on his way out. 'God keep you in good health and return you in good health.'

But when he is home of an evening reading the newspaper and comes across an item that engages his interest, he lets her in on it too. He shows her a picture of the Dionne quintuplets and explains exactly what happened out there in Callander, Ontario. This is a golden moment for her—she and Pa sitting over a newspaper discussing world events. Another time he shows her a picture of the Irish Sweepstakes winner. He won a hundred and fifty thousand, he tells her. She's entranced. *Mmm-mm-mm!* What she couldn't do with that money. They'd fix up the bathroom, paint the kitchen, clean out the backyard. *Mmm-mm-mm!* Pa says if we had that kind of money we could afford to put a match to a hundred-dollar bill, set fire to the house and buy a new one. She laughs at his wit. He's so clever, Pa. Christmas morning King George VI is speaking on the radio. She's rattling around in the kitchen, Pa calls her to come and hear the King of England. She doesn't understand a word of English, but pulls up a chair and sits listening. 'He stutters,' says Pa. This she won't believe. A king? Stutters? But if Pa says so it must be true. She bends an ear to the radio. Next day she has something to report to Mrs Oxenberg, our next-door neighbour.

I speak of Pa's impatience with her; I get impatient with her too. I'm always at her about one thing and another, chiefly about the weight she's putting on. Why doesn't she cut down on the bread, does she have to drink twenty glasses of tea a day? No wonder her feet are sore, carrying all that weight. (My ma's a short woman a little over five feet and weighs almost two hundred pounds.) 'Go ahead, keep getting fatter,' I tell her. 'The way you're going you'll never be able to get into a decent dress again.'

But it's Pa who finds a dress to fit her, a Martha Washington Cotton size 52, which but for the length is perfect for her. He finds a shoe she can wear, Romeo Slippers with elasticized sides. And it's Pa who gets her to soak her feet, then sits with them in his lap scraping away with a razor blade at the calluses and corns.

Ma is my father's second wife, and our stepmother. My father, now sixty-three, was widowed thirty years ago. My sister was six at the time, I was five, and my brother four when our mother died giving birth to a fourth child who lived only a few days. We were shunted around from one family to another who took us in out of compassion, till finally my father went to a marriage broker and put his case before him. He wanted a woman to make a home for his three orphans. An honest woman with a good heart, these were the two and only requirements. The marriage broker consulted his lists and said he thought he had two or three people who might fill the bill. Specifically, he had in mind a young woman from Russia, thirty years old, who was working without pay for relatives who had brought her over. She wasn't exactly an educated woman; in fact, she couldn't even read or write. As for honesty and heart, this he could vouch for. She was an orphan herself and as a child had been brought up in servitude.

Of the three women the marriage broker trotted out for him, my father chose Ma, and shortly afterward they were married.

A colostomy. So it is cancer. . . .

As of the second day Pa was in hospital I had taken to dropping in on him on my way home from work. 'Nothing yet,' he kept saying, 'maybe tomorrow they'll find out.'

After each of these visits, four in all, I reported to Ma that I had seen Pa. 'He looks fine. Best thing in the world for him, a rest in the hospital.'

'Pa's not lonesome for me?' she asked me once, and laughing, turned her head aside to hide her foolishness from me.

Yesterday Pa said to me, 'It looks a little more serious than I thought. I have to have an operation tomorrow. Don't say anything to Ma. And don't come here for at least two or three days.'

I take my time getting home. I'm not too anxious to face Ma —grinning like a monkey and lying to her the way I have been doing the last four days. I step into a hospital telephone booth to call my married sister. She moans. 'What are you going to say to Ma?' she asks.

I get home about half past six, and Ma's in the kitchen making a special treat for supper. A recipe given her by a neighbour and which she's recently put in her culinary inventory—pieces of cauliflower dipped in batter and fried in butter.

'I'm not hungry, Ma. I had something in the hospital cafeteria.' (We speak in Yiddish; as I mentioned before, Ma can't speak English.)

She continues scraping away at the cauliflower stuck to the bottom of the pan. (Anything she puts in a pan sticks.) 'You saw Pa?' she asks without looking up. Suddenly she thrusts the pan aside. 'The devil take it, I put in too much flour.' She makes a pot of tea, and we sit at the kitchen table drinking it. To keep from facing her I drink mine leafing through a magazine. I can hear her sipping hers through a cube of sugar in her mouth. I can feel her eyes on me. Why doesn't she ask me, How's Pa? Why doesn't she speak? She never stops questioning me when I come from hospital, drives me crazy with the same questions again and again. I keep turning pages, she's still sucking away at that cube of sugar—a maddening habit of hers. I look up. Of course her eyes are fixed on me, probing, searching.

I lash out at her. 'Why are you looking at me like that!'

Without answer she takes her tea and dashes it in the sink. She spits the cube of sugar from her mouth. (Thank God for that; she generally puts it back in the sugar bowl.) She resumes her place, puts her hands in her lap, and starts twirling her thumbs. No one in the world can twirl his thumbs as fast as Ma. When she gets them going they look like miniature windmills whirring around.

'She asks me why I'm looking at her like that,' she says, addressing herself to the twirling thumbs in her lap. 'I'm looking at her like that because I'm trying to read the expression in her face. She tells me Pa's fine, but my heart tells me different.'

Suddenly she looks up, and thrusting her head forward, splays her hands out flat on the table. She has a dark-complexioned strong face, masculine almost, and eyes so black the pupil is indistinguishable from the iris.

'Do you know who Pa is!' she says. 'Do you know who's lying in the hospital? I'll tell you who. The captain of our ship is lying in the hospital. The emperor of our domain. If the captain goes down, the ship goes with him. If the emperor leaves his throne, we can say good-bye to our domain. That's who's lying in the hospital. Now ask me why do I look at you like that.'

She breaks my heart. I want to put my arms around her, but I can't do it. We're not a demonstrative family, we never kiss, we seldom show affection. We're always hollering at each other. Less than a month ago I hollered at Pa. He had taken to dosing himself. He was forever mixing something in a glass, and I became irritated at the powders, pills, and potions lying around in every corner of the house like mouse droppings.

'You're getting to be a hypochondriac!' I hollered at him, not knowing what trouble he was in.

I reach out and put my hand over hers. 'I wouldn't lie to you, Ma. Pa's fine, honest to God.'

She holds her hand still a few seconds, then eases it from under and puts it over mine. I can feel the weight of her hand pinioning mine to the table, and in an unaccustomed gesture of tenderness we sit a moment with locked hands.

'You know I had a dream about Pa last night?' she says. 'I dreamt he came home with a basket of apples. I think that's a good dream?'

Ma's immigration to Canada had been sponsored by her Uncle Yankev. Yankev at the time he sent for his niece was in his mid-forties and had been settled a number of years in Toronto with his wife, Danyeh, and their six children. They made an odd pair, Yankev and Danyeh. He was a tall two-hundred-and-fifty-pound handsome man, and Danyeh, whom he detested, was a lackluster little woman with a pockmarked face, maybe weighing ninety pounds. Yankev was constantly abusing her. Old Devil, he called her to her face and in the presence of company.

Ma stayed three years with Yankev and his family, working like a skivvy for them and without pay. Why would Yankev pay his niece like a common servant? She was one of the family, she sat at table with them and ate as much as she wanted. She had a bed and even a room to herself, which she'd never had before. When Yankev took his family for a ride in the car to Sunnyside, she was included. When he bought ice-cream cones, he bought for all.

She came to Pa without a dime in her pocket.

Ma has a slew of relatives, most of them émigrés from a remote little village somewhere in the depths of Russia. They're a crude lot, loudmouthed and coarse, and my father (but for a few exceptions) had no use for any of them. The Russian Hordes, he called them. He was never rude; any time they came around to visit he simply made himself scarce.

One night I remember in particular; I must have been about seven. Ma was washing up after supper and Pa was reading a newspaper when Yankev arrived, with Danyeh trailing him. Pa folded his paper, excused himself, and was gone. The minute Pa was gone Yankev went to the stove and lifted the lids from the two pots. Just as he thought—*mamaliga* in one pot, in the other one beans, and in the frying pan a piece of meat their cat would turn its nose up at. He sat himself in the rocking chair he had given Ma as a wedding present, and rocking, proceeded to lecture her. He had warned her against the marriage, but if she was satisfied, he was content. One question and that's all. How had she bettered her lot? True, she was no longer an old maid. True, she was now mistress of her own home. He looked around him and snorted. A hovel. '*And* three snot-nose kids,' he said, pointing to us.

Danyeh, hunched over in a kitchen chair, her feet barely reaching the floor, said something to him in Russian, cautioning him, I think. He told her to shut up, and in Yiddish continued his tirade against Ma. He had one word to say to her. To *watch* herself. Against his advice she had married this no-good Rumanian twister, this murderer. The story of how he had kept his first wife pregnant all the time was now well known. Also well known was the story of how she had died in her ninth month with a fourth child. Over an ironing board. Ironing his shirts while he was out playing cards with his Rumanian cronies and drinking wine. He had buried one wife, and now was after burying a second. So Ma had better *watch* herself, that's all.

Ma left her dishwashing and with dripping wet hands took hold of a chair and seated herself facing Yankev. She begged him not to say another word. 'Not another word, Uncle Yankev, I beg you. Till the day I die I'll be grateful to you for bringing me over. I don't know how much money you laid out for my passage, but I tried my best to make up for it the three years I stayed with you, by helping out in the house. But maybe I'm still in your debt? Is this what gives you the right to talk against my husband?'

Yankev, rocking, turned up his eyes and groaned. '*You* speak to her,' he said to Danyeh. 'It's impossible for a *human being* to get through to her.'

Danyeh knew better than to open her mouth.

'Uncle Yankev,' Ma continued, 'every word you speak against my husband is like a knife stab in my heart.' She leaned forward, thumbs whirring away. '*Mamaliga?* Beans? A piece of meat your cat wouldn't eat? A crust of *bread* at his board, and I will still thank God every day of my life that he chose me from the other two the *shadchan* showed him.'

In the beginning my father gave her a hard time. I remember his bursts of temper at her rough ways in the kitchen. She never opened a kitchen drawer without wrestling it—wrenching it open, slamming it shut. She never put a kettle on the stove without its running over at the boil. A pot never came to stove without its lid being inverted, and this for some reason maddened him. He'd right the lid, sometimes scalding his fingers—and all hell would break loose. We never sat down to a set or laid table. As she had been used to doing, so she continued; slamming a pot down on the table, scattering a handful of cutlery, dealing out assorted-size plates. More than once, with one swipe of his hand my father would send a few plates crashing to the floor, and stalk out. She'd sit a minute looking in our faces, one by one, then start twirling her thumbs and talking to herself. What had she done now?

'Eat!' she'd admonish us, and leaving table would go to the mirror over the kitchen sink and ask herself face to face, 'What did I do now?' She would examine her face profile and front and then sit down to eat. After, she'd gather up the dishes, dump them in the sink, and running the water over them, would study herself in the mirror. 'He'll be better,' she'd tell herself, smiling. 'He'll be soft as butter when he comes home. You'll see,' she'd promise her image in the mirror.

Later in life, mellowed by the years perhaps (or just plain defeated—there was no changing her), he became more tolerant of her ways and was kinder to her. When it became difficult for her to get around because of her poor feet, he did her marketing. He attended to her feet, bought her the Martha Washingtons, the Romeo Slippers, and on a summer's evening on his way home from work, a brick of ice cream. She was very fond of it.

Three years ago he began promoting a plan, a plan to give Ma some pleasure. (This was during Exhibition time.) 'You know,' he said to me, 'it would be very nice if Ma could see the fireworks at the Exhibition. She's never seen anything like that in her life.

Why don't you take her?'

The idea of Ma going to the Ex for the fireworks was so preposterous, it made me laugh. She never went anywhere.

'Don't laugh,' he said. 'It wouldn't hurt you to give her a little pleasure once in a while.'

He was quite keen that she should go, and the following year he canvassed the idea again. He put money on the table for taxi and grandstand seats. 'Take her,' he said.

'Why don't you take her?' I said. 'She'll enjoy it more going with you.'

'Me? What will I do at the Exhibition?'

As children, we were terrified of Pa's temper. Once in a while he'd belt us around, and we were scared that he might take the strap to Ma too. But before long we came to know that she was the only one of us not scared of Pa, when he got mad. Not even from the beginning when he used to let fly at her was she intimidated by him, not in the least, and in later years was even capable of getting her own back by taking a little dig at him now and then about the 'aristocracy'—as she called my father's Rumanian connections.

Aside from his buddies in the back room of the ice-cream parlour on Augusta Avenue, my father also kept in touch with his Rumanian compatriots (all of whom had prospered), and would once in a while go to them for an evening. We were never invited, nor did they come to us. This may have been my father's doing, I don't know. I expect he was ashamed of his circumstances, possibly of Ma, and certainly of how we lived.

Once in a blue moon during Rosh Hashanah or Yom Kippur after shul, they would unexpectedly drop in on us. One time a group of four came to the house, and I remember Pa darting around like a gadfly, collecting glasses, wiping them, and pouring a glass of wine he'd made himself. Ma shook hands all around, then went to the kitchen to cut some slices of her honey cake, scraping off the burnt part. I was summoned to take the plate in to 'Pa's gentlefolk'. Pretending to be busy, she rattled around the kitchen a few seconds, then seated herself in the partially open door, inspecting them. Not till they were leaving did she come out again, to wish them a good year.

The minute they were gone, my father turned to her. 'Russian peasant! Tartar savage, you! Sitting there with your eyes popping out. Do you think they couldn't see you?'

'What's the matter? Even a cat may look at a king?' she said blandly.

'Why didn't you come out instead of sitting there like a caged animal?'

'Because I didn't want to shame you,' she said, twirling her thumbs and swaying back and forth in the chair Yankev had given her as a wedding present.

My father busied himself clearing table, and after a while he softened. But she wasn't through yet. 'Which one was Falik's wife?' she asked in seeming innocence. 'The one with the beard?'

This drew his fire again. 'No!' he shouted.

'Oh, the other one. The pale one with the hump on her back,' she said wickedly.

So . . . notwithstanding the good dream Ma had of Pa coming home with a basket of apples, she never saw him again. He died six days after the operation.

It was a harrowing six days, dreadful. As Pa got weaker, the more disputatious we became—my brother, my sister, and I—arguing and snapping at each other outside his door, the point of contention being should Ma be told or not.

Nurse Brown, the special we'd put on duty, came out once to hush us. 'You're not helping him by arguing like this. He can hear you.'

'Is he conscious, nurse?'

'Of course he's conscious.'

'Is there any hope?'

'There's always hope,' she said. 'I've been on cases like this before, and I've seen them rally.'

We went our separate ways, clinging to the thread of hope she'd given us. The fifth day after the operation I had a call from Nurse Brown: 'Your father wants to see you.'

Nurse Brown left the room when I arrived, and my father motioned me to undo the zipper of his oxygen tent. 'Ma's a good woman,' he said, his voice so weak I had to lean close to hear him. 'You'll look after her? Don't put her aside. Don't forget about her——'

'What are you talking about!' I said shrilly, then lowered my voice to a whisper. 'The doctor told me you're getting better. Honest to God, Pa, I wouldn't lie to you,' I whispered.

He went on as if I hadn't spoken. 'Even a servant if you had her for thirty years, you wouldn't put aside because you don't need her any more——'

'Wait a minute,' I said, and went to the corridor to fetch Nurse Brown. 'Nurse Brown, will you tell my father what you told me yesterday. You remember? About being on cases like this before, and you've seen them rally. Will you tell that to my father, please. He talks as if he's——'

I ran from the room and stood outside the door, bawling. Nurse Brown opened the door a crack. '*Ssh!* You'd better go now; I'll call you if there's any change.'

At five the next morning, my brother telephoned from hospital. Ma was sound asleep and didn't hear. 'You'd better get down here,' he said. 'I think the old man's checking out. I've already phoned Gertie.'

My sister and I arrived at the hospital within seconds of each other. My brother was just emerging from Pa's room. In the gesture of a baseball umpire he jerked a thumb over his shoulder, signifying OUT.

'Is he dead?' we asked our brother.

'Just this minute,' he replied.

Like three dummies we paced the dimly lit corridor, not speaking to each other. In the end we were obliged to speak; we had to come to a decision about how to proceed next.

We taxied to the synagogue of which Pa was a member, and roused the shamus. 'As soon as it's light I'll get the rabbi,' he said. 'He'll attend to everything. Meantime go home.'

In silence we walked slowly home. Dawn was just breaking, and Ma, a habitually early riser, was bound to be up now and in the kitchen. Quietly we let ourselves in and passed through the hall leading to the kitchen. We were granted an unexpected respite; Ma was not up yet. We waited ten minutes for her, fifteen—an agonizing wait. We decided one of us had better go and wake her; what was the sense of prolonging it? The next minute we changed our minds. To awaken her with such tidings would be inhuman, a brutal thing to do.

'Let's stop whispering,' my sister whispered. 'Let's talk in normal tones, do something, make a noise, she'll hear us and come out.'

In an access of activity we busied ourselves. My sister put the kettle on with a clatter; I took teaspoons from the drawer, clacking them like castanets. She was bound to hear, their bedroom was on the same floor at the front of the house—but five minutes elapsed and not a sound from the room.

'Go and see,' my sister said, and I went and opened the door to that untidy bedroom Pa used to rail against.

Ma, her black eyes circled and her hair in disarray, was sitting up in bed. At sight of me she flopped back and pulled the feather tick over her head. I approached the bed and took the covers from her face. 'Ma——'

She sat up. 'You are guests in my house now?'

For the moment I didn't understand. I didn't know the meaning of her words. But the next minute the meaning of them was clear—with Pa dead, the link was broken. The bond, the tie that held us together. We were no longer her children. We were now guests in her house.

'When did Pa die?' she asked.

'How did you know?'

'My heart told me.'

Barefooted, she followed me to the kitchen. My sister gave her a glass of tea, and we stood like mutes, watching her sipping it through a cube of sugar.

'You were all there when Pa died?'

'Just me, Ma,' my brother said.

She nodded. 'His kaddish. Good.'

I took a chair beside her, and for once without constraint or self-consciousness, put my arm around her and kissed her on the cheek.

'Ma, the last words Pa spoke were about you. He said you were a good woman. "Ma's a good woman," that's what he said to me.'

She put her tea down and looked me in the face.

'Pa said that? He said I was a good woman?' She clasped her hands. 'May the light shine on him in paradise,' she said, and wept silently, putting her head down to hide her tears.

Eight o'clock the rabbi telephoned. Pa was now at the funeral parlour on College near Augusta, and the funeral was to be at eleven o'clock. Ma went to ready herself, and in a few minutes called me to come and zip up her black crepe, the dress Pa had bought her six years ago for the Applebaum wedding.

The Applebaums, neighbours, had invited Ma and Pa to the wedding of their daughter, Lily. Right away Pa had declared he wouldn't go. Ma kept coaxing. How would it look? It would be construed as unfriendly, unneighbourly. A few days before the wedding he gave in, and Ma began scratching through her wardrobe for something suitable to wear. Nothing she exhibited pleased him. He went downtown and came back with the black crepe and an outsize corset.

I dressed her for the wedding, combed her hair, and put some powder on her face. Pa became impatient; he had already called a cab. What was I doing? Getting her ready for a beauty contest? The taxi came, and as Pa held her coat he said to me in English, 'You know, Ma's not a bad-looking woman?'

For weeks she talked about the good time she'd had at the Applebaum wedding, but chiefly about how Pa had attended her. Not for a minute had he left her side. Two hundred people at the wedding and not one women among them had the attention from her husband that she had had from Pa. 'Pa's a gentleman,' she said to me, proud as proud.

Word of Pa's death got around quickly, and by nine in the morning people began trickling in. First arrivals were Yankev and Danyeh. Yankev, now in his seventies and white-haired, was still straight and handsome. The same Yankev except for the white hair and an asthmatic condition causing him to wheeze and gasp for breath. Danyeh was wizened and bent over, her hands hanging almost to her knees. They approached Ma, Danyeh trailing Yankev. Yankev held out a hand and with the other one thumped his chest, signifying he was too congested to speak. Danyeh gave her bony hand to Ma and muttered a condolence.

From then on there was a steady influx of people. Here was Chaim the schnorrer! We hadn't seen him in years. Chaim the schnorrer, stinking of fish and in leg wrappings as always, instead of socks. Rich as Croesus he was said to be, a fish-peddling miser who lived on soda crackers and milk and kept his money in his leg wrappings. Yankev, a minute ago too congested for speech, found words for Chaim. 'How much money have you got in those *gutkess*? The truth, Chaim!'

Ma shook hands with all, acknowledged their sympathy, and to some she spoke a few words. I observed the Widow Spector, a gossip and trouble-maker, sidling through the crowd and easing her way toward Ma. 'The Post' she was called by people on the street. No one had the time of day for her; even Ma used to hide from her.

I groaned at the sight of her. As if Ma didn't have enough to contend with. But no! here was Ma welcoming the Widow Spector, holding a hand out to her. 'Give me your hand, Mrs Spector. Shake hands, we're partners now. Now I know the taste, I'm a widow too.' Ma patted the chair beside her. 'Sit down, partner. Sit down.'

At a quarter to eleven the house was clear of people. 'Is it time?' Ma asked, and we answered, Yes, it was time to go. We were afraid this would be the breaking point for her, but she went calmly to the bedroom and took her coat from the peg on the door and came to the kitchen with it, requesting that it be brushed off.

The small funeral parlour was jammed to the doors, every seat taken but for four left vacant for us. On a trestle table directly in front of our seating was the coffin. A pine box draped in a black cloth, and in its center a white Star of David.

Ma left her place, approached the coffin, and as she stood before it with clasped hands I noticed the uneven hemline of her coat, hiked up in back by that mound of flesh on her shoulders. I observed that her lisle stockings were twisted at the ankles, and was embarrassed for her. She stood silently a moment, then began to speak. She called him her dove, her comrade, her friend.

'Life is a dream,' she said. 'You were my treasure. You were the light of my eyes. I thought to live my days out with you—and look what it has come to.' (She swayed slightly, the black shawl slipping from her head—and I observed that could have done with a brushing too.) 'If ever I offended you or caused you even a twinge of discomfort, forgive me for it. As your wife I lived like a queen. Look at me now. I'm nothing. You were my jewel, my crown. With you at its head my house was a palace. I return now to a hovel. Forgive me for everything, my dove. Forgive me.'

('Russian peasant,' Pa used to say to her in anger, 'Tartar savage.' If he could see her now as she stood before his bier mourning him. Mourning him like Hecuba mourning Priam and the fall of Troy. And I a minute ago was ashamed of her hiked-up coat, her twisted stockings and dusty shawl.)

People were weeping; Ma resumed her place dry-eyed, and the rabbi began the service.

It is now a year since Pa died, and as he had enjoined me to do, I am looking after Ma. I have not put her aside. I get cross and holler at her as I always have done, but she allows for my testiness and does not hold it against me. I'm a spinster, an old maid now approaching my thirty-seventh year, and she pities me for it. I get bored telling her again and again that Pa's last words were Ma's a good woman, and sometimes wish I'd never mentioned it. She cries a lot, and I get impatient with her tears. But I'm good to her.

This afternoon I called Moodey's, booked two seats for the grandstand, and tonight I'm taking her to the Ex and she'll see the fireworks.

MARGARET LAURENCE

The Rain Child

I recall the sky that day—overcast, the flat undistinguished grey nearly forgotten by us here during the months of azure which we come to regard as rights rather than privileges. As always when the rain hovers, the air was like syrup, thick and heavily still, over-sweet with flowering vines and the occasional ripe paw-paw that had fallen and now lay yellow and fermented, a winery for ants.

I was annoyed at having to stay in my office so late. Annoyed, too, that I found the oppressive humidity just before the rains a little more trying each year. I have always believed myself particularly well-suited to this climate. Miss Povey, of course, when I was idiotic enough to complain one day about the heat, hinted that the change of life might be more to blame than the weather.

'Of course, I remember how bothersome you found the heat one season,' I parried. 'Some years ago, as I recollect.'

We work well together and even respect one another. Why must we make such petty stabs? Sitting depressed at my desk, I was at least thankful that when a breeze quickened we would receive it here. Blessings upon the founders of half a century ago who built Eburaso Girls' School at the top of the hill, for at the bottom the villagers would be steaming like crabs in a soup pot.

My leg hurt more than it had in a long time, and I badly wanted a cup of tea. Typical of Miss Povey, I thought, that she should leave yet another parental interview to me. Twenty-seven years here, to my twenty-two, and she still felt acutely uncomfortable with African parents, all of whom in her eyes were equally unenlightened. The fact that one father might be an illiterate cocoa farmer, while the next would possibly be a barrister from the city —such distinctions made no earthly difference to Hilda Povey. She was positive that parents would fail to comprehend the importance of sending their little girls to school with the proper clothing, and she harped upon this subject in a thoroughly tedious manner, as though the essence of education lay in the possession of six pairs of cotton knickers. Malice refreshed me for a moment. Then, as always, it began to chill. Were we still women, in actuality, who could bear only grudges, make venom for milk? I exaggerated for a while in this lamentably oratorical style, dramatizing the trivial for lack of anything great. Hilda, in point of fact, was an excellent headmistress. Like a budgerigar she darted and fussed through her days, but underneath the twittering there was a strong disciplined mind and a heart more pious than mine. Even in giving credit to her, however, I chose words churlishly—why had I not thought 'devout' instead of 'pious', with its undertones of self-righteousness? What could she possibly have said in my favour if she had been asked? That I taught English competently, even sometimes with love? That my irascibility was mainly reserved for my colleagues? The young ones in Primary did not find me terrifying, once they grew used to the sight of the lady in stout white drill skirt and drab lilac smock faded from purple, her greying hair arranged in what others might call a *chignon* but for me could only be termed a 'bun', a lady of somewhat uncertain gait, clumping heavily into the classroom with her ebony cane. They felt free to laugh, my forest children, reticent and stiff in unaccustomed dresses, as we began the alien speech. 'What are we doing, class?' And, as I sat down clumsily on the straight chair, to show them, they made their murmured and mirthful response—'We ah siddeen.' The older girls in Middle School also seemed to accept me readily enough. Since Miss Harvey left us to marry that fool of a government geologist, I have had the senior girls for English literature and composition. Once when we were taking *Daffodils*, Kwaale came to class with her arms full of wild orchids for me. How absurd Wordsworth seemed here then. I spoke instead about Akan poetry, and read them the drum prelude *Anyaneanyane* in their own tongue as well as the translation. Miss Povey, hearing of it, took decided umbrage. Well. Perhaps she would not have found much to say in my favour after all.

I fidgeted and perspired, beginning to wonder if Dr Quansah would show up that day at all. Then, without my having heard his car or footsteps, he stood there at my office door, his daughter Ruth beside him.

'Miss—' He consulted a letter which he held in his hand. 'Miss Violet Nedden?'

'Yes.' I limped over to meet him. I was, stupidly, embarrassed that he had spoken my full name. Violet, applied to me, is of course quite ludicrous and I detest it. I felt as well the old need to explain my infirmity, but I refrained for the usual reasons. I do not know why it should matter to me to have people realize I was not always like this, but it does. In the pre-sulpha days when I first came here, I developed a tropical sore which festered badly; this is the result. But if I mention it to Africans, they tend to become faintly apologetic, as though it were somehow their fault that I bear the mark of Africa upon myself in much the same way as any ulcerated beggar of the streets.

Dr Quansah, perhaps to my relief, did not seem much at ease either. Awkwardly, he transferred Miss Povey's typewritten instructions to his left hand in order to shake hands with me. A man in his middle fifties, I judged him to be. Thickly built, with hands which seemed too immense to be a doctor's. He was well dressed, in a beige linen suit of good cut, and there was about his eyes a certain calm which his voice and gestures lacked.

His daughter resembled him, the same strong coarse features, the same skin shade, rather a lighter brown than is usual here. At fifteen she was more plump and childish in figure than most of our girls her age. Her frock was pretty and expensive, a blue cotton with white daisies on it, but as she was so stocky it looked too old for her.

'I don't know if Miss Povey told you,' Dr Quansah began, 'but Ruth has never before attended school in this—in her own country.'

I must have shown my surprise, for he hastened on. 'She was born in England and has lived all her life there. I went there as a young man, you see, to study medicine, and when I graduated I had the opportunity to stay on and do malaria research. Ultimately my wife joined me in London. She—she died in England. Ruth has been in boarding schools since she was six. I have always meant to return here, of course. I had not really intended to stay away so long, but I was very interested in malaria research, and it was an opportunity that comes only once. Perhaps I have even been able to accomplish a certain amount. Now the government here is financing a research station, and I am to be in charge of it. You may have heard of it—it is only twenty miles from here.'

I could see that he had had to tell me so I should not think it odd for an African to live away from his own country for so many years. Like my impulse to explain my leg. We are all so anxious that people should not think us different. See, we say, I am not peculiar—wait until I tell you how it was with me.

'Well,' I said slowly, 'I do hope Ruth will like it here at Eburaso.'

My feeling of apprehension was so marked, I remember, that I attempted exorcism by finding sensible reasons. It was only the season, I thought, the inevitable tension before the rains, and perhaps the season of regrets in myself as well. But I was not convinced.

'I, too, hope very much she will like it here,' Dr Quansah said. He did not sound overly confident.

'I'm sure I shall,' Ruth said suddenly, excitedly, her round face beaming. 'I think it's great fun, Miss Nedden, coming to Africa like this.'

Her father and I exchanged quick and almost fearful glances. She had spoken, of course, as any English schoolgirl might speak, going abroad.

I do not know how long Ruth Quansah kept her sense of adventure. Possibly it lasted the first day, certainly not longer. I watched her as carefully as I could, but there was not much I could do.

I had no difficulty in picking her out from a group of girls, although she wore the same light green uniform. She walked differently, carried herself differently. She had none of their easy languor. She strode along with brisk intensity, and in consequence perspired a great deal. At meals she ate virtually nothing. I asked her if she had no appetite, and she looked at me reproachfully.

'I'm starving,' she said flatly. 'But I can't eat this food, Miss Nedden. I'm sorry, but I just can't. That awful mashed stuff, sort of greyish yellow, like some funny kind of potatoes—it makes me sick.'

'I'm afraid you'll have to get used to cassava,' I said, restraining a smile, for she looked so serious and so offended. 'African food is served to the girls here, naturally. Personally I'm very fond of it, groundnut stew and such. Soon you won't find it strange.'

She gave me such a hostile glance that I wondered uneasily what we would do if she really determined to starve herself. Thank heaven she could afford to lose a few pounds.

Our girls fetched their own washing water in buckets from our wells. The evening trek for water was a time of singing, of shouted gossip, of laughter, just as it was each morning for their mothers in the villages, taking the water vessels to the river. The walk was not an easy one for me, but one evening I stumbled rather irritably and unwillingly down the stony path to the wells.

Ruth was there, standing apart from the others. Each of the girls in turn filled a bucket, hoisted it up onto her head and sauntered off, still chattering and waving, without spilling a drop. Ruth was left alone to fill her bucket. Then, carrying it with both her hands clutched around the handle, she began to struggle back along the path. Perhaps foolishly, I smiled. It was done only in encouragement, but she mistook my meaning.

'I expect it looks very funny,' she burst out. 'I expect they all think so, too.'

Before I could speak she had swung the full bucket and thrown it from her as hard as she could. The water struck at the ground, turning the dust to ochre mud, and the bucket rattled and rolled, dislodging pebbles along its way. The laughter among the feathery *niim* trees further up the path suddenly stopped, as a dozen pairs of hidden eyes peered. Looking bewildered, as though she were surprised and shocked by what she had done, Ruth sat down, her sturdy legs rigid in front of her, her child's soft face creased in tears.

'I didn't know it would be like this, here,' she said at last. 'I didn't know at all.'

In the evenings the senior girls were allowed to change from their school uniforms to African cloth, and they usually did so, for they were very concerned with their appearances and they rightly believed that the dark-printed lengths of mammy-cloth were more becoming to them than their short school frocks. Twice a week it was my responsibility to hobble over and make the evening rounds of the residence. Ruth, I noticed, changed into one of her English frocks, a different one each time, it appeared. Tact had never been my greatest strength, but I tried to suggest that it might be better if she would wear cloth like the rest.

'Your father would be glad to buy one for you, I'm sure.'

'I've got one—it was my mother's,' Ruth replied. She frowned. 'I don't know how to put it on properly. They—they'd only laugh if I asked them. And anyway——'

Her face took on that defiance which is really a betrayal of uncertainty.

'I don't like those cloths,' she said clearly. 'They look like fancy-dress costumes to me. I'd feel frightfully silly in one. I suppose the people here haven't got anything better to wear.'

In class she had no restraint. She was clever, and she knew more about English literature and composition than the other girls, for she had been taught always in English, whereas for the first six years of their schooling they had received most of their instruction in their own language. But she would talk interminably, if allowed, and she rushed to answer my questions before anyone else had a chance. Abenaa, Mary Ansah, Yaa, Kwaale and all the rest would regard her with eyes which she possibly took to be full of awe for her erudition. I knew something of those bland brown eyes, however, and I believed them to contain only scorn for one who would so blatantly show off. But I was wrong. The afternoon Kwaale came to see me, I learned that in those first few weeks the other girls had believed, quite simply, that Ruth was insane.

The junior teachers live in residence in the main building, but Miss Povey and I have our own bungalows, hers on one side of the grounds, mine on the other. A small grove of bamboo partially shields my house, and although Yindo the garden boy deplores my taste, I keep the great spiny clumps of prickly pear that grows beside my door. Hilda Povey grows zinnia and nasturtiums, and spends hours trying to coax an exiled rosebush into bloom, but I will have no English flowers. My garden burns magnificently with jungle lily and poinsettia, which Yindo gently uproots from the forest and puts in here.

The rains had broken and the air was cool and lightened. The downpour began predictably each evening around dusk, so I was still able to have my tea outside. I was exceedingly fond of my garden chair. I discovered it years ago at Jillaram's Silk Palace, a tatty little Indian shop in the side streets of the city which I seldom visited. The chair was rattan with a high fan-shaped back like a throne or a peacock's tail, enamelled in Chinese red and decorated extravangantly with gilt. I had never seen anything so splendidly garish, so I bought it. The red had since been subdued by sun and the gilt was flaking, but I still sat enthroned in it each afternoon, my ebony sceptre by my side.

I did not hear Kwaale until she greeted me. She was wearing her good cloth, an orange one patterned with small black stars that wavered in their firmament as she moved. Kwaale had never been unaware of her womanhood. Even as a child she walked with that same slow grace. We did not need to hope that she would go on and take teacher training or anything of that sort. She would marry when she left school, and I believed that would be the right thing for her to do. But sometimes it saddened me to think of what life would probably be for her, bearing too many children in too short a span of years, mourning the inevitable deaths of some of them, working bent double at the planting and hoeing until her slim straightness was warped. All at once I felt ashamed in the presence of this young queen, who had only an inheritance of poverty to return to, ashamed of my comfort and my heaviness, ashamed of my decrepit scarlet throne and trivial game.

'Did you want to see me, Kwaale?' I spoke brusquely.

'Yes.' She sat down on the stool at my feet. At first they had thought Ruth demented, she said, but now they had changed their minds. They had seen how well she did on her test papers. She was sane, they had decided, but this was so much the worse for her, for now she could be held responsible for what she did.

'What does she do, Kwaale?'

'She will not speak with us, nor eat with us. She pretends not to eat at all. But we have seen her. She has money, you know, from her father. The big palm grove—she goes there, and eats chocolate and biscuits. By herself. Not one to anyone else. Such a thing.'

Kwaale was genuinely shocked. Where these girls came from, sharing was not done as a matter of moral principle, but as a necessary condition of life.

'If one alone eats the honey,' Kwaale said primly in Twi, 'it plagues his stomach.'

It was, of course, a proverb. Kwaale was full of them. Her father was a village elder in Eburaso, and although he did precious little work, he was a highly respected man. He spoke continuously in proverbs and dispensed his wisdom freely. He was a charming person, but it was his wife, with the cassava and peppers and medicinal herbs she sold in the market, who had made it possible for some of their children to obtain an education.

'That is not all,' Kwaale went on. 'There is much worse. She becomes angry, even at the young ones. Yesterday Ayesha spoke to her, and she hit the child on the face. Ayesha—if it had been one of the others, even——'

Ayesha, my youngest one, who had had to bear so much. Tears of rage must have come to my eyes, for Kwaale glanced at me, then lowered her head with that courtesy of the heart which forbids the observing of another's pain. I struggled with myself to be fair to Ruth. I called to mind the bleakness of her face as she trudged up the path with the water bucket.

'She is lonely, Kwaale, and does not quite know what to do. Try to be patient with her.'

Kwaale sighed. 'It is not easy—'

Then her resentment gained command. 'The stranger is like passing water in the drain,' she said fiercely.

Another of her father's proverbs. I looked at her in dismay.

'There is a different saying on that subject,' I said dryly, at last. 'We had it in chapel not so long ago—don't you remember? From Exodus. "Thou shalt not oppress a stranger, for ye know the heart of a stranger, seeing ye were strangers in the land of Egypt".'

But Kwaale's eyes remained implacable. She had never been a stranger in the land of Egypt.

When Kwaale had gone, I sat unmoving for a while in my ridiculous rattan throne. Then I saw Ayesha walking along the path, so I called to her. We spoke together in Twi, Ayesha and I. She had begun to learn English, but she found it difficult and I tried not to press her beyond her present limits. She did not even speak her own language very well, if it was actually her own language—no one knew for certain. She was tiny for her age, approximately six. In her school dress she looked like one of those stick figures I used to draw as a child—billowing garments, straight lines for limbs, and the same disproportionately large eyes.

'Come here, Ayesha.'

Obediently she came. Then, after the first moment of watchful survey which she still found necessary to observe, she scrambled onto my lap. I was careful—we were all careful here—not to establish bonds of too-great affection. As Miss Povey was fond of reminding us, these were not our children. But with Ayesha, the rule was sometimes hard to remember. I touched her face lightly with my hand.

'Did an older girl strike you, little one?'

She nodded wordlessly. She did not look angry or upset. She made no bid for sympathy because she had no sense of having been unfairly treated. A slap was not a very great injury to Ayesha.

'Why?' I asked gently. 'Do you know why she did that thing?'

She shook her head. Then she lifted her eyes to mine.

'Where is the monkey today?'

She wanted to ignore the slap, to forget it. Forgetfulness is her protection. Sometimes I wondered, though, how much could be truly forgotten and what happened to it when it was entombed.

'The monkey is in my house,' I said. 'Do you want to see her?'

'Yes.' So we walked inside and brought her out into the garden, my small and regal Ankyeo who was named, perhaps frivolously, after a great queen mother of this country. I did not know what species of monkey Ankyeo was. She was delicate-boned as a bird, and her fur was silver. She picked with her doll fingers at a pink hibiscus blossom, and Ayesha laughed. I wanted to make Ankyeo perform all her tricks, in order to hear again that rare laughter. But I knew I must not try to go too fast. After a while Ayesha tired of watching the monkey and sat cross-legged beside my chair, the old look of passivity on her face. We would have to move indoors before the rain started, but for the moment I left her as she was.

Ruth did not approach silently, as Kwaale and Ayesha had done, but with a loud crunching of shoes on the gravel path. When she saw Ayesha she stopped.

'I suppose you know.'

'Yes. But it was not Ayesha who told me.'

'Who, then?'

Of course I would not tell her. Her face grew sullen.

'Whoever it was, I think it was rotten of her to tell——'

'It did not appear that way to the girl in question. She was protecting the others from you, and that is a higher good in her eyes than any individual honour in not tattling.'

'Protecting—from me?' There was desolation in her voice, and I relented.

'They will change, Ruth, once they see they can trust you. Why did you hit Ayesha?'

'It was a stupid thing to do,' Ruth said in a voice almost inaudible with shame, 'and I felt awful about it, and I'm terribly sorry. But she—she kept asking me something, you see, over and over again, in a sort of whining voice, and I—I just couldn't stand it any more.'

'What did she ask you?'

'How should I know?' Ruth said. 'I don't speak Twi.'

I stared at her. 'Not—any? I thought you might be a little rusty, but I never imagined—my dear child, it's your own language, after all.'

'My father has always spoken English to me,' she said. 'My mother spoke in Twi, I suppose, but she died when I was under a year old.'

'Why on earth didn't you tell the girls?'

'I don't know. I don't know why I didn't——'

I noticed then how much thinner she had grown and how her expression had altered. She no longer looked like a child. Her eyes were implacable as Kwaale's.

'They don't know anything outside this place,' she said. 'I don't care if I can't understand what they're saying to each other. I'm not interested, anyway.'

Then her glance went to Ayesha once more.

'But why were they so angry—about her? I know it was mean, and I said I was sorry. But the way they all looked——'

'Ayesha was found by the police in Lagos,' I said reluctantly. 'She was sent back to this country because one of the constables recognized her speech as Twi. We heard about her and offered to have her here. There are many like her, I'm afraid, who are not found or heard about. She must have been stolen, you see, or sold when she was very young. She has not been able to tell us much. But the Nigerian police traced her back to several slave-dealers. When they discovered her she was being used as a child prostitute. She was very injured when she came to us here.'

Ruth put her head down on her hands. She sat without speaking. Then her shoulders, hunched and still, began to tremble.

'You didn't know,' I said. 'There's no point in reproaching yourself now.'

She looked up at me with a kind of naive horror, the look of someone who recognizes for the first time the existence of cruelty.

'Things like that really happen here?'

I sighed. 'Not just here. Evil does not select one place for its province.'

But I could see that she did not believe me. The wind was beginning to rise, so we went indoors. Ayesha carried the stool, Ruth lifted my red throne, and I limped after them, feeling exhausted and not at all convinced just then that God was in His heaven. What a mercy for me that the church in whose mission school I had spent much of my adult life did not possess the means of scrutinizing too precisely the souls of its faithful servants.

We had barely got inside the bungalow when Ayesha missed the monkey. She flew outside to look for it, but no amount of searching revealed Ankyeo. Certain the monkey was gone forever, Ayesha threw herself down on the damp ground. While the wind moaned and screeched, the child, who never wept for herself, wept for a lost monkey and would not be comforted. I did not dare kneel beside her. My leg was too unreliable, and I knew I would not be able to get up again. I stood there, lumpish and helpless, while Ruth in the doorway shivered in her thin and daisied dress.

Then, like a veritable angel of the Lord, Yindo appeared, carrying Ankyeo. Immediately I experienced a resurrection of faith, while at the same time thinking how frail and fickle my belief must be, to be so influenced by a child and a silver-furred monkey.

Yindo grinned and knelt beside Ayesha. He was no more than sixteen, a tall thin-wristed boy, a Dagomba from the northern desert. He had come here when he was twelve, one of the scores of young who were herded down each year to work the cocoa farms because their own arid land had no place for them. He was one of our best garden boys, but he could not speak to anyone around here except in hesitant pidgin English, for no one here knew his language. His speech lack never bothered him with Ayesha. The two communicated in some fashion without words. He put the monkey in her arms and she held Ankyeo closely. Then she made a slight and courtly bow to Yindo. He laughed and shook his head. Drawing from his pocket a small charm, he showed it to her. It was the dried head of a chameleon, with blue glass beads and a puff of unwholesome-looking fur tied around it. Ayesha understood at once that it was this object which had enabled Yindo to find the monkey. She made another and deeper obeisance and from her own pocket drew the only thing she had to offer, a toffee wrapped in silver foil which I had given her at least two weeks ago. Yindo took it, touched it to his talisman, and put both carefully away.

Ruth had not missed the significance of the ritual. Her eyes were dilated with curiosity and contempt.

'He believes in it, doesn't he?' she said. 'He actually believes in it.'

'Don't be so quick to condemn the things you don't comprehend,' I said sharply.

'I think it's horrible.' She sounded frightened. 'He's just a savage, isn't he, just a——'

'Stop it, Ruth. That's quite enough.'

'I hate it here!' she cried. 'I wish I were back at home.'

'Child,' I said, 'this is your home.'

She did not reply, but the denial in her face made me marvel at my own hypocrisy.

Each Friday Dr Quansah drove over to see Ruth, and usually on these afternoons he would call in at my bungalow for a few minutes to discuss her progress. At first our conversations were completely false, each of us politely telling the other that Ruth was getting on reasonably well. Then one day he dropped the pretence.

'She is very unhappy, isn't she? Please—don't think I am blaming you, Miss Nedden. Myself, rather. It is too different. What should I have done, all those years ago?'

'Don't be offended, Dr Quansah, but why wasn't she taught her own language?'

He waited a long moment before replying. He studied the clear amber tea in his cup.

'I was brought up in a small village,' he said at last. 'English came hard to me. When I went to Secondary School I experienced great difficulty at first in understanding even the gist of the lectures. I was determined that the same thing would not happen to Ruth. I suppose I imagined she would pick up her own language easily, once she returned here, as though the knowledge of one's family tongue was inherited. Of course, if her mother had lived——'

He set down the teacup and knotted his huge hands together in an unexpressed anguish that was painful to see.

'Both of them uprooted,' he said. 'It was my fault, I guess, and yet——'

He fell silent. Finally, his need to speak was greater than his reluctance to reveal himself.

'You see, my wife hated England, always. I knew, although she never spoke of it. Such women don't. She was a quiet woman, gentle and—obedient. My parents had chosen her and I had married her when I was a very young man, before I first left this country. Our differences were not so great, then, but later in those years in London—she was like a plant, expected to grow where the soil is not suitable for it. My friends and associates—the places I went for dinner—she did not accompany me. I never asked her to entertain those people in our house. I could not—you see that?'

I nodded and he continued in the same low voice with its burden of self-reproach.

'She was illiterate,' he said. 'She did not know anything of my life, as it became. She did not want to know. She refused to learn. I was—impatient with her. I know that. But——'

He turned away so I would not see his face.

'Have you any idea what it is like,' he cried, 'to need someone to talk to, and not to have even one person?'

'Yes,' I said. 'I have a thorough knowledge of that.'

He looked at me in surprise, and when he saw that I did know, he seemed oddly relieved, as though, having exchanged vulnerabilities, we were neither of us endangered. My ebony cane slipped to the ground just then, and Dr Quansah stooped and picked it up, automatically and casually, hardly noticing it, and I was startled at myself, for I had felt no awkwardness in the moment either.

'When she became ill,' he went on, 'I do not think she really cared whether she lived or not. And now, Ruth—you know, when she was born, my wife called her by an African name which means 'child of the rain'. My wife missed the sun so very much. The rain, too, may have stood for her own tears. She had not wanted to bear her child so far from home.'

Unexpectedly, he smiled, the dark features of his face relaxing, becoming less blunt and plain.

'Why did you leave your country and come here, Miss Nedden? For the church? Or for the sake of the Africans?'

I leaned back in my mock throne and re-arranged, a shade ironically, the folds of my lilac smock.

'I thought so, once,' I replied. 'But now I don't know. I think I may have come here mainly for myself, after all, hoping to find a place where my light could shine forth. Not a very palatable admission, perhaps.'

'At least you did not take others along on your pilgrimage.'

'No. I took no one. No one at all.'

We sat without speaking, then, until the tea grew cold and the dusk gathered.

It was through me that Ruth met David Mackie. He was an intent, lemon-haired boy of fifteen. He had been ill and was therefore out from England, staying with his mother while he recuperated. Mrs Mackie was a widow. Her husband had managed an oil palm plantation for an African owner, and when he died Clare Mackie had stayed on and managed the place herself. I am sure she made a better job of it than her husband had, for she was one of those frighteningly efficient women, under whose piercing eye, one felt, even the oil palms would not dare to slacken their efforts. She was slender and quick, and she contrived to look dashing and yet not unfeminine in her corded jodhpurs and open-necked shirt, which she wore with a silk paisley scarf at the throat. David was more like his father, thoughtful and rather withdrawn, and maybe that is why I had agreed to help him occasionally with his studies, which he was then taking by correspondence.

The Mackies' big whitewashed bungalow, perched on its cement pillars and fringed around with languid casuarina trees, was only a short distance from the school, on the opposite side of the hill to the village. Ruth came to my bungalow one Sunday afternoon, when I had promised to go the Mackies', and as she appeared bored and despondent, I suggested she come along with me.

After I had finished the lesson, Ruth and David talked together amicably enough while Mrs Mackie complained about the inadequacies of local labour and I sat fanning myself with a palm leaf and feeling grateful that fate had not made me one of Clare Mackie's employees.

'Would you like to see my animals?' I heard David ask Ruth, his voice still rather formal and yet pleased, too, to have a potential admirer for his treasures.

'Oh yes.' She was eager; she understood people who collected animals. 'What have you got?'

'A baby crocodile,' he said proudly, 'and a cutting-grass—that's a bush rat, you know, and several snakes, non-poisonous ones, and a lot of assorted toads. I shan't be able to keep the croc long, of course. They're too tricky to deal with. I had a duiker, too, but it died.'

Off they went, and Mrs Mackie shrugged.

'He's mad about animals. I think they're disgusting. But he's got to have something to occupy his time, poor dear.'

When the two returned from their inspection of David's private zoo, we drove back to the school in the Mackies' bone-shaking jeep. I thought no more about the visit until late the next week, when I realized that I had not seen Ruth after classes for some days. I asked her, and she looked at me guilelessly, certain I would be as pleased as she was herself.

'I've been helping David with his animals,' she explained enthusiastically. 'You know, Miss Nedden, he wants to be an animal collector when he's through school. Not a hobby—he wants to work at it always. To collect live specimens, you see, for places like Whipsnade and Regent's Park Zoo. He's lent me a whole lot of books about it. It's awfully interesting, really it is.'

I did not know what to say. I could not summon up the sternness to deny her the first friendship she had made here. But of course it was not 'here', really. She was drawn to David because he spoke in the ways she knew, and of things which made sense to her. So she continued to see him. She borrowed several of my books to lend to him. They were both fond of poetry. I worried, of course, but not for what might be thought the obvious reasons. Both Ruth and David needed companionship, but neither was ready for anything more. I did not have the fears Miss Povey would have harboured if she had known. I was anxious for another reason. Ruth's friendship with David isolated her more than ever from the other girls. She made even less effort to get along with them now, for David was sufficient company.

Only once was I alarmed about her actual safety, the time when Ruth told me she and David had found an old fishing pirogue and had gone on the river in it.

'The river——' I was appalled. 'Ruth, don't you know there are crocodiles there?'

'Of course.' She had no awareness of having done anything dangerous. 'That's why we went. We hoped to catch another baby croc, you see. But we had no luck.'

'You had phenomenal luck,' I snapped. 'Don't you ever do that again. Not ever.'

'Well, all right,' she said regretfully. 'But it was great fun.'

The sense of adventure had returned to her, and all at once I realized why. David was showing Africa to her as she wanted to be shown it—from the outside.

I felt I should tell Dr Quansah, but when I finally did he was so upset that I was sorry I had mentioned it.

'It is not a good thing,' he kept saying. 'The fact that this is a boy does not concern me half so much, to be frank with you, as the fact that he is a European.'

'I would not have expected such illogicalities from you, Dr Quansah.' I was annoyed, and perhaps guilty as well, for I had permitted the situation.

Dr Quansah looked thoughtfully at me.

'I do not think it is that. Yes—maybe you are right. I don't know. But I do not want my daughter to be hurt by any—stupidity. I know that.'

'David's mother is employed as manager by an African owner.'

'Yes,' Dr Quansah said, and his voice contained a bitterness I had not heard in it before, 'but what does she say about him, in private?'

I had no reply to that, for what he implied was perfectly true. He saw from my face that he had not been mistaken.

'I have been away a long time, Miss Nedden,' he said, 'but not long enough to forget some of the things that were said to me by Europeans when I was young.'

I should not have blurted out my immediate thought, but I did.

'You have been able to talk to me——'

'Yes.' He smiled self-mockingly. 'I wonder if you know how much that has surprised me?'

Why should I have found it difficult then, to look at him, at the face whose composure I knew concealed such aloneness? I took refuge, as so often, in the adoption of an abrupt tone.

'Why should it be surprising? You liked people in England. You had friends there.'

'I am not consistent, I know. But the English at home are not the same as the English abroad—you must have realized that. You are not typical, Miss Nedden. I still find most Europeans here as difficult to deal with as I ever did. And yet—I seem to have lost touch with my own people, too. The young laboratory technicians at the station—they do not trust me, and I find myself getting so very impatient with them, losing my temper because they have not comprehended what I wanted them to do, and——'

He broke off. 'I really should not bother you with all this.'

'Oh, but you're not.' The words came out with an unthinking swiftness which mortified me later when I recalled it. 'I haven't so many people I can talk with, either, you know.'

'You told me as much, once,' Dr Quansah said gently. 'I had not forgotten.'

Pride has so often been my demon, the tempting conviction that one is able to see the straight path and to point it out to others. I was proud of my cleverness when I persuaded Kwaale to begin teaching Ruth Quansah the language of her people. Each afternoon they had lessons, and I assisted only when necessary to clarify some point of grammar. Ruth, once she started, became quite interested. Despite what she had said, she was curious to know what the other girls talked about together. As for Kwaale, it soothed her rancour to be asked to instruct, and it gave her an opportunity to learn something about Ruth, to see her as she was and not as Kwaale's imagination had distorted her. Gradually the two became, if not friends, at least reasonably peaceful acquaintances. Ruth continued to see David, but as her afternoons were absorbed by the language lessons, she no longer went to the Mackies' house quite so often.

Then came the Odwira. Ruth asked if she might go down to the village with Kwaale, and as most of the girls would be going, I agreed. Miss Povey would have liked to keep the girls away from the local festivals, which she regarded as dangerously heathen, but this quarantine had never proved practicable. At the time of the Odwira the girls simply disappeared, permission or not, like migrating birds.

Late that afternoon I saw the school lorry setting off for Eburaso, so I decided to go along. We swerved perilously down the mountain road, and reached the village just in time to see the end of the procession, as the chief, carried in palanquin under his saffron umbrella, returned from the river after the rituals there. The palm-wine libations had been poured, the souls of the populace cleansed. Now the Eburasahene would offer the new yams to the ancestors, and then the celebrations would begin. Drumming and dancing would go on all night, and the next morning Miss Povey, if she were wise, would not ask too many questions.

The mud and thatch shanties of the village were empty of inhabitants and the one street was full. Shouting, singing, wildly excited, they sweated and thronged. Everyone who owned a good cloth was wearing it, and the women fortunate enough to possess gold earrings or bangles were flaunting them before the covetous eyes of those whose bracelets and beads were only coloured glass. For safety I remained in the parked lorry, fearing my unsteady leg in such a mob.

I spotted Kwaale and Ruth. Kwaale's usual air of tranquillity had vanished. She was all sun-coloured cloth and whirling brown arms. I had never seen anyone with such a violence of beauty as she possessed, like surf or volcano, a spendthrift splendour. Then, out of the street's turbulence of voices I heard the low shout of a young man near her.

'Fire a gun at me.'

I knew what was about to happen, for the custom was a very old one. Kwaale threw back her head and laughed. Her hands flicked at her cloth and for an instant she stood there naked except for the white beads around her hips, and her *amoanse*, the red cloth between her legs. Still laughing, she knotted her cloth back on again, and the young man put an arm around her shoulders and drew her close to him.

Ruth, tidy and separate in her frock with its pastel flowers, stared as though unable to believe what she had seen. Slowly she turned and it was then that she saw me. She began to force her way through the crowd of villagers. Instantly Kwaale dropped the young man's hand and went after her. Ruth stood beside the lorry, her eyes appealing to me.

'You saw—you saw what she—'

Kwaale's hand was clawing at her shoulder then, spinning her around roughly.

'What are you telling her? It is not for you to say!'

Kwaale thought I would be bound to disapprove. I could have explained the custom to Ruth, as it had been explained to me many years ago by Kwaale's father. I could have told her it used to be 'Shoot an arrow', for Mother Nyame created the sun with fire, and arrows of the same fire were shot into the veins of mankind and became life-blood. I could have said that the custom was a reminder that women are the source of life. But I did not, for I was by no means sure either Kwaale or the young man knew the roots of the tradition or that they cared. Something was permitted at festival time—why should they care about anything other than the beat of their own blood?

'Wait, Ruth, you don't understand—'

'I understand what she is,' Ruth said distinctly. 'She's nothing but a —'

Kwaale turned upon her viciously.

'Talk, you! Talk and talk. What else could you do? No man here would want you as his wife—you're too ugly.'

Ruth drew away, shocked and uncertain. But Kwaale had not finished.

'Why don't you go? Take all your money and go! Why don't you?'

I should have spoken then, tried to explain one to the other. I think I did, after a paralysed moment, but it was too late. Ruth, twisting away, struggled around the clusters of people and disappeared among the trees on the path that led back to the mountain top.

The driver had trouble in moving the lorry through the jammed streets. By the time we got onto the hill road Ruth was not there. When we reached the school I got out and limped over to the Primary girls who were playing outside the main building. I asked if they had seen her, and they twirled and fluttered around me like green and brown leaves, each trying to outdo the others in impressing me with their display of English.

'Miss Neddeen, I seein' she. Wit' my eye I seein' she. She going deah——'

The way they pointed was the road to the Mackies' house.

I did not especially want the lorry to go roaring into the Mackies' compound as though the errand were urgent or critical, so when we sighted the casuarina trees I had the driver stop. I walked slowly past David's menagerie, where the cutting-grass scratched in its cage and the snakes lay in bright apathetic coils. Some sense of propriety made me hesitate before I had quite reached the house. Ruth and David were on the verandah, and I could hear their voices. I suppose it was shameful of me to listen, but it would have been worse to appear at that moment.

'If it was up to me——' David's voice was strained and tight with embarrassment. 'But you know what she's like.'

'What did she say, David? What did she say?' Ruth's voice, desperate with her need to know, her fear of knowing.

'Oh, well—nothing much.'

'Tell me!'

Then David, faltering, ashamed, tactless.

'Only that African girls mature awfully young, and she somehow got the daft notion that—look here, Ruth, I'm sorry, but when she gets an idea there's nothing anyone can do. I know it's a lot of rot. I know you're not the ordinary kind of African. You're almost—almost like a—like us.'

It was his best, I suppose. It was not his fault that it was not good enough. She cried out, then, and although the casuarina boughs hid the two from my sight, I could imagine their faces well enough, and David's astounded look at the hurt in her eyes.

'Almost——' she said. Then, with a fury I would not have believed possible, 'No, I'm not! I'm not like you at all. I won't be!'

'Listen, Ruth——'

But she had thrust off his hand and had gone. She passed close to the place where I stood but she did not see me. Once again I watched her running. Running and running, into the forest where I could not follow.

I was frantic lest Miss Povey should find out and notify Dr Quansah before we could find Ruth. I had Ayesha go all through the school and grounds, for she could move more rapidly and unobtrusively than I. I waited, stumping up and down my garden, finally forcing myself to sit down and assume at least the appearance of calm. At last Ayesha returned. Only tiredness showed in her face, and my heart contracted.

'You did not find her, little one?'

She shook her head. 'She is not here. She is gone.'

Gone. Had she remained in the forest, then, with its thorns and strangular vines, its ferned depths that could hide death, its green silences? Or had she run as far as the river, dark and smooth as oil, deceptively smooth, with its saurian kings who fed of whatever flesh they could find? I dared not think.

I did something then that I had never before permitted myself to do. I picked up Ayesha and held the child tightly, not for her consoling but for my own. She reached out and touched a finger to my face.

'You are crying. For her?'

Then Ayesha sighed a little, resignedly.

'Come then,' she said. 'I will show you where she is.'

Had I known her so slightly all along, my small Ayesha whose childhood lay beaten and lost somewhere in the shanties and brothels of Takoradi or Kumasi, the airless upper rooms of palm-wine bars in Lagos or Kaduna? Without a word I rose and followed her.

We did not have far to go. The gardeners' quarters were at the back of the school grounds, surrounded by *niim* trees and a few banana palms. In the last hut of the row, Yindo sat cross-legged on the packed-earth floor. Beside him on a dirty and torn grass mat Ruth Quansah lay, face down, her head buried in her arms.

Ayesha pointed. Why had she wanted to conceal it? To this day I do not really know, nor what the hut recalled to her, nor what she felt, for her face bore no more expression than a pencilled stick-child's, and her eyes were as dull as they had been when she first came to us here.

Ruth heard my cane and my dragged foot. I know she did. But she did not stir.

'Madam——' Yindo's voice was nearly incoherent with terror. 'I beg you. You no give me sack. I Dagomba man, madam. No got bruddah dis place. I beg you, mek I no go lose dis job——'

I tried to calm him with meaningless sounds of reassurance.

Then I asked him to tell me. He spoke in a harsh whisper, his face averted.

'She come dis place like she crez'. She say—do so.' He gestured unmistakably 'I—I try, but I can no do so for she. I too fear.'

He held out his hands then in an appeal both desperate and hopeless. He was a desert man. He expected no mercy here, far from the dwellings of his tribe.

Ruth still had not moved. I do not think she had even heard Yindo's words. At last she lifted her head, but she did not speak. She scanned slowly the mud walls, the tin basin for washing, the upturned box that served as table, the old hurricane lamp, and in a niche the grey and grinning head of the dead chameleon, around it the blue beads like naive eyes shining and beside it the offering of a toffee wrapped in grimy silver paper.

I stood there in the hut doorway, leaning on my ebony cane to support my cumbersome body, looking at the three of them but finding nothing simple enough to say. What words, after all, could possibly have been given to the outcast children?

I told Dr Quansah. I did not spare him anything, nor myself either. I imagined he would be angry at my negligence, my blundering, but he was not.

'You should not blame yourself in this way,' he said. 'I do not want that. It is—really, I think it is a question of time, after all.'

'Undoubtedly. But in the meantime?'

'I don't know.' He passed a hand across his forehead. 'I seem to become tired so much more than I used to. Solutions do not come readily any more. Even for a father like myself, who relies so much on schools, it is still not such an easy thing, to bring up a child without a mother.'

I leaned back in my scarlet chair. The old rattan received my head, and my absurdly jagged breath eased.

'No,' I said. 'I'm sure it can't be easy.'

We were silent for a moment. Then with some effort Dr Quansah began to speak, almost apologetically.

'Coming back to this country after so long away—you know, I think that is the last new thing I shall be able to do in my life. Does that seem wrong? When one grows older, one is aware of so many difficulties. Often they appear to outweigh all else.'

My hands fumbled for my cane, the ebony that was grown and

carved here. I found and held it, and it both reassured and mocked me.

'Perhaps,' I said deliberately. 'But Ruth——'

'I am taking her away. She wants to go. What else can I do? There is a school in the town where a cousin of mine lives.'

'Yes. I see. You cannot do anything else, of course.'

He rose. 'Goodbye,' he said, 'and——'

But he did not finish the sentence. We shook hands, and he left.

At Eburaso School we go on as before. Miss Povey and I still snipe back and forth, knowing in our hearts that we rely upon our differences and would miss them if they were not there. I still teach my alien speech to the young ones, who continue to impart to it a kind of garbled charm. I grow heavier and I fancy my lameness is more pronounced, although Kwaale assures me this is not the case. In few enough years I will have reached retirement age.

Sitting in my garden and looking at the sun on the prickly pear and the poinsettia, I think of that island of grey rain where I must go as a stranger, when the time comes, while others must remain as strangers here.

MONIQUE BOSCO

The Old Woman's Lamentations on Yom Kippur

Day of Atonement, when I asked nothing but to meditate, repent.

Day of Atonement, Remembrance Day. They set aside whole days like this for us to clear up our bad accounts, to feel remorse and regret. On this day of silence thunder made a hellish racket all the same, on this September day. I don't even know any more what it was I wanted to forget, erase, blot out, by making this artificial fast so I could be absolved, forgiven.

But I was thirsty.

I did drink, just little sips at first, then big gulps. Once I'd taken a drink—broken the rule of abstinence—my guilt made me ashamed, so I ate too, just to relieve my pangs of anxiety. For a week now I've been scared of these attacks of weakness that come over me and shake me up inside.

Everything has been difficult since . . . since when? To say everything has always been difficult would be more like it.

This tremendous tiredness. I'm getting up. I'm going to get up. I do get up, then crawl right back again under the thick ba-ba-blankets. One more try and . . . I'm senile, you say? Sure, I don't deny it. Age has got nothing to do with it. Neither has the weather. 'Doctor, would you like me to describe my symptoms?' He actually seems to be listening. That's enough to make me keep quiet. I have no idea any more whether I'd want to be like other people, all those people wandering around all over the world. Look at them, energetically coming and going, charging around in subways and buses, criss-crossing the whole island from dawn to dusk. No sooner are these hordes settled in front of the TV, to watch their game or their 'great film', than other hordes start coming out of the woodwork—a different type altogether—full of vitality for going dancing, or gambling, or knocking themselves out all night at porno shows, or simply getting ready to take over at the head of the class, or from yesterday's promotion. Ah! the handsome mahogany desks that have to be freshly polished for the morning!

I feel dizzy, my head is spinning. All these organized people, with their union cards and their daily routines of thinking about what's best. I myself, for months now, for years, have been unemployed.

That, too, has been taken away from me, that one comforting alibi. Comforting for the rest of them, obviously. That's why, when they'd ask about me, I used to make a big show of announcing grandly, 'I'm working, you know. Full time.'

What's to say from now on? 'I'm unemployed. Full time.'

Full time, that's for sure. I have all the time in the world to get upset about the state of the earth, the planet, to take inventory of the disasters, floods, plagues, outbreaks of cholera, that are claiming new victims—and that's not to mention AIDS. This way I'll never be idle. I'll make myself a bunch of files on everything. If I had anyone to talk to, I'd be able to provide them with exact references, with up-to-date figures and statistics on the entire universe. It's fabulous, believe me, what goes on. I've got a passion for everything, now that there's never any passion to interrupt my sleep. I sleep all the time, since I can no longer sleep snuggled up, once in a while, beside a living body.

'You're at least eating properly?'

This doctor hears nothing, apparently. I hate the way he looks as much as his voice, when he inspects me this way, skulking behind his white coat. What does he see? My legs, like chicken legs? —one of their famous 'barnyard' chickens, one that wasn't stuffed full of hormones, but scratched frantically in the gravel, crazy with hunger. My arms? Let's not talk about them. Sometimes, when I can't sleep, I get a strange feeling that I've grown old all of a sudden, and find myself rattling around in my casket. Still, very nice that I should have a right to a real pine casket for my 'final resting-place'. I wonder what they'll invent, should it take me a long time, that will be 'durable and economical'. Stainless steel? Sheet metal? I ought to look into that. They're going to make fun of me again. 'Old lady, what's it to you—when, or what kind of saucepan we cook your goose in?' They're right, I don't care. Maybe they've salvaged the old crematoriums, who knows? They let on there was never any such thing.

But there I have to stop.

I dread weeping my eyes out, letting myself stir up the past, raking through the coals and ashes.

My old grandfather, the one on my father's side, the Polish side, when yet one more affliction would strike them, he didn't hesitate to spread ashes all over his face, his clothes. To let out—in public—the most ghastly blood-curdling shrieks. Nowadays we're ashamed of those old people. I miss them. I can't stand the old women my age—the ones of my own generation—with no sense of shame, no religion, yet still terrified of God and the devil. Yes, in the old days they had staying power, something to hold onto. I should have worn a corset, I should have, I should.

He persists: 'Are you really eating properly, Madam?' Don't you know I'm on 'welfare', as they call it? Naturally, I have to watch every penny. I save coupons for 'bargains'. I walk, doctor, regularly, to work up an appetite. I roam the aisles of Steinberg's for hours, keeping an eye out for the stupendous moment when the 'bargains' show up. I never miss one of them. Just try and make a balanced diet when, purely to economize I can assure you, I buy a slightly limp bunch of celery-hearts, or a not-too-fresh cauliflower. The other people go by. They dodge in and out, glide past, bump into me, sometimes they excuse themselves for jostling me—but I can tell that I'm annoying them, there with my little shopping bag that's still good, even though it's been folded a thousand times. As if I'd buy a new one just to please them. Yes, I deliberate over everything, I calculate. I add and add again.

No matter what I do, it's thought out, and it's not my fault I've come to this. But the hardest of all is not 'this'.

The hardest of all

Sorrow hidden in the heart, the pit that hides 'way down in the heart of the juiciest peach

The hardest of all is, quite simply, growing old

Where the keynote is less

I see less, I hear less, my hands tremble so much they can't even manage to give a gentle, reassuring little pat to the cheek or the hand of a child.

'Grandmother, why do you have such big teeth?'

The way he used to laugh, little Samuel, when we'd play Little Red Riding Hood together.

He was four then, and I was forty.

Today I'm a hundred, for sure. Pointless to add up the number of years, that's the way I feel, in my bones. A hundred years.

One Hundred Years of Solitude.

'For they are everyone and I am alone,' said the Underground Man. And yesterday when, just to spoil myself a bit, I went out to take a walk up and down Sherbrooke Street—a nice long tour, all the way from Guy to Peel—I got the shock of my life. It was too hot for this time of year. But I was wearing my suit anyway, or, I should say the ex-suit of my cousin Zelda, to be more precise. Zelda's a 'tightwad', but the things she buys for her 'affairs', things that she wants to 'last', as she says, she pays a bundle for. After ten years with this hound's-tooth outfit, Zelda'd had enough of it and handed it down to me. And I wear it whenever I'm really down in the dumps, or for special occasions. Say what you like, having expensive clothes really sets you up. I get the feeling that people bump into me less, and sometimes even absent-minded young people make room for me. Anyway, I was wearing my suit and doing some very careful window-shopping. I was taking in every detail of each display: porcelain from China or Limoges; antiques—easy to call them antiques, they're hardly ever, at the outside, as old as I am; furs: magnificent minks—grey, silver, white. I love Sherbrooke Street—not a price tag in sight to risk spoiling our contemplation. I find that discreet, tasteful. On the other side of the street was the Museum. I wasn't sure whether to cross or not. A tour of the Museum might have been pleasant, and it's free one day a week. But I didn't have enough courage to go and ask what day. So I continued on the same sidewalk. In front of the Ritz I hesitated again. It looked like they'd completely renovated it. The doorman intimidated me. But I made up a little story—a waste of time because I went right in with no trouble at all. I swear, the high ceilings, the rich wall-coverings, and the huge leather chairs took my breath away. I sat in one of them. Nothing happened. No one even noticed me.

So, even an old woman on welfare can have the luxury of watching, in comfort, and, as a matter of fact, for the good of her welfare, the passing scene.

I watched. I listened.

Well—they were an ordinary-looking crowd, very ordinary in fact. Nothing elegant, not the least bit of chic.

Zelda would have been a sensation. Even I, in her old suit, I thought I was pretty elegant, almost dignified.

I probably should have gone to synagogue for Yom Kippur.

To pray with them, for them, to wail and sing with them:

'Next year in Jerusalem.'

No, no Lord, not in Jerusalem,

Next year

No, thank you very much

It's too kind

No thanks, not for me

I beg of you

'Somewhere out of this world' would suit me better.

Translated by Patricia Sillers

LOUISE MAHEUX-FORCIER

Discretion

Maud never spoke without a hand over her mouth, never laughed except to herself, neither creasing her face nor showing her teeth, and never cried but in secret, behind the raised lid of her desk or the trunk of the big oak tree that shaded the playground.

Her movements were inaudible, and if suddenly you turned around to find her following you, she would be the image of Lot's wife—pale as salt, dumb-founded, her eyes unseeing, a statue unstirred by any of the usual impulses: 'I like you', or 'Come and study with me tonight', or 'Comfort me, my mother hates me, my father beats me up'.

Of Maud's house we knew nothing but the outside, if that. We couldn't have said if it was stone or brick, because of the vines that crept the length and breadth of its walls.

Of Maud's family we knew little more than what you guess at dusk, when lamplight casts silhouettes behind drawn curtains.

We had the impression that with Maud, life must be something not for living but for hiding away. Now and then, we would even go so far as to whisper that Maud didn't have any—that she had no life at all.

Nothing but silence. Absence. A heart you never heard beating. A fly you couldn't hear. An ethereal little thing, unsubstantial, almost abstract. A mystery.

From one diploma after another, we had reached puberty without knowing any more of her than of a sphinx.

That year, just before the summer, when according to custom we were taunting each other with tales of cruises and sunny faraway shores (knowing very well that most of us would be building our sand-castles-in-Spain on the neighbourhood pavement), I caught a glimpse in Maud's eyes of something other than the scorn our wanderings to romantic lands of milk and honey usually provoked in her, something far more dramatic and serious: in the desperate blue of those eyes were all the depths of the sea. I was sure that at last Maud would find oblivion there, and the numbered days of her vacation would sink into that sea without a murmur, leaving not a ripple behind.

She came back safe and sound, but more transparent than ever, as if the fresh air had blown her colour away instead of reviving it; and more impassive, as if the imaginary journeys we were so full of had left in her—the one who really had gone away—not a trace.

Unlike Maud, I was unmistakably physical, a noisy type, and, to top it off, so fond of praise that I almost expected cheers for the feat of cracking an egg without breaking the yolk.

So on the famous day in October when Maud returned my smile and invited me to her house, I thought my moment of glory had arrived, just for drawing her out of her shell. Convinced I was off to desecrate the tomb of a pharaoh, at the very least, I started rehearsing my report, polishing the mysteries I was bound to shed light on the following day, and counting in advance on the highlights, the gems that were going to secure me a pre-eminent place in the class and in the world.

Well, of all that I saw, learned, and guessed that evening, I have never said a word. It may even be on account of that day after, forty years ago, that now I am teased for my colourlessness, my overly discreet temperament, which takes fright at the slightest confidence, and my total lack of vanity, which makes the slightest honour painful and distressing.

On the way, then, to my glory, arm in arm with a Maud who, haloed in autumn leaves, was suddenly concrete, chatty, and attentive to the point of carrying my book-bag; yet I think at the same time I felt a terrible uneasiness mixed with fear: at my side was a phantom all at once stepping out of her shroud, passing from supernatural to tangible. Not only had Maud too suddenly come to life—what troubled me even more was the realization, from a glance at the rounded profile of her blouse and an inquisitive touch at the border of the fabric, that long before the rest of us, in the span of a single vacation, she had passed from childhood to maturity.

I said I hadn't told my mother where I was going, but Maud assured me she wouldn't keep me for long and, anyway, no one was going to send the police after me just for being late one more time! . . . I swelled with pride . . . So Maud was aware of my habits. Before making her choice she had studied me, and found out for herself I was not some little dog on a leash, or a coward afraid of a spanking.

That pleased her. And I appreciated the honour all the more since I had always been a sissy at heart, ready to run away fast . . . But Maud was smiling at me, her face all crinkled with pleasure, showing her even white teeth. Already her practised hands had parted the curtain of vines that hung over the door, and she was telling me to wipe my feet on the mat.

Once through the half-light of the vestibule, where Maud left my book-bag, I saw nothing at first but the staircase. A superb staircase that turned on itself, unrolling up to the second floor its spiral of wrought iron and varnished steps, like the coils of a snake. That sounds crazy, of course, but at a distance images sometimes take a curious twist, as if the past, having already linked them to the future, projected them to us in foreshortened perspective, laying one on top of another . . . It was when I entered Maud's room that I saw the snake, not in the attractive form of a spiral staircase but in its small and disgusting reality. It was curled around itself in the middle of a miniature vivarium, and I probably wouldn't have noticed it so quickly if the fluorescent tube that served as sun for the reptile had not also been the source of light for the whole room.

Maud muffled my cry with a hand so brisk it was almost a slap, then pressed it over my mouth like a gag until, with the commanding blue of her eyes, she had made me so ashamed that never since then have I lost my composure or cried out, either at the peak of joy or in the depths of the worst fear, pain, or disaster.

While I was catching my breath, sitting on the floor at the foot of the bed, Maud had gone to the window. I had watched her vainly attempt to tear the vines away from the frame—intending, no doubt, to let the last rays of dusk into the room. With a sigh, she had given up and lit the wick of a pretty oil lamp with an orange globe, which cast around it a warm autumn glow. Like a gift. Then, having stationed herself, erect, before the mirror of a large wardrobe, she had begun to undress.

There is no other way for me to tell these things. I can't slow them down. Or speed them up. The memory is there, after forty years. In profile. Piece by piece, Maud takes off her clothes, raising her arms for the ones with sleeves and straps, letting the rest slip, billowing, to her feet. She looks at herself.

Then she speaks. But there is a filter over her words.

'I'd rather have had a rattlesnake. With rattles that worked, really venomous. Or a cobra. With a fine point on his fangs . . . That one . . .' and for a moment her gaze travels to the top of the reptile's coils, seeks the small glassy eyes as they open . . . 'that one is good for nothing but sleeping and gulping dead flies . . . Go to the table beside my bed and take a box of matches, a blue one. The red ones really have matches in them . . . Take a blue box and feed him . . . I know it makes you sick, but you have to do it; after, you'll be prouder of this than all the other things you boast about . . .'

She leans over. I don't move. She rolls her stockings down to her ankles, takes them off. Maud is naked in front of her mirror. For me, in profile.

Then she speaks. But the voice is husky, as if full of tears. If Maud had been hidden behind the big oak in the schoolyard at that moment, those tears would have washed down her face, but she holds them back in her throat because I am there to see. With Maud, life cancels itself out.

'Don't you notice anything? . . .' and with caressing hands she traces circles all over her body . . . 'I'm pregnant . . . Come . . . You have to touch, press your ear close, to understand . . . There's something living in me . . . There . . .' She moulds herself with her hands, as if wanting to balloon even now.

I don't move. But someone in the next room does, passing the closed door. I hear the heavy sound of heavy shoes receding, step by step . . .

It's late. I have to go. They'll be worrying about me at home. Maybe calling the police . . . But Maud said I was brave, courageous, and that was why she chose me . . . One should always ask advice from someone more solid and experienced than oneself. What advice, Maud? What advice can a little girl give, trapped in a pharaoh's tomb? What secret can she share?

'That's my father going down to dinner. Don't panic, little bird, my father only forces my door at night, when my mother's asleep. You see, that's why I wanted a real cobra, like the one he took me to see at the Jardin des Plantes, in Paris, this summer . . .' for a flash, her eyes seek mine, mocking my imaginary safaris and cruises down the Nile, then she goes on, 'instead of that useless little grass snake that can't hurt anything but flies . . . Don't make a mistake . . . I said: a blue box . . . There's nothing for consumption in the others . . . they're for combustion!'

Maud starts to laugh, but to herself, wrapping herself in the bedspread. Then she dances, holding the oil-lamp, towards her bedside table.

Sitting on my book-bag, at the other side of the neighbourhood, I watched for a long time as the orange flames lit the autumn clouds.

The fire that razed the house of vines to the ground that night caused such an uproar, my parents didn't even ask where I'd been the day before. That made things much easier for me at the cemetery; I was able to weep and shudder in peace as they buried the three of them, first the two deaf-mutes, then their daughter . . . It was particularly useful when the police opened the inquest, since I'd had the time to think and prepare my alibi. Everyone is entitled to slip away once in a while, even if it's just to go to the movies, to see *Aurore l'enfant-martyre* . . .

—No, no one ever set foot in Maud's house . . . Yes, she carried my book-bag that day, but she gave it back to me a minute later, at the corner . . . No, she didn't have any girl-friends . . . No, there were no boys hanging around . . . No, I didn't know her parents couldn't speak or hear . . . how could they have travelled, like that? . . . What I mean is . . . Leave me alone, I don't know anything! . . . All I know is that with Maud, life didn't make any noise . . . How can I explain? . . . It crept . . . And I've always been scared of anything that creeps, even a baby on a carpet, or a hand running along the bannister of a staircase.

Translated by Sally Livingston

ALICE MUNRO

The Peace of Utrecht

I have been at home now for three weeks and it has not been a success. Maddy and I, though we speak cheerfully of our enjoyment of so long and intimate a visit, will be relieved when it is over. Silences disturb us. We laugh immoderately. I am afraid—very likely we are both afraid—that when the moment comes to say goodbye, unless we are very quick to kiss, and fervently, mockingly squeeze each other's shoulders, we will have to look straight into the desert that is between us, and acknowledge that we are not merely indifferent; at heart we reject each other, and as for that past we make so much of sharing we do not really share it at all, but each keep it jealously to ourselves, thinking privately that the other has turned alien, and forfeited her claim.

And I am wondering why this should be.

At night we often sit out on the steps of the veranda, and drink gin and smoke diligently to defeat the mosquitoes and postpone until very late the moment of going to bed. It is hot; the evening takes a long time to burn out. The high brick house, which stays fairly cool until mid-afternoon, holds the heat of the day trapped until long after dark. It was always like this, and Maddy and I recall how we used to drag our mattress downstairs onto the veranda, where we lay counting falling stars and trying to stay awake till dawn. We never did, falling asleep each night about the time a chill drift of air came up off the river, carrying a smell of reeds and the black ooze of the riverbed. At half-past ten a bus goes through the town, not slowing much; we see it go by at the end of our street. It is the same bus I used to take when I came home from college, and I remember coming into Jubilee on some warm night, seeing the earth bare around the massive roots of the trees, the drinking-fountain surrounded by little puddles of water on the main street, the soft scrawls of blue and red and orange light that said BILLIARDS AND CAFE; feeling as I recognized these signs a queer kind of oppression and release, as I exchanged the whole holiday world of school, of friends, and later on, of love, for the dim world of continuing disaster, of home. Maddy making the same journey four years earlier must have felt the same thing. I want to ask her: is it possible that children growing up as we did lose the ability to believe in—to be at home in—any ordinary and peaceful reality? But I don't ask her; we never talk about any of that. 'No exorcising here,' says Maddy in her thin, bright voice with the slangy quality I had forgotten, 'we're not going to depress each other.' So we haven't.

One night Maddy took me to a party at the Lake, which is about thirty miles west of here. The party was held in a cottage a couple of women from Jubilee had rented for the week. Most of the women there seemed to be widowed, single, separated, or divorced; the men were mostly young and unmarried—those from Jubilee so young that I remember them only as little boys in the lower grades. There were two or three older men, not with their wives. But the women—they reminded me surprisingly of certain women familiar to me in my childhood, though of course I never saw their party-going personalities, only their activities in the stores and offices, and not infrequently in the Sunday-schools, of Jubilee. They differed from the married women in being more aware of themselves in the world, a little brisker, sharper, and coarser (though I can think of only one or two whose respectability was ever in question). They wore resolutely stylish though matronly clothes, which tended to swish and rustle over their hard rubber corsets, and they put perfume, quite a lot of it, on their artificial flowers. Maddy's friends were considerably modernized; they had copper rinses on their hair, and blue eyelids, and a robust capacity for drink. Maddy I thought did not look one of them, with her slight figure and her still carelessly worn dark hair; her face has grown thin and strained without losing entirely its girlish look of impertinence and pride. But she speaks with the harsh twang of the local accent, which we used to make fun of, and her expression as she romped and drank was determinedly undismayed. It seemed to me that she was making every effort to belong with these people and that shortly she would succeed. It seemed to me too that she wanted me to see her succeeding, to see her repudiating that secret, exhilarating, really monstrous snobbery which we cultivated when we were children together, and promised ourselves, of course, much bigger things than Jubilee.

During the game in which all the women put an article of clothing—it begins decorously with a shoe—in a basket, and then all the men come in and have a race trying to fit things onto their proper owners, I went out and sat in the car, where I felt lonely for my husband and my friends and listened to the hilarity of the party and the waves falling on the beach and presently went to sleep. Maddy came much later and said, 'For Heaven's sake!' Then she laughed and said airily like a lady in an English movie, 'You find these goings-on distasteful?' We both laughed; I felt apologetic, and rather sick from drinking and not getting drunk. 'They may not be much on intellectual conversation but their hearts are in the right place, as the saying goes.' I did not dispute this and we drove at eighty miles an hour from Inverhuron to Jubilee. Since then we have not been to any more parties.

But we are not always alone when we sit out on the steps. Often we are joined by a man named Fred Powell. He was at the party, peaceably in the background remembering whose liquor was whose and amiably holding someone's head over the rickety porch railing. He grew up in Jubilee as we did, but I do not remember him, I suppose because he went through school some years ahead of us and then went away to the war. Maddy surprised me by bringing him home to supper the first night I was here, and then we spent the evening, as we have spent many since, making this strange man a present of our childhood, or of that version of our childhood which is safely preserved in anecdote, as in a kind of mental cellophane. And what fantasies we build around the frail figures of our childselves, so that they emerge beyond recognition incorrigible and gay. We tell stories together well. 'You girls have got good memories,' Fred Powell says, and sits watching us with an air of admiration and something else—reserve, embarrassment, mild deprecation—which appears on the faces of these mild deliberate people as they watch the keyed-up antics of their entertainers.

Now thinking of Fred Powell I admit that my reaction to this—this *situation* as I call it—is far more conventional than I would have expected; it is even absurd. And I do not know what situation it really is. I know that he is married. Maddy told me so, on the first evening, in a merely informative voice. His wife is an invalid. He has her at the Lake for the summer, Maddy says, he's very good to her. I do not know if he is Maddy's lover and she will never tell me. Why should it matter to me? Maddy is well over thirty. But I keep thinking of the way he sits on our steps with his hands set flat on his spread knees, his mild full face turned almost indulgently toward Maddy as she talks; he has an affable masculine look of being diverted but unimpressed. And Maddy teases him, tells him he is too fat, will not smoke his cigarettes, involves him in private, nervous, tender arguments which have no meaning and no end. He allows it. (And this is what frightens me, I know it now: he allows it; *she needs it*.) When she is a little drunk she says in tones of half-pleading mockery that he is her only real friend. 'He speaks the same language,' she says. 'Nobody else does.' I have no answer to that.

Then again I begin to wonder: *is* he only her friend? I had forgotten certain restrictions of life in Jubilee—and this holds good whatever the pocket novels are saying about small towns—and also what strong, respectable, never overtly sexual friendships can flourish within these restrictions and be fed by them, so that in the end such relationships may consume half a life. This thought depresses me (unconsummated relationships depress outsiders perhaps more than anybody else) so much that I find myself wishing for them to be honest lovers.

The rhythm of life in Jubilee is primitively seasonal. Deaths occur in the winter; marriages are celebrated in the summer. There is good reason for this; the winters are long and full of hardship and the old and weak cannot always get through them. Last winter was a catastrophe, such as may be expected every ten or twelve years; you can see how the pavement in the streets is broken up, as if the town had survived a minor bombardment. A death is dealt with then in the middle of great difficulties; there comes time now in the summer to think about it, and talk. I find that people stop me in the street to talk about my mother. I have heard from them about her funeral, what flowers she had and what the weather was like on that day. And now that she is dead I no longer feel that when they say the words 'your mother' they deal a knowing, cunning blow at my pride. I used to feel that; at those words I felt my whole identity, that pretentious adolescent construction, come crumbling down. Now I listen to them speak of her, so gently and ceremoniously, and I realize that she became one of the town's possessions and oddities, its brief legends. This she achieved in spite of us, for we tried, both crudely and artfully, to keep her at home, away from that sad notoriety; not for her sake, but for ours, who suffered such unnecessary humiliation at the sight of saliva dribbling over her chin, her eyes rolling back in her head in a temporary paralysis of the eye-muscles, at the sound of her thickened voice, whose embarrassing pronouncements it was our job to interpret to outsiders. So bizarre was the disease she had in its effects that it made us feel like crying out in apology (though we stayed stiff and white) as if we were accompanying a particularly tasteless and badly done sideshow. All wasted, our pride, our purging its rage in wild caricatures we did for each other (no, not caricatures, for she was one herself: imitations). We should have let the town have her; it would have treated her better.

About Maddy and her ten-years' vigil they say very little; perhaps they want to spare my feelings, remembering that I was the one who went away and here are my two children to show for it, while Maddy is alone and has nothing but that discouraging house. But I don't think so; in Jubilee the feelings are not spared this way. And they ask me point-blank why I did not come home for the funeral; I am glad I have the excuse of the blizzard that halted air travel that week, for I do not know if I would have come anyway, after Maddy had written so vehemently urging me to stay away. I felt strongly that she had a right to be left alone with it, if she wanted to be, after all this time.

After all this time. Maddy was the one who stayed. First, she went away to college, then I went. 'You give me four years, I'll give you four years,' she said. But I got married. She was not surprised; she was exasperated at me for my wretched useless feelings of guilt. She said that she had always meant to stay. She said that Mother no longer 'bothered' her. 'Our Gothic Mother,' she said, 'I play it out now, I let her be. I don't keep trying to make her *human* any more. You know.' It would simplify things so much to say that Maddy was religious, that she felt the joys of self-sacrifice, the strong, mystical appeal of total rejection. But about Maddy who could say that? When we were in our teens, and our old aunts, Aunt Annie and Auntie Lou, spoke to us of some dutiful son or daughter who had given up everything for an ailing parent, Maddy would quote impiously the opinions of modern psychiatry. Yet she stayed. All I can think about that, all I have ever been able to think, to comfort me, is that she may have been able and may even have chosen to live without time and in perfect imaginary freedom as children do, the future untampered with, all choices always possible.

To change the subject, people ask me what it is like to be back in

Jubilee. But I don't know, I am still waiting for something to tell me, to make me understand that I am back. The day I drove up from Toronto with my children in the back seat of the car I was very tired, on the last lap of a twenty-five hundred mile trip. I had to follow a complicated system of highways and side roads, for there is no easy way to get to Jubilee from anywhere on earth. Then about two o'clock in the afternoon I saw ahead of me, so familiar and unexpected, the gaudy, peeling cupola of the town hall, which is no relation to any of the rest of the town's squarely-built, dingy-grey and red-brick architecture. (Underneath it hangs a great bell, to be rung in the event of some mythical disaster.) I drove up to the main street—a new service-station, new stucco front on the Queen's Hotel—and turned into the quiet, decaying side streets where old maids live, and have bird-baths and blue delphiniums in their gardens. The big brick houses that I knew, with their wooden verandas and gaping, dark-screened windows, seemed to me plausible but unreal. (Anyone to whom I have mentioned the dreaming, sunken feeling of these streets wants to take me out to the north side of town where there is a new soft-drink bottling plant, some new ranch-style houses, and a Tastee-Freez.) Then I parked my car in a little splash of shade in front of the house where I used to live. My little girl, whose name is Margaret, said neutrally yet with some disbelief, 'Mother, is that your house?'

And I felt that my daughter's voice expressed a complex disappointment (to which, characteristically, she seemed resigned, or even resigned *in advance*); it contained the whole flatness and strangeness of the moment in which is revealed the source of legends, the unsatisfactory, apologetic, and persistent reality. The red brick of which the house is built looked harsh and hot in the sun, and was marked in two or three places by long grimacing cracks; the veranda, which always had the air of an insubstantial decoration, was visibly falling away. There was—there *is*—a little blind window of coloured glass beside the front door. I sat staring at it with a puzzled lack of emotional recognition. I sat and looked at the house and the window-shades did not move, the door did not fly open, no one came out on the veranda; there was no one at home. This was as I had expected, since Maddy works now in the office of the Town Clerk, yet I was surprised to see the house take on such a closed, bare, impoverished look, merely by being left empty. And it was brought home to me, as I walked across the front yard to the steps, that after all these summers on the Coast I had forgotten the immense inland heat, which makes you feel as if you have to carry the whole burning sky on your head.

A sign pinned to the front door announced, in Maddy's rather sloppy and flamboyant hand: *Visitors Welcome, Children Free, Rates to be Arranged Later (You'll be sorry), Walk In.* On the hall table was a bouquet of pink phlox whose velvety scent filled the hot air of a closed house on a summer afternoon. 'Upstairs!' I said to the children, and I took the hand of the little girl and her smaller brother, who had slept in the car and who rubbed against me, whimpering, as he walked. Then I paused, one foot on the bottom step, and turned to greet, matter-of-factly, the reflection of a thin, tanned, habitually watchful woman, recognizably a Young Mother, whose hair, pulled into a knot on top of her head, exposed a jawline no longer softly fleshed, a brown neck rising with a look of tension from the little sharp knobs of the collarbone—this in the hall mirror that had shown me, last time I looked, a commonplace pretty girl, with a face as smooth and insensitive as an apple, no matter what panic and disorder lay behind it.

But this was not what I had turned for; I realized that I must have been waiting for my mother to call, from her couch in the dining-room, where she lay with the blinds down in the summer heat, drinking cups of tea which she never finished, eating—she had dispensed altogether with mealtimes, like a sickly child—little bowls of preserved fruit and crumblings of cake. It seemed to me that I could not close the door behind me without hearing my mother's ruined voice call out to me and feeling myself go heavy all over as I prepared to answer it. Call, 'Who's there?'

I led my children to the big bedroom at the back of the house, where Maddy and I used to sleep. It has thin, almost worn-out white curtains at the windows and a square of linoleum on the floor; there is a double bed, a washstand which Maddy and I used as a desk when we were in high school, and a cardboard wardrobe with little mirrors on the inside of the doors. As I talked to my children I was thinking—but carefully, not in a rush—of my mother's state of mind when she called out *Who's there?* I was allowing myself to hear—as if I had not dared before—the cry for help—undisguised, oh, shamefully undisguised and raw and supplicating—that sounded in her voice. A cry repeated so often, and, things being as they were, so uselessly, that Maddy and I recognized it only as one of those household sounds which must be dealt with so that worse may not follow. *You go and deal with Mother,* we would say to each other, or *I'll be out in a minute, I have to deal with Mother.* It might be that we had to perform some of the trivial and unpleasant services endlessly required, or that we had to supply five minutes' expediently cheerful conversation, so remorselessly casual that never for a moment was there a recognition of the real state of affairs, never a glint of pity to open the way for one of her long debilitating sieges of tears. But the pity denied, the tears might come anyway—the melodramatic sobs rising out of the half-paralysed throat in an unbearable celebration of misery, so that we were defeated; we were forced, to stop that noise, into the most frightful parodies of love, in which she tried, through her creaking throat, to plead for kisses in coy pitiable childish tones, and we gave them, she watching with a little cunning at the bottom of her glazed eyes for the signs, in us, of revulsion or coldness at which she might weep again. But we grew cunning too, unfailing in cold solicitude; we took away from her our anger and impatience and disgust, took all emotion away from our dealings with her, as you might take away meat from a prisoner to weaken him, till he died.

We would tell her to read, to listen to music and enjoy the changes of season and be grateful that she did not have cancer. We added that she did not suffer any pain, and that is true, if imprisonment is not pain. While she demanded our love in every way she knew, without shame or sense, as a child will. And how could we have loved her, I say desperately to myself, the resources of love we had were not enough, the demand on us was too great; we were only children when the disease took hold of her and our father was dead, we were alone with her. Nor would it have changed anything.

'Everything has been taken away from me,' she would say. To strangers, to friends of ours whom we tried always unsuccessfully to keep separate from her, to old friends of hers who came guiltily infrequently to see her, she would speak like this, in the very slow and mournful voice that was not intelligible or quite human; we would have to interpret. Such theatricality humiliated us almost to death; yet now I think that without that egotism feeding stubbornly even on disaster she might have sunk rapidly into some dim vegetable life. She kept herself as much in the world as she could, not troubling about her welcome; restlessly she wandered through the house and into the streets of Jubilee. Oh, she was not resigned; she must have wept and struggled in that house of stone (as I can but will not imagine) until the very end.

But I find the picture is still not complete. Our Gothic Mother, with the cold appalling mask of the shaking palsy laid across her features, shuffling, weeping, devouring attention wherever she can get it, eyes dead and burning, fixed inward on herself: this is not all. For the disease is erratic and leisurely in its progress—some mornings (gradually growing fewer and fewer and farther apart) she wakes up better; she goes out to the yard and straightens up a plant in such a simple housewifely way; she says something calm and lucid to us; she listens attentively to the news. She has wakened out of a bad dream; she tries to make up for lost time, tidying the house, forcing her stiff trembling hands to work a little while at the sewing-machine. She makes us one of her specialities, a banana-cake or a lemon-meringue pie. Occasionally since she died I have dreams of her (I never dreamt of her when she was alive) in which she is doing something like this, and I think, why did I exaggerate so to myself, see, she is all right, only that her hands are trembling . . .

At the end of these periods of calm a kind of ravaging energy would come over her: she would make conversation insistently and with less and less coherence; she would demand that we rouge her cheeks and fix her hair; sometimes she might even hire a dressmaker to come in and make clothes for her, working in the dining-room where she could watch (spending her time again more and more on the couch). This was extravagant, unnecessary from any practical point of view (for why did she need these clothes, where did she wear them?), and nerve-racking, because the dressmaker did not understand what she wanted and sometimes neither did we. I remember after I went away receiving from Maddy several amusing, distracted, quietly overwrought letters describing these sessions with the dressmaker. I read them with sympathy but without being able to enter into the once-familiar atmosphere of frenzy and frustration which my mother's demands could produce. In the ordinary world it was not possible to recreate her. The picture of her face which I carried in my mind seemed too terrible, unreal. Similarly the complex strain of living with her, the feelings of hysteria which Maddy and I once dissipated in a great deal of brutal laughter, now began to seem partly imaginary; I felt the beginnings of a secret, guilty estrangement.

I stayed in the room with my children for a little while, because it was a strange place, for them it was only another strange place to go to sleep. Looking at them in this room I felt that they were particularly fortunate and that their life was safe and easy, which may be what most parents think at one time or another. I looked in the wardrobe but there was nothing there, only a hat trimmed with flowers from the five-and-ten, which one of us must have made for some flossy Easter. When I opened the drawer of the washstand I saw that it was crammed full of pages from a loose-leaf notebook. I read: *The Peace of Utrecht, 1713, brought an end to the War of the Spanish Succession.* It struck me that the handwriting was my own. Strange to think of it lying there for ten years—more; it looked as if I might have written it that day.

For some reason reading these words had a strong effect on me; I felt as if my old life were lying around me, waiting to be picked up again. Only then for a few moments in our old room did I have this feeling. The brown halls of the old High School (a building since torn down) were reopened for me, and I remembered the Saturday nights in spring, after the snow had melted and all the country people crowded into town. I thought of us walking up and down the main street, arm-in-arm with two or three other girls, until it got dark, then going into Al's to dance, under a string of little coloured lights. The windows in the dance-hall were open, they let in the raw spring air with its smell of earth and the river; the hands of farm boys crumpled and stained our white blouses when we danced. And now an experience which seemed not at all memorable at the time (in fact Al's was a dismal place and the ritual of walking up and down the street to show ourselves off we thought crude and ridiculous, though we could not resist it) had been transformed into something curiously meaningful for me, and complete; it took in more than the girls dancing and the single street, it spread over the whole town, its rudimentary pattern of streets and its bare trees and muddy yards just free of the snow, over the dirt roads where the lights of cars appeared, jolting towards the town, under an immense pale wash of sky.

Also: we wore ballerina shoes and full black taffeta skirts, and short coats of such colours as robin's egg blue, cerise red, lime green. Maddy wore a great funereal bow at the neck of her blouse and a wreath of artificial daisies in her hair. These were the fashions, or so we believed, of one of the years after the war. Maddy; her bright skeptical look; my sister.

I ask Maddy, 'Do you ever remember what she was like before?'

'No,' says Maddy. 'No, I can't.'

'I sometimes think I can,' I say hesitantly. 'Not very often.' Cowardly tender nostalgia, trying to get back to a gentler truth.

'I think you would have to have been away,' Maddy says. 'You would have to have been away these last—quite a few—years to get those kind of memories.'

It was then she said: 'No exorcising.'

And the only other thing she said was, 'She spent a lot of time sorting things. All kinds of things. Greeting cards. Buttons and yarn. Sorting and putting them into little piles. It would keep her quiet by the hour.'

2

I have been to visit Aunt Annie and Auntie Lou. This is the third time I have been there since I came home and each time they have been spending the afternoon making rugs out of dyed rags. They are very old now. They sit on a hot little porch that is shaded by bamboo blinds; the rags and the half-finished rugs make an encouraging, domestic sort of disorder around them. They do not go out any more, but they get up early in the mornings, wash and powder themselves and put on their shapeless print dresses trimmed with rickrack and white braid. They make coffee and porridge and then they clean the house, Aunt Annie working upstairs and Auntie Lou down. Their house is very clean, dark, and varnished, and it smells of vinegar and apples. In the afternoon they lie down for an hour and then put on their afternoon dresses, with brooches at the neck, and sit down to do handwork.

They are the sort of women whose flesh melts or mysteriously falls away as they get older. Auntie Lou's hair is still black, but it looks stiff and dry in its net as the dead end of hair on a ripe ear of corn. She sits straight and moves her bone-thin arms in very fine, slow movements; she looks like an Egyptian, with her long neck and small sharp face and greatly wrinkled, greatly darkened skin. Aunt Annie, perhaps because of her gentler, even coquettish manner, seems more humanly fragile and worn. Her hair is nearly all gone, and she keeps on her head one of those pretty caps designed for young wives who wear curlers to bed. She calls my attention to this and asks if I do not think it is becoming. They are both adept at these little ironies, and take a mild delight in pointing out whatever is grotesque about themselves. Their company manners are exceedingly light-hearted, and their conversation with each other falls into an accomplished pattern of teasing and protest. I have a fascinated glimpse of Maddy and myself, grown old, caught back in the web of sisterhood after everything else has disappeared, making tea for some young, loved, and essentially unimportant relative—and exhibiting just such a polished relationship; what will anyone ever know of us? As I watch my entertaining old aunts I wonder if old people play such stylized and simplified roles with us because they are afraid that anything more honest might try our patience, or if they do it out of delicacy, to fill the social time, when in reality they feel so far away from us that there is no possibility of communicating with us at all.

At any rate I felt held at a distance by them, at least until this third afternoon when they showed in front of me some signs of disagreement with each other. I believe this is the first time that has happened. Certainly I never saw them argue in all the years when Maddy and I used to visit them, and we used to visit them often, not only out of duty, but because we found the atmosphere of sense and bustle reassuring after the comparative anarchy, the threatened melodrama, of our house at home.

Aunt Annie wanted to take me upstairs to show me something. Auntie Lou objected, looking remote and offended, as if the whole subject embarrassed her. And such is the feeling for discretion, the tradition of circumlocution in that house, that it was unthinkable for me to ask them what they were talking about.

'Oh, let her have her tea,' Auntie Lou said, and Aunt Annie said, 'Well. When she's *had* her tea.'

'Do as you like then. That upstairs is hot.'

'Will you come up, Lou?'

'Then who's going to watch the children?'

'Oh, the children. I forgot.'

So Aunt Annie and I withdrew into the darker parts of the house. It occurred to me, absurdly, that she was going to give me a five-dollar bill. I remembered that sometimes she used to draw me into the front hall in this mysterious way and open her purse. I do not think that Auntie Lou was included in that secret either. But we went on upstairs, and into Aunt Annie's own bedroom, which looked so neat and virginal, papered with timid flowery wallpaper, the dressers spread with white scarves. It was really very hot, as Auntie Lou had said.

'Now,' Aunt Annie said, a little breathless. 'Get me down that box on the top shelf of the closet.'

I did, and she opened it and said with her wistful conspirator's gaiety, 'Now I guess you wondered what became of all your mother's clothes?'

I had not thought of it. I sat down on the bed, forgetting that in this house the beds were not to be sat on; the bedrooms had one straight chair apiece for that. Aunt Annie did not check me. She began to lift things out, saying, 'Maddy never mentioned them, did she?'

'I never asked her,' I said.

'No. Nor I wouldn't. I wouldn't say a word about it to Maddy. But I thought I might as well show you. Why not? Look,' she said. 'We washed and ironed what we could and what we couldn't we sent to the cleaner's. I paid the cleaning myself. Then we mended anything needed mending. It's all in good condition, see?'

I watched helplessly while she held up for my inspection the underwear which was on top. She showed me where things had been expertly darned and mended and where the elastic had been renewed. She showed me a slip which had been worn, she said, only once. She took out nightgowns, a dressing-gown, knitted bedjackets. 'This was what she had on the last time I saw her,' she said. 'I think it was. Yes.' I recognized with alarm the peach-coloured bedjacket I had sent for Christmas.

'You can see it's hardly used. Why, it's hardly used at all.'

'No,' I said.

'Underneath is her dresses.' Her hands rummaged down through those brocades and flowered silks, growing yearly more exotic, in which my mother had wished to costume herself. Thinking of her in these peacock colours, even Aunt Annie seemed to hesitate. She drew up a blouse. 'I washed this by hand, it looks like new. There's a coat hanging up in the closet. Perfectly good. She never wore a coat. She wore it when she went into the hospital, that was all. Wouldn't it fit you?'

'No,' I said. '*No.*' For Aunt Annie was already moving towards the closet. 'I just got a new coat. I have several coats. Aunt Annie!'

'But why should you go and buy,' Aunt Annie went on in her mild stubborn way, 'when there are things here as good as new.'

'I would rather buy,' I said, and was immediately sorry for the coldness in my voice. Nevertheless I continued, 'When I need something, I do go and buy it.' This suggestion that I was not poor any more brought a look of reproach and aloofness into my aunt's face. She said nothing. I went and looked at a picture of Aunt Annie and Auntie Lou and their older brothers and their mother and father which hung over the bureau. They stared back at me with grave accusing Protestant faces, for I had run up against the simple unprepossessing materialism which was the rock of their lives. Things must be used; everything must be used up, saved and mended and made into something else, and used again; clothes were to be worn. I felt that I had hurt Aunt Annie's feelings and that furthermore I had probably borne out a prediction of Auntie Lou's, for she was sensitive to certain attitudes in the world that were too sophisticated for Aunt Annie to bother about, and she had very likely said that I would not want my mother's clothes.

'She was gone sooner than anybody would have expected,' Aunt Annie said. I turned around surprised and she said, 'Your mother.' Then I wondered if the clothes had been the main thing after all; perhaps they were only to serve as the introduction to a conversation about my mother's death, which Aunt Annie might feel to be a necessary part of our visit. Auntie Lou would feel differently; she had an almost superstitious dislike of such rituals of emotionalism; such a conversation could never take place with her about.

'Two months after she went into the hospital,' Aunt Annie said. 'She was gone in two months.' I saw that she was crying distractedly, as old people do, with miserably scanty tears. She pulled a handkerchief out of her dress and rubbed at her face.

'Maddy told her it was nothing but a checkup,' she said. 'Maddy told her it would be about three weeks. Your mother went in there and she thought she was coming out in three weeks.' She was whispering as if she was afraid of us being overheard. 'Do you think she wanted to stay in there where nobody could make out what she was saying and they wouldn't let her out of her bed? She wanted to come home!'

'But she was too sick,' I said.

'No, she wasn't, she was just the way she'd always been, just getting a little worse and a little worse as time went on. But after she went in there she felt she would die, everything kind of closed in around her, and she went down so fast.'

'Maybe it would have happened anyway,' I said. 'Maybe it was just the time.'

Aunt Annie paid no attention to me. 'I went up to see her,' she said. 'She was so glad to see me because I could tell what she was saying. She said "Aunt Annie, they won't keep me in here for good, will they?" And I said to her, "No." I said, "No." '

'And she said, "Aunt Annie ask Maddy to take me home again or I'm going to die." She didn't want to die. Don't you ever think a person wants to die, just because it seems to everybody else they have got no reason to go on living. So I told Maddy. But she didn't say anything. She went to the hospital every day and saw your mother and she wouldn't take her home. Your mother told me Maddy said to her, "I won't take you home." '

'Mother didn't always tell the truth,' I said. 'Aunt Annie, you know that.'

'Did you know your mother got out of the hospital?'

'No,' I said. But strangely I felt no surprise, only a vague physical sense of terror, a longing not to be told—and beyond this a feeling that what I would be told I already knew, I had always known.

'Maddy, didn't she tell you?'

'No.'

'Well she got *out*. She got out the side door where the ambulance comes in, it's the only door that isn't locked. It was at night when they haven't so many nurses to watch them. She got her dressing-gown and her slippers on, the first time she ever got anything on herself in years, and she went out and there it was January, snowing, but she didn't go back in. She was away down the street when they caught her. After that they put the board across her bed.'

The snow, the dressing-gown and slippers, the board across the bed. It was a picture I was much inclined to resist. Yet I had no doubt that this was true, all this was true and exactly as it had happened. It was what she would do; all her life as long as I had known her led up to that flight.

'Where was she going?' I said, but I knew there was no answer.

'I don't know. Maybe I shouldn't have told you. Oh, Helen, when they came after her she tried to run. She tried to *run*.'

The flight that concerns everybody. Even behind my aunt's soft familiar face there is another, more primitive old woman, capable of panic in some place her faith has never touched.

She began folding the clothes up and putting them back in the box. 'They nailed a board across her bed. I saw it. You can't blame the nurses. They can't watch everybody. They haven't the time.'

'I said to Maddy after the funeral, ''Maddy, may it never happen like that to you.'' I couldn't help it, that's what I said.' She sat down on the bed herself now, folding things and putting them back in the box, making an effort to bring her voice back to normal —and pretty soon succeeding, for having lived this long who would not be an old hand at grief and self-control?

'We thought it was hard,' she said finally. 'Lou and I thought it was hard.'

Is this the last function of old women, beyond making rag rugs and giving us five-dollar bills—making sure the haunts we have contracted for are with us, not one gone without?

She was afraid of Maddy, through fear had cast her out for good. I thought of what Maddy had said: *nobody speaks the same language*.

When I got home Maddy was out in the back kitchen making a salad. Rectangles of sunlight lay on the rough linoleum. She had taken off her high-heeled shoes and was standing there in her bare feet. The back kitchen is a large untidy pleasant room, with a view behind the stove and the drying dish towels of the sloping backyard, the CPR station, and the golden, marshy river that almost encircles the town of Jubilee. My children, who had felt a little repressed in the other house, immediately began to play under the table.

'Where have you been?' Maddy asked.

'Nowhere. Just to see the Aunts.'

'Oh, how are they?'

'They're fine. They're indestructible.'

'Are they? Yes I guess they are. I haven't been to see them for a while. I don't actually see that much of them any more.'

'Don't you?' I said, and she knew then what they had told me.

'They were beginning to get on my nerves a bit, after the funeral. And Fred got me this job and everything and I've been so busy—' She looked at me, waiting for what I would say, smiling a little derisively, patiently.

'Don't be guilty, Maddy,' I said softly. All this time the children were running in and out and shrieking at each other between our legs.

'I'm not guilty,' she said. 'Where did you get that? I'm not guilty.' She went to turn on the radio, talking to me over her shoulder.

'Fred's going to eat with us again since he's alone. I got some raspberries for dessert. Raspberries are almost over for this year. Do they look all right to you?'

'They look all right,' I said. 'Do you want me to finish this?'

'Fine,' she said. 'I'll go and get a bowl.'

She went into the dining-room and came back carrying a pink cut-glass bowl for the raspberries.

'I couldn't go on,' she said. 'I wanted my life.'

She was standing on the little step between the kitchen and the dining-room and suddenly she lost her grip on the bowl, either because her hands had begun to shake or because she had not picked it up properly in the first place; it was quite a heavy and elaborate old bowl. It slipped out of her hands and she tried to catch it and it smashed on the floor.

Maddy began to laugh. 'Oh, hell,'she said. 'Oh, hell, oh *Hel-en*,' she said, using one of our old foolish ritual phrases of despair. 'Look what I've done now. In my bare feet yet. Get me the broom.'

'Take your life, Maddy. Take it.'

'Yes I will,' Maddy said. 'Yes I will.'

'Go away, don't stay here.'

'Yes I will.'

Then she bent down and began picking up the pieces of broken pink glass. My children stood back looking at her with awe and she was laughing and saying, 'It's no loss to me. I've got a whole shelf full of glass bowls. I've got enough glass bowls to do me the rest of my life. Oh, don't stand there looking at me, go and get me the broom!' I went around the kitchen looking for the broom because I seemed to have forgotten where it was kept and she said, 'But why can't I, Helen? *Why can't I?*'

JANE RULE

Invention for Shelagh

'What does your face mean now?'

'I'll write it to you,' I say, and Shelagh smiles, easy, knowing either I really will or that I'll tell her some other time when there aren't quite so many people as there are now: Haron, Leith, Fran, as well as Shelagh, Helen and I. Or maybe, in a way, Shelagh's reading my face and letting me know, the way she lets Haron know by touching him.

When I get home, I go to my desk, open my journal and write: Shelagh's space-place (in me?)

The post-American gothic window, Leith's American gothic face. That's what broke it open for me—immediate nourishment?—what came then was how much in that space I'd cast there, not just Grandmother's maroon plates and cups, her card table, Helen's mother's chairs, but *even* Haron. How much challenged me there—the Bridget Riley poster—never mind Doris Lessing. The old records, which do make me remember Garberville as well as private South Fork. And how does it happen a) that Shelagh doesn't really want me there for a year and b) that I find my imagination, scattered for months in interesting but thin places, coming together in the fragments of her place. One image: that I'm a piece of pottery smashed, the shards everywhere. Another: in Shelagh's space I am finally the altogetherness of being about to make a coherent statement. And I *really* wonder what it's like for her to live in *our* space. Does that complex focus of herself happen to her? I wrote an edgy story out of her cottage on the lane. If this isn't simply drunken sharp edges, I'd like to write 'Shelagh's space-place' from zoo sheets to rock-plexiglass rock-actual room, a love song of how we put each other together in nephews and plates and loving Helen. And this vision is partly an assertion against my grief about Doris Lessing, the immediacy of not wanting Fran to ride on that bird, Helen to distance herself so much as not to be primarily offended, Shelagh to be wooed by *any* energy. I do feel as if I knew, with passion, about the wrong of that book, as simple as knowing the lobster is bad, don't eat it. And have the vocabulary, but not shared, to say so: to say Don't. For the sake of Life, DON'T. And feel guilt only because of the urgency I have to make my own vision clear. My love: Haron and Leith and Shelagh and Fran and Helen, I love you. Don't ride on that bird. It's a chairlift into arrogant desolation, into a lie about not only the stars but ourselves. I, who live daily close to madness and its wily justifications, love too much to go there, and I cannot stand anyone else taking an energy ride out of that perverse imagination. But I don't want my power to cut out. I wanted to go away, to live in myself, unoffending, somewhere else.

Notes for me, not for Shelagh.

'I'll write it to you' doesn't weigh on my conscience, but it does on my imagination. Shelagh and I talk about writing sometimes, writing to each other, and we sometimes have, but not ever, or not yet, in the way we imagine we might. Our letters have been personal. Personal doesn't mean anything. Timely, then, about planes to meet, changes of plan, ongoing fragments of our own and our friends' lives. What we have in mind instead is some kind of elaborate conversation, I think, and I could try to write, from those notes, a letter. Or I could simply read those notes to Shelagh and we could talk. But I want to climb up through process to make something, as I understand it and can come to understand it. And that is what I meant when I said, 'I'll write it to you.'

The way the maze at Hampton Court this summer is something other than how Shelagh wrote about it to Haron or how we all learn to tell it together at parties now that we are out of it and at home. My maze? My invention? Well, yes. And I'll wait to know what that is, as I waited for months before we went into the maze with the tag line, 'Something amazing, a boy falling out of the sky.' And never once thought of myself as Icarus, never mind Daedalus, some sort of old testament woman rather, with a face like dissolving rock under the heat of someone else's mortal fire.

And still do, obviously, as I shout at Fran. 'Get off Doris Lessing's bird!' And get out of that two bit satire about the Greek gods. You, too, I want to say to myself, feeling a brief temptation of my own.

Shelagh writes on her walls on strips of newsprint. The people who visit often, like Leith and Haron, have to choose whether to read what is written there or not. Shelagh reads what she has written to Helen and me after she has taken it down, typed it and carried it 7000 miles. Shelagh takes down her walls and brings them to England. We sit in our rented house there and listen to her walls. That is how Shelagh makes home with us. Her nephews come and build roads and airstrips in the rock garden. Helen and Shelagh and I can cook together in a space four feet square. We think of putting flour on the floor to see how our feet do it. Shelagh is the only one who always remembers to give the gardener his tea. Shelagh got us out of the maze that day. 'The way out is the way in,' she said. We followed her there. Out. Without flour or bread crumbs. Otherwise Helen would have slashed down the privet hedge with the power of her imagination. One of us always does something.

We showed Shelagh the house in Chelsea where we might have stayed. She and Helen both believed that somehow they could have imagined themselves into it, though neither would have wanted to. We went through it like tourists, and I could see the invisible velvet ropes strung across bedroom doors, but Shelagh and Helen went in, set feet right down on the carpets, pointed at the drapes, found the cracks in the wall paper that were cupboard doors, peered at a white china blue bird in a niche, and said to each other, 'We could have done it. We could.' I couldn't. It was hard enough to crack an ice tray open and pour drinks from my own bottle in that parody of a rich man's town house, all mirrors and crystal chandeliers. In the maid's room there is a picture of a cow mooing. But in that room also there are bars on the windows. *I* got us out of there.

Written in my journal at 1:40 a.m.: 'Rereading what I wrote today —"Invention for Shelagh" it's probably called—I have a fantasy about phoning her now, saying, "this is suicide time"—like that kid at Concord who couldn't ask to talk after lights were out unless she'd done something as important as slitting her wrists. Sexual tides, Shelagh's and mine, sometimes pull us apart. I wonder if she knows my regret as well as I sometimes know hers, not for lack of sexual saying between us, for the tides themselves. We are generous there, too. Shelagh never takes suicide space. Neither do I. I give us stars for that. Should I?'

In the light of day, yes. Suicide space excludes the whole clutter of living which we so welcome in each other. Shelagh says, 'I've decided there should be one slob in the house, and I'm it.' Because she likes books and clothes and old coffee cups to decide for themselves, a democracy of objects about her. I bully what I own, order furniture and china and papers about in military frenzy. Helen coaxes things into place, makes them comfortable where they belong. Is it because there is no morality in it that Shelagh can late at night set the breakfast table with me as companionably as if we were laying out a game of double solitaire? She has done it even on her way home to her own place, simply to set me in order where I like to be. But playing our orderly games in her own place is too much more than once a year, borrowing chairs from Larry so that everyone can sit at the table, gathering up all the papers, making the bed so that Haron can show off the fine zoo sheets he's brought back from California. They wake to leering giraffes and smug hippopotamuses. Haron's jeans hang in careful arrangement against one living room wall, the ones he drew on the first time he dropped acid, complementing Bridget Riley. The serial photographs of rocks are mounted as if in an art gallery, VERY IMPORTANT, the rock itself on the floor on a piece of paper. The writing walls are in the bedroom. Shelagh, when she orders things, does so to see them. My order makes things invisible, as if I were preparing for black-out or blindness and only cared not to stumble. Looking, really looking, at anything but the human face is something I have to remind myself to do. Without Helen, without Shelagh I would go functionally blind for days at a time.

I stay home, go out, travel, to see people. I simply learn to complain at the Tate about the heads that get in the way of the paintings. Only a remarkable portrait is more interesting than any face in the crowd, no portrait as interesting as Helen's face or Shelagh's face looking at it. The Turners? They force me to acknowledge the existence of the sky. Take away the human face. Take away the sky under which I occasionally know I live. Offer me in geometric metaphor the quality of light, the tension of objects in space, the absolute command of the vision to be seen, my eyes torn free of their migraine, myopic defenses, I will resist.

Helen and Shelagh walk me through the Hayward Gallery to see the Bridget Riley show as if I were just out of hospital. The guards all wear sunglasses, characters in a Cocteau movie. The spaces of the rooms are as huge and empty as the space in dreams, nothing there to order into invisibility, only the commands on the walls. Know with your eyes. Helen has such natural courage, Shelagh such joy in the energy, the acute intelligence. I couldn't go alone into that light, and, even now, two months later, Shelagh and Helen appear to me as much nurses and jailors as companions in that space.

If the escape from the peopled maze is into a Bridget Riley painting, then I *am* Icarus falling into the sea.

We all three need so much more of the world than any one is willing to risk alone that each of us can agree, for a time, to be invalid victim to another's courage. Is that true? It is for me. Helen would have other words for it; so would Shelagh, who asked once this summer after serving one of my invented days, 'Is it worth it . . . for you?' 'Yes,' I said. And grew a little moral vision from that exchange but don't know that will transplant to any other occasion.

When Shelagh defended me against Rick's charge that I was 'good with people', she wanted nothing of the con artist in it, nothing of manipulation. I did what I cared to do, caring about people. Yes. But I have taught us all automatic pilot amiability so that we can not only cook in four square feet but stand to linear hours of people without knowing how we do it. I rarely ask why either. But I do know, yes. If I am on those occasions sometimes nurse and jailor as well as companion, I can be.

On a train from Wallington to London, a sick child howls, monotonous, as rhythmic as breathing, either retarded or very ill, perhaps both. Everyone in the carriage is restless. Someone shouts 'Shut up!' We wait through a long four minutes to the next station, get out and get into another carriage, not sharing whatever guilty or fearful memories we might have, sharing only the resolution to move. We usually sit through even bad plays, as helpless to change them, perhaps as troubled, but we talk afterwards about Osborne's stinking, stupid politics, the 'acky-acky-acky' melodrama of the last act, and finally laugh about the exact duplication of Haron's holey jeans on the stage American who is allowed only, 'Shit, shit, shit' to articulate the revolution. About the child we say nothing.

Shelagh says the pictures Helen took this summer are full of processions of asses. I had noticed instead how often we walked or stood, apparently inattentive to each other, like horses in a field; beyond the backs of our heads, the characteristic body stances, always a great tower or an expanse of field. The pictures Avis took in the house, the pictures Helen has taken over the years at home, show us either alone for the camera, Helen picking flowers, Shelagh modeling her new trousers, me writing my journal, or obviously together at the breakfast or dinner table, engaged. I don't feel sorry for us in those large landscapes, but there is something about us that is always a bit bewildered, patient, abstracted under Turner skies.

The pictures my mind took: Shelagh at Victoria station, Gate 9, with pack sack, straw basket, brief case, laughing, pleased with herself. 'I even have my ticket.' (My snapshots move and talk.) Shelagh at the front door, welcoming us home from a week-end, tired of running the house herself but determined to go on with it for the rest of the day. Shelagh and Helen high up behind me on the theatre stairs, laughing to each other, with the same relief I feel that we've all made it again. Shelagh and Helen in the upstairs hall late at night, conspiratorial as children who have been told to go straight to bed.

Since Shelagh had posters made for us, I have wanted all memory to be life size. Instead of Che and Mao, Shelagh gave us herself and Ted bottling wine, drunk and hilarious, Helen's mother standing in blue jeans in her beloved farm fields, my grandmother standing in the hollow of a redwood tree. Since, we have added Rick on the Cutty Sark, my great grandmother in a row boat with a good sized steelhead. They are in the garage, along with our Bridget Riley poster, and they are fading with the weather. But I renew rather than replace memory.

'Once you take it all away, getting married, having children, even remembering to comb your hair, what is there left to being female? And does it matter?' Shelagh is sitting next to me in the seminar we share for the Women's Studies course and posing the question to fifteen other people but as importantly to herself. Is she tempted to answer it? To try, probably. I'm not sure it is a question for me. But I would go back as far as I had to to remember when it still was. For Shelagh, I would. Years back, then, to about the age of 25 or 26, still vulnerable to descriptions of other women, 'She never married', still threatened by the sexual gossip of men looking for 'good tits', 'a piece of ass', and simply frightened by the prospect of taking my life in my own hands, never having taken earning a living very seriously. Could I live with all those tags of failure, no husband, no child, at the bottom of the academic ladder with no inclination to take even the first step up into a PhD, six or seven years of unpublished manuscripts stuffed into filing drawers? 'Does it matter?' For the proud and frightened, of course it matters, at that point. And no decision against retreating into the success of MRS or PhD or both is made without pig-headed refusal to be humiliated. The only consolation I had was that no man as proud as I could ever risk it. So what was left? That sense of immunity that is also part of the package of being female. If the world doesn't take you seriously to begin with, your failure in it can't be all that much of a disaster. Yeats' poem about failure, 'Be secret and exult.' By now I think I have also forgotten or left behind my immunity. As Shelagh leaves hers when she says about getting up to speak before a crowd, 'It does matter. If you are going to get up and do it, you've got to leave all that tentativeness and apology behind. It's private. Get through it at home. That's what a bathroom's for. Then stand up and say what you have to say without anything left of being "just a woman".'

That's one line for the answer to take, and it gets us somewhere but not as far as Shelagh's question pushes. For standing there without any of those conventional definitions, protections, limitations, something is surely left, and it may matter. To ourselves as well as the audience. I really don't know.

For over a year, and more obviously this summer in London, I have been taken as often for a man as for a woman. Shelagh could believe the funny story about the young salesman at my front door, asking first for my mother, then for my wife, finally for 'the lady of the house'. But she did not believe that as often as not during a day, I was called 'sir' rather than 'madam' until we were all getting out of a cab at the theatre. The doorman greeted Helen with 'Good evening, Madam,' Shelagh with 'Good evening, Miss,' and me with 'good evening, Sir.' I have not chosen a disguise. I have not changed my hairstyle or my way of dressing for twenty years. It is men who have grown their hair, put bright scarves around their necks, and altered their voices to gentleness. Their choices have not only changed my social sexual identity but also my age. For lack of a beard, for a low pitched but light voice, I am not a forty year old woman, but a twenty year old boy. There are obviously a number of twenty year old boys, without my height, who are being called 'miss' and still don't find it threatening or humiliating enough to cut their hair.

Last spring, when Gladys had her baby, Shelagh told me she could not bring herself to ask whether it was a boy or a girl. What do we mean by the phrase 'private parts'? What is public sexuality?

A dream reported in my class last night: a young woman was on an operating table, a nurse pushing down on her belly, asking whether she wanted to know now if it was dead or alive. No, she would wait until it was born to be told. The nurse shone a flashlight into her, then ran to get the doctor, a great bulbous man. The young woman then found herself being ushered into a room without furniture. She was exhausted, too uncomfortable to be willing to sit on the floor, very angry. Another young woman in a hospital gown came in and said, 'I had a boy. What did you have?' 'A light bulb.'

The man who delivered a light bulb into the world was proud of it. Why not turn nightmare into daydream or even fact?

Stand up with a wedding ring, be eight and a half months pregnant, and you are still 'just a woman'. Add a career. You are not then more but suspected of being even less. So the terms of reference we have won't work. We do have to throw them out, all of them. Yes, the baby with the bath water, the lot. With no immunity, with no certainty at all about what is left, begin again.

Shelagh told me last night that she must go into the hospital in a few days' time to have a cone biopsy. She is under thirty. She has to convince the doctor that the potential of her uterus is not more important to her than the protection of her own life, that his decisions must be based on her set of values rather than his own.

She also said, 'It doesn't bother *me* when Helen cries.'

In any evening, we all have marvellous ideas, but Shelagh's have a vehemence that Helen remembers, believes, and often acts on the next morning: trying to order a game pie from Selfridge's ('Madame, game is out of season'), dialing a poem. Today I found myself caught up in one of Shelagh's late night schemes, left to me because she has gone out of town for the week-end. I know only half way into it that it is another game pie. So I tell the story out of season.

Are we inclined to see the difficulties in each other's lives and admire the courage rather than the ease which makes our several choices possible? Perhaps I don't think about Shelagh's life when it is easy to. I think of it, apart from mine, only when she is impatiently casting off domestic involvement while at the same time guiltily describing the 'uncomfortable space' she must live in, crowded with people who require and delight her attention.

'I have no domestic peace, except with the two of you here,' and she mistrusts herself if she stays in it for very long. She needs the stress of crowded singularity. There it is, in negative terms. Freedom from domestic involvement, from accountability in those daily terms gives her the energy to spend herself as she does.

Events of any day smash against this invention like birds against my study window. They don't break the glass, but I can't entirely rid the process of that mortal thumping. From Helen's study, she can hear, day after day, the obscene saws and the breaking rush and shudder of the trees going down in the ravine. I don't know Shelagh's sounds. I do know she looks out of her window at a corrugated iron building on which are printed the letters, V.I.E.W.

Helen talks of turning this house into a commune, by which she means that perhaps Shelagh would share it with us. Commune is a word like fuck: political. Not for Helen, for me. I have to walk round it and come in at the private entrance. I am exclusive, hoarding of my little authorities, jealous of my own time. The smallest shift in responsibility, whether more or less, requires great deliberation. I am more comfortable sharing negative fantasies: room and board somewhere for $85.00 a month. Is having my own money different from simply having money? My own space different from space? Well, I like to give them both away, grandly, and that's ridiculous, so beautifully ridiculous that I might talk myself into one final grand gesture, about which we could all rollick with laughter. I mean, if I put all my vast sums of money into the common till, what's less grand about that than buying Helen a painting or keeping the liquor bill a secret from Shelagh, who knows how much it is anyway? Nobody needs to give up paintings or liquor. And surely I really am past needing to make money for the sake of having made it, to pay for the right to my own space. I don't really need 'my own' in that sense. This house is always a clutter of people, some delighted in, some endured.

While Shelagh moves through restless days toward Thursday's operation, Helen and I are planning menus for Shelagh's mother and then for Shelagh when she comes home. But we are also, in our imaginations, moving beds around and bank accounts. It may be a game pie, but when we dialed a poem, we heard a poem every night for the nights after Shelagh had left England.

Last night Shelagh said, 'Maybe we've got rid of the baby, but what about all this bath water?' We were talking with our seminar group about the competition and justification that goes on in relationship. People must ask each other for money and freedom, justify those needs each time they occur. Answers? Pool all moneys, pay for the necessities and divide what is left equally. Assert freedom. Don't ever ask for it. Simple as that. There is resigned laughter from most people in the room, vehement hope only from the young woman who lives in a commune, but she also talks a great deal about limiting one's needs, self-sacrifice, attitudes I don't have much real respect for. Why? She would teach the painter to need no more physical space than the writer, no more money for materials, and sees all such activities essentially as 'hobbies'. I am not interested in anyone's adjusting needs for the sake of a group, for the sake of any other person, except in circumstances of emergency. Shelagh says she does adjust to someone else's need, ignoring her own, until she is furious, which doesn't take long.

'Why should *I* go home when he's sleepy?' she demands. 'He can go home any time he likes.'

Well, Haron agrees.

Then Shelagh demands, 'Why aren't you angry with me?'

A happy fight with ranges of comic anger. We should indulge more in expressing our interior logics, their fierce, ludicrous power. Why translate into the justifiable? I live more comfortably with outrageous needs than moral imperatives, in me and in the people around me.

Leith and both Ricks have called, wanting news of Shelagh. Her mother and Helen and I talk briefly about problems that may come up about visitors while Shelagh is in the hospital. There are so many people.

Haron and Shelagh's mother are sitting in the dining room over morning coffee where last night at nine-thirty she and Ted sat having a late supper. Mrs Jelking has made another pot of coffee and is now washing windows. Haron has brought Shelagh's clothes and the zoo sheets to wash in our machine. I have just finished reading Reich's *The Sexual Revolution*, an analysis of the failure of communes in Russia.

'When are you going to see Shelagh?' Haron asks me.

'I don't want to be selfish,' Shelagh's mother says to me.

I'm not going to the hospital at all unless, for some reason, Shelagh needs to see me. I stay in the centre of the house, like someone keeping a boat balanced. That is where I like to be, in my psychic space. There are plenty of people just now to take care of Shelagh. Helen and I take care for her.

'What does your face mean now?'

That I am discovering the space we live in, how incredibly crowded it is with who I am, who each of us is, how much room there seems to be. I don't feel sure-footed, but I feel together we are. When I want to know why, I try to read answers in Grandmother's plates, Haron's face, the Bridget Riley poster, which is as hard and fine as we know how to make Christmas. Or I listen again to what we say to each other. We so rarely get in each other's way. Or maybe like to be there. We do not make laws so much as come upon patterns, those comic, invisible footprints on the kitchen floor, these words on the page.

GLORIA SAWAI

The Day I Sat with Jesus

ON THE SUN DECK AND A WIND CAME UP AND BLEW MY KIMONO OPEN AND HE SAW MY BREASTS

When an extraordinary event takes place in your life, you're apt to remember with unnatural clarity the details surrounding it. You remember shapes and sounds that weren't directly related to the occurrence but hovered there in the periphery of the experience. This can even happen when you read a great book for the first time—one that unsettles you and startles you into thought. You remember where you read it, what room, who was nearby.

I can remember, for instance, where I read *Of Human Bondage*. I was lying on a top bunk in our high school dormitory, wrapped in a blue bedspread. I lived in a dormitory then because of my father. He was a religious man and wanted me to get a spiritual kind of education: to hear the WORD and know the LORD, as he put it. So he sent me to St John's Lutheran Academy in Regina for two years. He was confident, I guess, that's where I'd hear the WORD. Anyway, I can still hear Mrs Sverdren, our house-mother, knocking on the door at midnight and whispering in her Norwegian accent, 'Now, Gloria, it iss 12 o'clock. Time to turn off the lights. Right now.' Then scuffing down the corridor in her bedroom slippers. What's interesting here is that I don't remember anything about the book itself except that someone in it had a club foot. But it must have moved me deeply when I was sixteen, which is some time ago now.

You can imagine then how distinctly I remember the day Jesus of Nazareth, in person, climbed the hill in our back yard to our house, then up the outside stairs to the sundeck where I was sitting. And how he stayed with me for a while. You can surely understand how clear those details rest in my memory.

The event occurred on Monday morning, 11 September, 1972 in Moose Jaw, Saskatchewan. These facts in themselves are more unusual than they may appear to be at first glance. September's my favourite month, Monday my favourite day, morning my favourite time. And although Moose Jaw may not be the most magnificent place in the world, even so, if you happen to be there on a Monday morning in September it has its beauty.

It's not hard to figure out why these are my favourites, by the way. I have five children and a husband. Things get hectic, especially on weekends and holidays. Kids hanging around the house, eating, arguing, asking me every hour what there is to do in Moose Jaw. And television. The programs are always the same; only the names change! Roughriders, Stampeders, Blue Bombers, whatever. So when school starts in September I bask in freedom, especially on Monday. No quarrels. No TV. The morning, crisp and lovely. A new day. A fresh start.

On the morning of 11 September, I got up at 7, the usual time, cooked Cream of Wheat for the kids, fried a bit of sausage for Fred, waved them all out of the house, drank a second cup of coffee in peace and decided to get at last week's ironing. I wasn't dressed yet but still in the pink kimono I'd bought years ago on my trip to Japan—my one and only overseas trip, a $300 quick tour of Tokyo and other cities. I'd saved for this while working as a library technician in Regina, and I'm glad I did. Since then I've hardly been out of Saskatchewan. Once in a while a trip to Winnipeg, and a few times down to Medicine Lake, Montana, to visit my sister.

I set up the ironing-board and hauled out the basket of week-old sprinkled clothes. When I unrolled the first shirt it was completely dry and smelled stale. The second was covered with little grey blots of mould. So was the third. Fred teaches junior-high science here in Moose Jaw. He uses a lot of shirts. I decided I'd have to unwrap the whole basketful and air everything out. This I did, spreading the pungent garments about the living-room. While they were airing I would go outside and sit on the deck for a while since it was such a clear and sunny day.

If you know Moose Jaw at all, you'll know about the new subdivision at the southeast end called Hillhurst. That's where we live, right on the edge of the city. In fact, our deck looks out on flat land as far as the eye can see, except for the backyard itself, which is a fairly steep hill leading down to a stone quarry. But from the quarry the land straightens out into the Saskatchewan prairie. One clump of poplars stands beyond the quarry to the right, and high weeds have grown up among the rocks. Other than that it's plain—just earth and sky. But when the sun rises new in the morning, weeds and rocks take on an orange and rusty glow that is pleasing. To me at least.

I unplugged the iron and returned to the kitchen. I'd take a cup of coffee out there, or maybe some orange juice. To reach the juice at the back of the fridge my hand passed right next to a bottle of dry red Calona. Now here was a better idea. A little wine on Monday morning, a little relaxation after a rowdy weekend. I held the familiar bottle comfortably in my hand and poured, anticipating a pleasant day.

I slid open the glass door leading to the deck. I pulled an old canvas folding-chair into the sun, and sat. Sat and sipped. Beauty and tranquillity floated toward me on Monday morning, 11 September, around 9.40.

First he was a little bump on the far, far-off prairie. Then he was a mole way beyond the quarry. Then a larger animal, a dog perhaps, moving out there through the grass. Nearing the quarry, he became a person. No doubt about that. A woman perhaps, still in her bathrobe. But edging out from the rocks, through the weeds, toward the hill, he was clear to me. I knew then who he was. I knew it just as I knew the sun was shining.

The reason I knew is that he looked exactly the way I'd seen him 5000 times in pictures, in books and Sunday School pamphlets. If there was ever a person I'd seen and heard about, over and over, this was the one. Even in grade school those terrible questions. Do you love the Lord? Are you saved by grace alone through faith? Are you awaiting eagerly the glorious day of his Second Coming? And will you be ready on that Great Day? I'd sometimes hidden under the bed when I was a child, wondering if I really had been saved by grace alone, or, without realizing it, I'd been trying some other method, like the Catholics, who were saved by their good works and would land in hell. Except for a few who knew in their hearts it was really grace, but they didn't want to leave the church because of their relatives. And was this it? Would the trumpet sound tonight and the sky split in two? Would the great Lord and King, Alpha and Omega, holding aloft the seven candlesticks, accompanied by a heavenly host that no man could number, descend from heaven with a mighty shout?

And was I ready? Rev. Hanson in his high pulpit in Swift Current, Saskatchewan, roared in my ears and clashed against my eardrums.

And there he was. Coming. Climbing the hill in our backyard, his body bent against the climb, his robes ruffling in the wind. He was coming. And I was not ready. All those mouldy clothes scattered about the living-room, and me in this faded old thing, made in Japan, and drinking—in the middle of the morning.

He had reached the steps now. His hand touched the railing. His right hand was on my railing. Jesus' fingers were curled around my railing. He was coming up. He was ascending. He was coming up to me here on the sundeck.

He stood on the top step and looked at me. I looked at him. He looked exactly right, exactly the same as all the pictures: white robe, purple stole, bronze hair, creamy skin. How had all those queer artists, illustrators of Sunday School papers, how had they gotten him exactly right like that?

He stood at the top of the stairs. I sat there holding my glass. What do you say to Jesus when he comes? How do you address him? Do you call him *Jesus*? I supposed that was his first name. Or *Christ*? I remembered the woman at the well, the one living in adultery who'd called him *Sir*. Perhaps I could try that. Or maybe I should pretend not to recognize him. Maybe, for some reason, he didn't mean for me to recognize him. Then he spoke.

'Good morning,' he said. 'My name is Jesus.'

'How do you do,' I said. 'My name is Gloria Johnson.'

My name is Gloria Johnson. That's what I said, all right. As if he didn't know.

He smiled, standing there at the top of the stairs. I thought of what I should do next. Then I got up and unfolded another canvas chair.

'You have a nice view here,' he said, leaning back against the canvas and pressing his sandaled feet against the iron bars of the railing.

'Thank you,' I said. 'We like it.'

Nice view. Those were his very words. Everyone who comes to our house and stands on the deck says that. Everyone.

'I wasn't expecting company today.' I straightened the folds of my pink kimono and tightened the cloth more securely over my knees. I picked up the glass from the floor where I'd laid it.

'I was passing through on my way to Winnipeg. I thought I'd drop by.'

'I've heard a lot about you,' I said. 'You look quite a bit like your pictures.' I raised the glass to my mouth and saw that his hands were empty. I should offer him something to drink. Tea? Milk? How should I ask him what he'd like to drink? What words should I use?

'It gets pretty dusty out there,' I finally said. 'Would you care for something to drink?' He looked at the glass in my hand. 'I could make you some tea,' I added.

'Thanks,' he said. 'What are you drinking?'

'Well, on Mondays I like to relax a bit after the busy weekend with the family all home. I have five children you know. So sometimes after breakfast I have a little wine.'

'That would be fine,' he said.

By luck I found a clean tumbler in the cupboard. I stood by the sink, pouring the wine. And then, like a bolt of lightning, I realized my situation. Oh, Johann Sebastian Bach. Glory. Honour. Wisdom. Power. George Frederick Handel. King of Kings and Lord of Lords. He's on my sundeck. Today he's sitting on my sundeck. I can ask him any question under the sun, anything at all, he'll know the answer. Hallelujah. Hallelujah. Well now, wasn't this something for a Monday morning in Moose Jaw.

I opened the fridge door to replace the bottle. And I saw my father. It was New Year's morning. My father was sitting at the kitchen table. Mother sat across from him. She'd covered the oatmeal pot to let it simmer on the stove. I could hear the lid bumping against the rim, quietly. Sigrid and Freda sat on one side of the table, Raymond and I on the other. We were holding hymn books, little black books turned to page one. It was dark outside. On New Year's morning we got up before sunrise. Daddy was looking at us with his chin pointed out. It meant be still and sit straight. Raymond sat as straight and stiff as a soldier, waiting for Daddy to notice how nice and stiff he sat. We began singing. Page one. Hymn for the New Year. Philipp Nicolai. 1599. We didn't really need the books. We'd sung the same song every New Year's since the time of our conception. Daddy always sang the loudest.

The Morning Star upon us gleams; How full of grace and truth His beams,
How passing fair His splendour. Good Shepherd, David's proper heir,
My King in heav'n Thou dost me bear Upon Thy bosom tender.
Near—est, Dear—est, High—est, Bright—est, Thou delight—est.

Still to love me, Thou so high enthroned a—bove me.

I didn't mind, actually, singing hymns on New Year's, as long as I was sure no-one else would find out. I'd have been rather embarrassed if any of my friends ever found out how we spent New Year's. It's easy at a certain age to be embarrassed about your family. I remember Alice Olson, how embarrassed she was about her father, Elmer Olson. He was an alcoholic and couldn't control his urine. Her mother always had to clean up after him. Even so, the house smelled. I suppose she couldn't get it all. Anyway, I know Alice was embarrassed when we saw Elmer all tousled and sick-looking, with urine stains on his trousers. Actually, I don't know what would be harder on a kid—having a father who's a drunk, or one who's sober on New Year's and sings *The Morning Star*.

I walked across the deck and handed Jesus the wine. I sat down, resting my glass on the flap of my kimono. Jesus was looking out over the prairie. He seemed to be noticing everything out there. He was obviously in no hurry to leave, but he didn't have much to say. I thought of what to say next.

'I suppose you're more used to the sea than to the prairie.'

'Yes,' he answered. 'I've lived most of my life near water. But I like the prairie too. There's something nice about the prairie.' He turned his face to the wind, stronger now, coming toward us from the east.

Nice again. If I'd ever used that word to describe the prairie, in an English theme at St John's, for example, it would have had three red circles around it. At least three. I raised my glass to the wind. Good old St John's. Good old Pastor Solberg, standing in front of the wooden altar, holding the gospel aloft in his hand.

In the beginning wass the Word,
And the Word wass with God,
And the Word wass God.

All things were made by him;
And without him wass not anything made
That wass made.

I was sitting on a bench by Paul Thorson. We were sharing a hymnal. Our thumbs touched at the centre of the book. It was winter. The chapel was cold—an army barracks left over from World War 2. We wore parkas and sat close together. Paul fooled around with this thumb, pushing my thumb to my own side of the book, then pulling it back to his side. The wind howled outside. We watched our breath as we sang the hymn.

In thine arms I rest me, Foes who would molest me
Cannot reach me here; Tho' the earth be shak—ing,
Ev—ry heart be quak—ing, Jesus calms my fear;
Fires may flash and thunder crash,
Yea, and sin and hell as—sail me,
Jesus will not fai—l me. . . .

And here he was. Alpha and Omega. The Word. Sitting on my canvas chair, telling me the prairie's nice. What could I say to that?

'I like it too,' I said.

Jesus was watching a magpie circling above the poplars just beyond the quarry. He seemed very nice actually. But he wasn't like my father. My father was perfect, mind you, but you know about perfect people—busy, busy. He wasn't as busy as Elsie though. Elsie was the busy one. You could never visit there without her having to do something else at the same time. Wash the leaves of her plants with milk or fold socks in the basement while you sat on a bench by the washing-machine. I wouldn't mind sitting on a bench in the basement if that was all she had, but her living-room was full of big soft chairs that no-one ever sat in. Now Christ here didn't seem to have any work to do at all.

The wind had risen now. His robes puffed about his legs. His hair swirled around his face. I set my glass down and held my kimono together at my knees. The wind was coming stronger now out of the east. My kimono flapped about my ankles. I bent down to secure the bottom, pressing the moving cloth close against my legs. A Saskatchewan wind comes up in a hurry, let me tell you. Then it happened. A gust of wind hit me straight on, seeping into the folds of my kimono, reaching down into the bodice, billowing the cloth out, until above the sash, the robe was fully open. I knew without looking. The wind was suddenly blowing on my breasts. I felt it cool on both my breasts. Then as quickly as it came, it left, and we sat in the small breeze of before.

I looked at Jesus. He was looking at me. And at my breasts. Looking right at them. Jesus was sitting there on the sundeck, looking at my breasts.

What should I do? Say excuse me and push them back into the kimono? Make a little joke of it? Look what the wind blew in, or something? Or should I say nothing? Just tuck them in as inconspicuously as possible? What do you say when a wind comes up and blows your kimono open and he sees your breasts?

Now, there are ways and there are ways of exposing your breasts. I know a few things. I read books. And I've learned a lot from my cousin Millie. Millie's the black sheep in the family. She left the Academy without graduating to become an artist's model in Winnipeg. A dancer too. Anyway, Millie's told me a few things about body exposure. She says, for instance, that when an artist wants to draw his model he has her either completely nude and stretching and bending in various positions so he can sketch her from different angles. Or he drapes her with cloth, satin usually. He covers one section of the body with the material and leaves the rest exposed. But he does so in a graceful manner, draping the cloth over her stomach or ankle. Never over the breasts. So I realized that my appearance right then wasn't actually pleasing, either aesthetically or erotically—from Millie's point of view. My breasts were just sticking out from the top of my old kimono. And for some reason that I certainly can't explain, even to this day, I did nothing about it. I just sat there.

Jesus must have recognized my confusion, because right then he said, quite sincerely I thought, 'You have nice breasts.'

'Thanks,' I said. I didn't know what else to say, so I asked him if he'd like more wine.

'Yes, I would,' he said, and I left to refill the glass. When I returned he was watching the magpie swishing about in the tall weeds of the quarry. I sat down and watched with him.

Then I got a very, very peculiar sensation. I know it was just an illusion, but it was so strong it scared me. It's hard to explain because nothing like it had ever happened to me before. The magpie began to float toward Jesus. I saw it fluttering toward him in the air as if some vacuum were sucking it in. When it reached him, it flapped about on his chest, which was bare now because the top of his robe had slipped down. It nibbled at his little brown nipples and squawked and disappeared. For all the world, it seemed to disappear right into his pores. Then the same thing happened with a rock. A rock floating up from the quarry and landing on the breast of Jesus, melting into his skin. It was very strange, let me tell you, Jesus and I sitting there together with that happening. It made me dizzy, so I closed my eyes.

I saw the women in a public bath in Tokyo. Black-haired women and children. Some were squatting by faucets that lined a wall. They were running hot water into their basins, washing themselves with white cloths, rubbing each other's backs with the soapy washcloths, then emptying their basins and filling them again, pouring clean water over their bodies for the rinse. Water and suds swirled about on the tiled floor. Others were sitting in the hot pool on the far side, soaking themselves in the steamy water as they jabbered away to one another. Then I saw her. The woman without the breasts. She was squatting by a faucet near the door. The oldest woman I've ever seen. The thinnest woman I've ever witnessed. Skin and bones. Literally. Just skin and bones. She bowed and smiled at everyone who entered. She had three teeth. When she hunched over her basin, I saw the little creases of skin where her breasts had been. When she stood up the wrinkles disappeared. In their place were two shallow caves. Even the nipples seemed to have disappeared into the small brown caves of her breasts.

I opened my eyes and looked at Jesus. Fortunately, everything had stopped floating.

'Have you ever been to Japan?' I asked.

'Yes,' he said, 'a few times.'

I paid no attention to his answer but went on telling him about Japan as if he'd never been there. I couldn't seem to stop talking about that old woman and her breasts.

'You should have seen her,' I said. 'She wasn't flat-chested like some women even here in Moose Jaw. It wasn't like that at all. Her breasts weren't just flat. They were caved in, as if the flesh had sunk right there. Have you ever seen breasts like that before?'

Jesus' eyes were getting darker. He seemed to have sunk farther down into his chair.

'Japanese women have smaller breasts to begin with, usually,' he said.

But he'd misunderstood me. It wasn't just her breasts that held me. It was her jaws, teeth, neck, ankles, heels. Not just her breasts.

I said nothing for a while. Jesus, too, was not talking.

Finally I asked, 'Well, what do you think of breasts like that?'

I knew immediately that I'd asked the wrong question. If you want personal and specific answers, you ask personal and specific questions. It's as simple as that. I should have asked him, for instance, what he thought of them from a sexual point of view. If he were a lover, let's say, would he like to hold such breasts in his hand and play on them with his teeth and fingers? Would he now? The woman, brown and shiny, was bending over her basin. Tiny bubbles of soap drifted from the creases of her chest down to her navel. Hold them. Ha.

Or I could have asked for some kind of aesthetic opinion. If he were an artist, a sculptor, let's say, would he travel to Italy and spend weeks excavating the best marble from the hills near Florence, and then would he stay up night and day in his studio, without eating or bathing, and with matted hair and glazed eyes, chisel out those little creases from his great stone slab?

Or if he were a curator in a large museum in Paris, would he place these wrinkles on a silver pedestal in the centre of the foyer?

Or if he were a patron of the arts, would he attend the opening of this grand exhibition and stand in front of these white caves in his purple turtleneck, sipping champagne and nibbling on the little cracker with the shrimp in the middle, and would he turn to the one beside him, the one in the sleek black pants, and would he say to her, 'Look, darling. Did you see this marvellous piece? Do you see how the artist has captured the very essence of the female form?'

These are some of the things I could have said if I'd had my wits about me. But my wits certainly left me that day. All I did say, and I didn't mean to—it just came out—was, 'It's not nice and I don't like it.'

I lifted my face, threw my head back, and let the wind blow on my neck and breasts. It was blowing harder again. I felt small grains of sand scrape against my skin.

Jesus lover of my soul, let me to thy bosom fly.
While the nearer waters roll, while the tempest still is
nigh . . .

When I looked at him again, his eyes were blacker still and his body had shrunk considerably. He looked almost like Jimmy that time in Prince Albert. Jimmy's an old neighbour from Regina. On his twenty-seventh birthday he joined a motorcycle gang, The Grim Reapers to be exact, and got into a lot of trouble. He ended up in maximum security in PA. One summer on a camping trip up north we stopped to see him—Fred and the kids and I. It wasn't a good visit, by the way. If you're going to visit inmates you should do it regularly. I realize this now. Anyway, that's when his eyes looked black like that. But maybe he'd been smoking. It's probably not the same thing. Jimmy Lebrun. He never did think it was funny when I'd call him a Midnight Raider instead of a Grim Reaper. People are sensitive about their names.

Then Jesus finally answered. Everything seemed to take him a long time, even answering simple questions.

But I'm not sure what he said because something so strange happened that whatever he did say was swept away. Right then the wind blew against my face, pulling my hair back. My kimono swirled about every which way, and I was swinging my arms in the air, like swimming. And there right below my eyes was the roof of our house. I was looking down on the top of the roof. I saw the row of shingles ripped loose from the August hail storm. And I remember thinking—Fred hasn't fixed those shingles yet. I'll have to remind him when he gets home from work. If it rains again the back bedroom will get soaked. Before I knew it I was circling over the sundeck, looking down on the top of Jesus' head. Only I wasn't. I was sitting in the canvas chair watching myself hover over his shoulders. Only it wasn't me hovering. It was the old woman in Tokyo. I saw her grey hair twisting in the wind and her shiny little bum raised in the air, like a baby's. Water was dripping from her chin and toes. And soap bubbles trailed from her elbows like tinsel. She was floating down toward his chest. Only it wasn't her. It was me. I could taste bits of suds sticking to the corners of my mouth and feel the wind on my wet back and in the hollow caves of my breasts. I was smiling and bowing, and the wind was blowing in narrow wisps against my toothless gums. Then quickly, so quickly, like a flock of winter sparrows diving through snow into the branches of the poplar, I was splitting up into millions and millions of pieces and sinking into the tiny, tiny, holes in his chest. It was like the magpie and the rock, like I had come apart into atoms or molecules, or whatever it is we really are.

After that I was dizzy. I began to feel nauseated, there on my canvas chair. Jesus looked sick too. Sad and sick and lonesome. Oh, Christ, I thought, why are we sitting here on such a fine day pouring our sorrows into each other?

I had to get up and walk around. I'd go into the kitchen and make some tea.

I put the kettle on to boil. What on earth had gotten into me? Why had I spent this perfectly good morning talking about breasts? My once chance in a lifetime and I'd let it go. Why didn't I have better control? Why was I always letting things get out of hand? *Breasts.* And why was my name Gloria? Such a pious name for one who can't think of anything else to talk about but breasts. Why wasn't it Lucille? Or Millie? You could talk about breasts all day if your name was Millie. But Gloria. Gloria. Glo-o-o-o-o-o-o-o-oria. I knew then why so many Glorias hang around bars, talking too loud, laughing shrilly at stupid jokes, making sure everyone hears them laugh at the dirty jokes. They're just trying to live down their name, that's all. I brought out the cups and poured the tea.

Everything was back to normal when I returned except that Jesus still looked desolate sitting there in my canvas chair. I handed him the tea and sat down beside him.

Oh, Daddy. And Phillip Nicolai. Oh, Bernard of Clairvoux. Oh, Sacred Head Now Wounded. Go away for a little while and let us sit together quietly, here in this small space under the sun.

I sipped the tea and watched his face. He looked so sorrowful I reached out and put my hand on his wrist. I sat there a long while, rubbing the little hairs on his wrist with my fingers. I couldn't help it. After that he put his arm on my shoulder and his hand on the back of my neck, stroking the muscles there. It felt good. Whenever anything exciting or unusual happens to me my neck is the first to feel it. It gets stiff and knotted up. Then I usually get a headache, and frequently I become nauseous. So it felt very good having my neck rubbed.

I've never been able to handle sensation very well. I remember when I was in grade three and my folks took us to the Saskatoon Exhibition. We went to see the grandstand show—the battle of Wolfe and Montcalm on the Plains of Abraham. The stage was filled with Indians and pioneers and ladies in red, white and blue dresses, singing 'In Days of Yore From Britain's Shore'. It was very spectacular but too much for me. My stomach was upset and my neck ached. I had to keep my head on my mother's lap the whole time, just opening my eyes once in a while so I wouldn't miss everything.

So it felt really good having my neck stroked like that. I could almost feel the knots untying and my body becoming warmer and more restful. Jesus too seemed to be feeling better. His body was back to normal. His eyes looked natural again.

Then, all of a sudden, he started to laugh. He held his hand on my neck and laughed out loud. I don't know to this day what he was laughing about. There was nothing funny there at all. But hearing him made me laugh too. I couldn't stop. He was laughing so hard he spilled the tea over his purple stole. When I saw that I laughed even harder. I'd never thought of Jesus spilling his tea before. And when Jesus saw me laugh so hard and when he looked at my breasts shaking, he laughed harder still, till he wiped tears from his eyes.

After that we just sat there. I don't know how long. I know we watched the magpie carve black waves in the air above the rocks. And the rocks stiff and lovely among the swaying weeds. We watched the poplars twist and bend and rise again beyond the quarry. And then he had to leave.

'Goodbye, Gloria Johnson,' he said, rising from his chair. 'Thanks for the hospitality.'

He leaned over and kissed me on my mouth. Then he flicked my nipple with his finger. And off he went. Down the hill. Through the quarry, and into the prairie. I stood on the sundeck and watched. I watched until I could see him no longer. Until he was only some dim and ancient star on the far horizon.

I went inside the house. Well, now, wasn't that a nice visit. Wasn't that something. I examined the clothes, dry and sour in the living-room. I'd have to put them back in the wash, that's all. I couldn't stand the smell. I tucked my breasts back into my kimono and lugged the basket downstairs.

That's what happened to me in Moose Jaw in 1972. It was the main thing that happened to me that year.

JOY KOGAWA

Obasan

She is sitting at the kitchen table when I come in. She is so deaf now that my knocking does not rouse her and when she sees me she is startled.

'O,' she says, and the sound is short and dry as if there is no energy left to put any inflection into her voice. She begins to rise but falters and her hands outstretched in greeting, fall to the table. She says my name as a question.

I put my shoulder bag down, remove the mud-caked boots and stand before her.

'Obasan,' I say loudly and take her hands. My aunt is not one for hugs and kisses.

She peers into my face. 'O,' she says again.

I nod in reply. We stand for a long time in silence. I open my mouth to ask, 'Did he suffer very much?' but the question feels pornographic.

'Everyone dies some day,' she says eventually. She tilts her head to the side as if it's all too heavy inside.

I hang my jacket on a coat peg and sit beside her.

The house is familiar but has shrunk over the years and is even more cluttered than I remember. The wooden table is covered with a plastic table cloth over a blue and white cloth. Along one edge are African violets in profuse bloom, salt and pepper shakers, a soya sauce bottle, an old radio, a non-automatic toaster, a small bottle full of toothpicks. She goes to the stove and turns on the gas flame under the kettle.

'Everyone dies some day,' she says again and looks in my direction, her eyes unclear and sticky with a gum-like mucous. She pours the tea. Tiny twigs and bits of popcorn circle in the cup.

When I last saw her nine years ago, she told me her tear ducts were clogged. I have never seen her cry. Her mouth is filled with a gummy saliva as well. She drinks warm water often because her tongue sticks to the roof of her false plate.

'Thank you,' I say, taking the cup in both hands.

Uncle was disoriented for weeks, my cousin's letter told me. Towards the end he got dizzier and dizzier and couldn't move without clutching things. By the time they got him to the hospital, his eyes were rolling.

'I think he was beginning to see everything upside down again,' she wrote, 'the way we see when we are born.' Perhaps for Uncle, everything had started reversing and he was growing top to bottom, his mind rooted in an upstairs attic of humus and memory, groping backwards through cracks and walls to a moist cellar. Down to water. Down to the underground sea.

Back to the fishing boat, the ocean, the skiff moored off Vancouver Island where he was born. Like Moses, he was an infant of the waves, rocked to sleep by the lap lap and *'Nen, nen, korori'*, his mother's voice singing the ancient Japanese lullaby. His father, Japanese craftsman, was also a son of the sea which had tossed and coddled his boatbuilding ancestors for centuries. And though he had crossed the ocean from one island as a stranger coming to an island of strangers, it was the sea who was his constant landlord. His fellow tenants, the Songhee Indians of Esquimalt, and the fishermen, came from up and down the BC coast to his workshop in Victoria, to watch, to barter and to buy.

In the framed family photograph hanging above the sideboard, Grandfather sits on a chair with his short legs not quite square on the floor. A long black cape hangs from his shoulders. His left hand clutches a pair of gloves and the top of a cane. On a pedestal beside him is a top hat, open end up. Uncle stands slightly to his right, and behind, with his hand like Napoleon's in his vest. Sitting to their left is Grandmother in a lace and velvet suit with my mother in her arms. They all look in different directions, carved and rigid with their expressionless Japanese faces and their bodies pasted over with Rule Britannia. There's not a ripple out of place.

And then there is the picture, not framed, not on display, showing Uncle as a young man smiling and proud in front of an exquisitely detailed craft. Not a fishing boat, not an ordinary yacht—a creation of many years and many winter evenings—a work of art. Uncle stands, happy enough for the attention of the camera, eager to pass on the message that all is well. That forever and ever all is well.

But many things happen. There is the voice of the RCMP officer saying 'I'll keep that one,' and laughing as he cuts through the water. 'Don't worry, I'll make good use of her.' The other boats are towed away and left to rot. Hundreds of Grandfather's boats belonging to hundreds of fishermen.

The memories are drowned in a whirlpool of protective silence. 'For the sake of the children,' it is whispered over and over. '*Kodomo no tame*.'

And several years later, sitting in a shack on the edge of a sugar beet field in southern Alberta, Obasan is watching her two young daughters with their school books doing homework in the light of a coal oil lamp. Her words are the same. '*Kodomo no tame*.' For their sakes, they will survive the dust and the wind, the gumbo, the summer oven sun. For their sakes, they will work in the fields, hoeing, thinning acres of sugar beets, irrigating, topping, harvesting.

'We must go back,' Uncle would say on winter evenings, the ice thick on the windows. But later, he became more silent.

'*Nen nen*.' Rest, my dead uncle. The sea is severed from your veins. You have been cut loose.

They were feeding him intravenously for two days, the tubes sticking into him like grafting on a tree. But Death won against the medical artistry.

'Obasan, will you be all right?' I ask.

She clears her throat and wipes dry skin off her lips but does not speak. She rolls a bit of dried up jam off the table cloth. She isn't going to answer.

The language of grief is silence. She knows it well, its idioms, its nuances. She's had some of the best tutors available. Grief inside her body is fat and powerful. An almighty tapeworm.

Over the years, Grief has roamed like a highwayman down the channels of her body with its dynamite and its weapons blowing up every moment of relief that tried to make its way down the road. It grew rich off the unburied corpses inside her body.

Grief acted in mysterious ways, its melancholy wonders to perform. When it had claimed her kingdom fully, it admitted no enemies and no vengeance. Enemies belonged in a corridor of experience with sense and meaning, with justice and reason. Her Grief knew nothing of these and whipped her body to resignation until the kingdom was secure. But inside the fortress, Obasan's silence was that of a child bewildered.

'What will you do now?' I ask.

What choices does she have? Her daughters, unable to rescue her or bear the silent rebuke of her suffering have long since fled to the ends of the earth. Each has lived a life in perpetual flight from the density of her inner retreat—from the rays of her inverted sun sucking in their lives with the voracious appetite of a dwarf star. Approaching her, they become balls of liquid metal—mercurial—unpredictable in their moods and sudden departures. Especially for the younger daughter, departure is as necessary as breath. What metallic spider is it in her night that hammers a constant transformation, lacing open doors and windows with iron bars.

'What will you do?' I repeat.

She folds her hands together. I pour her some more tea and she bows her thanks. I take her hands in mine, feeling the silky wax texture.

'Will you come and stay with us?' Are there any other words to say? Her hands move under mine and I release them. Her face is motionless. 'We could leave in a few days and come back next month.'

'The plants. . . .'

'Neighbours can water them.'

'There is trouble with the house,' she says. 'This is an old house. If I leave. . . .'

'Obasan,' I say nodding, 'it is your house.'

She is an old woman. Every homemade piece of furniture, each pot holder and child's paper doily, is a link in her lifeline. She has preserved in shelves and in cupboards, under layers of clothing in closets—a daughter's rubber ball, colouring books, old hats, children's dresses. The items are endless. Every short stub pencil, every cornflake box stuffed with paper bags and old letters is of her ordering. They rest in the corners of the house like parts of her body, hair cells, skin tissue, food particles, tiny specks of memory. This house is now her blood and bones.

She is all old women in every hamlet in the world. You see her on a street corner in a village in southern France, in her black dress and her black stockings. She is squatting on stone steps in a Mexican mountain village. Everywhere she stands as the true and rightful owner of the earth, the bearer of love's keys to unknown doorways, to a network of astonishing tunnels, the possessor of life's infinite personal details.

'I am old,' she says.

These are the words my grandmother spoke that last night in the house in Victoria. Grandmother was too old then to understand political expediency, race riots, the yellow peril. I was too young.

She stands up slowly. 'Something in the attic for you,' she says.

We climb the narrow stairs one step at a time carrying a flashlight with us. Its dull beam reveals mounds of cardboard boxes, newspapers, magazines, a trunk. A dead sparrow lies in the nearest corner by the eaves.

She attempts to lift the lid of the trunk. Black fly corpses fall to the floor. Between the wooden planks, more flies fill the cracks. Old spider webs hang like blood clots, thick and black from the rough angled ceiling.

Our past is as clotted as old webs hung in dark attics, still sticky and hovering, waiting for us to adhere and submit or depart. Or like a spider with its skinny hairy legs, the past skitters out of the dark, spinning and netting the air, ready to snap us up and ensnare our thoughts in old and complex perceptions. And when its feasting is complete, it leaves its victims locked up forever, dangling like hollowed out insect skins, a fearful calligraphy, dry reminders that once there was life flitting about in the weather.

But occasionally a memory that refuses to be hollowed out, to be categorized, to be identified, to be explained away, comes thudding into the web like a giant moth. And in the daylight, what's left hanging there, ragged and shredded is a demolished fly trap, and beside it a bewildered eight-legged spinning animal.

My dead refuse to bury themselves. Each story from the past is changed and distorted, altered as much by the present as the present is shaped by the past. But potent and pervasive as a prairie dust storm, memory and dream seep and mingle through cracks, settling on furniture, into upholstery. The attic and the living room encroach onto each other, deep into their invisible places.

I sneeze and dust specks pummel across the flashlight beam. Will we all be dust in the end—a jumble of faces and lives compressed and powdered into a few lines of statistics—fading photographs in family albums, the faces no longer familiar, the clothing quaint, the anecdotes lost?

I use the flashlight to break off a web and lift the lid of the trunk. A strong whiff of mothballs assaults us. The odour of preservation. Inside, there are bits of lace and fur, a 1920s nightgown, a shoe box, red and white striped socks. She sifts through the contents, one by one.

'That's strange,' she says several times.

'What are you looking for?' I ask.

'Not here. It isn't here.'

She turns to face me in the darkness. 'That's strange,' she says and leaves her questions enclosed in silence.

I pry open the folds of a cardboard box. The thick dust slides off like chocolate icing sugar—antique pollen. Grandfather's boat building tools are wrapped in heavy cloth. These are all he brought when he came to this country wearing a western suit, western shoes, a round black hat. Here is the plane with a wooden handle which he worked by pulling it towards him. A fundamental difference in workmanship—to pull rather than push. Chisels, hammer, a mallet, a thin pointed saw, the handle extending from the blade like that of a kitchen knife.

'What will you do with these?' I ask.

'The junk in the attic,' my cousin's letter said, 'should be burned. When I come there this summer, I'll have a big bonfire. It's a fire trap. I've taken the only things that are worth keeping.'

Beneath the box of tools is a pile of *Life* magazines dated in the 1950s. A subscription maintained while the two daughters were home. Beside the pile is another box containing shoe boxes, a metal box with a disintegrating elastic band, several chocolate boxes. Inside the metal box are pictures, duplicates of some I have seen in our family albums. Obasan's wedding photo—her mid-calf dress hanging straight down from her shoulders, her smile glued on. In the next picture, Uncle is a child wearing a sailor suit.

The shoe box is full of documents.

Royal Canadian Mounted Police, Vancouver, BC, March 4, 1942. A folded mimeographed paper authorizes Uncle as the holder of a numbered Registration Card to leave a Registered Area by truck for Vernon where he is required to report to the local Registrar of Enemy Aliens, not later than the following day. It is signed by the RCMP superintendant.

Uncle's face, young and unsmiling looks up at me from the bottom right hand corner of a wallet size ID card. 'The bearer whose photograph and specimen of signature appear hereon, has been duly registered in compliance with the provisions of Order-in-Council PC 117.' A purple stamp underneath states 'Canadian Born'. His thumb print appears on the back with marks of identification specified—scar on back of right hand.

There is a letter from the Department of the Secretary of State. Office of the Custodian. Japanese Evacuation Section. 506 Royal Bank Bldg. Hastings and Granville. Vancouver, BC.

Dear Sir.

Dear Uncle. With whom were you corresponding and for what did you hope? That the enmity would cease? That you could return to your boats? I have grown tired, Uncle, of seeking the face of the enemy hiding in the thick forests of the past. You were not the enemy. The police who came to your door were not the enemy. The men who rioted against you were not the enemy. The Vancouver alderman who said 'Keep BC White' was not the enemy. The men who drafted the Order-in-Council were not the enemy. He does not wear a uniform or sit at a long meeting table. The man who read your timid letter, read your polite request, skimmed over your impossible plea, was not your enemy. He had an urgent report to complete. His wife was ill. The phone rang all the time. The senior staff was meeting in two hours. The secretary was spending too much time over coffee breaks. There were a billion problems to attend to. Injustice was the only constant in a world of flux. There were moments when expedience demanded decisions which would later be judged unjust. Uncle, he did not always know what he was doing. You too did not have an all compassionate imagination. He was just doing his job. I am just doing my work, Uncle. We are all just doing our jobs.

My dear dead Uncle. Am I come to unearth our bitterness that our buried love too may revive?

'Obasan, what shall we do with these?'

She has been waiting at the top of the stairs, holding the railing with both hands. I close the shoe box and replace the four interlocking flaps of the cardboard box. With one hand I shine the flashlight and with the other, guide her as I precede her slowly down the stairs. Near the bottom she stumbles and I hold her small body upright.

'Thank you, thank you,' she says. This is the first time my arms have held her. We walk slowly through the living room and back to the kitchen. Her lips are trembling as she sits on the wooden stool.

Outside, the sky of the prairie spring is painfully blue. The trees are shooting out their leaves in the fierce wind, the new branches elastic as whips. The sharp-edged clarity is insistent as trumpets.

But inside, the rooms are muted. Our inner trees, our veins, are involuted, cocooned, webbed. The blood cells in the trunks of our bodies, like tiny specks of light, move in a sluggish river. It is more a potential than an actual river—an electric liquid—the current flowing in and between us, between our generations. Not circular, as in a whirlpool, or climactic and tidal as in fountains or spray—but brooding. Bubbling. You expect to hear barely audible pip-pip electronic tones, a pre-concert tuning up behind the curtains in the darkness. Towards the ends of our branches and fingertips, tiny human-shaped flames or leaves break off and leap towards the shadows. My arms are suffused with a suppressed urge to hold.

At the edges of our flesh is a hint of a spiritual osmosis, an eagerness within matter, waiting to brighten our dormant neurons, to entrust our stagnant cells with movement and dance.

Obasan drinks her tea and makes a shallow scratching sound in her throat. She shuffles to the door and squats beside the boot tray. With a putty knife, she begins to scrape off the thick clay like mud that sticks to my boots.

AUDREY THOMAS

If One Green Bottle . . .

When fleeing, one should never look behind. Orpheus, Lot's wife . . . penalties grotesque and terrible await us all. It does not pay to doubt . . . to turn one's head . . . to rely on the confusion . . . the smoke . . . the fleeing multitudes . . . the satisfaction of the tumbling cities . . . to distract the attention of the gods. Argus-eyed, they wait, he waits . . . the golden chessmen spread upon the table . . . the opponent's move already known, accounted for. . . . Your pawns, so vulnerable . . . advancing with such care (if you step on a crack, then you'll break your mother's back). Already the monstrous hand trembles in anticipation . . . the thick lips twitch with suppressed laughter . . . then pawn, knight, castle, queen scooped up and tossed aside. 'Check,' and (click click) 'check . . . mmmate.' The game is over, and you . . . surprised (but why?) . . . petulant . . . your nose still raw from the cold . . . your galoshes not yet dried . . . really, it's indecent . . . inhumane (why bother to come? answer: the bother of not coming) . . . and not even the offer of a sandwich or a cup of tea . . . discouraging . . . disgusting. The great mouth opens . . . like a whale really . . . he strains you, one more bit of plankton, through his teeth (my mother had an ivory comb once). 'Next week . . .? At the same time . . .? No, no, not at all. I do not find it boring in the least. . . . Each time a great improvement. Why, soon,' the huge lips tremble violently, 'ha, ha, you'll be beating me.' Lies . . . all lies. Yet, even as you go, echoes of Olympian laughter in your ears, you know you will return, will once more challenge . . . and be defeated once again. Even plankton have to make a protest . . . a stand . . . what else can one do? 'Besides, it passes the time . . . keeps my hand in . . . and you never know. . . . One time, perhaps . . . a slip . . . a flutter of the eyelids. . . . Even the gods grow old.'

The tropical fan, three-bladed, omniscient, omnipotent, inexorable, churns up dust and mosquitoes, the damp smell of coming rain, the overripe smell of vegetation, of charcoal fires, of human excrement, of fear . . . blown in through the open window, blown up from the walls and the floor. All is caught in the fan's embrace, the efficient arms of the unmoved mover. The deus in the machina, my old chum the chess-player, refuses to descend . . . yet watches. Soon they will let down the nets and we will lie in the darkness, in our gauze houses, like so many lumps of cheese . . . protected . . . revealed. The night-fliers, dirty urchins, will press their noses at my windows and lick their hairy lips in hunger . . . in frustration. Can they differentiate, I wonder, between the blood of my neighbour and mine? Are there aesthetes among the insects who will touch only the soft parts . . . between the thighs . . . under the armpits . . . along the inner arm? Are there vintages and connoisseurs? I don't like the nights here: that is why I wanted it over before the night. One of the reasons. If I am asleep I do not know who feeds on me, who has found the infinitesimal rip and invited his neighbours in. Besides, he promised it would be over before the night. And one listens, doesn't one? . . . one always believes . . . absurd to rely on verbal consolation . . . clichés so worn they feel like old coins . . . smooth . . . slightly oily to the touch . . . faceless.

Pain, the word, I mean, derived (not according to Skeat) from 'pay' and 'Cain'. How can there, then, be an exit . . . a way out? The darker the night, the clearer the mark on the forehead . . . the brighter the blind man's cane at the crossing . . . the louder the sound of footsteps somewhere behind. Darkness heightens the absurd sense of 'situation' . . . gives the audience its kicks. But tonight . . . really . . . All Souls' . . . it's too ridiculous. . . . Somebody goofed. The author has gone too far; the absurdity lies in one banana skin, not two or three. After one, it becomes too painful . . . too involved . . . too much like home. Somebody will have to pay for this . . . the reviews . . . tomorrow . . . all will be most severe. The actors will sulk over their morning cup of coffee . . . the angel will beat his double breast above the empty pocketbook . . . the director will shout and stamp his feet. . . . The whole thing should have been revised . . . rewritten . . . we knew it from the first.

(This is the house that Jack built. This is the cat that killed the rat that lived in the house that Jack built. We are the maidens all shaven and shorn, that milked the cow with the crumpled horn . . . that loved in the hearse that Joke built. Excuse me, please, was this the Joke that killed the giant or the Jack who tumbled down . . . who broke his crown? Crown him with many crowns, the lamb upon his throne. He tumbled too . . . it's inevitable. . . . It all, in the end, comes back to the nursery. . . . Jill, Humpty Dumpty, Rock-a-bye baby . . . they-kiss-you, they-kiss-you . . . they all fall down. The nurses in the corner playing Ludo . . . centurions dicing. We are all betrayed by Cock-a-Doodle-Doo. . . . We all fall down. Why, then, should I be exempt? . . . presumptuous of me . . . please forgive.)

Edges of pain. Watch it, now, the tide is beginning to turn. Like a cautious bather, stick in one toe . . . both feet . . . 'brr' . . . the impact of the ocean . . . the solidity of the thing, now that you've finally got under . . . like swimming in an ice cube really. 'Yes, I'm coming. Wait for me.' The shock of the total immersion . . . the pain breaking over the head. Don't cry out . . . hold your breath . . . so. 'Not so bad, really, when one gets used to it.' That's it . . . just the right tone . . . the brave swimmer. . . . Now wave a gay hand toward the shore. Don't let them know . . . the indignities . . . the chattering teeth . . . the blue lips . . . the sense of isolation. . . . Good.

And Mary, how did she take it, I wonder, the original, the appalling announcement . . . the burden thrust upon her? 'No, really, some other time . . . the spring planting . . . my aged mother . . . quite impossible. Very good of you to think of me, of course, but I couldn't take it on. Perhaps you'd call in again next year.' (Dismiss him firmly . . . quickly, while there's still time. Don't let him get both feet in the door. Be firm and final. 'No, I'm sorry, I never accept free gifts.') And then the growing awareness, the anger showing quick and hot under the warm brown of the cheeks. The voice . . . like oil. . . . 'I'm afraid I didn't make myself clear.' (Like the detective novels. . . . 'Allow me to present my card . . . my credentials.' The shock of recognition . . . the horror. 'Oh, I see. . . . Yes . . . well, if it's like that. . . . Come this way.' A gesture of resignation. She allows herself one sigh . . . the ghost of a smile.) But no, it's all wrong. Mary . . . peasant girl . . . quite a different reaction implied. Dumbfounded . . . remember Zachary. A shocked silence . . . the rough fingers twisting together like snakes . . . awe . . . a certain rough pride ('Wait until I tell the other girls. The well . . . tomorrow morning. . . . I won't be proud about it, not really. But it is an honour. What will Mother say?') *Droit de seigneur* . . . the servant summoned to the bedchamber . . . honoured . . . afraid. Or perhaps like Leda. No preliminaries . . . no thoughts at all. Too stupid . . . too frightened . . . the thing was, after all, over so quickly. That's it . . . stupidity . . . the necessary attribute. I can hear him now. 'That girl . . . whatzername? . . . Mary. Mary will do. Must be a simple woman. . . . That's where we made our first mistake. Eve too voluptuous . . . too intelligent . . . this time nothing must go wrong.'

And the days were accomplished. Unfair to gloss that over . . . to make so little of the waiting . . . the months . . . the hours. They make no mention of the hours; but of course, men wrote it down. How were they to know? After the immaculate conception, after the long and dreadful journey, after the refusal at the inn . . . came the maculate delivery . . . the manger. And all that noise . . . cattle lowing (and doing other things besides) . . . angels blaring away . . . the eerie light. No peace . . . no chance for sleep . . . for rest between the pains . . . for time to think . . . to gather courage. Yet why should she be afraid . . . downhearted . . .? Hadn't she had a sign . . . the voice . . . the presence of the star? (And notice well, they never told her about the other thing . . . the third act.) It probably seemed worth it at the time . . . the stench . . . the noise . . . the pain.

Robert the Bruce . . . Constantine . . . Noah. The spider . . . the flaming cross . . . the olive branch. . . . With these signs. . . . I would be content with something far more simple. A breath of wind on the cheek . . . the almost imperceptible movement of a curtain . . . a single flash of lightning. Courage consists, perhaps, in the ability to recognize signs . . . the symbolism of the spider. But for me . . . tonight . . . what is there? The sound of far-off thunder . . . the smell of the coming rain which will wet, but not refresh . . . that tropical fan. The curtain moves . . . yes, I will allow you that. But for me . . . tonight . . . there is only a rat behind the arras. Jack's rat. This time there is no exit . . . no way out or up.

(You are not amused by my abstract speculations? Listen . . . I have more. Time. Time is an awareness, either forward or backward, of Then, as opposed to Now . . . the stasis. Time is the moment between thunder and lightning . . . the interval at the street corner when the light is amber, neither red nor green, but shift gears, look both ways . . . the oasis of pleasure between pains . . . the space between the darkness and the dawn . . . the conversations between courses . . . the fear in the final stroke of twelve . . . the nervous fumbling with cloth and buttons, before the longed-for contact of the flesh . . . the ringing telephone . . . the solitary coffee cup . . . the oasis of pleasure between pains. Time . . . and time again.)

That time when I was eleven and at Scout camp . . . marching in a dusky serpentine to the fire tower . . . the hearty counselors with sun-streaked hair and muscular thighs . . . enjoying themselves, enjoying ourselves . . . the long hike almost over. 'Ten green bottles standing on the wall. Ten green bottles standing on the wall. If one green bottle . . . should accidentally fall, there'd be nine green bottles standing on the wall.' And that night . . . after pigs in blankets . . . cocoa . . . campfire songs . . . the older girls taught us how to faint . . . to hold our breath and count to 30 . . . then blow upon our thumbs. Gazing up at the stars . . . the sudden sinking back into warmth and darkness . . . the recovery . . . the fresh attempt . . . delicious. In the morning we climbed the fire tower (and I, afraid to look down or up, climbing blindly, relying on my sense of touch), reached the safety of the little room on top. We peered out the windows at the little world below . . . and found six baby mice, all dead . . . curled up, like dust kitties in the kitchen drawer. 'How long d'you suppose they've been there?' 'Too long. Ugh.' 'Throw them away.' 'Put them back where you found them.' Disturbed . . . distressed . . . the pleasure marred. 'Let's toss them down on Rachel. She was too scared to climb the tower. Baby.' 'Yes, let's toss them down. She ought to be paid back.' (Everything all right now . . . the day saved. Ararat . . . Areopagus. . . .) Giggling, invulnerable, we hurled the small bodies out the window at the Lilliputian form below. Were we punished? Curious . . . I can't remember. And yet the rest . . . so vivid . . . as though it were yesterday . . . this morning . . . five minutes ago. . . . We must have been punished. Surely they wouldn't let us get away with that?

Waves of pain now . . . positive whitecaps . . . breakers. . . . Useless to try to remember . . . to look behind . . . to think. Swim for shore. Ignore the ringing in the ears . . . the eyes half blind with water . . . the waves breaking over the head. Just keep swimming . . . keep moving forward . . . rely on instinct . . . your sense of direction . . . don't look back or forward . . . there isn't time for foolish speculation. . . . See? Flung up . . . at last . . . exhausted, but on the shore. Flotsam . . . jetsam . . . but there, you made it. Lie still.

The expected disaster is always the worst. One waits for it . . . is obsessed by it . . . it nibbles at the consciousness. Jack's rat. Far better the screech of brakes . . . the quick embrace of steel and shattered glass . . . or the sudden stumble from the wall. One is prepared through being unprepared. A few thumps of the old heart . . . like a brief flourish of announcing trumpets . . . a roll of drums . . . and then nothing. This way . . . tonight . . . I wait for the crouching darkness like a child waiting for that movement from the shadows in the corner of the bedroom. It's all wrong . . . unfair . . . there ought to be a law. . . . One can keep up only a given number of chins . . . one keeps silent only a given number of hours. After that, the final humiliation . . . the loss of self-control . . . the oozing out upon the pavement. Dumpty-like, one refuses (or is unable?) to be reintegrated . . . whimpers for morphia and oblivion . . . shouts and tears her hair. . . . That must not happen. . . . Undignified . . . déclassé. I shall talk to my friend the fan . . . gossip with the night-fliers . . . pit my small light against the darkness, a miner descending the shaft. I have seen the opening gambit . . . am aware of the game's inevitable conclusion. What does it matter? I shall leap over the net . . . extend my hand . . . murmur, 'Well done', and walk away, stiff-backed and shoulders high. I will drink the hemlock gaily . . . I will sing. Ten green bottles standing on the wall. If one green bottle should accidentally fall. . . . When it is over I will sit up and call for tea . . . ignore the covered basin . . . the bloody sheets (but what do they do with it afterward . . . where will they take it? I have no experience in these matters). They will learn that the death of a part is not the death of the whole. The tables will be turned . . . and overturned. The shield of Achilles will compensate for his heel.

And yet, were we as ignorant as all that . . . as naïve . . . that we never wondered where the bottles came from? I never wondered. . . . I accepted them the way a small child draws the Christmas turkey . . . brings the turkey home . . . pins it on the playroom wall . . . and then sits down to eat. One simply doesn't connect. Yet there they were . . . lined up on the laboratory wall . . . half-formed, some of them . . . the tiny vestigial tails of the smallest . . . like corpses of stillborn kittens . . . or baby mice. Did we think that they had been like that always . . . swimming forever in their little formaldehyde baths . . . ships in bottles . . . snowstorms in glass paperweights? The professor's voice . . . droning like a complacent bee . . . tapping his stick against each fragile glass shell . . . cross-pollinating facts with facts . . . our pencils racing over the paper. We accepted it all without question . . . even went up afterward for a closer look . . . boldly . . . without hesitation. It was all so simple . . . so uncomplex . . . so scientific. Stupidity, the necessary attribute. And once we dissected a guinea pig, only to discover that she had been pregnant . . . tiny little guinea pigs inside. We . . . like children presented with one of those Russian dolls . . . were delighted . . . gratified. We had received a bonus . . . a free gift.

Will they do that to part of me? How out of place it will look, bottled with the others . . . standing on the laboratory wall. Will the black professor . . . the brown-eyed students . . . bend their delighted eyes upon this bonus, this free gift? (White. 24 weeks. Female . . . or male.) But perhaps black babies are white . . . or pink . . . to begin. It is an interesting problem . . . one which could be pursued . . . speculated upon. I must ask someone. If black babies are not black before they are born, at what stage does the dark hand of heredity . . . of race . . . touch their small bodies? At the moment of birth perhaps? . . . like silver exposed to the air. But remember their palms . . . the soles of their feet. It's an interesting problem. And remember the beggar outside the central post office . . . the terrible burned place on his arm . . . the new skin . . . translucent . . . almost a shell pink. I turned away in disgust . . . wincing at the shared memory of scalding liquid . . . the pain. But really . . . in retrospect . . . it was beautiful. That pink skin . . . that delicate . . . Turneresque tint . . . apple blossoms against dark branches.

That's it . . . just the right tone. . . . Abstract speculation on birth . . . on death . . . on human suffering in general. Remember only the delicate tint . . . sunset against a dark sky . . . the pleasure of the Guernica. It's so simple, really . . . all a question of organization . . . of aesthetics. One can so easily escape the unpleasantness . . . the shock of recognition. Cleopatra in her robes . . . her crown. . . . 'I have immortal longings in me.' No fear . . . the asp suckles peacefully and unreproved. . . . She wins . . . and Caesar loses. Better than Falstaff babbling 'of green fields'. One needs the transcendentalism of the tragic hero. Forget the old man . . . pathetic . . . deserted . . . broken. The grey iniquity. It's all a question of organization . . . of aesthetics . . . of tone. Brooke, for example. 'In that rich earth a richer dust concealed. . . .' Terrified out of his wits, of course, but still organizing, still posturing.

(The pain is really quite bad now . . . you will excuse me for a moment? I'll be back. I must not think for a moment . . . must not struggle . . . must let myself be carried over the crest of the wave . . . face downward . . . buoyant . . . a badge of seaweed across the shoulder. It's easier this way . . . not to think . . . not to struggle. . . . It's quicker . . . it's more humane.)

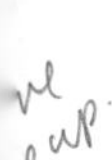

Still posturing. See the clown . . . advancing slowly across the platform . . . dragging the heavy rope. . . . Grunts . . . strains . . . the audience shivering with delight. Then the last . . . the desperate . . . tug. And what revealed? . . . a carrot . . . a bunch of grapes . . . a small dog . . . nothing. The audience in tears. . . . 'Oh, God . . . how funny. . . . One knows, of course . . . all the time. And yet it never fails to amuse . . . I never fail to be taken in.' Smothered giggles in the darkened taxi . . . the deserted streets. . . . 'Oh, God, how amusing. . . . Did you see? The carrot . . . the bunch of grapes . . . the small dog . . . nothing. All a masquerade . . . a charade . . . the rouge . . . the powder . . . the false hair of an old woman . . . a clown.' Babbling of green fields.

Once, when I was ten, I sat on a damp rock and watched my father fishing. Quiet . . . on a damp rock . . . I watched the flapping gills . . . the frenzied tail . . . the gasps for air . . . the refusal to accept the hook's reality. Rainbow body swinging through the air . . . the silver drops . . . like tears. Watching quietly from the haven of my damp rock, I saw my father struggle with the fish . . . the chased and beaten silver body. 'Papa, let it go, Papa . . . please!' My father . . . annoyed . . . astonished . . . his communion disrupted . . . his chalice overturned . . . his paten trampled underfoot. He let it go . . . unhooked it carelessly and tossed it lightly toward the centre of the pool. After all, what did it matter . . . to please the child . . . and the damage already done. No recriminations . . . only, perhaps (we never spoke of it), a certain loss of faith . . . a fall, however imperceptible . . . from grace?

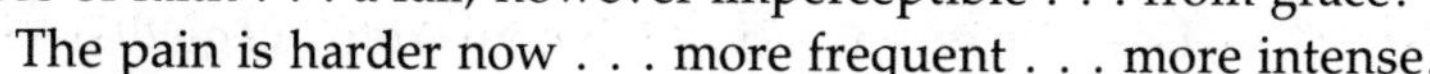

The pain is harder now . . . more frequent . . . more intense.

Don't think of it . . . ignore it . . . let it come. The symphony rises to its climax. No more andante . . . no more moderato . . . clashing cymbals . . . blaring horns. . . . Lean forward in your seat . . . excited . . . intense . . . a shiver of fear . . . of anticipation. The conductor . . . a wild thing . . . a clockwork toy gone mad. . . . Arms flailing . . . body arched . . . head swinging loosely . . . dum de dum de DUM DUM DUM. The orchestra . . . the audience . . . all bewitched . . . heads nodding . . . fingers moving, yes, oh, yes . . . the orgasm of sound . . . the straining . . . letting go. An ecstasy . . . a crescendo . . . a coda . . . it's over. 'Whew.' 'Terrific.' (Wiping the sweat from their eyes.) Smiling . . . self-conscious . . . a bit embarrassed now. . . . 'Funny how you can get all worked up over a bit of music.' Get back to the formalities. . . . Get off the slippery sand . . . onto the warm, safe planks of conversation. 'Would you like a coffee . . . a drink . . . an ice?' The oasis of pleasure between pains. For me, too, it will soon be over . . . and for you.

Noah on Ararat . . . high and dry . . . sends out the dove to see if it is over. Waiting anxiously . . . the dove returning with the sign. Smug now . . . self-satisfied . . . know-it-all. . . . All those drowned neighbours . . . all those doubting Thomases . . . gone . . . washed away . . . full fathoms five. . . . And he, safe . . . the animals pawing restlessly, scenting freedom after their long confinement . . . smelling the rich smell of spring . . . of tender shoots. Victory . . . triumph . . . the chosen ones. Start again . . . make the world safe for democracy . . . cleansing . . . purging . . . Guernica . . . Auschwitz . . . God's fine Italian hand. Always the moral . . . the little tag . . . the cautionary tale. Willie in one of his bright new sashes/fell in the fire and was burnt to ashes. . . . Suffering is good for the soul . . . the effects on the body are not to be considered. Fire and rain . . . cleansing . . . purging . . . tempering the steel. Not much longer now . . . and soon they will let down the nets. (He promised it would be over before the dark. I do not like the dark here. Forgive me if I've mentioned this before.) We will sing to keep our courage up. Ten green bottles standing on the wall. Ten green bottles standing on the wall. If one green bottle. . . .

The retreat from Russia . . . feet bleeding on the white snow . . . tired . . . discouraged . . . what was it all about anyway? . . . we weren't prepared. Yet we go on . . . feet bleeding on the white snow . . . dreaming of warmth . . . smooth arms and golden hair

. . . a glass of kvass. We'll get there yet. (But will we ever be the same?) A phoenix . . . never refusing . . . flying true and straight . . . into the fire and out. Plunge downward now . . . a few more minutes . . . spread your wings . . . the moment has come . . . the fire blazes . . . the priest is ready . . . the worshippers are waiting. The battle over . . . the death within expelled . . . cast out . . . the long hike over . . . Ararat. Sleep now . . . and rise again from the dying fire . . . the ashes. It's over . . . eyes heavy . . . body broken but relaxed. All over. We made it, you and I. . . . It's all, is it not . . . a question of organization . . . of tone? Yet one would have been grateful . . . at the last . . . for a reason . . . an explanation . . . a sign. A spider . . . a flaming cross . . . a carrot . . . a bunch of grapes . . . a small dog. Not this nothing.

HÉLÈNE OUVRARD

The Angel

The tall redhead was posing. In that careless manner typical of everything about her. Actually she seemed not to be posing at all, but simply to be there, as if waiting at a street corner for she-alone-knew-what, but it could only have been something commonplace. A bus, her lover, her son returning from school. She wasn't beautiful, she really wasn't, with her round shoulders, slack thighs, sagging breasts. An ordinary woman at an ordinary moment in her life. Sitting there, nude, she looked as if she never smoked—which she surely did—in front of her bathroom mirror in the morning. A smell of cigarette smoke and a sound of scuffing slippers trailed this woman everywhere.

Judith moved among the easels. The students had clearly captured this—a woman no one notices, or one who doesn't care if she is noticed. A woman with no need in her life for other people's attention. And to whom their attention will make not a particle of difference. A woman who exists solely, supremely, for herself. This woman was present on each sheet of paper. This woman lived. She was extraordinarily alive.

From one drawing to another, as Judith passed along in front of the easels, the angle of the pose altered, as if, from sheet to sheet, the model herself were turning, revealing not merely a flat two-dimensional representation, but a woman of complete dimensions, identifiable through the relations of the lines that defined her—breasts in front, buttocks behind—as a unique being, sturdily self-contained, whose features were not in the least difficult to portray. Even down to the circles under the eyes, the corners of the mouth, the heavy coil of untidy hair on the nape; even the curve in the nape, where the hollow of it met the neck when the model shifted position slightly; all this came to life remarkably. And when the woman finally moved, her hour of posing having come to an end, Judith was astonished not to see one sheet of paper after another conveying that movement, a completely ordinary one of reaching for her washed-out purple chenille bathrobe and her pack of cigarettes.

And she also ought to have been on every sheet when she sat down and crossed her legs, making the calves bulge unattractively, and rubbed her swollen ankle. Judith thought she could very likely be found in just such a pose, wearing that same bathrobe and with that cigarette in her mouth, sitting on the edge of the bathtub in the morning, talking to her lover while he combed his beard in front of the mirror.

She thought then of the hairs that would inevitably fall into the sink, and gave a little start of irritation, as if having to repeat for the hundredth time that she absolutely detested seeing whiskers or hairs of any kind on the porcelain. All at once she became aware of her absorption and glanced around, blushing, but the students of the evening class were busy changing their drawing paper for the next sketch, so no one had noticed her fitful, nervous gesture, an unaccountable gesture that was entirely inappropriate here. She felt like blaming the model, whose singularly unstudied manner had drawn her, in spite of herself, into a banality that was repellent to her; but the platform was vacant, and she suddenly remembered that she herself must hurry and undress because it was now her turn to pose.

She met the tall redhead emerging from behind the screen, still doing up her buttons, one hand behind her back, and a cigarette dangling from her lips. 'Good evening,' the redhead said, and a bit of cigarette ash fell onto her old red sweater, which was every bit as worn as the faded purple bathrobe. And Judith was unable to reply because just then the woman's odour—a peculiar blend of cigarette smoke, old clothing, and the scent of her body mingled with that of the fine soap redheads use for their fair skin —drew her into the room in which she imagined the redhead getting ready for class, amid the disorder that was as unimportant to her as her posture, her slumped shoulders, her worn clothes, or her son, who would share his bowl of milk with the cat before leaving for school—'Bye Mom!' the child would call out—and Judith's heart tightened, possibly with envy.

She pulled down her zipper and kicked off her soaked shoes. It was mild out and the streets were covered with melting snow —there was a hint of spring tonight in the breeze that ruffled the bare treetops caught in clouds—and she had come across town on foot, despite the slush that seeped into her light overshoes, the ones she wore winter or summer now, ever since she had decided to live at all times according to her inner weather, which could make winter of summer, or summer of winter, just as it pleased.

'They want to have the model lying down: a ''reclining nude'',' the professor said. Then he added, 'They tell me you're their favourite model—they'd like to have you for every course this year.' He smiled with satisfaction, and Judith bowed her head to hide her embarrassment, which he noticed, but thought had been caused by the pleasure he had given her rather than by the tall redhead, who had just entered Judith's thoughts—her purple bathrobe wide open to display the red flame of her sex, and an orange towel round her neck because, now that both lover and son had left, it was her turn to use the bathroom.

Disregarding their wishes, she assumed an entirely different pose, one that delighted them. It seemed that her body moulded itself, of its own accord, into compact forms and curves, its lines settling themselves one upon the other, seeking each other, intermingling, marrying; she was like a sculpture that would eventually articulate itself and, in fact, once the work began she seemed to feel as heavy as bronze, her body dividing itself into three sections, like the tremendous statue by a famous contemporary artist adorning a public square in the business district of the city, the cost of which had so incensed people that as soon as this abstract figure of a woman had appeared they threatened to dismember it—essential parts had been left out of the composition and anyone might have walked off with head, pelvis, or feet; but that pose, she thought, would convey nothing more than an empty block, so no sooner had she assumed it than she made a great effort to extricate herself from the three sections, leaving the students nothing to feed their starving charcoals—which attacked her all over like forks—but empty lines, less lived-in even than those of the woman from the business district, who had a tiny head and stumps of arms, a concave stomach, and feet—God knows what they were, what kind of feet did that statue have anyway?—but it didn't matter, the feet were the first part of her body that she withdrew, thinking to test their insensibility by trying to feel them without moving so much as a muscle of her toes; no, she didn't feel a thing, neither in her feet nor anywhere else, she had actually become an empty form, or rather, a full one, full of matter, just as the statue was full of metal but empty in itself, for needless to say, when a form—whether of flesh or of metal, empty or full—has attained absolute immobility, it is of no consequence.

Released from her body now, she floated on an ethereal plane somewhere above the easels, and to soar higher, right up to the huge skylight at the top of the studio, was merely a matter of twisting what used to be her hips, and she found herself gasping like someone looking into a shop-window at Christmas time; the students, meanwhile, were splintering their charcoals over the uninhabited, uninhabitable, unfamiliar forms that she had left them—she could hear them complaining, sighing, tearing up their paper, for some of them were professional designers who spent their days drawing plans, designing machines or buildings with straight lines, and these specialists in mechanics, accustomed to axes and rigid lines, couldn't begin to master the curves, the shifting perspectives, and devilish compressions of the pose the model had taken against their wishes. As for the women, they failed utterly to harmonize the young model's catatonic pallor with the cushions and draperies of the room they had chosen to install her in for their portraits, but no one suspected that Judith had left her body—though all they had to do was look up in order to see her flapping her wings, yes, wings, because at the tips of her long feathers she could feel a slight air resistance, and she gaily allowed herself to fall, wings folded, whereupon she knew the terror of Icarus, and then she rose again with a single wingbeat, slid along the dizzying, but unslippery, slide, mounted once more, and remained there, immobile, transported, wingtips trembling ever so slightly, like the fins of a fish in the midst of the current, and watched the stars twinkling, bright as stars in a winter sky.

The distant clouds were rushing towards the plain, she could see them whipped by the spring breeze, hurrying to the city gates, and once they had swept by them and were above the streets, they turned pink—they were not unlike children dressing up for Hallowe'en, and Judith suddenly longed to join in the fun, so she beat her wings and made her way through the skylight and found herself right in the midst of the clouds, laughing, somersaulting, gliding with wings extended, and then she pirouetted, brushing the treetops, vroom! which ducked their heads, so very high and mighty they were—they were English trees surrounding an English museum—and winded now, she went to sit down on the roof of a stone house below, one she had noticed many times —those times when she had been obliged to walk with freezing feet through the icy slush, heading into the wind that engulfed everything at the moment—and she had to admit feeling a thrill of pleasure at being seated, stark naked, on the roof of this respectable house with the Union Jack flying from it, naked except for the long feathery wings that she folded round herself because it was no warmer on the roofs of English houses than it was inside them, brrr . . . 'Judith! Time to rest!' came to her ears suddenly, making her jump so that she tumbled, shivering, from the roof, wrenching the flag from its pole on the way down, and swathed in the Union Jack she sailed through the skylight, which shattered with a sound of tinkling ice, and in an instant she reconstituted herself into the truncated statue from the business district, which—as soon as the blood began recirculating through the inert members of her body, permitting her to stand and walk —immediately recombined into a single entity, though there was still time for her to catch a glimpse of the Union Jack disintegrating into little red, white, and blue strips before the students, smiling and blissfully admiring their clever drawings, appeared again before her.

Judith, wearing her dressing gown, moved among the easels silently, with her wings down. She looked dispiritedly at the mechanical maidens, the whipped-cream Renoirs that all of them, in their wisdom, had created. But where was she to be found? Where was she in all these drawings? Had no one looked beyond the surface? Oh, she didn't ask them to be surprised by the angelic state, no, certainly not! She merely begged them to retain a tiny portion of her real essence. Hadn't they understood that if she took the trouble to come all the way across the city to expose herself in this place, it was only to discover from their observation of her what had escaped her own notice? To have them confirm that she existed, that she was alive? But she had eluded their sketches as easily as she had escaped from her own body. Perhaps one doesn't truly exist when one is unable to be grasped either by oneself or by others. . .

And what about the tall redhead? That same tall redhead who was present in the merest line?

The tall redhead was arranging her paints and brushes. The tall English redhead was an artist who posed in order to pay for her courses. Her paint-stained holdall didn't look like anything that might have come from an artist's supply shop. The tall redhead continued putting away her charcoal and red chalk as Judith, who had stopped in front of her easel, contemplated the image she had given her: it was that of an angel with slightly sunken eyes, thighs that sagged a little, and wings that were beginning to moult—an angel that was turning into a woman.

Translated by Patricia Sillers

MARGARET ATWOOD

Polarities

Gentle and just pleasure
It is, being human, to have won from space
This unchill, habitable interior
—MARGARET AVISON, 'New Year's Poem'

He hadn't seen her around for a week, which was unusual: he asked her if she'd been sick.

'No,' she said, 'working.' She always spoke of what she had been doing with organizational, almost military briskness. She had a little packsack in which she carried around her books and notebooks. To Morrison, whose mind shambled from one thing to another, picking up, fingering, setting down, she was a small model of the kind of efficiency he ought to be displaying more of. Perhaps that was why he had never wanted to touch her: he liked women who were not necessarily more stupid but lazier than himself. Sloth aroused him: a girl's unwashed dishes were an invitation to laxity and indulgence.

She marched beside him along the corridor and down the stairs, her short clipped steps syncopating with his own lank strides. As they descended, the smell of straw, droppings and formaldehyde grew stronger: a colony of overflow experimental mice from the science building lived in the cellar. When he saw that she was leaving the building too and probably going home, he offered her a lift.

'Only if you're heading that way anyway.' Louise didn't accept favours, she had made that clear from the start. When he'd asked her if she wanted to take in a film with him she said, 'Only if you let me pay for my own ticket.' If she had been taller he might have found this threatening.

It was colder, the weak red sun almost down, the snow purpling and creaky. She jumped up and down beside the car till he got the plug-in engine heater untangled and the door opened, her head coming out of the enormous second-hand fur coat she wore like a gopher's out of its burrow. He had seen a lot of gophers on the drive across, many of them dead; one he had killed himself, an accident, it had dived practically under the car wheels. The car itself hadn't held up either: by the time he'd made it to the outskirts—though later he realized that this was in fact the city—a fender had come off and the ignition was failing. He'd had to junk it, and had decided stoically to do without a car until he found he couldn't.

He swung the car onto the driveway that led from the university. It bumped as though crossing a metal-plated bridge: the tires were angular from the cold, the motor sluggish. He should take the car for long drives more often; it was getting stale. Louise was talking more than she normally did; she was excited about something. Two of her students had been giving her a hassle, but she told them they didn't have to come to class. 'It's your heads, not mine.' She knew she had won, they would shape up, they would contribute. Morrison was not up on the theories of group dynamics. He liked the old way: you taught the subject and forgot about them as people. It disconcerted him when they slouched into his office and mumbled at him, fidgeting and self-conscious, about their fathers or their love lives. He didn't tell them about his father or his love life and he wished they would observe the same reticence, though they seemed to think they had to do it in order to get extensions on their term papers. At the beginning of the year one of his students had wanted the class to sit in a circle but luckily the rest of them preferred straight lines.

'It's right here,' she said; he had been driving past it. He crunched the car to a halt, fender against the rockbank, snowbank. Here they did not take the snow away; they spread sand on it, layer by layer as it fell, confident there would be no thaw.

'It's finished; you can come in and see it,' she said, suggesting but really demanding.

'What's finished?' he asked. He hadn't been paying attention.

'I told you. My place, my apartment, that's what I've been working on.'

The house was one of the featureless two-storey boxes thrown up by the streetful in the years after the war when there was a housing boom and materials were scarce. It was stuccoed with a greyish gravel Morrison found spiritually depleting. There were a few older houses, but they were quickly being torn down by developers; soon the city would have no visible past at all. Everything else was highrises, or worse, low barrack-shaped multiple housing units, cheaply tacked together. Sometimes the rows of flimsy buildings—snow on their roofs, rootless white faces peering suspiciously out through their windows, kids' toys scattered like trash on the walks—reminded him of old photographs he had seen of mining camps. They were the houses of people who did not expect to be living in them for long.

Her apartment was in the basement. As they went around to the back and down the stairs, avoiding on the landing a newspaper spread with the overshoes and boots of the family living upstairs, Morrison remembered vividly and with a recurrence of panic his own search for a place, a roof, a container, his trudges from address to address, his tours of clammy, bin-like cellars hastily done up by the owners in vinyl tile and sheets of cheap panelling to take advantage of the student inflow and the housing squeeze. He'd known he would never survive a winter buried like that or closed in one of the glass-sided cardboard-carton apartment buildings. Were there no real ones, mellowed, interesting, possible? Finally he had come upon an available second storey; the house was pink gravel instead of grey, the filth was daunting and the landlady querulous, but he had taken it immediately just to be able to open a window and look out.

He had not known what to expect of Louise's room. He had never visualized her as living anywhere, even though he had collected her and dropped her off outside the house a number of times.

'I finished the bookshelves yesterday,' she said, waving at a wall-length structure of varnished boards and cement blocks. 'Sit down, I'll make you some cocoa.' She went into the kitchen, still with her fur coat on, and Morrison sat down in the leatherette swivel armchair. He swivelled, surveying, comparing it with the kind of interior he thought of himself as inhabiting but never got around to assembling.

She had obviously put a lot of energy into it, but the result was less like a room than like several rooms, pieces of which had been cut out and pasted onto one another. He could not decide what created this effect: it was the same unity in diversity he had found in the motels on the way across, the modernish furniture, the conventional framed northern landscapes on the walls. But her table was ersatz Victorian and the prints Picasso. The bed was concealed behind a partly drawn dyed burlap curtain at the end of the room, but visible on the bedside rug were two light blue fuzzy slippers that startled, almost shocked him: they were so unlike her.

Louise brought the cocoa and sat down opposite him on the floor. They talked as usual about the city: they were both still looking for things to do, a quest based on their shared eastern assumption that cities ought to be entertaining. It was this rather than mutual attraction which led them to spend as much time together as they did; most of the others were married or had been here too long and had given up.

The films changed slowly; the one theatre, with its outdated popular comedies, they had sneered at. They had gone to the opera together when it had come, though: local chorus and imported stars—*Lucia,* it had been, and really quite well done, considering. At intermission Morrison had glanced around at the silent, chunky audience in the lobby, some of the women still in early-sixties pointed-toe spike heels, and murmured to Louise that it was like tourist brochures from Russia.

One Sunday before the snow came they had gone for an impromptu drive; at her suggestion they had aimed for the zoo twenty miles from the city. After they made it through the oil derricks there had been trees; not the right kind of trees—he had felt, as he had on the way across, that the land was keeping itself apart from him, not letting him in, there had to be more to it than this repetitive, non-commital drabness—but still trees; and the zoo once they reached it was spacious, the animals kept in enclosures large enough for them to run in and even hide in if they wanted to.

Louise had been there before—how, since she had no car, he didn't ask—and showed him around. 'They choose animals that can survive the winter,' she said. 'It's open all year. They don't even know they're in a zoo.' She pointed out the artificial mountain made of cement blocks for the mountain goats to climb on. Morrison didn't as a rule like any animal bigger and wilder than a cat, but these kept far enough away to be tolerable. That day she had told him a little about herself, a departure: mostly she talked about her work. She had travelled in Europe, she told him, and had spent a year studying in England.

'What are you doing here?' he had asked.

She shrugged. 'They gave me money; nobody else would.'

Essentially it was his reason too. It wasn't the draft; he was really over-age, though here they kept wanting to think he was a dodger, it made his presence more acceptable to them. The job market had been tight back in the States and also, when he tried later, in what they called here the East. But in all fairness it hadn't been only the money or the dismalness of the situation back home. He had wanted something else, some adventure; he felt he might learn something new. He had thought the city would be near the mountains. But except for the raw gully through which the brownish river curved, it was flat.

'I don't want you to think of it as typical,' Louise was saying. 'You ought to see Montreal.'

'Are *you* typical?' he asked.

She laughed. 'None of us is typical, or do we all look alike to you? I'm not typical, I'm all-inclusive.'

She let her fur coat fall down from around her shoulders as she said this, and he wondered again whether he was expected to make a move, to approach her. He ought to approach someone or something; he was beginning to feel isolated inside his clothes and skin. His students were out of the question. Besides, they were so thick, so impermeable; the girls, even the more slender ones, made him think of slabs of substance white and congealed, like lard. And the other single women on staff were much older than he was: in them Louise's briskness had degenerated into a pinpointing, impaling quality.

There must be a place where he could meet someone, some nice loosely structured girl with ungroomed, seedy breasts, more thing than idea, slovenly and gratuitous. They existed, he was familiar with them from what he had begun to think of as his previous life, but he had not kept in touch with any of them. They had all been good at first but even the sloppiest had in time come to require something from him he thought he was not yet ready to give: they wanted him to be in love with them, an exertion of the mind too strenuous for him to undertake. His mind, he felt, was needed for other things, though he wasn't quite sure what they were. He was tasting, exploring: goals would come later.

Louise wasn't at all like them; she would never lend him her body for nothing, even temporarily, though she had the fur spread out around her now like a rug and had raised one corduroy-trousered knee, letting him see in profile the taut bulge of her somewhat muscular thigh. She probably went skiing and ice skating. He imagined his long body locked in that athletic, chilly grip, his eyes darkened by fur. Not yet, he thought, raising his half-full cocoa cup between them. I can do without, I don't need it yet.

It was the weekend and Morrison was painting his apartment as he habitually did on weekends; he had been at it off and on since he moved in.

'You'll have to have it painted, of course,' he'd said smoothly to the landlady when inspecting it, but he had already shown himself too eager and she'd outfoxed him. 'Well, I don't know, there's another boy wants it says he'll paint it himself. . . .' So of course Morrison had to say he would too. This was the third coat.

Morrison's vision of wall-painting had been drawn from the paint ads—spot-free housewives gliding it on, one-handed and smiling—but it wasn't easy. The paint got on the floor, on the furniture, in his hair. Before he could even begin he had to cart out the accumulated discards of several generations of previous tenants: baby clothes, old snapshots, an inner tube, heaps of empty liquor bottles, and (intriguingly) a silk parachute. Messiness interested him only in women; he could not live surrounded by it himself.

One wall of the livingroom had been pink, one green, one orange and one black. He was painting them white. The last tenants, a group of Nigerian students, had left weird magic-looking murals on the walls: a sort of swamp, in black on the orange wall, and an upright shape, in pink on the green wall, was either a very poorly done Christ Child or—could it be?—an erect penis with a halo around it. Morrison painted these two walls first, but it made him uneasy to know the pictures were still there underneath the paint. Sometimes as he rollered his way around the room he wondered what the Nigerians had thought the first time it hit forty below.

The landlady seemed to prefer foreign students, probably because they were afraid to complain: she had been aggrieved when Morrison had demanded a real lock for his door. The cellar was a warren of cubbyholes; he was not sure yet exactly who lived in them. Soon after he had moved in a Korean had appeared at his door, hopefully smiling. He wanted to talk about income tax.

'I'm sorry,' Morrison had said, 'some other time, okay? I have a lot of work to do.' He was nice enough, no doubt, but Morrison didn't want to get involved with someone he didn't know; and he did have work to do. He felt picayune about it later when he discovered the Korean had a wife and child down in his cubbyhole with him; often in the fall they had put fishes out to dry, stringing them on the clotheslines where they twirled in the wind like plastic gas-station decorations.

He was doing the ceiling, craning his neck, with the latex oozing down the handle of the roller onto his arm, when the buzzer went. He almost hoped it was the Korean, he seldom saw anyone on the weekends. But it was Louise.

'Hi,' he said, surprised.

'I just thought I'd drop in,' she said. 'I don't use the phone any more.'

'I'm painting,' he said, partly as an excuse: he wasn't sure he wanted her in the house. What would she demand from him?

'Can I help?' she asked, as though it was a big treat.

'Actually I was about to stop for the day,' he lied. He knew she would be better at it than he was.

He made tea in the kitchen and she sat at the table and watched him.

'I came to talk about Blake,' she said. 'I have to do a paper.' Unlike him she was only a Graduate Assistant, she was taking a course.

'What aspect?' Morrison asked, not interested. Blake wasn't his field. He didn't mind the earlier lyrics but the prophecies bored him and the extravagant letters in which Blake called his friends angels of light and vilified his enemies he found in bad taste.

'We each have to analyze one poem in *Songs of Experience.* I'm supposed to do the "Nurse's Song". But they don't know what's going on in that course, he doesn't know what's going on. I've been trying to get through to them but they're all doing the one-up thing, they don't know what's happening. They sit there and pull each other's papers apart, I mean, they don't know what poetry's supposed to be *for.*' She wasn't drinking her tea.

'When's it due?' he asked, keeping on neutral ground.

'Next week. But I'm not going to do it, not the way *they* want.

I'm giving them one of my own poems. That says it all. I mean, if they have to read one right there in the class they'll get what Blake was trying to do with *cadences.* I'm getting it xeroxed.' She hesitated, less sure of herself. 'Do you think that'll be all right?'

Morrison wondered what he would do if one of his own students tried such a ploy. He hadn't thought of Louise as the poetry-writing type. 'Have you checked with the professor about it?'

'I try to talk to him,' she said. 'I try to *help* him but I can't get *through* to him. If they don't get what I mean though I'll know they're all phonies and I can just walk out.' She was twisting her cup on the table top, her lips were trembling.

Morrison felt his loyalties were being divided; also he didn't want her to cry, that would involve dangerous comforting pats, even an arm around her shoulder. He tried to shut out an involuntary quick image of himself on top of her in the middle of the kitchen floor, getting white latex all over her fur. *Not today,* his mind commanded, pleaded.

As if in answer the reverberations of an organ boomed from beneath their feet, accompanied by a high quavering voice: *Rock of a-ges, cleft for me . . . Let me* HIIIDE *myself. . . .* Louise took it as a signal. 'I have to go,' she said. She got up and went out as abruptly as she had come, thanking him perfunctorily for the tea she hadn't drunk.

The organ was a Hammond, owned by the woman downstairs, a native. When her husband and nubile child were home she shouted at them. The rest of the time she ran the vacuum cleaner or picked out hymn tunes and old favourites on the organ with two fingers, singing to herself. The organ was to Morrison the most annoying. At first he tried to ignore it; then he put on opera records, attempting to drown it out. Finally he recorded it with his tape recorder. When the noise got too aggravating he would aim the speakers down the hot air register and run the tape through as loudly as possible. It gave him a sense of participation, of control.

He did this now, admiring the way the tape clashed with what she was currently playing: 'Whispering Hope' with an overlay of 'Annie Laurie'; 'The Last Rose of Summer' counterpointing 'Come to the Church in the Wildwood'. He was surprised at how much he was able to hate her: he had only seen her once, looking balefully out at him from between her hideous flowered drapes as he wallowed through the snow on his way to the garage. Her husband was supposed to keep the walk shovelled but didn't.

Louise came back the next day before Morrison was up. He was awake but he could tell by the chill in the room—his breath was visible—and by the faint smell of oil that something had gone wrong with the furnace again. It was less trouble to stay in bed, at least till the sun was well risen, than to get up and try the various ways of keeping warm.

When the buzzer went he pulled a blanket around himself and stumbled to the door.

'I thought of something,' Louise said tragically. She was in the door before he could fend her off.

'I'm afraid it's cold in here,' he said.

'I had to come over and tell you. I don't use the phone any more. You should have yours taken out.'

She stomped the snow from her boots while Morrison retreated into the livingroom. There was a thick crust of frost on the insides of the windows; he lit the gas fireplace. Louise stalked impatiently around the uncarpeted floor.

'You aren't listening,' she said. He looked out obediently at her from his blanket. 'What I thought of is this: *The city has no right to be here.* I mean, why is it? No city should be here, this far north; it isn't even on a lake or an important river, even. Why is it here?' She clasped her hands, gazing at him as though everything depended on his answer.

Morrison, standing on one bare foot, reflected that he had often since his arrival asked himself the same question. 'It started as a trading post,' he said, shivering.

'But it doesn't *look* like one. It doesn't look like anything, it doesn't *have* anything, it could be anywhere. Why is it *here*?' She implored; she even clutched a corner of his blanket.

Morrison shied away. 'Look,' he said, 'do you mind if I get some clothes on?'

'Which room are they in?' she asked suspiciously.

'The bedroom,' he said.

'That's all right. That room's all right,' she said.

Contrary to his fear she made no attempt to follow him in. When he was dressed he returned to find her sitting on the floor with a piece of paper. 'We have to complete the circle,' she said. 'We need the others.'

'What others?' He decided she was overtired, she had been working too hard: she had deep red blotches around her eyes and the rest of her face was pale green.

'I'll draw you a diagram of it,' she said. But instead she sat on the floor, jabbing at the paper with the pencil point. 'I wanted to work out my own system,' she said plaintively, 'but they wouldn't let me.' A tear slid down her cheek.

'Maybe you need to talk to someone,' Morrison said, over-casually.

She raised her head. 'But I'm talking to you. Oh,' she said, reverting to her office voice, 'you mean a shrink. I saw one earlier. He said I was very sane and a genius. He took a reading of my head: he said the patterns in my brain are the same as Julius Caesar's, only his were military and mine are creative.' She started jabbing with the pencil again.

'I'll make you a peanut butter sandwich,' Morrison said, offering the only thing he himself wanted right then. It did not occur to him until months later when he was remembering it to ask himself how anyone could have known about the patterns in Julius Caesar's brain. At the moment he was wondering whether Louise might not in fact be a genius. He felt helpless because of his own inability to respond; she would think him as obtuse as the others, whoever they were.

At first she did not want him to go into the kitchen: she knew the telephone was in there. But he promised not to use it. When he came out again with a piece of bread on which he had spread with difficulty the gelid peanut butter, she was curled inside her coat in front of the fire, sleeping. He laid the bread gently beside her as if leaving crumbs on a stump for unseen animals. Then he changed his mind, retrieved it, took it on tiptoe into the kitchen and ate it himself. He turned on the oven, opened the oven door, wrapped himself in a blanket from the bedroom and read Marvell.

She slept for nearly three hours; he didn't hear her get up. She appeared in the kitchen doorway, looking much better, though a greyish-green pallor still lingered around her mouth and eyes.

'That was just what I needed,' she said in her old brisk voice. 'Now I must be off; I have lots of work to do.' Morrison took his feet off the stove and saw her to the door.

'Don't fall,' he called after her cheerfully as she went down the steep wooden steps, her feet hidden under the rim of her coat. The steps were icy, he didn't keep them cleared properly. His landlady was afraid someone would slip on them and sue her.

At the bottom Louise turned and waved at him. The air was thickening with ice fog, frozen water particles held in suspension; if you ran a horse in it, they'd told him, the ice pierced its lungs and it bled to death. But they hadn't told him that till after he'd trotted to the university in it one morning when the car wouldn't start and complained aloud in the coffee room about the sharp pains in his chest.

He watched her out of sight around the corner of the house. Then he went back to the living room with a sense of recapturing lost territory. Her pencil and the paper she had used, covered with dots and slashing marks, an undeciphered code, were still by the fireplace. He started to crumple the paper up, but instead folded it carefully and put it on the mantelpiece where he kept his unanswered letters. After that he paced the apartment, conscious of his own work awaiting him but feeling as though he had nothing to do.

Half an hour later she was back again; he discovered he had been expecting her. Her face was mournful, all its lines led downwards as though tiny hands were pulling at the jawline skin.

'Oh, you have to come out,' she said, pleading. 'You have to come out, there's too much fog.'

'Why don't you come in?' Morrison said. That would be easier to handle. Maybe she'd been into something, if that was all it was he could wait it out. He'd been cautious himself; it was a small place and the local pusher was likely to be one of your own students; also he had no desire to reduce his mind to oatmeal mush.

'No,' she said, 'I can't go through this door any more. It's wrong. You have to come out.' Her face became crafty, as though she was planning. 'It will do you good to get out for a walk,' she said reasonably.

She was right, he didn't get enough exercise. He pulled on his heavy boots and went to find his coat.

As they creaked and slid along the street Louise was pleased with herself, triumphant; she walked slightly ahead of him as if determined to keep the lead. The ice fog surrounded them, deadened their voices, it was crystallizing like a growth of spruce needles on the telephone wires and the branches of the few trees which he could not help thinking of as stunted, though to the natives, he supposed, they must represent the normal size for trees. He took care not to breathe too deeply. A flock of grosbeaks whirred and shrilled up ahead, picking the last few red berries from a mountain ash.

'I'm glad it isn't sunny,' Louise said. 'The sun was burning out the cells in my brain, but I feel a lot better now.'

Morrison glanced at the sky. The sun was up there somewhere, marked by a pale spot in the otherwise evenly spread grey. He checked an impulse to shield his eyes and thereby protect his brain cells: he realized it was an attempt to suppress the undesired knowledge that Louise was disturbed or, out with it, she was crazy.

'Living here isn't so bad,' Louise said, skipping girlishly on the hard-packed snow. 'You just have to have inner resources. I'm glad I have them; I think I have more than you, Morrison. I have more than most people. That's what I said to myself when I moved here.'

'Where are we going?' Morrison asked when they had accomplished several blocks. She had taken him west, along a street he was not familiar with, or was it the fog?

'To find the others, of course,' she said, glancing back at him contemptuously. 'We have to complete the circle.'

Morrison followed without protest; he was relieved there would soon be others.

She stopped in front of a medium-tall highrise. 'They're inside,' she said. Morrison went towards the front door, but she tugged at his arm.

'You can't go in that door,' she said. 'It's facing the wrong way. It's the wrong door.'

'What's the matter with it?' Morrison asked. It might be the wrong door (and the longer he looked at it, plate glass and shining evilly, the more he saw what she meant), but it was the only one.

'It faces east,' she said. 'Don't you know? The city is polarized north and south; the river splits it in two; the poles are the gas plant and the power plant. Haven't you ever noticed the bridge joins them together? That's how the current gets across. We have to keep the poles in our brains lined up with the poles of the city, that's what Blake's poetry is all about. You can't break the current.'

'Then how do we get in?' he said. She sat down in the snow; he was afraid again she was going to cry.

'Listen,' he said hastily, 'I'll go in the door sideways and bring them out; that way I won't break the current. You won't have to go through the door at all. Who are they?' he asked as an afterthought.

When he recognized the name he was elated: she wasn't insane after all, the people were real, she had a purpose and a plan. This was probably just an elaborate way of arranging to see her friends.

They were the Jamiesons. Dave was one of those with whom Morrison had exchanged pleasantries in the hallways but nothing further. His wife had a recent baby. Morrison found them in their Saturday shirts and jeans. He tried to explain what he wanted, which was difficult because he wasn't sure. Finally he said he needed help. Only Dave could come, the wife had to stay behind with the baby.

'I hardly know Louise, you know,' Dave volunteered in the elevator.

'Neither do I,' said Morrison.

Louise was waiting behind a short fir tree on the front lawn. She came out when she saw them. 'Where's the baby?' she said. 'We need the baby to complete the circle. We *need* the baby. Don't you know the country will split apart without it?' She stamped her foot at them angrily.

'We can come back for it,' Morrison said, which pacified her. She said there were only two others they had to collect; she explained that they needed people from both sides of the river. Dave Jamieson suggested they take his car, but Louise was now off cars: they were as bad as telephones, they had no fixed directions. She wanted to walk. At last they persuaded her onto the bus, pointing out that it ran north and south. She had to make certain first that it went over the right bridge, the one near the gas plant.

The other couple Louise had named lived in an apartment overlooking the river. She seemed to have picked them not because they were special friends but because from their livingroom, which she had been in once, both the gas plant and the power plant were visible. The apartment door faced south; Louise entered the building with no hesitation.

Morrison was not overjoyed with Louise's choice. This couple was foremost among the local anti-Americans: he had to endure Paul's bitter sallies almost daily in the coffee room, while Leota at staff parties had a way of running on in his presence about the wicked Americans and then turning to him and saying, mouth but not eyes gushing, 'Oh, but I forgot—*you're* an American.' He had found the best defence was to agree. 'You Yanks are coming up and taking all our jobs,' Paul would say, and Morrison would nod affably. 'That's right, you shouldn't let it happen. I wonder why you hired me?' Leota would start in about how the Americans were buying up all the industry, and Morrison would say, 'Yes, it's a shame. Why are you selling it to us?' He saw their point, of course, but he wasn't Procter and Gamble. What did they want him to do? What were they doing themselves, come to think of it? But Paul had once broken down after too many beers in the Faculty Club and confided that Leota had been thin when he married her but now she was fat. Morrison held the memory of that confession as a kind of hostage.

He had to admit though that on occasion Paul was much more efficient than he himself was capable of being. Paul saw at once what it had taken Morrison hours, perhaps weeks, to see: that something was wrong with Louise. Leota decoyed her into the kitchen with a glass of milk while Paul conspired single-handedly in the livingroom.

'She's crazy as a coot. We've got to get her to the loony bin. We'll pretend to go along with her, this circle business, and when we get her downstairs we'll grab her and stuff her into my car. How long has this been going on?'

Morrison didn't like the sound of the words 'grab' and 'stuff'. 'She won't go in cars,' he said.

'Hell,' said Paul, 'I'm not walking in this bloody weather. Besides, it's miles. We'll use force if necessary.' He thrust a quick beer at each of them, and when he judged they ought to have finished they all went into the kitchen and Paul carefully told Louise that it was time to go.

'Where?' Louise asked. She scanned their faces: she could tell they were up to something. Morrison felt guilt seeping into his eyes and turned his head away.

'To get the baby,' Paul said. 'Then we can form the circle.'

Louise looked at him strangely. 'What baby? What circle?' she said testing him.

'*You* know,' Paul said persuasively. After a moment she put down her glass of milk, still almost full, and said she was ready.

At the car she balked. 'Not in there,' she said, planting her feet. 'I'm not going in there.' When Paul gripped her arm and said, soothingly and menacingly, 'Now be a good girl,' she broke away from him and ran down the street, stumbling and sliding. Morrison didn't have the heart to run after her; already he felt like a traitor. He watched stupidly while Dave and Paul chased after her, catching her at last and half-carrying her back; they held her wriggling and kicking inside her fur coat as though it was a sack. Their breath came out in white spurts.

'Open the back door, Morrison,' Paul said, sergeant-like, giving him a scornful glance as though he was good for nothing else. Morrison obeyed and Louise was thrust in, Dave holding her more or less by the scruff of the neck and Paul picking up her feet. She did not resist as much as Morrison expected. He got in on one side of her; Dave was on the other. Leota, who had waddled down belatedly, had reached the front seat; once they were in motion she turned around and made false, cheering-up noises at Louise.

'Where are they taking me?' Louise whispered to Morrison. 'It's to the hospital, isn't it?' She was almost hopeful, perhaps she had been depending on them to do this. She snuggled close to Morrison, rubbing her thigh against his; he tried not to move away.

As they reached the outskirts she whispered to him again. 'This is silly, Morrison. They're being silly, aren't they? When we get to the next stoplight, open the door on your side and we'll jump out and run away. We'll go to my place.'

Morrison smiled wanly at her, but he was almost inclined to try it. Although he knew he couldn't do anything to help her and did not want the responsibility anyway, he also didn't want his mind burdened with whatever was going to happen to her next. He felt like someone appointed to a firing squad: it was not his choice, it was his duty, no one could blame him.

There was less ice fog now. The day was turning greyer, bluer: they were moving east, away from the sun. The mental clinic was outside the city, reached by a curving, expressionless driveway. The buildings were the same assemblage of disparate once-recent styles as those at the university: the same jarring fragmentation of space, the same dismal failure at modishness. Government institutions, Morrison thought; they were probably done by the same architect.

Louise was calm as they went to the reception entrance. Inside was a glass-fronted cubicle, decorated with rudimentary Christmas bells cut from red and green construction paper. Louise stood quietly, listening with an amused, tolerant smile, while Paul talked with the receptionist; but when a young intern appeared she said,

'I must apologize for my friends; they've been drinking and they're trying to play a practical joke on me.'

The intern frowned enquiringly. Paul blustered, relating Louise's theories of the circle and the poles. She denied everything and told the intern he should call the police; a joke was a joke but this was a misuse of public property.

Paul appealed to Morrison: he was her closest friend. 'Well,' Morrison hedged, 'she *was* acting a little strange, but maybe not enough to. . . .' His eyes trailed off to the imitation-modern interior, the corridors leading off into god knew where. Along one of the corridors a listless figure shuffled.

Louise was carrying it off so well, she was so cool, she had the intern almost convinced; but when she saw she was winning she lost her grip. Giving Paul a playful shove on the chest, she said, 'We don't need *your* kind here. *You* won't get into the circle.' She turned to the intern and said gravely, 'Now I have to go. My work is very important, you know. I'm preventing the civil war.'

After she had been registered, her few valuables taken from her and locked in the safe ('So they won't be stolen by the patients,' the receptionist said), her house keys delivered to Morrison at her request, she disappeared down one of the corridors between two interns. She was not crying, nor did she say goodbye to any of them, though she gave Morrison a dignified, freezing nod. 'I expect you to bring my notebook to me,' she said with a pronounced English accent. 'The black one, I need it. You'll find it on my desk. And I'll need some underwear. Leota can bring that.'

Morrison, shamed and remorseful, promised he would visit.

When they got back to the city they dropped Dave Jamieson off at his place; then the three of them had pizza and cokes together. Paul and Leota were friendlier than usual: they wanted to find out more. They leaned across the table, questioning, avid, prying; they were enjoying it. This, he realized, was for them the kind of entertainment the city could best afford.

Afterwards they all went to Louise's cellar to gather up for her those shreds of her life she had asked them to allow her. Leota found the underwear (surprisingly frilly, most of it purple and black) after an indecently long search through Louise's bureau drawers; he and Paul tried to decide which of the black notebooks on her desk she would want. There were eight or nine of them;

Paul opened a few and read excerpts at random, though Morrison protested weakly. References to the poles and the circle dated back several months; before he had known her, Morrison thought.

In her notebooks Louise had been working out her private system, in aphorisms and short poems which were thoroughly sane in themselves but which taken together were not; though, Morrison reflected, the only difference is that she's taken as real what the rest of us pretend is only metaphorical. Between the aphorisms were little sketches like wiring diagrams, quotations from the English poets, and long detailed analyses of her acquaintances at the university.

'Here's you, Morrison,' Paul said with a relishing chuckle. ' "Morrison is not a complete person. He needs to be completed, he refuses to admit his body is part of his mind. He can be in the circle possibly, but only if he will surrender his role as a fragment and show himself willing to merge with the greater whole." Boy, she must've been nutty for months.'

They were violating her, entering her privacy against her will. 'Put that away,' Morrison said, more sharply than he ordinarily dared speak to Paul. 'We'll take the half-empty notebook, that must be the one she meant.'

There were a dozen or so library books scattered around the room, some overdue: geology and history for the most part, and one volume of Blake. Leota volunteered to take them back.

As he was about to slip the catch on the inside lock Morrison glanced once more around the room. He could see now where it got its air of pastiche: the bookcase was a copy of the one in Paul's livingroom, the prints and the table were almost identical with those at the Jamiesons'. Other details stirred dim images of objects half-noted in the various houses, at the various but nearly identical get-acquainted parties. Poor Louise had been trying to construct herself out of the other people she had met. Only from himself had she taken nothing; thinking of his chill interior, embryonic and blighted, he realized it had nothing for her to take.

He kept his promise and went to see her. His first visit was made with Paul and Leota, but he sensed their resentment: they seemed to think their countrywoman should be permitted to go mad without witness or participation by any Yanks. After that he drove out by himself in his own car.

On the second visit Louise initially seemed better. They met in a cramped cubicle furnished with two chairs; Louise sat on the edge of hers, her hands folded in her lap, her face polite, withholding. Her English accent was still noticeable, though hard r's surfaced in it from time to time. She was having a good rest, she said; the food was all right and she had met some nice people but she was eager to get back to her work; she worried about who was looking after her students.

'I guess I said some pretty crazy things to you,' she smiled.

'Well . . .' Morrison stalled. He was pleased by this sign of her recovery.

'I had it all wrong. I thought I could put the country together by joining the two halves of the city into a circle, using the magnetic currents.' She gave a small disparaging laugh, then dropped her voice. 'What I hadn't figured out though was that the currents don't flow north and south, like the bridge. They flow east and west, like the river. And I didn't *need* to form the circle out of a bunch of incomplete segments. I didn't even need the baby. I mean,' she said in a serious whisper, dropping her accent completely, 'I *am* the circle. I have the poles within myself. What I have to do is keep myself in one piece, it *depends* on me.'

At the desk he tried to find out what was officially wrong with Louise but they would not tell him anything; it wasn't the policy.

On his next visit she spoke to him almost the whole time in what to his untrained ear sounded like perfectly fluent French. Her mother was a French Protestant, she told him, her father an English Catholic. *'Je peux vous dire tout ceci,'* she said, *'parce que vous êtes americain*. You are outside it.' To Morrison this explained a lot; but the next time she claimed to be the daughter of an Italian opera singer and a Nazi general. 'Though I also have some Jewish blood,' she added hastily. She was tense and kept standing up and sitting down again, crossing and recrossing her legs; she would not look at Morrison directly but addressed her staccato remarks to the centre of his chest.

After this Morrison stayed away for a couple of weeks. He did not think his visits were doing either of them any good, and he had papers to mark. He occupied himself once more with the painting of his apartment and the organ music of the woman downstairs; he shovelled his steps and put salt on them to melt the ice.

His landlady, uneasy because she had still not supplied him with a lock, unexpectedly had him to tea, and the tacky plastic grotesqueries of her interior decoration fueled his reveries for a while. The one good thing in her bogus ranch-style bungalow had been an egg, blown and painted in the Ukrainian manner, but she had dismissed it as ordinary, asking him to admire instead a cake of soap stuck with artificial flowers to resemble a flowerpot; she had got the idea out of a magazine. The Korean came up one evening to ask him about life insurance.

But the thought of Louise out there in the windswept institution grounds with nothing and no one she knew bothered him in twinges, like a mental neuralgia, goading him finally into the section of the city that passed for downtown; he would buy her a gift. He selected a small box of water-colour paints: she ought to have something to do. He was intending to mail it, but sooner than he expected he found himself again on the wide deserted entrance driveway.

They met once more in the visitors' cubicle. He was alarmed by the change in her: she had put on weight, her muscles had slackened, her breasts drooped. Instead of sitting rigidly as she had done before, she sprawled in the chair, legs apart, arms hanging; her hair was dull and practically uncombed. She was wearing a short skirt and purple stockings, in one of which there was a run. Trying not to stare at this run and at the white, loose thigh flesh it revealed, Morrison had the first unmistakably physical stirrings of response he had ever felt towards her.

'They have me on a different drug,' she said. 'The other one was having the wrong effect. I was allergic to it.' She mentioned that someone had stolen her hairbrush, but when he offered to bring her another one she said it didn't matter. She had lost interest in the circle and her elaborate system and did not seem to want to talk much. What little she said was about the hospital itself: she was trying to help the doctors, they didn't know how to treat the patients but they wouldn't listen to her. Most of those inside were getting worse rather than better; many had to stay there because no one would take the responsibility of looking after them, even if they were drugged into manageability. They were poor, without relations; the hospital would not let them go away by themselves. She told him about one girl from further north who thought she was a cariboo.

She hardly glanced at the water-colour paints, though she

thanked him sluggishly. Her eyes, normally wide and vivacious, were puffed shut nearly to slits and her skin appeared to have darkened. She reminded him of someone, though it took him several minutes to remember: it was an Indian woman he had seen early in the fall while he was still searching for a place to have a civilized drink. She had been sitting outside a cheap hotel with her legs apart, taking off her clothes and chanting, 'Come on boys, what're you waiting for, come on boys, what're you waiting for.' Around her a group of self-conscious, sniggering men had gathered. Morrison, against his will and appalled at her, the men, and himself, had joined them. She was naked to the waist when the police got there.

When he rose to say goodbye Louise asked him, as if it was a matter of purely academic interest, whether he thought she would ever get out.

On his way out to the car it struck him that he loved her. The thought filled him like a goal, a destiny. He would rescue her somehow; he could pretend she was his cousin or sister; he would keep her hidden in the apartment with all his dangerous implements, razors, knives, nailfiles, locked away; he would feed her, give her the right drugs, comb her hair. At night she would be there in the sub-zero bedroom for him to sink into as into a swamp, warm and obliterating.

This picture at first elated, then horrified him. He saw that it was only the hopeless, mad Louise he wanted, the one devoid of any purpose or defence. A sane one, one that could judge him, he would never be able to handle. So this was his dream girl then, his ideal woman found at last: a disintegration, mind returning to its component shards of matter, a defeated formless creature on which he could inflict himself like shovel on earth, axe on forest, use without being used, know without being known. Louise's notebook entry, written when she had surely been saner than she was now, had been right about him. Yet in self-defence he reasoned that his desire for her was not altogether evil: it was in part a desire to be reunited with his own body, which he felt less and less that he actually occupied.

Oppressed by himself and by the building, the prison he had just left, he turned when he reached the main road away from the city instead of towards it: he would take his car for a run. He drove through the clenched landscape, recalling with pain the gentle drawl of the accommodating hills east and south, back in that settled land which was so far away it seemed not to exist. Here everything was tightlipped, ungiving, good for nothing and nothing.

He was halfway to the zoo before he knew he was going there. Louise had said it was kept open all winter.

Not much of the day was left when he reached the entrance: he would be driving back in darkness. He would have to make his visit short, he did not want to be caught inside when they locked the gates. He paid the admission fee to the scarfed and muffled figure in the booth, then took his car along the empty drives, glancing out the side window at the herds of llama, of yak, the enclosure of the Siberian tiger in which only the places a tiger might hide were to be seen.

At the buffalo field he stopped the car and got out. The buffalo were feeding near the wire fence, but at his approach they lifted their heads and glared at him, then snorted and rocked away from him through the haunch-deep snowdunes.

He plodded along the fence, not caring that the wind was up and chilling him through his heavy coat, the blood retreating from his toes. Thin sinister fingers of blown snow were creeping over the road; on the way back he would have to watch for drifts. He imagined the snow rising up, sweeping down in great curves, in waves over the city, each house a tiny centre of man-made warmth, fending it off. By the grace of the power plant and the gas plant: a bomb, a catastrophe to each and the houses would close like eyes. He thought of all the people he barely knew, how they would face it, chopping up their furniture for firewood until the cold overcame. How they were already facing it, the Koreans' fishes fluttering on the clothesline like defiant silver flags, the woman downstairs shrilling 'Whispering Hope' off-key into the blizzard, Paul in the flimsy armour of his cheap nationalism, the landlady holding aloft torchlike her bar of soap stuck with artificial flowers. Poor Louise, he saw now what she had been trying desperately to do: the point of the circle, closed and self-sufficient, was not what it included but what it shut out. His own efforts to remain human, futile work and sterile love, what happened when it was all used up, what would he be left with? Black trees on a warm orange wall; and he had painted everything white. . . .

Dizzy with cold, he leaned against the fence, forehead on mittened hand. He was at the wolf pen. He remembered it from his trip with Louise. They had stood there for some time waiting for the wolves to come over to them but they had kept to the far side. Three of them were near the fence now though, lying in its shelter. An old couple, a man and a woman in nearly identical grey coats, were standing near the wolves. He had not noticed them earlier, no cars had passed him, they must have walked from the parking lot. The eyes of the wolves were yellowish grey: they looked out through the bars at him, alert, neutral.

'Are they timber wolves?' Morrison said to the old woman. Opening his mouth to speak, he was filled with a sudden chill rush of air.

The woman turned to him slowly: her face was a haze of wrinkles from which her eyes stared up at him, blue, glacial.

'You from around here?' she asked.

'No,' Morrison said. Her head swung away; she continued to look through the fence at the wolves, nose to the wind, short white fur ruffled up on edge.

Morrison followed her fixed gaze: something was being told, something that had nothing to do with him, the thing you could learn only after the rest was finished with and discarded. His body was numb; he swayed. In the corner of his eye the old woman swelled, wavered, then seemed to disappear, and the land opened before him. It swept away to the north and he thought he could see the mountains, white-covered, their crests glittering in the falling sun, then forest upon forest, after that the barren tundra and the blank solid rivers, and beyond, so far that the endless night had already descended, the frozen sea.

MARIE-CLAIRE BLAIS

The Forsaken

She was just an ordinary person. There were, far away, individuals, tragic events, but that was far off in countries bathed in blood, while here, in this part of the world where she had been tucked away since the day she was born, one met nothing but ordinary people and, without being happy, never had to suffer a single tragic event. Sometimes she wondered whether she really existed, or whether through some blind act of cruelty whoever it was that had placed her here, said to be God, had not insidiously abandoned her inside this body that resembled so many others, even though she constantly doubted the reality of her earthly existence. Like everyone else who had not reached the age of discretion and whose lives, plagued by monotony, she could see close at hand, she was just as much a monster on a small scale, fond of games and skirmishes, as ready as the next one to take part in those sly applications of fingernails to skin and, when she was less bored, in their greedy buzzing around the life of the senses. The days followed one upon the other, the seasons too, and not one catastrophe came along to alter her miserable fate of being nobody, always nobody, of being held captive in this body, inside this ordinary person. The only things she could feel were: the burden of her alien existence, which was silently growing; the skin of those she approached, touched in hopes of breaking through the haze that separated her from herself, which was by turns oily, sweaty, or hot, and if they were old, often insensible to her caresses. She would kiss them or hug them, aware that they too were oppressed, uncommunicative creatures, and whatever soul or existence they had was devoid of calamity because they had also been forsaken within their lives, those cramped cells of flesh where they had been condemned to feel that nothing ever happened, where there was never anything to fear, not even the fear itself of a great misfortune.

In winter there was the stale odour of snow, or perhaps there was no odour at all. The warlike contraptions she kept seeing in her dreams would be used here for nothing but clearing the streets and sidewalks of the mountains of grimy snow, underneath which it was forbidden to lie down and go to sleep, calm and breathless. Those machines had ground the featureless lives of her friends to bits, and nothing of them had been recovered but bloody fragments, a foot, a hand—they had died in pieces, just as others were dying in far off places, mowed down by ghastly machines. But here one did not perish gloriously in the carnage of a war, one died in solitude, without anyone knowing, a death already submitted to and lacking all hope of resurrection in memories or hearts.

In summer one gulped down the dust from the streets while running, a heady feeling, voluptuous, even for an ordinary person. Life would suddenly catch at you, like the pernicious spikes that run along the fences around buildings: she stopped running, looked at the sun that seemed to want to obliterate everything, and remembered that she was merely a drab creature that had been overlooked here on the sidewalk, under the vast white sky that glittered and offended her sight. Could it be that she was more miserable than the real wretches who were dying in distant places under the bombs, and, if she did resemble, without knowing them, those creatures who were subjected to genuine suffering—out there—what was she doing here, in this body that pretended to breathe, play, live, like all the others? She would have done better to leave, like the victims, carrying her few belongings in a wheelbarrow. But in the midst of all those mortals who had no personal destiny other than the common fate of being people to whom nothing would happen, she diverted her numbed spirits by going through the same motions each day, sleeping at night, rising in the morning, eating with no appetite, fingering the hollows created by hunger in this body that could shudder without existing and that had never known the evils of famine and death, the unending curse that, right now, in some other place, was weighing upon all those whom misfortune had not forsaken.

One morning, while lounging against a red brick wall that bruised her hands and elbows, a wall whose bricks were hot under a sky that was setting fire with its dull flame to the whole world, she had the temerity to think she, too, would leave. She did not yet know where it was that she would be going, but she would follow the lead of those who headed out towards distant parts with a wheelbarrow, a few objects, a bit of clothing and food, for one did not sleep, did not eat on such a journey, there was time only to flee, under the bombs, in the whirlwind of an avenging sky. She had to leave this red brick wall because, by leaning her sweat-soaked back, her elbows, the palms of her hands against it too hard, was she not running a risk of imprinting into the rough substance, which was about to melt in the sun, the outline of this body that she was not sure she inhabited? Her heart was pounding deep inside her chest as if it had been left by itself with its persistent beating motion inside a subterranean passage. Now, she was leaving. The sky was white and harsh, her wheelbarrow, which she dragged clumsily behind her, held the spade and the knife for the rats that might swarm over the stone or concrete walls; but the rats themselves were drowsy from the heat and did not venture out of their thornbushes, and the lecherous drunkards, whom she feared as much as the rat-bites, also seemed to be asleep in their shacks, with the blinds down. The sky was silent, white and still, with its unblinking sun overhead. The sun, to some extent, illuminated the way through the dust; she had by now walked for so long that her hair was sticking to her temples. From time to time she would pause before a landscape that she had never seen before this day, a lush part of the world, and spend hours there, waiting for the tragic event that was not taking place, for no threat of any kind erupted from the heavens. She ran through the tall, cool grass, telling herself that the far-off war had perhaps come to an end, she would soon be able, she thought, to inhabit her body, to live, breathe, like everyone else. They would very likely come looking for her during the night, and would tell her again not to run away—because she was only an ordinary person—but here, in this fresh patch of green that was a new landscape, a new vision of a world to come, with her face lifted towards the sun, she had felt that it was time for her to make her peace with all those dead people who passed through her dreams at night, and with the living ones who preyed on her mind during the day, those whom misfortune had forgotten.

Translated by Patricia Sillers

SANDRA BIRDSELL

The Wednesday Circle

Betty crosses the double planks that span the ditch in front of Joys' yard. Most people have only one plank. But Mrs Joy needs two. Mrs Joy is a possible candidate for the circus. Like sleeping with an elephant, Betty's father says often. But Mr and Mrs Joy, the egg people, don't sleep together. Betty knows this even though she's never gone further than inside their stale smelling kitchen.

The highway is a smeltering strip of gunmetal grey at her back. It leads to another town like the one she lives in. If you kept on going south, you would get to a place called Pembina in the States and a small dark tavern where a woman will serve under-age kids beer. Laurence, Betty's friend, knows about this. But if you turn from the highway and go west, there are dozens of villages and then the Pembina Hills which Betty has seen on one occasion, a school trip to the man-made lake at Morden. Home of the rich and the godly, Betty's father calls these villages. Wish the godly would stay home. Can't get a seat in the parlour on Friday nights.

Beyond her lies a field in summer fallow and a dirt road rising to a slight incline and then falling as it meets the highway. Before her is the Joys' crumbling yellow cottage, flanked on all sides by greying bales of straw which have swollen and broken free from their bindings and are scattered about the yard. Behind the cottage is the machine shed. Behind the machine shed and bumping up against the prairie is the chicken coop.

Because Mika, Betty's mother, sends her for the eggs instead of having them delivered by Mr Joy, she gets them cheaper.

Betty balances the egg cartons beneath her chin and pushes open the gate. It shrieks on its rusty hinges. The noise doesn't affect her as it usually does. Usually, the noise is like a door opening into a dark room and she is filled with dread. Today, she is prepared for it. Today is the day for the Wednesday Circle. The church ladies are meeting at her home. Even now, they're there in the dining room, sitting in a circle with their Bibles in their laps. It's like women and children in the centre. And arrows flying. Wagons are going up in flames and smoke. The goodness and matronly wisdom of the Wednesday Circle is a newly discovered thing. She belongs with them now. They can reach out to protect her even here, by just being what they are. And although she wants nothing to happen today, she is prepared for the worst.

'Come on in,' Mrs Joy calls from the kitchen.

Betty sets the egg cartons down on the steps and enters the house. Mrs Joy's kitchen resembles a Woolworth store. There are porcelain dogs and cats in every corner on knick-knack shelves. Once upon a time, she used to love looking at those figurines but now she thinks they're ugly.

The woman sits in her specially made chair which is two chairs wired together. Her legs are stretched out in front resting up on another chair. Out of habit, Betty's heart constricts because she knows the signs. Mrs Joy is not up to walking back to the chicken coop with her. And that's how it all began.

'Lo, I am with you always even unto the end of the world,' her mind recites.

These verses rise unbidden. She has memorized one hundred of them and won a trip to a summer Bible camp at Lake Winnipeg. She has for the first time seen the ocean on the prairie and tried to walk on water. The waves have lifted and pulled her out where her feet couldn't touch the sandy bottom and she has been swept beneath that mighty sea and heard the roaring of the waves in her head and felt the sting of fish water in her nostrils. Like a bubble of froth she is swept beneath the water, back and forth by the motion of the waves. She is drowning. What happens is just as she's heard. Her whole life flashes by. Her head becomes a movie screen playing back every lie and swearing, malicious and unkind deeds, thoughts, words. There is not one thing that makes her look justified for having done or said them. And then her foot touches a rock and she pushes herself forward in desperation, hoping it's the right direction.

Miraculously, it is. She bounces forward from the depths to where she can tip-toe to safety, keeping her nose above the waves. She runs panting with fear to her cabin. She pulls the blankets over her. She tells no one. But that evening in the chapel during devotions, the rustling wind in the poplars against the screen causes her to think of God. When they all sing, 'Love Lifted Me', the sunset parts the clouds above the water so there is a crack of gold where angels hover, watching. So she goes forward to the altar with several others and has her name written in the Book of Life. They tell her the angels are clapping and she thinks she can hear them there at that crack of gold which is the door to heaven. She confesses every sin she's been shown in the water except for one. For some reason, it wasn't there in the movie. And they are such gentle, smiling nice people who have never done what she's done. So she can't bring herself to tell them that Mr Joy puts his hands in her pants.

'Rainin' today, ain't it child?' Mrs Joy asks.

'No, not yet,' Betty says. 'It's very muggy.'

'Don't I know it,' she says.

'Are your legs sore?' Betty asks.

'Oh Lord, yes, how they ache,' Mrs Joy says and rolls her eyes back into her head. Her jersey dress is a tent stretched across her knees. She cradles a cookie tin in her lap.

'That's too bad,' Betty says.

A chuckle comes from deep inside her mammoth chest. 'You sound just like your mother,' she says. 'And you're looking more and more like her each time I see you. You're just like an opal, always changing.'

God's precious jewels, Mrs Joy calls them when she visits Mika. She lines them up verbally, Betty and her sisters and brothers, comparing chins, noses. This one here, she says about Betty, she's an opal. You oughta keep a watch over that one. Always changing. But it just goes to show, His mysteries does He perform. Not one of them the same.

'Thank you,' Betty says, but she hates being told she looks like her mother. Mika has hazel eyes and brown hair. She is blonde and blue-eyed like her Aunt Elizabeth.

'Well, you know where the egg pail is,' Mrs Joy says, dismissing her with a flutter of her pudgy hand.

'Aren't you coming?' Betty asks.

'Not today, girl. It aches me so to walk. You collect the eggs and then you jest find Mr Joy and you pay him. He gets it in the end anyhow.'

Betty looks around the kitchen. His jacket is missing from its hook on the wall. She goes over to the corner by the window and feigns interest in the porcelain figures. She picks one up, sets it down. His truck is not in the yard.

'Where is he?'

'Went to town for something,' Mrs Joy says. 'But I thought he'd be back by now. Doesn't matter though, jest leave the money in the back porch.'

The egg pail thumps against her leg as she crosses the yard to the chicken coop. She walks toward the cluttered wire enclosure, past the machine shed. The doors are open wide. The hens scratch and dip their heads in her direction as she approaches. Hope rises like an erratic kite as she passes the shed and there are no sounds coming from it. She stamps her feet and the hens scatter before her, then circle around and approach her from behind, silently. She quickly gathers three dozen of the warm, straw-flecked eggs, and then steps free of the stifling smelly coop out into the fresh moist air. She is almost home-free. She won't have to face anything today. It has begun to rain. Large spatters spot her white blouse, feel cool on her back. She sets the pail down on the ground beside the egg cartons and begins to transfer the eggs.

'Here, you don't have to do that outside.' His sudden voice, as she fills the egg cartons, brings blood to her face, threatens to pitch her forward over the pail.

He strides across the yard from the shed. 'Haven't got enough sense to come in out of the rain,' he says. 'Don't you know you'll melt? Be nothing left of you but a puddle.'

He carries the pail, she carries the cartons. He has told her: Mrs Joy is fat and lazy, you are my sunshine, my only sunshine. I would like six little ones running around my place too, but Mrs Joy is fat and lazy. His thin hand has gone from patting her on the head with affection, to playfully slapping her on the behind, graduated then to tickling her armpits and ribs and twice now, his hands have been inside her underpants.

'Be not afraid,' a verse leaps into her head. 'For I am with you.' She will put her plan into action. The Wednesday Circle women are strong and mighty. She knows them all, they're her mother's friends. She'll just go to them and say, Mr Joy feels me up, and that will be the end of it.

She walks behind him, her heart pounding. He has an oil rag hanging from his back pocket and his boots are caked with clay, adding inches to his height.

'I'm waiting for my parts,' he says over his shoulder. 'Can't do anything until I get that truck fixed.' Sometimes he talks to her as though she were an adult. Sometimes as though she were ten again and just coming for the eggs for the first time. How old are you, he'd asked the last time and was surprised when she said, fourteen. My sunshine has grown up.

They enter the machine shed and he slides the doors closed behind them, first one and then the other, leaving a sliver of daylight beaming through where the doors join. A single light bulb dangles from a wire, shedding a circle of weak yellow light above the truck, not enough to clear the darkness from the corners.

'Okay-dokey,' he says and puts the pail of eggs on the workbench. 'You can work here. I've got things to do.' He goes over to the truck, disappears beneath its raised hood.

Then he's back at the workbench, searching through his tool box. 'Seen you with your boyfriend the other day,' he says. 'That Anderson boy.'

'He's not my boyfriend,' she says.

'I saw you,' he says. His usual bantering tone is missing. 'The two of you were in the coulee.' Then his breath is warm on the side of her face as he reaches across her. His arms knock against her breast, sending pain shooting through her chest. I need a bra, she has told Mika. Whatever for? Wear an undershirt if you think you really need to.

'Do you think it's a good idea to hang around in the coulee with your boyfriend?'

'He's not my boyfriend,' she says. 'I told you.'

He sees her flushed cheeks, senses her discomfort. 'Aha,' he says. 'So he is. You can't fool me.'

She moves away from him. Begins to stack the cartons up against her chest, protection against his nudgings. Why is it that everyone but her own mother notices that she has breasts now?

'Don't rush off,' he says. 'Wait until the rain passes.' The sound of it on the tin roof is like small pebbles being dropped one by one.

He takes the cartons from her and sets them back on the workbench. He smiles and she can see that perfect decayed circle between his front teeth. His hair is completely grey even though he's not as old as her father. He starts to walk past her, back towards the truck and then suddenly he grasps her about the waist and begins to tickle her ribs. She is slammed up against him and gasping for breath. His whiskers prickle against her neck. She tastes the bitterness of his flannel shirt.

She pushes away. 'Stop.'

He holds her tighter. 'You're so pretty,' he says. 'No wonder the boys are chasing you. When I'm working in here, know what I'm thinking all the time?'

'Let me go.' She continues to push against his bony arms.

'I'm thinking about all the things I could do to you.'

Against her will, she has been curious to know. She feels desire rising when he speaks of what he would like to do. He has drawn vivid word-pictures that she likes to reconstruct until her face burns. Only it isn't Mr Joy in the pictures, it's Laurence. It's what made her pull aside her underpants so he could fumble inside her moist crevice with his grease-stained fingers.

'Show me your tits,' he whispers into her neck. 'I'll give you a dollar if you do.'

She knows the only way out of this is to tell. When the whole thing is laid out before the Wednesday Circle, she will become whiter than snow. 'No,' she says.

'What do you mean, no,' he says, jabbing her in the ribs once again.

'I'm going to tell,' she says. 'You can't make me do anything anymore because I'm going to tell on you.' She feels as though a rock has been taken from her stomach. He is ugly. He is like a salamander dropping from the sky after a rainstorm into a mince-meat pail. She doesn't know how she could ever have liked him.

'Make you?' he says. 'Make you? Listen here, girlie, I've only done what you wanted me to do.'

She knows this to be true and not true. She isn't certain how she has come to accept and even expect his fondling. It has happened over a course of four years, gradually, like growing.

She walks to the double doors where the light shines through. 'Open them, please,' she says.

'Open them yourself,' he says. She can feel the presence of the Wednesday Circle. The promise of their womanly strength is like a lamp unto her feet. They will surround her and protect her. Freedom from his word-pictures will make her a new person.

'You say anything,' he says. 'You say one thing and I'll have some pretty stories to tell about you. You betcha.'

'That woman,' Mika is saying to the Wednesday Circle as Betty enters the dining room. 'That woman. She has absolutely no knowledge of the scriptures. She takes everything out of context.' Mika is standing at the buffet with a china tea cup in her hand.

Betty steps into the circle of chairs and sits down in Mika's empty one. Mika stops talking, throws her a look of surprise and question. The other women greet her with smiles, nods.

'Did you get the eggs?' Mika asks.

Betty feels her mouth stretching, moving of its own accord into a silly smile. She knows the smile irritates Mika but she can't help it. At times like these, her face moves on its own. She can hear her own heartbeat in her ears, like the ocean, roaring.

'What now?' Mika asks, worried.

'What do you mean, she takes everything out of context?' Mrs Brawn asks, ignoring Betty. It's her circle. She started it off, arranging for the church women to meet in each others' homes twice a month to read scripture and sew things which they send to a place in the city where they are distributed to the poor. The women are like the smell of coffee to Betty and at the same time, they are like the cool opaque squares of Mika's lemon slice which is arranged on bread and butter plates on the table. They are also like the sturdy varnished chairs they sit on. To be with them now is the same as when she was a child and thought that if you could always be near an adult when you were ill, you wouldn't die.

'My, my,' Mika mimicks someone to demonstrate to Mrs Brawn what she means. She places her free hand against her chest in a dramatic gesture. 'They are different, ain't they? God's precious jewels. Just goes to show, His mysteries does He perform.'

Betty realizes with a sudden shock that her mother is imitating Mrs Joy.

Mrs Brawn takes in Mika's pose with a stern expression and immediately Mika looks guilty, drops her hand from her breast and begins to fill cups with coffee.

'I suppose that we really can't expect much from Mrs Joy,' Mika says with her back to them. Betty hears the slight mocking tone in her voice that passes them by.

Heads bent over needlework nod their understanding. The women's stitches form thumbs, forest-green fingers; except for the woman who sits beside Betty. With a hook she shapes intricate spidery patterns to lay across varnished surfaces, the backs of chairs. What the poor would want with those, I'll never know, Mika has said privately. But they include the doilies in their parcels anyway because they have an understanding. They whisper that this white-haired woman has known suffering.

She works swiftly. It seems to Betty as though the threads

come from the ends of her fingers, white strings with a spot of red every few inches. It looks as though she's cut her finger and secretly bleeds the colour into the lacy scallops. The women all unravel and knit and check closely for evenness of tension.

Mika enters the circle of chairs then, carrying the tray of coffee, and begins to make her way around it. She continues to speak of Mrs Joy.

'Are you looking forward to school?' the white-haired woman asks Betty. Her voice is almost a whisper, a knife peeling skin from a taut apple. Betty senses that it has been difficult for her to speak, feels privileged that she has.

'Yes, I miss school.'

The woman blinks as she examines a knot in her yarn. She scrapes at it with her large square thumbnail which is flecked oddly with white fish-hook-shaped marks. 'Your mother tells us you were at camp,' she says. 'What did you do there?'

Mika approaches them with the tray of coffee. 'I just wish she hadn't picked me out, that's all,' Mika says. 'She insists on coming over here in the morning and it's impossible to work with her here. And Mr Joy is just as bad. I send Betty for the eggs now because he used to keep me at the door talking.'

Mr Joy is just as bad. Mr Joy makes me ashamed of myself and I let him do it. The woman shakes loose the doily; it unfolds into the shape of a star as she holds it up.

'You like it?' the white-haired woman asks Betty.

'It's pretty.'

'Maybe I give it to you.'

'Ah, Mika,' a woman across the circle says, 'she just knows where she can find the best baking in town.'

Then they all laugh; even the quiet woman beside Betty has a dry chuckle over the comment, only Mrs Brawn doesn't smile. She stirs her coffee with more force than necessary and sets the spoon alongside it with a clang.

'Obesity is no laughing matter,' she says. 'Mrs Joy is a glutton and that's to be pitied. We don't laugh at sin, the wages of sin is death.'

'But the gift of God is eternal life through Jesus Christ our Lord,' the woman says so softly, the words are nail filings dropping into her lap. If Betty hadn't seen her lips moving, she wouldn't have heard it. 'God forgives,' the woman says then, louder. She is an odd combination of young and old. Her voice and breasts are young but her hair is white.

Mika stands before them with the tray of coffee. 'Not always,' Mika says. 'There's the unpardonable sin, don't forget about that.' She seems pleased to have remembered this.

'Which is?' the woman asks.

'Well, suicide,' Mika says. 'It has to be, because when you think of it, it's something you can't repent of once the deed is done.' Mika smiles around the circle as if to say to them, see, I'm being patient with this woman who has known suffering.

'Perhaps there is no need to repent,' the woman says.

'Pardon?'

'In Russia,' the woman begins and then stops to set her thread down into her lap. She folds her hands one on top of the other and closes her eyes. The others, sensing a story, fall silent.

'During the revolution in Russia, there was once a young girl who was caught by nine soldiers and was their prisoner for two weeks. She was only thirteen. These men had their way with her many times, each one taking their turn, every single night. In the end, she shot herself. What about her?'

'I've never heard of such a case,' Mika says. She sounds as though she resents hearing of it now.

'There are always such cases,' the woman says. 'If God knows the falling of a single sparrow, He is also merciful. He knows we're only human.'

Mrs Brawn sets her knitting down on the floor in front of her chair, leans forward slightly. 'Oh, He knows,' she says. 'But He never gives us more than we can bear. When temptation arises, He gives us the strength to resist.' She closes her statement with her hands, like a conductor pinching closed the last sound.

Betty watches as the white-haired woman twists and untwists her yarn into a tight ring around her finger. 'I don't believe for one moment,' she says finally, 'that God would condemn such a person to hell. Jesus walked the earth and so He knows.'

'No, no,' Mika says from the buffet. 'He doesn't condemn us, don't you see? That's where you're wrong. We condemn ourselves. We make that choice.'

'And what choice did that young girl have?' the woman asks. 'It was her means of escape. God provided the gun.'

Mika holds the tray of lemon squares up before her as though she were offering them to the sun. She looks stricken. Deep lines cut a sharp V above her nose. 'You don't mean that,' she says. 'Suicide is unpardonable. I'm sure of it. Knowing that keeps me going. Otherwise, I would have done it myself long ago.'

There is shocked silence and a rapid exchange of glances around the circle, at Betty, to see if she's heard.

'You shouldn't say such things,' Mrs Brawn says quietly. 'For shame. You have no reason to say that.'

The white-haired woman speaks with a gaunt smile. 'Occasionally,' she says, 'in this room, someone dares to speak the truth.'

'What do you mean?' asks Mrs Brawn.

'Look at us,' the woman says. 'We're like filthy rags to Him in our self-righteousness. We obey because we fear punishment, not because we love.'

Betty sees the grease spot on her blouse where his arm has brushed against her breast. Her whole body is covered with handprints. The stone is back in her stomach. She feels betrayed. For a moment the women are lost inside their own thoughts and they don't notice as she rises from her chair and sidles over to the door. Then, as if on some signal, their conversation resumes its usual level, each one waiting impatiently for the other to be finished so they can speak their words. Their laughter and goodwill have a feeling of urgency, of desperation. Betty stands at the door; a backward glance and she sees the white-haired woman bending over her work once again, eyes blinking rapidly, her fingers moving swiftly and the doily, its flecked pattern spreading like a web across her lap.

EDNA ALFORD

Tuesday, Wednesday, Thursday

cold and in the winter weather
comfort is denied
doors are fast but still the weather
rages inside

CHRISTOPHER WISEMAN
'Winter Song' from
waiting for the barbarians

Tuesday morning Arla stood at the porch window watching the sky which was frozen in red and grey streaks across the glass. She stood as if she too were paralyzed by the anesthetic cold administered by the January wind from around the corners of the lodge.

She knew she shouldn't have been standing there. She was already late for work. Her bus had been delayed by the drifting snow and had crawled up to her stop almost half an hour late. She had climbed on and had sat through her part of the route with glazed, unseeing eyes directed toward the frosted window beside her. She was not noticed; the other passengers this morning were similar, sightless, huddled in pairs on their seats, facing the front of the bus. Their bulky winter coats and scarves exuded a musty odour, human, that mingled with the bus exhaust, fumes from the gas heater, and the cold patches of air which swarmed up the icy steps of the vehicle when its door creaked open and closed at each stop.

She intended to go to Mrs Langland right after finishing with Mrs Mandel, to make sure she was dressed for breakfast, but her mind just now was only an expansion of the frozen space outside the lodge. She simply stood, her hands in the pockets of her spotless uniform, and gazed, unthinking, out the window. Not until

Matron Benstone's sharp voice over the public address system commanded the ladies to breakfast in fifteen minutes did she at last even stir. Then she moved toward the porch door, out and into the hallway, still slowly, still without conscious direction.

Mrs Langland's room was two doors down from the porch and her door was ajar. Her room was lit only by a dim, unreal light that filtered through the grey and red streaks on her window.

In the moment before Arla switched on the light, she indifferently observed the old woman. Mrs Langland sat erect on the side of her unmade bed. A tangle of stark white hair sat awkwardly on her head. The hair was curled and artificial looking, like the synthetic hair on the head of a plastic doll. Only where the skin should have descended from the hair, fat-plastic and smooth with permanently rouged cheeks, there was a long white bony forehead, wrinkled and interrupted by heavy tufted white brows. Beneath these brows were two bluish grey hollows which were her eye sockets, and deep in those sockets hung two enormous clear grey eyes, vacant, staring, not at Arla, but apparently at nothing.

The remainder of her face was very long and thin and bony, punctuated only by two high sharp cheekbones, the grey shadows of the sunken cheeks, and two pale blue lines for lips. Her neck was engraved with almost symmetrical wrinkles and was scrawny, like the dowel neck of a wooden puppet; it was stuck into a hollow between the woman's bony shoulders. She was wearing a faded pink flannelette nightgown, short and with lace at the neck. Her legs, like sucker sticks, stuck out over the side of the bed, and the skin on these was paper thin and you could see all the veins running cold blue beneath it. Skeleton feet somehow hung precariously onto the ends of these legs.

She was, therefore, precisely the same this morning as all the other mornings Arla had found her, undressed and unwilling to prepare herself for another day, much less for breakfast. There were occasional exceptions. Sometimes Arla found her still lying in her bed with only her head sticking out of the covers, her large vacant eyes fixed on a patch of ceiling above her.

Arla could feel the anger climbing the walls of her throat, as if this emotional calisthenic could somehow lessen the frustration of the old woman's perversity and indifference.

She flicked on the light. 'Mrs Langland, you're late,' she said, and when she could not see even the flicker of a response, she continued in a loud detached voice that sounded as if it came from somewhere else in the room, not her own mouth. 'I said you're going to be late again, for your breakfast. You have to get dressed.'

Arla walked over to the closet in the corner, opened the door and pulled a cotton housedress from a metal hanger; it clinked against the other empty hangers in the closet. She carried the dress over her arm carefully, with repugnance. She glanced at it briefly. It was white and flecked with tiny black ferny leaves that made it look to Arla as if it were covered with fly specks. She laid the dress on the bed beside Mrs Langland who did not notice.

Next Arla went to the dresser beside the bed; the mirror on the dresser reflected wavily the red and grey streaked sky, its image already altered through the yellow film of the cracked windowpane. She accidentally pulled open the third drawer. Piled neatly there were new clothes, most of them still in their plastic wrappers with printing on them which said things like 'Machine Washable', and 'Permanent Press'. New colourful nightgowns, blouses, slips, and several arnel dresses, neatly folded, took up three-quarters of the space in the drawer. The remainder was filled with unopened cartons of pink and lavender soaps, flower-shaped, and perfume bottles still in their boxes, Avon mostly.

These were all gifts from Mrs Langland's nieces who lived in the city and who only came to visit her at Christmas and at Easter. Each time a new present arrived, Arla or one of the other practical nurses took it to Mrs Langland who sat and stared at it. The nurse would then open it and show it to Mrs Langland who would not respond. Then the nurse would open the third drawer and set it neatly on top or beside its fellows according to the nature of the gift.

Arla closed this department store drawer and automatically reached for the handle on the middle drawer where she knew the underclothes were stored. She took out a worn, stained pair of heavy perforated cotton bloomers and a cotton undershirt which was skinny and had thin straps at the top. Mrs Langland obviously didn't need a brassiere, Arla thought. Her breasts were empty, flat and wrinkled like crushed tin foil. They disgusted Arla who was young and well-endowed with tight resilient skin enveloping her own breasts. She took a plain white slip from the drawer. The slip had one strap broken and this was attached to the garment by a large chrome safety pin squashed permanently closed in the laundry mangle downstairs.

She approached Mrs Langland with the undergarments and held them out to her. Mrs Langland only stared at them.

'You have to get dressed now, Mrs Langland,' Arla repeated mechanically. 'Stand up.' The old woman gripped the edge of the mattress and rose slowly, like a ghost. 'Take off your nightie,' Arla directed, but the woman did not respond. Arla reached down and pulled the nightie up over the body, exposing it to the morbid glare of the lightbulb in the ceiling.

A faint fecal odour filtered through the body's skin and mingled with the dead air in the room. Arla turned her head away and said, 'Lift up your arms, Mrs Langland.' She did and Arla said, 'There, that's it.'

'Now put on your undershirt.' The woman did not move. Arla slipped it on over her head, unrolling it downward over her vacant breasts. 'Now, your pants, Mrs Langland. Sit down.' Mrs Langland sat and Arla stooped; she stuck the first bony foot into one hole of the garment, then the second into the other, and grabbing the top elastic on either side she pulled the underpants up both legs to the parchment thighs. 'Stand up,' said Arla. The old woman stood. Arla tucked the undershirt into the pants, realizing that she could have saved the old woman the trouble of standing up the last time had she put the underpants on first.

What's done is done, Arla thought. Bad enough that she should be expected to encourage this old woman each and every morning to dress herself, to do what she would not do. Was it any wonder she was confused herself. And it wasn't as if Mrs Langland was the only lodger who had to be 'done' each morning, either. There was Miss Bole and Mrs Mandel and that new lady, Mrs Eagleton and, of course, old Mrs Torpor. And these were the ones who had to be dressed from top to toe, so to speak, not to mention the ones who had to have help buttoning, zippering, putting on stockings, combing and pinning their sparse white hair.

When she had finished tucking in the undershirt, Arla again spoke to Mrs Langland who stared back in response, 'You put on your slip and your dress. They're right beside you on the bed. I'll be back in a few minutes.' Arla left the old woman standing and almost fled from the room, turning left down the hallway. She had to check on Miss Bole in room five. Arla didn't actually expect Mrs Langland to do what she was told but it had become a habit with her to mouth the instructions. Matron Oliver had told her exactly what to say.

Mrs Langland remained standing, motionless except for an almost imperceptible shiver which vibrated her body, a kind of movement you'd think would make a noise, perhaps a hum. Shortly after Arla left, a large brown-yellow stain began to spread over the back of Mrs Langland's white cotton underpants. Soon it hung heavy inside the cloth and then it escaped through the bottom of her bloomers and ran straight down her right leg, crossing over the maze of cold blue veins till it reached her ankle. Then it swerved forward and oozed over her foot onto the dull brown linoleum floor where it rapidly formed a large pool of warm, yellowish, almost fluid mass that seemed to vaporize into a cloud of stench and rise from the floor, creeping silently upward, back over her body toward her head. Gradually it sent fingers of fumet toward the doorway, out into the hall. So Arla detected it before she actually entered the room, and when she confirmed its source, she grimaced, moved stiffly toward the creature standing at its centre.

'Hold up your hands, Mrs Langland,' she ordered. The woman obeyed. 'Of all mornings to come up with a stunt like this,' Arla hissed at her in a voice not loud enough to be heard outside the door but loud enough for the oblivious old woman to hear, had she so wished. 'You're already late and now you'll be another fifteen minutes or more.' And what about the others who needed help in the meantime, thought Arla. How in God's name could she be expected to be in fourteen places at the same time. She couldn't do it—they would have to make out by themselves this morning, or go to breakfast in their housecoats or help each other for a change.

Arla peeled off the undershirt, careful not to touch the tucked in portion which had been contaminated and which yellow-streaked up Mrs Langland's back as it was lifted up over her head. Some of it caught in her hair.

Arla began to unroll the bloomers downward, delicately, as if they contained a bomb which could, if not handled respectfully, explode in her hands and over her clean white uniform. Then she placed her arm around the thin old body and braced herself against the bed. She directed Mrs Langland to lift her feet, quickly, each in turn. Now she was holding her breath for long intervals and when she did breathe, it was through her mouth, not her nostrils.

The soiled underclothing removed, she left Mrs Langland standing by the bed and ran out of the room, down the hall to the bathroom. As she rinsed the garments in the porcelain bowl of the sink, her face betrayed her feeling toward them and toward her task. She hated the clothes, found them more repulsive than if they had been snakes she fingered in the yellowing water.

Back in her room, Mrs Langland stood, visibly shivering now so that, had the movement made noise, there would have been heard a loud hum interrupted by spasmodic silences where the old body would jerk into a new set of shivers.

At one such interval, Mrs Langland moved her foot and began to slip on the ooze that was now under it; in a second, she had moved the other foot to regain her balance but it, too, found footing in the mass beneath her and suddenly, grotesquely, she was catapulted into the air by the sordid conspiracy of these skeleton feet and her own feces. Her thin limbs like pick-up sticks, straight and brittle, scrambled around each other, whacked the bed, the night table, the floor. Throughout, small inhuman squeaks were emitted from the mouth of the white body.

Finally the movement and the squeaks stopped. The rancid air was quiet. The old woman lay naked, rigid with fear, and again she began to shiver. Her eyes appeared to have grown permanently monstrous, shone silver with horror. The yellow mass oozed beneath her and found its way to the edges of her body where some escaped around her bony hips and some just above her armpits, near her shoulders. She held her legs straight out before her, suspended a little above the floor, which gave the body the appearance that it was about to levitate, had already begun to rise.

Shortly after the fall, Arla returned from the laundry room where she had deposited the wet bundle of garments. She carried towels, washcloth, and a basin full of warm water. She saw the old woman right away, jerked violently and sucked in her breath as if someone had struck her chest and knocked the wind out of her. She held onto the basin of water but only because it was locked in her hands by some other power than her own will.

Her face looked like a blank sheet of paper, her eyes large, almost silver, mirroring the eyes of the old woman lying on the floor. The longer Arla stared obliquely at the body, the more she recognized or remembered something familiar in the old woman's frozen face, something unholy in the humiliating posture of the crooked old bone body, framed in the yellow ooze of its own feces. Arla couldn't say exactly what it was she recognized there, but she knew it was somehow part of herself. And although she would never really know why, it tore like a ragged fish-knife through the flesh of her indifference, her only ally at times like this, left her with a deeper repugnance, a more palpable fear and disgust than she had ever felt before, even at Pine Mountain Lodge. There was something she saw here, something she smelled in the sulphuric acrid air that made her think of hell, the long-forgotten Sunday School hell of a four-year-old girl.

It took some time before she realized what might happen if the matrons or one of the other lodgers came along and saw Mrs Langland naked on the floor and her just standing there, doing nothing. She held the basin with one hand and jerked the free hand round to slam the door.

The two women stared at each other silently, as if they were in a play and had been directed to 'freeze', motionless, suspended in time. And although neither spoke or moved, this was the first honest communication between them, the only time Arla had ever been able to imagine the old woman as an ordinary human being —stirring soup, maybe, or out in the garden on her knees under a loving sun, warm and lazy on the back of her head. The first time Mrs Langland looked out at her from wherever it was she had been hiding, day in, day out as long as Arla had worked at the lodge.

The winter sun rose behind the red and grey streaks of cloud on the windowpane, illuminated them, sent red and grey shafts of light over the white body on the floor. A red streak slid over Mrs Langland's face, lit upon the bulbous silver eyes, and only for a moment Arla thought she saw the old lady's eyes on fire, thought she saw flames licking out from her eyelids, then consumed and rekindled in the grey-white irises and finally smothered in the blackness of her tiny, precise pupils.

The light reflected on the old woman's body rekindled Arla's memory, haunted her with infernal childish notions she couldn't seem to shake this time. She almost took leave of her senses, screamed and dropped the basin, ran out of the room, out of the lodge, out of the city. Yet, somewhere within her she knew there was nowhere far enough to run, no escape from what she had learned. And so she began to move toward Mrs Langland, very slowly at first, as if she were a robot or hypnotized. She felt her flesh soften, release her, allow her back into herself. She became aware that the old woman might have broken bones, that she might have died or might still die as a result of the accident.

By the time she had set her basin down on the night table and was reaching out toward the body, her limbs operated efficiently, like a well-tuned machine, and she had the old rigid body on the bed, washed, and dressed in an exceptionally short time. She sat Mrs Langland on a chair, brushed her hair, then rushed off for a can of Lysol. The fecal smell remained, was only camouflaged, but she had done the best she could. After spraying the room, she approached Mrs Langland again, said, 'Stand up, Mrs Langland, it's time to go to breakfast.' But this time, her voice was gentle, respectful.

She led the old woman out to the sun porch and sat her down at a small card table in the corner of the room. Her breakfast sat on the table in the form of a cold, greyish lump of oatmeal rising out of a little sea of milk and spattered with blotches of brown sugar.

On the left side of the bowl lay two cold crusty pieces of toast, the butter already congealed like wax. On the side of the bread and butter plate leaned a tiny white cardboard cup of jam with white and yellow chunks and specks mashed into it, Mrs Langland's medication. She would take it no other way—in fact, was not aware she was taking it at all. A stainless steel teapot full of strong, lukewarm tea and a cup and saucer sat on the right-hand side of the tray.

Mrs Langland picked up a spoon and began poking disinterestedly at the oatmeal. Arla sat in a chair in the opposite end of the sun porch and occasionally glanced up at the old woman who, in her dress covered with simulated fly specks, sat imitating someone eating breakfast. At one point, when Arla looked up at her, she felt cold, began to shiver, went to the closet for her sweater and returned to the porch.

Not long after Mrs Langland had begun poking her breakfast, Mrs Mackenzie waddled into the sun porch and settled her huge mass of flesh into a blue plastic-covered armchair across from Arla. Mrs Mackenzie was Scottish and wore a full apron and a navy wool cardigan sent to her from the old country. She had just finished breakfast. She belched and looked around the room to make sure no one else had beat her to the sun porch. She prided herself on being the first one here after every meal.

She picked up an old issue of *Woman's Day Magazine* donated to the lodge by the Ladies' Auxiliary, plunked it on her lap and began to look through it, deliberately licking her thumb each time she turned to a new page.

Arla got up, walked over to Mrs Langland and said, 'Why don't you have a bite to eat, Mrs Langland? Maybe if I give you a hand.' She spread the yellow and white-speckled jam on a half piece of toast. Mrs Langland didn't look up but took the toast, dipped it in her tea and pushed it, bird-like, into her mouth; then she began to chew absently, smacked her lips and continued chewing mechanically long after she had swallowed the toast.

When Arla returned to her chair, Mrs Mackenzie leaned toward her and although she half-cupped her hand over her mouth in a token effort to prevent Mrs Langland from hearing what she was about to say, she began in a loud whisper to Arla, 'She came here from the asylum, you know. She shouldn't even be here—she belongs in the mental, that's what I say. I don't know why they let her out.'

'Is that so, Mrs Mackenzie?' said Arla. 'Where'd you hear that? You know what she was in there for?'

'You never knew Matron Diamond, did you dear? She was before your time, I think. She told me about Mrs Langland. We don't know for sure why she went there, o'course,' Mrs Mackenzie leaned closer to Arla but continued to whisper loudly, 'but the way I heard it she watched her house afire, burned to the ground and her children in it at the time. They say she was never the same since. If you were to ask me, I'd say she's still seeing it. She shouldn't even be here, among the likes of us—that's what I say.'

Mrs Mackenzie gave a self-righteous, accusatory nod toward Arla and continued, 'O'course, we all of us had our hardships in them days, on the prairies, but some was weaker and some of us was stronger. O'course, some just couldn't take it at all.' Mrs Mackenzie glanced furtively over her shoulder at Mrs Langland who was still playing with her porridge. Mrs Mackenzie then settled her stout frame back into her chair, licked her thumb and continued looking at her magazine, feeling rightfully that she had said her piece and was finished with speaking.

Mrs Mackenzie could not have known how this information affected Arla; in fact, she was unaware of any response whatsoever. But Arla stared at Mrs Mackenzie's bowed head without seeing it or anything else in the room.

What she saw, behind her eyes, was Mrs Langland—in her flannelette nightgown, younger, standing in the snow in front of a blazing farmhouse. She saw flames reflected off the snow, red and orange and licking, their glow melting down the rigid body of the woman. They played in her hair and mocked her with fire cries from within the house, infected her with fire inside herself, licking through her eyes and ears. And all she could do was just stand there, more rigid every second than the one before.

The reenactment was followed by the image of the old woman, this morning, staring up from the yellow pool of her own feces, naked, stiff, horrified. Arla remembered with guilt the red shafts of light playing over the woman's body and rekindling the acrid, flesh melting fire behind the bulbous silver eyes.

One of her first feelings after cleaning the old woman had been that of relief, thanking God she didn't die. How could she have explained that to the matrons, account for what had happened? Now her own incompetence and thoughtlessness converged on her. She could have done better. She should have known she couldn't leave the old woman standing by herself.

Yet the information Mrs Mackenzie had volunteered fit into a vague puzzle of remarks Matron Oliver had used to describe Mrs Langland when Arla began her job at the lodge, remarks like, 'She's not the same as the other ladies here, requires more care—had a very unfortunate time of it—not quite right, you know.' No, it wasn't the actual revelation of that past event that had so shaken Arla; she had suspected some horror in Mrs Langland's past life. But the details, both imagined and imparted by Mrs Mackenzie, together with the fall this morning, had given the experience an unearthly kind of aura. And most of all, more terrifying than anything else, had been the vague, still undefined recognition of some part of herself in the disintegrating mind and body of the old woman, a recognition so deep it seemed to shake her from within.

Now Arla began to shake externally, through her hands. Realizing this, and afraid that it would soon be noticeable to Mrs Mackenzie, she stood and rushed out of the sun porch to the kitchen where she sat by herself on the grey plastic stool for some time. When she felt ready, she stood and walked confidently back to the sun porch as if she felt nothing. Again the efficiency of the limbs returned.

She picked up the breakfast tray without looking at Mrs Langland and took it back to the dining hall, then went back to check on the slow ladies, to make sure they had been given breakfast. Miss Bole was piqued that she had to go to breakfast without her hair pinned properly but everyone had been fed except for Mrs Torpor. Arla took a tray to her room. Later she gathered all the ladies into the chapel for morning prayer and from then on, everything went according to her regular work routine at the lodge for that day.

Wednesday morning on the way to work in the bus filled with eyeless frozen riders, Arla resolved to treat Mrs Langland more kindly. Although she couldn't seem to bring herself to look at the old woman's eyes, she was gentle with her and dressed her as carefully as she could, even though Mrs Langland was perverse and unyielding. At breakfast, she sat with Mrs Langland the whole time, quietly and gently encouraging her to eat, helping her in every possible way.

Yet there was no response. Always the old woman's silence, her oppressive, enigmatic silence stood between them. And it bothered Arla even more now, after what had happened, after what they had shared, unwillingly, unmercifully—but shared nonetheless. After all that Arla thought she understood. The old woman still passively resisted any attempt to help her, refusing to do even the simplest jobs for herself, even those Arla had seen her do before, till now.

After dinner on Wednesday Mrs Mackenzie sat in her same chair on the sun porch and read the obituary column, looking for friends and acquaintances who may have died since yesterday. Arla was sitting by Mrs Langland, trying to get her to eat while Mrs Langland refused even so much as a mouthful. Arla could almost imagine her vaporizing out of existence, she looked so thin.

Mrs Mackenzie looked up from her paper and spoke, 'I see you're still havin' trouble with Mrs Langland, dear.'

'No, not really—she hasn't been much trouble, really,' Arla replied without facing Mrs Mackenzie.

'Don't tell *me* that, my girl. I was walking by the door yesterday mornin' and I saw her lyin' on the floor in her altogether in the middle of her own mess. I don't know how you could stand it, cleanin' up that kind of mess. I don't know why they keep her here. It's not right for the rest of us.'

So someone had seen after all, thought Arla; someone else knew, sympathised with her, even if it was only old Mrs Mackenzie. Someone else knew at least a little of what it had been like. Rather than being frightened of someone else knowing, as she thought she'd be, Arla felt unaccountably relieved, somehow justified, vindicated. But Mrs Mackenzie didn't know all of it, hadn't felt what Arla had, and it occurred to her to say to Mrs Mackenzie that it could have been her, could still be, another day, another nurse. But Arla couldn't say it even though the words were all there. Instead she said, 'We have to remember what she's been through. We have to try and understand.'

And Arla really did try to understand, tried to remember. Still, the woman had to be dressed and fed, every day of the week, over and over.

Thursday morning when the sun streaked red across the window pane in Mrs Langland's room, remembering became progressively more difficult. Mrs Langland was particularly perverse and unresponsive today. She refused to help Arla dress her, even to the extent of raising or lowering her bony arms so that Arla could slip on her underclothes or dress, but held them rigidly at her sides.

Finally, after pulling up the old woman's stockings, Arla knelt on the floor and tried to put shoes on the skeleton feet. Mrs Langland curled her toes into hard, high lumps and Arla couldn't even push the feet into the perforated black leather oxfords. 'If only you got some satisfaction out of being perverse,' she hissed in a voice not loud enough to be heard outside the door but loud enough for the oblivious old woman to hear, had she so wished, 'but you don't. You just stare and stare.'

Patches of perspiration began to crawl out from the underarms of Arla's uniform. She became brutal, grew determined to force the rebellious toes into their proper places. Angry now, forgetting grew easy for her, understanding impossible—both finally of the same thing—that these could be her feet, her toes, her somewhere, some other distant time.

Now all she could see was Mrs Langland's face, like stone, her eyes like glass that saw nothing, appeared to feel nothing, but only glinted sparkle-like, red and orange-yellow reflections of sunlight off the Thursday morning snow, Tuesday morning's smaller shadow.

DIONNE BRAND

Sans Souci

Rough grass asserted itself everywhere, keeping the earth damp and muddy. It inched its way closer and closer to doorsteps and walls until some hand, it was usually hers, ripped it from its tendrilled roots. But it soon grew back again. It kept the woman in a protracted battle with its creeping mossyness. She ripping it out; shaking the roots of earth. It grew again the minute she turned her back. The house, like the others running up and down the hill, could barely be seen from the struggling road, covered as it was by lush immortelle trees with coarse vine spread among them so that they looked like women with great bushy hair, embracing.

In Sans Souci, as the place was called, they said that the people were as rough as the grass.

She may have looked that way but it was from walking the hills and tearing out grass which grew until she was afraid of it covering her. It hung like tattered clothing from her hips, her breasts, her whole large body. Even when her arms were lifted to carry water to the small shack, she felt weighed down by the bush. Great green patches of leaves, bougainvillea, almond, karili vine fastened her ankles to her wrists. She kept her eyes to the floor of the land. Her look tracing, piercing the bush and marking her steps to the water, to the tub, to the fire, to the road, to the land. The woman turning into a tree, though she was not even old yet. As time went on she felt her back harden like a crab's, like the bark of a tree, like its hard brown meat. A man would come often, but it was difficult to know. When she saw him coming, she would never know him until he said her name, 'Claudine'. Then she would remember him vaguely. A bee near her ear, her hand brushing it away. Sometimes she let the bush grow as tall as it wanted. It overwhelmed her. Reaching at her each new spore or shoot burdened her. Then someone would pass by and not see the house and say that she was minding snakes. Then she would cut it down.

She climbed the hill often when the bush was low around the house. Then she went for water, or so it seemed because she carried a pot. Reaching the top, her feet caking with mud, she would sit on the ground near the edge of the cliff. Then she would look down into the sea and rehearse her falling—a free fall, a dive into the sea. How fast the sea would come toward her—probably not—the cliff was not vertical enough. Her body would hit tufts of grass before reaching the bottom. She could not push off far enough to fall into the water. Musing on whether it would work or not she would lie down on the ground, confused. Spread out, the pot beneath her head, she would be faced by the sky. Then her eyes would close, tired of the blue of the sky zooming in and out at her gaze, and she would be asleep. She never woke up suddenly. Always slowly, as if someone else was there moving in on her sleep. Even when it rained a strong rain which pushed her into the ground or when she slept till the sky turned purple.

Her children knew where she was. They would come up the hill when they did not see her or go to their grandmother's. She never woke up suddenly here, even when the three of them screamed her name—'Claudine!' The boy with his glum face turning cloudier and the girl and the little boy looking hungry.

Three of them. In the beginning she had bathed them and oiled their skins in coconut and dressed them in the wildest and brightest of colours and played with them and shown them off to the other inhabitants of the place. Then they were not good to play with any more. They cried and felt her hands. They cried for the roughness of her hands and the slap. If he was there he would either say 'don't hit them' or 'why don't you hit those children?' His ambiguity caused her to hesitate before each decision on punishment. Then she decided not to touch the children, since either instruction he gave, he gave in an angry and distant voice and for her the two had to be separate thoughts, clear opposites. So after a time the children did not get bathed and dressed and after a time they did not get beaten either.

The people around spoke well of him, described his physical attributes which were in the main two cheloidal scars on his chin and face. When he came he told them of his escapades on the bigger island. Like the time he met the famous criminal Weapon and he and Weapon spent the night drinking and touring the whore houses and the gambling dens and Weapon stuck a knife into the palm of a man who touched his drink. He brought new fashions to the place. The wearing of a gold ring on his little finger and the growing of an elegant nail to set it off. The men, they retold his stories until he came with new ones. They wore copper rings on their little fingers.

If she wasn't careful they would come into the house and tell her what to do again. The shacks up and down the hill were arranged like spiders crawling towards her. One stong rain and they'd be inside of her house which was not at the bottom of the hill so there was no real reason to think that it would actually happen. Looking at them, the other people, they made gestures towards her as they did to each other, to everyone else. They brought her things and she gave them things and they never noticed, nor did she, that she was not her mother's child nor her sister's sister nor an inhabitant of the place, but the woman turning into a tree. They had pressed her with their eyes and their talk and their complicit winks first into a hibiscus switch then into a shrub and now this . . . a tree.

He didn't live there. The dirt path beside the house ran arbitrarily up the hill. Whenever he came he broke a switch with which to scare the children. This was his idea of being fatherly. Coming through the path, he made his stern face up to greet the children and the woman. He came and went and the people in the place expected him to come for her and made excuses when he did not. They expected her to be his. They assumed this as they assumed the path up the hill, the steady rain in March. He is a man, you're a woman, that's how it is.

Those times, not like the first, he would sit on her bed—a piece of wood, his face blunt in the air, dense and unmoving, he had no memory, almost like the first, his breathing and his sweat smelling the same furry thickness as before. Like something which had walked for miles with rain falling and insects biting and the bush and trees slapping some green and murky scent onto its body, a scent rough from years of instinct, and horrible. Now he grew his fingernails and splashed himself with cheap scent but sometimes when he lifted his arm she recalled and forgot quickly. And sometimes she saw his face as before. Always, in and out of seeing him and not seeing him; or wondering who he was and disbelieving when she knew.

Those times he would sit on her bed and tell her about a piece of land which his maternal grandmother had left him. He was just waiting for the day that they built the road across Sans Souci and that was the day that he was going to be a rich man. Because it was good agricultural land and only a road was holding it back. He went on about how he would work the land and how he was really a man of the earth. She listened even though she knew that his mouth was full of nonsense. He had said that for the last many years.

How many . . . was he the same as the first . . . somehow she had come to be with him. Not if he was the first, not him.

His hands with their long fingernails, the elegant long nail on the right finger could never dig into the soil. She listened to him even though she knew that he was lying. But he really wasn't lying to deceive her. He liked to hear himself. He liked to think that he sounded like a man of ideas, like a man going somewhere. Mostly he repeated some phrase which he heard in a popular reggae song about having the heights of jah-jah or something he had heard at the occasional north-american evangelist meeting. He had woven these two into a thousand more convolutions than they already were and only he could understand them. He, the other men in the place and Claudine who couldn't really understand either but liked the sound of him. The sound confused her, it was different, not like the pig squealing that sorrowful squealing as it hung in front of the knife nor its empty sound as it hung for days . . . years . . . its white belly bloodless when it hung with no one seeing it. None around except the air of the yard folding and sealing pockets of flesh, dying. The sound covered an afternoon or so for her above the chorus of the pig's squeal at once mournful and brief in its urgency. The startling incidence of its death mixed with commonplaceness and routine. She liked to have him sit with her as if they were husband and wife.

II

She had met uncle Ranni on the Carenage, she never thought that he would ever get old, he used to be quick and smooth, with golden rings on his fingers. Each time he smiled or laughed that challenging sweet laugh of his the sun would catch the glint of his rings and throw it onto his teeth so that they looked yellow. He would throw his head way back revealing the gold nugget on his thick chain. He was a small man really but you would never know, looking at him when he laughed.

Then even when he talked of killing a man he laughed that sweet laugh, only his eyes were different.

They cut across your face for the briefest of moments like the knife that he intended to use. Once he even threatened to kill his father and his father believed him and slapped his face and never spoke with him again. She poured everything out to him now hoping he would kill the man this time.

Everything about Prime's exhortations and his lies. It came out of her mouth and she didn't know who was saying it. Uncle Ranni's laugh only changed slightly. No one in the family ever really believed that he'd ever kill anyone but no one ever dared not to believe either. Something about his laugh said that he'd never kill a man if he didn't have to and if he did, it would be personal. With a knife or a machete, never with a gun, but close so that the dying man would know who had killed him and why. She'd caught a glimpse of him once, under a tamarind tree, talking about cutting a man's head off and the eyes of the head open, as it lay apart from its body in the dirt. He had told it and the men around, kicking the dust with their toes, had laughed, weakly. Claudine told him everything, even some things that she only thought happened, but happened. These didn't make the case against Prime any worse, they just made her story more lyrical —inspiring the challenging laugh from Ranni. 'This man don't know who your uncle is, or what?' This only made her say more, Prime had lied to her and left her with three children to feed.

The new child, the fourth, moved in her like the first, it felt green and angry. Her flesh all around it, forced to hang there protecting this green and angry thing. It reached into her throat sending up bubbles and making her dizzy all the time. It was not that she hated it, she only wanted to be without it. Out, out, out, out, never to have happened. She wanted to be before it, to never know or have known about it. He had said that the land was in her name, he had even shown her papers which said so and now he had run off, taken a boat to St Croix. 'St Croix? It don't have a place that man can hide; he don't know me,' uncle Ranni said. Claudine got more and more frightened and more and more excited as she talked the story. It would serve Prime right to have uncle Ranni chop him up with a knife, she would like to see it herself. Uncle Ranni was old now. Sixty-four, but when he laughed like that she could see his mouth still full of his white teeth. It surprised her.

Her mother's brother—he had looked at her once back then as if she had made it happen. Looked at her as if she were a woman and contemptible, but it passed quickly like his other looks.

She'd only been talking to an old man about her trouble. She had not been paying attention. His old face had lit up briefly with that look and his teeth were as white as when he was young. His skin was tight and black as she remembered it years ago. He seemed to laugh out of a real joy. She remembered liking to hear him laugh and see his white teeth against his beautiful skin. He would spit afterward as if there was something too sweet in his mouth. Now when she'd first seen him on the Carenage she had seen an old man with grey eyelashes and a slight stubble of grey on parts of his skin and face. She had told him everything in a surge of relief and nostalgia, never expecting him to do anything but it was he, uncle Ranni, she had told. She almost regretted saying anything but she needed to say it to someone.

The look across her face as before, cutting her eyes away, cutting her lips, her head, slicing her, isolating sections of her for scrutiny and inevitable judgment. Her hand reached to touch her face, to settle it, dishevelled as it was, to settle it on her empty chest. All that she had said was eaten up by the old man's face, and thrown at her in a transient lacerating look which he gave back. Her eyes sniffed the quickly sealed cut and turned, fell on a wrecked boat in the Carenage.

A little boy jumped off the end not submerged in the water. The glum-faced boy at home came to her. She hurriedly made excuses to uncle Ranni about having to go and ran with a kind of urgency toward the tied-up boat to Cast Island. Disappearing into its confusion of provisions, vegetables and goats. She did what she always had to do. She pretended to live in the present. She looked at the awful sky. She made its insistent blueness define the extent of what she could see. Before meeting uncle Ranni she had walked along pretending that the boat was not there; that she did not have to go; wishing she could keep walking; that the Carenage would stretch out into the ocean, that the water of the ocean was a broad floor and the horizon a shelf which divided and forgot. An end to things completely. Where she did not exist. The line of her eyes furthest look burned her face into the sunset of yellow, descending. The red appearing behind her eyelids, rubbing the line with her head. She had wished that the water between the jetty and the lapping boat was wider and fit to drink so that she could drink deeply, become like sand, change places with the bottom of the ocean, sitting in its fat-legged deepness and its immutable width.

III

After the abortion, she went to Mama's Bar, even though she was in pain and even though she knew that she should lie down. Mama's was a wooden house turned into a restaurant and bar and Mama was a huge woman who had an excellent figure. Mama dominated the bar; she never shouted; she raised her eyebrows lazily when challenged. There were other women in the bar, regulars, who imitated Mama's walk and Mama's eyelids but deferred to Mama and faded, when Mama was in the bar. Mama always sat with her back to the door, which proved just how dangerous she was.

The walls of the bar, at unaccounted intervals, had psychedelic posters in fluorescent oranges and blues. One of them was of an aztec-like mountain—dry, mud brown, cracked, strewn with human bones. Nothing stood on it except bones of feet and ribs and skulls. It would be a foreboding picture if it weren't so glossy. Instead it looked sickly and distant. It was printed by someone in California and one of Mama's visitors had bought it at a head shop in San Diego. Mama thought that it was high art and placed it so that people entering the bar could see it immediately.

Claudine walked down the steps to the bar, closed her eyes anticipating the poster then opened them too soon and felt her stomach reach for her throat.

Mama's eyes watched her walk to the counter, ask for a rum, down it and turning to leave bump into the man with the limp. A foamy bit of saliva hung onto the stubble on his face. He grabbed Claudine to save himself from falling and then they began dancing to Mama's crackling stereo.

They danced until lunch time, until the saliva from the limping man's face stretched onto the shoulder of Claudine's dress. Mama had not moved either. She controlled all of it with her eyes and when they told Claudine to leave, she sat the man with the limp onto a stool and left. Going somewhere, averting her stare from the mountain strewn with human bones.

IV

She went to the address on the piece of paper someone had given her—29 Ponces Road. When she got to the street there was no number on any of the houses. She didn't know the woman's name. It was best in these situations not to know anyone's name or to ask anyone where. She walked up and down the street looking at the houses. Some were back from the curb and faced the next street over so there was no way of telling. Maybe something about the house would tell her—what does a house where a woman does that look like, she asked herself—she walked up and down the street thinking that maybe it was this one with the blue veranda or that one with the dog tied to a post. No, she couldn't tell. Maybe this was a sign or something. She gave up, suddenly frightened that it may just be a sign—holy mary mother of god—and bent her head walking very fast up the street for the last time.

She passed a house with nine or ten children in the yard. Most of them were chasing after a half-dressed little boy. They were screaming and pointing at something he was chewing. She hadn't seen the woman on the wooden veranda until one of the children ran towards her saying something breathless and pointing to the woman on the veranda. Then she saw her as the woman on the veranda reached out into the yard and hit a flying child. It didn't seem as if she wanted to hit this one in particular or any one in particular. The group of children gave a common flinch (accustomed to these random attacks on their chasing and rushing around), then continued after the boy. Faced with finally doing this Claudine didn't know anymore. She hesitated, looked at the woman's face for some assurance. But nothing. The woman looked unconcerned waiting for her, and then turning and walking into the ramshackle house, her back expecting Claudine to follow. Claudine walked toward the yard not wanting to stand in the street. Now she moved because of the smallest reasons, now she was trapped by even tinier steps, by tinier reasons. She moved so that her feet would follow each other, so that she could get away from the road, so that she could make the distance to the house, so that it would be over. Nothing had come from the woman's face, no sign of any opinion. Claudine had seen her face, less familiar than a strangers'. Later when she tried she would never remember the face, only as a disquieting and unresolved meeting. Like waking in between sleep and catching a figure, a movement in the room.

V

He had raped her. That is how her first child was born. He had grabbed her and forced her into his little room and covered her mouth so that his mother would not hear her screaming. She had bitten the flesh on his hand until there was blood and still he had exploded her insides, broken her. His face was dense against her crying. He did it as if she was not there, not herself, not how she knew herself. Anyone would have seen that he was killing her but his dense face told her that he saw nothing. She was thirteen, she felt like the hogs that were strung on the limbs of trees and slit from the genitals to the throat. That is how her first child was born. With blood streaming down her legs and feeling broken and his standing up and saying 'Nothing is wrong, go home and don't tell anyone.' And when she ran through the bush crying that she would tell her mother and stood at the stand pipe to wash the blood off her dress and to cool the pain between her thighs, she knew she could tell no one.

Up the hill to the top overlooking the water, she wanted to dive into the sea. The water would hit her face it would rush past her ears quickly it would wash her limbs and everything would be as before and this would not have happened—a free fall, a dive into the sea. Her body would hit the tuft of grass before reaching the bottom and it would hurt even more. She could not push off far enough to fall into the water.

She said nothing. She became sick and puffy. And her stepfather told her mother that she was pregnant and she begged her mother not to believe him, it was a lie, and her mother sent her to the doctor and told her not to come back home if it was true. When the doctor explained the rape, he said 'Someone put a baby in your belly.' And she could not go home. And when it was dark that night and she was alone on the road because everyone—her aunt first and then her grandmother had said 'go home', she saw her mother on the road coming down with a torchlight. Her mother, rakish and holding her skirt coming toward her. Both of them alone on the road. And she walked behind her all the way home silent, as her mother cursed and told her that she'd still have to do all the work and maybe more. Every day until the birth her mother swore and took care of her.

He denied it when the child was coming and she screamed it was 'you, you, you!' loud and tearing so that the whole village could hear, that it was he. He kept quiet after that and his mother bore his shame by feeding her and asking her 'How're things?'

From then, everyone explained the rape by saying that she was his woman. In fact they did not even say it they did not have to. Only they made her feel, as if she was carrying his body around. In their looking at her and their smiles which moved to one side of the cheek and with their eyelids, uncommonly demuring, or round and wide and gazing she came into the gaze of all of them no longer a child, much less a child who had been raped, now—a man's body. All she remembered was his face as if he saw nothing when he saw her and his unusual body resembling the man who slaughtered pigs for the village—so gnarled and horrible, the way he moved. Closing her eyes he seemed like a tamarind tree—sour and unclimbable—her arms could not move, pinned by his knotted hands and she could not breathe, her breathing took up all the time and she wanted to scream, not breathe—more screaming than breathing.

That is how her first child with him was born. Much as she tried her screaming did not get past the bush and the trees even though she tried to force it through the blades of grass and the coarse vines. Upon every movement of the bush her thin and piercing voice grabbed for the light between but the grass would move the other way making the notes which got through dissonant and unconnected, not like the sound of a killing.

ARITHA VAN HERK

Never Sisters

You would never believe that we are sisters. If you see us together, you might think we are friends or cousins, but never sisters. Unless you are perceptive enough to notice that we have the same hurried walk, the same unsympathetic way of speaking. But she is far more beautiful than I am, emanating a suggestion of whispy frailness that completely contradicts my stocky build. And in contrast to her dark hair and eyes, I am fair and freckled, without the clear olive tone of her skin. Or the decisiveness of her actions. Whatever I may seem like, I am not jealous. Although I will admit, as a child I worried that she would be forever beyond my grasp. Older, slimmer, always an edge of knowledge, her hands flying easily where mine fumbled. That is the advantage an older sister will perpetually have: she experiences long before you possibly can.

She is older than I am by eight years. An odd situation. I have a menage of brothers (four of them), but only this one sister. My brothers used to be important, but that has changed and now it is my sister who preoccupies me. I suppose we ought to be close. But somehow, in the patterns of years, we have admitted distance. Eight years is an enormous gap when you are young. And perhaps it was for the best. Throughout my childhood she was my second mother, a surrogate. Now that I am old enough to be called adult, there are those years between us so that we do not compete, there is no severing dragon of jealousy. Instead, time interfered. We are not close; I must say that. We never were.

I was ten when she left home. I stand at the window and watch the car drive away; Hannike sits very straight on the front seat beside my father. The picture has the clarity of illusion: she wears a creamy blouse and a wine-coloured jumper and in her ears are the pearl earrings my mother has given her that morning. In that instant I see only a flash of her fine dark hair drawn back off her forehead and then the car is gone.

In a certain sense, she ceased to exist, no longer the cool inviolable sister who moved among my brothers so effortlessly. And so unlike me. I fought and kicked and yelled, learned all of the boys' bad habits and none of the good. My mother often wished aloud that I had been born a boy so that she could treat me like one. Sometimes she even dared to ask me why I was not more like Hannike. I pretended not to care, but I felt hurt, secondhand.

Hannike and I shared the same bedroom. When the car turned out of the driveway, it was that I thought of, her sleeping beside me for as long as I could remember. For the first time, I would sleep alone. The idea paralysed me—not that I would sleep alone, but that *she* would sleep alone far away in a strange bed while I had the comfort of our familiar room. And lying still and awake that night I cried for her more than for myself.

In bed. I suppose that was when we were the closest. After all, we spent little time together during the day. I was locked into my child's world of play while she had gone a step further into the labyrinth of chores and responsibility. It was her room. She was the oldest and she shared it with me, but it was still her room. There was never any question about that. I was tolerated. Still, there was an intimacy about it that I appreciate only now.

I was a pretender. I lie awake in bed until she comes upstairs and closes the bedroom door behind her. I lie perfectly still with my eyes shut until she thinks she is sure that I am asleep. I can peek through my eyelashes at her without her ever guessing that I am awake. She hesitates and stands at the window for a moment, looking out into the darkness. Then she turns back to the room, stilled and reluctant, almost compliant. I thought that she was cautious and quiet for me, but now I believe her stillness was something else.

She was the first naked woman I ever saw. My own nakedness was shameful and wretched—I had the straight body of a boy. Watching her step out of her skirt and shuck off her blouse to stand fragile and a little stooped in white panties and bra emphasized my inadequacy, how hopelessly far behind I was. I could have watched her for hours, the turns of her body as smooth and pale as those of a ceramic figure. And it was not her sexuality, the white cotton bra easily unhooked and flung onto the dresser, the panties kicked from around her ankles, that made me hold my breath, but the fragility of her bones, the angularity of her back and hips, her long slender legs moving in a blurred sibilance of lambent skin. I wanted to touch that skin, feel the texture of it, but I never did, knowing my grimy child's hand would be a kind of violation.

Propped against the pillows, with the book resting on her knees, she would read. I shifted closer and closer until through my eyelashes, I could almost see the page. I didn't want to read her book, I only wanted to be close to her, to watch her read. But she sensed my awareness always, caught me immediately.

'Get over on your own side!'

I am instantly quiet as a shell, feigning perfect slumber.

'You can't fool me, Marikje. Turn over and get to sleep.'

That was the year I could never fall asleep. I lay awake for hours, listening to the sounds the old house made around me. And always she was there, Hannike my sister, the sprawl of her dark hair, the fluidity of her body in sleep, even the smell of her faint and dark like thin-skinned oranges at Christmas.

If she was angry, she would shove me over, her hands pushing at my rigid and resistant body. I never said a word, as if I thought silence would confirm my innocence, that I wasn't really awake at all. She was never cruel. Rather, she used a form of practicality on me that was sometimes humiliating, sometimes comforting.

'Go to sleep. You'll be too tired to go to school tomorrow.'

That was true. In the mornings I could not move; I had to be prodded and shoved and pulled at until I was walking down the driveway to the end of the road to wait for the school bus.

She was different at school, one of the older kids who moved smoothly between the separate circles of home and learning. For us they were still two isolated worlds, so radically different we could hardly think of them together, let alone merge them. The long and jolting bus ride divided them completely.

For her, there was no separation. Outwardly at least, she made the transitions easily. I am still envious that she could have become an adult before I was even aware that I was a child, or so it seemed to me. It was strange that she was old enough to be a babysitter and a stand-in mother, but young enough to have to listen to my parents. Her eight years superiority became my incessant preoccupation. When I'm as old as Hannike. . . . Of course, I will never catch up.

She will tell you that we were very different, but neither of us is remembering the way I used to imitate her, emulate her, wish to be her. To all outward appearances, I have given that up now and so the memory remains unjogged. But her shape was always there. My childhood has no memories that do not include her.

Did I say that she was an adult before I was even a child? She had to be. We were all younger than she; we were all her responsibility. I know she wishes she had been the youngest, had been absolved of our weight. But there it was; older children do what they have to do and then leave home.

When she was left with us she was the boss, we had to listen to her. Of course we were unwilling, disobedient, eager to imagine new forms of misbehaviour. Jan broke his ankle jumping out of the hayloft. Dad found the horse in the next county after we let her out. And always Hannike was stoic and responsible. I think she sometimes even took the blame.

The old bureau in the attic was full of pictures and books and boxes of letters. They were the leftovers of my parents' past; a lock of my grandmother's hair, a christening gown wrapped in tissue. We were allowed to play drum corps in the attic but were supposed to stay out of the bureau. I didn't open the drawer and find the picture of my father in a uniform, holding a gun, but we were suddenly fighting over it and then we tore it. I remember her lighting among the five of us like a hailstorm, yanking at us in a silent fury. Her small fists useless against us, she flashed away and in a moment was back wielding my mother's wooden butter paddle. How could she possibly catch us? We were Indians, monkeys, devils going in five directions at once. And she chased us all, furiously and frantically while we laughed and ran and whooped at her. It was only when she stomped back to the house with such anger written in every line of her body, the paddle dangling from her hand, that we stopped, sobered.

She locked us out of the house that afternoon. Locked all the doors and wouldn't open them for anything. Left us to our own devices as if she didn't care if we were dead, or would all kill ourselves. We slunk around the porch, hoping she would relent, hoping for anger rather than icy withdrawal. We knew only that she was crying, crying and crying with that helpless inevitability that we sometimes glimpsed in her. And we were terrifyingly ashamed.

And then there is the other picture. I stand at the end of the driveway with Hannike and my brothers waiting for the bus. The trees are heavy with frost, the bus is late, and we have been waiting for fifteen minutes. I am in grade two. I carry a lunchkit but no books. Inside my red mittens my hands are cold, so cold I am unable to hang onto the handle and I drop the lunchpail with a clatter. I curl my hands into fists but they only seem to be getting colder.

Hannike is looking down the road for the bus, squinting into the brilliant ice-sun as if she would challenge it. Her boots scrunch the snow and she is standing beside me. 'Are you cold, Marikje?'

I nod, huddled inside my coat like a turtle.

'Stamp!' she says.

I stamp my feet hard on the ground so that needles of fire race through my legs.

'It's my hands.'

'Put them in your pockets.'

I shove them into the pockets of my coat but still they feel stiff and bloodless.

'Are they still cold?'

I nod, miserable. 'Isn't the bus coming?'

'It's probably stuck.' She takes my mittened hands in hers, rubs them absently. Suddenly she turns her back to me. 'Here. Take off your mitts and put your hands under my coat.'

I drop my stiff mittens at my feet and shove my hands under her coat, into the warmth trapped there.

'Is that better?' she says over her shoulder.

'Yes.' My hands are still curled into fists.

'Put them under my sweater.'

I fumble with the layers of clothing, the suddenly acute sensation of rough wool on the backs of my hands in opposition to the smoother crispness of her blouse on my palms and fingertips. And suddenly I am afraid, afraid of touching her. I pull my hands away from her blouse, her body underneath it.

'Marikje, you're letting all the cold air under my sweater!' She is suddenly ruthless, authoritative. 'Look, put your hands under my shirt and on my back and stand still.'

For an instant I am petrified, then slowly, slowly I obey her, moving deeper under the cocoon of her clothes, my fingers stumbling onto the incredible softness of her warm skin. Entranced, I open my hands and touch her, lay my spread palms on her. It is as if I am touching some magical source of heat that thaws my fingers immediately, but more, leaves them with a tingling ache of sensation. Her skin is like warm water, perfectly still and smooth, unshrinking. Under my fingers I can even feel the shape of her ribs. I marvel at that now, the intimacy of it, the liberty she allowed me, my cold hands warming themselves on the flush of her skin. That was my sister.

When I am twelve, she comes home on weekends. Now she is totally beyond me, a woman from another place who does not belong here anymore. She even laughs with me. She is free of having to protect me, free of having to punish me. I am fascinated by her. She is free of my parents too; free as I know I will never be, too young and malleable to tear myself away. The turn of her head and the fine line of bone along her chin have left us behind completely, another transition accomplished. While she has grown more graceful, I have become clumsy and awkward. I break dishes and stumble; my hair is lank and colourless.

She still sleeps in the big bed with me and now she talks to me before we go to sleep. About the residence and about going to university and about taking courses and becoming a teacher. I want to do exactly what she is doing; I want to retrace every step she makes. Her life seems as perfect to me as mine is not. She falls asleep before I do and I lie staring at the sloping ceiling above me and wishing I could be her, free of having to wait, waiting for everything. Beside me her body is restless and suddenly she turns over.

'No,' she mumbles. 'No.'

I am instantly motionless. 'What? Hannike?'

'Mmmn.'

She is still asleep; her voice comes out of the depths of her dreams. I am suddenly frightened, something somewhere has leaped beyond me.

She flings out her arms. 'No. I don't want to.'

I sit up and stare down at her. Now I am even afraid to touch her, to waken her.

She mumbles something else and then is quiet.

I sit frozen upright, not wanting to hear, yet I cannot stop myself from listening and I cannot bring myself to wake her.

She stirs. 'I won't,' she says clearly. 'I hate them all. I won't take care of them anymore.'

'Hannike, Hannike.' I shake her shoulder hard. 'Wake up. Don't you feel well?'

She opens her eyes for a moment, then sighs and turns her back to me.

'Go to sleep, Marikje,' she says. 'Go to sleep. You have to go to school in the morning.'

I lay awake besider her then, trying to fit the pieces together. Her endless stooped endurance, the oldest of the six of us, the liberties she allowed us, the gleam of her creamy skin in the light. And I knew that she had made a transition that I would never even get to, let alone make, a spoiled child with an older sister.

When Hannike was married, two years later, I was fourteen. I was her youngest bridesmaid; I wore a yellow dress and carried pink flowers. But what I remember most is her standing in her bathrobe before she put on her dress, standing lost and defenseless as if she would cry, as if there were no hope or escape. I was dispassionate. I didn't want to be like her anymore. I would never marry and have children. I had decided.

And I remember that my father cried, that he stood beside my mother and the tears slipped down his brown face. He never cried when I got married, eight years later. I know because I watched him. I wanted to see if he would. That was the difference between Hannike and I.

A year later she was heavy and awkward with her first child, as if she had never denied anything, only affirmed it. She had slipped away from me. At fifteen I did not understand pregnancy and I did not like small children. Her body seemed to be a gross intrusion on her small, light frame and I was afraid for her. She did not want my fear. She was happy, she said, and the corners of her mouth tilted upwards.

Now everyone says that her daughter looks like me when I was a child. I do not see the resemblance. She seems to me to look more like Hannike. But then, I do not see her often. Only often enough to remind her of my strangeness and that I am a disinterested aunt. Hannike and I live in the same city but we are far away from each other. She has four children now. I have none.

When we are home together, my father sometimes asks me when will I have a child and I smile and say, 'Not yet, Dad.' And Hannike looks at me very quickly out of the corner of her eye, but she says nothing.